BLOSSOMING PATH

BOOK FOUR

BLOSSOMING PATH

BOOK FOUR

Carlos Calma

Podium

To my family,

Thank you for your unwavering support and encouragement, even though we all know I'm the least artistically gifted among us

All rights reserved. No part of this publication may be reproduced, stored in a retrieval system, or transmitted in any form or by any means electronic, mechanical, photocopying, recording, or otherwise without prior written permission from Podium Publishing.

This is a work of fiction. Names, characters, places, and incidents are either products of the author's imagination or used fictitiously. Any resemblance to actual events, locales, or persons, living, dead, or undead, is entirely coincidental.

Copyright © 2026 by Carlos Calma

Cover design by Kongsi

ISBN: 978-1-0394-8859-5

Published in 2026 by Podium Publishing
www.podiumentertainment.com

BLOSSOMING PATH

BOOK FOUR

CHAPTER ONE

Winter's Embrace

Winter's breath clawed at my cheeks the moment I stepped outside, biting through the heavy layers of the Iron Boar cloak and bracers crafted by Wang Jun. The thick, insulated leather felt sturdy, a shield against the season's fury, but its weight was something I was still getting used to.

The wind howled, its sharpness carrying an unnatural chill. By all rights, the worst of winter should have been behind us. Instead, it clung tighter, thickening the air and layering the landscape in snow so deep my boots sank with every step.

I paused at the edge of my porch, scanning the village. Gentle Wind Village had weathered the month well, given the circumstances. The preparations were coming along steadily, with new structures rising on foundations Li Wei had designed and laid before the first heavy snow. The extra supplies and seeds sent by Feng Wu's sect were a blessing, easing the strain of rebuilding after Narrow Stone Peak. Still, their absence lingered in my mind, a shadow that refused to leave.

The Heavenly Flame Mantra had been another focus of my days. Training in its movements, channeling qi through my palms, and being forbidden from utilizing the Rooted Banyan Stance or the Bamboo Reprisal Counter made it difficult. Yet, there were victories, small sparks of progress that kept me going, like the moment I first felt the searing heat manifest without trembling, steady and controlled, instead of a fleeting flicker of warmth.

> *Heavenly Flame Mantra (Level 1):*
> *A martial style that channels the essence of fire into the cultivator's attacks. The Heavenly Flame Mantra infuses the cultivator's strikes with searing heat, generating flames that radiate outward from their body. Each movement embodies the principles of fire: aggressive, adaptable, and consuming.*

> *Next Stage: Radiant Flame Mantra*
> *Requirements:*
> *Heavenly Flame Mantra Proficiency—Level 10*
> *Inflict at least fifty successful strikes using flame-imbued techniques.*
> *Sustain the mantra for thirty hours.*

I trusted Elder Ming's guidance, and only ever practiced my techniques separately. In time, I'd become proficient enough to use them both in tandem.

I tightened the cloak around me and trudged toward the greenhouse. Its structure stood resilient against the frost, its translucent walls glowing faintly with the life it sheltered. Inside, the temperature was warm and welcoming, a contrast to the icy world outside.

My gaze wandered over the rows of vibrant plants, their colors defying the season. Deep greens, fiery reds, and bright yellows filled the space because of the hybrids I had cultivated. Leaves twisted into unfamiliar shapes; stems bore unexpected fruits . . . and vegetables.

And at the very edge of the greenhouse stood the Golden Bamboo, a single stalk rising above the rest, its golden sheen shimmering under the filtered light. It was taller than I remembered, its growth almost unnatural in its speed. The thought brought a small smile to my face.

The memory of that quest resurfaced; how I had struggled to figure out how to elicit its growth.

My initial attempts had been met with frustration, thinking the lack of sunlight was the problem. But then I realized yang energy wasn't limited to the sun. Not for me, at least.

By infusing it with the essence of plants like Sunfire Blade Grass and ginseng, I had nourished the bamboo despite the winter. The technique wasn't perfect, but it worked, and the quest rewarded me with a Technique Token for my efforts.

The bamboo's rapid growth under essence infusion hinted at the potential I hadn't yet fully explored. Each day it stretched taller, its presence commanding attention like a beacon amid the other hybrids. The process of sustaining its growth had become a delicate dance, feeding it just enough energy to thrive without overwhelming its natural balance.

Despite the harshness of the season, it thrived.

And soon, I'd be able to harvest it.

My footsteps carried me farther into the greenhouse, each step a reminder of how much had changed. With every sprouting hybrid, every repaired fence, and every snow-dusted roof standing firm, hope felt less like an illusion and more like a certainty.

But winter wasn't done with us yet. The chill outside had grown sharper, and the snow deeper. Something in the air felt wrong, as though the season itself had turned hostile. For now, though, the garden was thriving, and the village was safe.

And yet, as I stood amid the thriving life of my greenhouse, a thought lingered. Would it be enough? Would *I* be enough when the next storm came?

> *Heavenly Interface: Kai Liu*
> *Perk(s):*
> *Interface Manipulator*—Allows manipulation of the Heavenly Interface and access to special features.
> *Dao Pioneer*—Grants a unique status that softens the rigid thresholds that usually constrain skill acquisition and evolution, allowing for more fluid and spontaneous development of skills and cultivation techniques.
> *Race: Human*
> *Vitality: Sufficient*
> *Primary*
> *Affinity*—Wood and Fire
> *Cultivation Rank: Qi Initiation—Rank 1*
> *Qi: Qi Initiation Stage—Rank 5 (. . .)*
> *Mind: Qi Initiation Stage—Rank 2 (. . .)*
> *Body: Mortal Realm—Rank 5 (. . .)*
> *Skills*
> *Spiritual Herbalism—6 (. . .)*
> *Nature's Attunement—6 (. . .)*
> *Accelerated Reading—9 (. . .)*
> *Cultivation Techniques*
> *Rooted Banyan Stance—4 (. . .)*
> *Crimson Lotus Purification—1 (. . .)*
> *Bamboo Reprisal Counter—1 (. . .)*
> *Memory Palace Technique—1 (. . .)*
> *Refinement Simulation Technique—1 (. . .)*
> *Heavenly Flame Mantra—1 (. . .)*
> *Currency*
> *Technique Token—2*

I shook my head, trying to dispel the doubts before they could take root. Worry wouldn't cultivate strength. It never did. Action would.

It was easy to forget when I was surrounded by so many exceptional people, but my overall rank was at the Qi Initiation stage. Above average for a third-class disciple. Even though it was carried by my comparatively large reserve of qi, it didn't change the fact that I was a cultivator. Physical training and recovering through the use of pills and Tianyi's power allowed my body to break through into the final stage of the mortal realm.

I stretched out my hands and summoned the Heavenly Flame Mantra. Heat surged through my body, pooling in my palms before erupting into a searing glow. The faint red glow danced along my fingers, warming them, the heat an anchor in the biting cold of my thoughts. With Elder Ming's support and my continuous efforts, I've developed my affinity for fire. Although it wasn't innate like my affinity for wood, it meant that my training in Elder Ming's martial art was affecting my cultivation.

"No room for hesitation. Keep moving forward," I murmured to myself.

I extinguished the technique and set to work, tending to the plants and checking their vitality. It was a careful process, ensuring each hybrid received just the right balance of care and essence infusion. When the last vine was supported and the final stalk was watered, I stepped back, satisfied for now.

> *Quest: Mastery of Spiritual Plant Cultivation*
> *—Cultivate and grow fifty viable and different plant hybrids. (48/50)*

I was almost done with my quest. But finding the last two combinations had been difficult.

But today, I'd get another hybrid down.

The chill hit me again as I exited the greenhouse and made my way back to the house. Inside, the warmth was welcoming, and the scent of dried herbs hanging near the hearth lingered in the air. I crossed the room to a low shelf, retrieving a jar of rice seeds. Elder Wen had given them freely, even after I stole his horse to kidnap Zhao Wen.

"Kai," a voice called softly from across the room. I turned to see Tianyi, her lithe form draped in her human guise. She sat near the window, her posture calm but her gaze piercing. "Are you working again?"

Her tone carried more emotion than before—curiosity, maybe even a hint of amusement. She was becoming more expressive by the day, her growth as a person as startling as her martial prowess.

"Just a little," I replied, setting the jar on the workbench. "And I'll need you and Windy to protect me while I work. You know, from marauding bandits or roving snow demons."

"Snow demons?" she repeated. "I see no demons, but if they come, I will defend this garden." She paused, then added, "May I watch this time?"

"Sure." I waved her over as I began preparing the jar. "It's not the most exciting thing, but feel free."

She approached, her movements as fluid as ever. Windy, coiled tightly on a windowsill nearby, hissed softly as we passed. His temperament had grown pricklier in the cold, his usual grace replaced by a moody vigilance. I gave him a wide berth, letting him brood in peace.

"This," I began, gesturing to the jar of rice seeds, "is the beginning of something new. The process isn't complicated, but it took a lot of trial and error to figure out."

Tianyi leaned in, her sharp eyes tracking my movements as I unscrewed the jar and spread the seeds across the workbench. "Why start with seeds?" she asked, her tone genuinely curious.

"Because it's easier to integrate new essence while the plant is still in its potential stage," I explained. "Fully grown plants have established structures, and while you can still infuse them, the results are less stable. Seeds are like blank slates—they absorb the essence more evenly, leading to better hybrids."

She nodded, her gaze unwavering as I placed a small sprig of Sunfire Blade Grass beside the seeds. "This is the infusion step," I continued. "The essence of the Sunfire Blade Grass will combine with the seeds, giving them yang energy and a measure of cold resistance. It's delicate work, though. Too much energy, and you could destabilize the entire batch."

I pressed my palm against the Sunfire Blade Grass, channeling a controlled stream of qi to extract its essence. The grass wilted instantly, its energy flowing into my palms. With practiced precision, I guided the glowing energy into the seeds, watching as they absorbed the infusion. A faint red hue spread across their surfaces, a sign of success.

> *Quest: Mastery of Spiritual Plant Cultivation*
> *—Cultivate and grow fifty viable and different plant hybrids. (49/50)*

"I'll call it Heavenly Flame Rice," I said, stepping back to admire the result. "If it works the way I hope, it could grow earlier in the season, even in cold climates. Maybe even enhance cattle feed. And if I'm lucky, it'll give it a nourishing effect, like a minor pill."

Tianyi's brow furrowed slightly. "What happens if you do this to all the seeds? Will it work for everyone?"

"That's the tricky part," I admitted. I grimaced upon remembering the drawback of the infusion skill. "These hybrids can't reproduce hybrids. The seeds from this rice won't carry the same traits; they'll revert or be weaker. So, the only way to scale this is for me to create more manually."

Her eyes narrowed. "That seems . . . inefficient."

"It is," I agreed with a sigh. "But even if it's not a farming revolution, it's still useful. Small-scale production can make a difference. I'll take what I can get."

I carefully returned the infused seeds to the jar, sealing it tightly before bringing it with me. Tianyi's gaze lingered on the jar, her expression contemplative.

"Take care of the house," I said, turning to her with a small smile. "I'm heading out to check on the village."

She bowed, clasping her hands together in a respectful gesture. "I will guard it well. And if the snow demons come, I will call for Windy."

"Perfect plan," I said with a chuckle as I pulled on my cloak and braced myself for the cold once more.

The village bustled with activity despite the thick snow that blanketed every surface. The crunch of my boots accompanied the muffled hammering of wood and the rhythmic calls of workers coordinating their efforts. As I made my way toward the construction site, I couldn't help but marvel at the scene.

The artisans brought in by the Verdant Lotus Sect were working closely with Li Wei, and the sight was nothing short of comical. The boy, barely into his teenage years, stood amid seasoned carpenters and builders, pointing at various sections of the half-built courtyard. His voice carried above the din, issuing instructions that the artisans followed without hesitation.

I stopped a few paces away, leaning against a snow-dusted post to watch. My chest swelled with smug satisfaction. Feng Wu had doubted my words when I'd spoken of Li Wei's genius. He thought I was exaggerating. But now, seeing how the artisans treated the boy as an equal—no, as a peer—it was clear just how wrong Feng Wu had been.

The courtyard house itself was impressive. Positioned away from the village square, it was large enough to accommodate two dozen people, with training grounds integrated into the layout. Its rapid construction over the past few weeks was proof of the combined efforts of the Verdant Lotus artisans and the villagers, who'd thrown themselves into the work with gusto.

I tipped my head toward Li Wei, who caught my eye mid-instruction. He nodded and waved before returning to his task. Shaking my head with a grin of my own, I moved on, heading toward the Soaring Swallow Teahouse.

The teahouse had become the temporary home of the second-class disciples from the Verdant Lotus Sect while the courtyard was being built. It stood at the edge of the square, its windows glowing warmly against the winter's stark white backdrop. As I stepped inside, the scent of tea and freshly baked pastries enveloped me, a welcome contrast to the cold.

Inside, Lan-Yin was a blur of motion, darting between the kitchen and dining area with an energy that defied her condition. Despite the faint bump visible beneath her robes, she moved with athletic grace, balancing trays laden with steaming cups and plates. Her parents, seated near the back, wore identical expressions of exasperation as they watched her flit about. No doubt they had tried to convince her to rest, but Lan-Yin was nothing if not stubborn.

Even the disciples, seated in groups around low tables, seemed impressed by her nimbleness. Their surprise was evident in their occasional glances and murmured comments. And yet, I knew this was only part of her routine. She still attended Elder Ming's morning practice sessions, though she'd wisely refrained from sparring.

"Lan-Yin!" I called out, stepping further into the room. The disciples turned toward me, offering respectful nods and greetings.

"Good morning, Kai," one of them, Jian Feng, said with a small bow.

"Morning, everyone," I replied, nodding in return. Though I wasn't as close to these disciples as I was with Feng Wu or even Lan Sheng, I appreciated their dedication. Within days of their arrival, they'd established patrol schedules and taken their duties seriously. It was comforting to know they had the village's safety in mind.

Lan-Yin approached, her expression harried but bright. "What can I get you?" she asked, balancing a tray in one hand while reaching for a tea towel with the other.

I reached into my cloak and pulled out the jar of Heavenly Flame Rice, handing it to her. "This is for you," I said. "A gift. It's a hybrid rice I just cultivated. Prepare it when you get a chance, and let me know what you think. If it's good, I'll grow more for the disciples."

Lan-Yin's eyes widened slightly as she took the jar, holding it up to inspect the faint red hue of the grains. "You're spoiling me, Kai," she said with a small laugh. "I'll make sure it's done right, but you'll have to wait a few days. Husking it will take some time."

"No rush," I said, smiling. "I'm curious about how it turns out. If it's good enough, it might even make its way onto your teahouse's menu."

She laughed again, the sound light and genuine, before tucking the jar under her arm and disappearing into the kitchen. I watched her go, marveling at her determination despite everything. Lan-Yin let nothing slow her down—not her condition, not the added workload, not even the cold.

As I lingered in the teahouse, the Verdant Lotus disciples relaxed around their tables, their conversation dipping in and out of patrol schedules, cultivation techniques, and everything in between. I caught Jian Feng's eye and approached his table, drawing their attention with a casual wave.

"You all seem settled," I said, pulling up a chair and sitting across from him. The other disciples nodded politely, their postures straightening as if they expected some kind of formal conversation.

"It's a peaceful village," Jian Feng replied. "A good place to train in. Gathering energy is quite easy here."

"Glad to hear it." I let a pause hang in the air, then leaned forward, my tone light. "Speaking of training, have you considered engaging in some friendly sparring with the villagers? Or maybe teaching the more able-bodied adults a few exercises?"

The disciples exchanged quick glances, and one of them, a sharp-eyed woman named Mei Rong, spoke up. "Feng Wu mentioned something similar before we left. We can't teach sect techniques, of course, but basic drills and self-defense? That's within reason."

Jian Feng nodded in agreement. "If it helps strengthen the village, we're happy to assist. Just let us know how you'd like to organize it."

"Oh, I've got an idea," I said, my grin turning mischievous. "In fact, we've got something to show you all that might help with your efforts."

CHAPTER TWO

Blows and Balance

The forge loomed ahead, a squat building exhaling thin plumes of smoke into the frigid air. Its doors were cracked open, spilling a warm orange glow that flickered against the snow-covered ground. The rhythmic clang of metal striking metal carried through the cold, mingling with the muted crunch of boots on snow as I led the second-class disciples toward it.

"Here we are." I said, gesturing to the forge with a grin.

The forge's heat was a welcome reprieve from the biting cold outside. Inside, Master Qiang stood at his anvil, his powerful arms swinging a hammer with practiced precision. Sparks flew as he struck a glowing piece of metal, shaping it with a precision that belied his gruff demeanor. Wang Jun stood nearby, his hands stained with soot as he inspected a row of freshly forged blades laid out on a workbench.

"Master Qiang! Wang Jun!" I called out over the clamor, stepping into the forge. Both men looked up, their faces breaking into smiles at the sight of us.

"Kai," Wang Jun said, wiping his hands on a cloth. His gaze flicked to the disciples behind me, curiosity sparking in his eyes. "Brought company, I see."

"Thought it was about time they saw what you've been working on," I said, motioning for the disciples to follow. "Everyone, meet Master Qiang, our resident blacksmith, and Wang Jun, his apprentice and Gentle Wind's soon-to-be best blacksmith."

"Soon-to-be?" Wang Jun quipped, raising an eyebrow. "You mean I'm not already?"

"Not while I'm alive, you ain't!" his master barked out.

The disciples chuckled politely as they stepped further into the forge, their eyes scanning the weapons lined up on the workbench. Swords, spears, and daggers gleamed under the forge's light, their designs simple but sturdy. Some were smaller, clearly intended for younger hands, while others bore the heft and length of weapons meant for adults.

"This," I began, gesturing to the array, "is part of our effort to prepare the village. We're not expecting to turn them into warriors overnight, but having a weapon in hand can make a world of difference in an emergency."

Jian Feng picked up a short blade, turning it over in his hands. "These are well made," he said, his tone betraying a hint of surprise. "And the variety . . . You've thought about this."

"I try," I said with a shrug. "Every villager, no matter their size or strength, should have something they can wield. That's where Master Qiang and Wang Jun come in. They've been working tirelessly to produce weapons both for you and the village."

Master Qiang grunted, setting down his hammer. "Kai here's been pushing us hard," he said, his voice gruff but good-natured. "Won't stop talking about making sure everyone's prepared. Can't say I disagree, though."

"And speaking of preparation," Wang Jun cut in, his eyes gleaming with a familiar spark of determination, "how about a demonstration? A spar, maybe?"

The disciples perked up at that, their curiosity clearly piqued. Mei Rong, ever the cautious one, folded her arms. "A spar? Against whom?"

"Me, of course." Wang Jun said with a grin, already pulling off his heavy apron. "No one better to test the weapons against than the one who made it, I'd say."

I leaned against the workbench, watching Wang Jun with a mix of amusement and pride. Over the past month, he'd been a whirlwind of energy, throwing himself into training and forging with a fervor that bordered on obsession. Ever since Lan-Yin's diagnosis, he'd been different. More focused, more driven. He'd pestered me endlessly for spars and advice on how to get stronger, even volunteering to test some of my experimental medicines.

I couldn't help but think how fitting it was for him to be a father. The weight of responsibility had sharpened him, turning his usual bluster into something more resolute. The events after Narrow Stone Peak had left their mark on all of us, but Wang Jun . . . he'd risen to the challenge in a way that made me proud to call him a friend.

We walked into a clearing just behind the building, where Wang Jun and Master Qiang chopped and stored the wood to fuel their forge.

It had been hastily shoveled free of snow, the ground underneath packed hard from years of foot traffic and work. A faint haze of heat still clung to the air from the forge's fires, keeping the chill at bay. Wang Jun rolled his shoulders, testing the grip of his hammer as he glanced at me with a lopsided grin.

"So," I said, crossing my arms, "how's it been, using that hammer in your fighting style?"

"Good," Wang Jun replied, hefting the hammer and giving it a few experimental swings. The head cut through the air with a satisfying whoosh. "Almost too good, honestly. Feels natural, like it's been part of me all along. Guess that's what happens when you spend years wielding one."

I nodded, watching as he fell into a comfortable stance. "Makes sense. You've been swinging that thing since you were a kid, right? It's just muscle memory now, honed into something lethal."

From the corner of my eye, I noticed the disciples huddled together, murmuring among themselves. Their attention soon shifted to a small game of *slug, snake, frog*, deciding who would spar with Wang Jun.

The game was quick, with fingers snapping into shapes and groans or cheers accompanying each round. Jian Feng lost with a sigh, stepping forward to claim a weapon. His hand hovered over a short sword before settling on a staff. He gave it an experimental twirl, murmuring quietly to himself.

"Well-balanced."

"You don't have to use it if you don't want to," Wang Jun offered, spinning his hammer idly. His tone was casual, but there was an edge of anticipation in his voice.

Jian Feng shook his head, planting the staff in the ground with a solid thud. "It's not my primary weapon, but every sparring match is a learning opportunity. And who knows? It might teach me something new."

The disciples murmured their approval, and Jian Feng stepped into the clearing, spinning the staff once more before settling into a ready stance. "Custom dictates I give you the first three moves," he said with a wry smile. "Use them wisely."

Wang Jun didn't hesitate.

He surged forward, hammer held low as he closed the distance with alarming speed. For someone of his size and wielding such a heavy weapon, his movement was fluid, his footwork surprisingly light. His first strike was a sweeping arc aimed at Jian Feng's side, the head of the hammer whistling through the air.

Jian Feng reacted instantly, pivoting on his back foot to deflect the strike with his staff. The clash made a loud noise, but Jian Feng's stance remained firm even with Wang Jun's full weight bearing down on him. He shifted slightly, ready for the next attack.

Wang Jun's second move came just as quickly, a feint upward that transitioned into a quick jab toward the disciple's midsection. The staff spun, deflecting the blow with a loud crack. Undeterred, he followed with a downward swing, his hammer crashing toward Jian Feng with a force that could split wood.

Jian Feng sidestepped, the hammer slamming into the packed earth with a dull thud. He spun his staff in a fluid arc, stepping back into his stance, with the same faint smile on his lips.

"Your strength is impressive," Jian Feng said, his tone admiring but measured. "But strength alone isn't enough."

Wang Jun grunted, pulling his hammer free from the ground and resetting his stance. His face was set in determination, his jaw clenched as he stepped forward to close the gap again.

I watched, my arms folded, as Wang Jun pressed the offensive. His strikes were relentless, each one precise and deliberate, a reflection of his years spent forging steel. The hammer wasn't just a weapon in his hands; it was an extension of his body, moving with a rhythm honed by years at the forge.

And yet, as impressive as he was, Jian Feng remained several steps ahead. The senior disciple's movements were calculated, almost effortless as he parried and dodged each attack. He wasn't just defending; his eyes were sharp as they followed every swing of Wang Jun's hammer.

The blacksmith had a natural gift. His strength, combined with the technical refinement gained from years of smithing, made him a formidable opponent. If I compared him to myself at the same stage in our journeys, I had to admit; Wang Jun was stronger. He didn't have the raw power of someone like Ping Hai, but there was something undeniably solid about him.

If Ping Hai was an ox, Wang Jun was a horse: strong, agile, and athletic.

It stung just a little to realize this. I'd spent so much time as a child envying Wang Jun's constitution, bemoaning how he seemed to have the perfect base for a fighter while I'd struggled to find my footing in the beginning of my journey. His strength came naturally, while I had to claw for every inch of progress.

But even as the old pang of envy surfaced, I felt a swell of pride. Wang Jun had taken what he was given and worked hard to refine it. That determination, that grit, was something I couldn't help but admire.

The sparring match came to a decisive end when Jian Feng shifted from defense to offense. His staff moved like a blur, striking Wang Jun's hammer in a way that forced him to overextend. In the same motion, Jian Feng swept his staff low, catching Wang Jun's leg and sending him sprawling onto his back.

For a moment, the clearing was silent except for the sound of Wang Jun's heavy breathing. Then, Jian Feng stepped back, lowering his staff and bowing slightly.

"You've got potential," Jian Feng said, his tone even. "For someone with no formal training under a sect or clan, you're impressive."

Wang Jun grunted as he sat up, wiping sweat from his brow. His expression was a mix of frustration and respect. "Thanks," he muttered, pulling himself to his feet. "I learned well."

I clapped him on the shoulder as he dusted himself off. "You did great," I said with a grin. "Besides, you can't expect to win against someone like Jian Feng on your first try. He's probably been training since he could walk."

Wang Jun chuckled, the tension easing from his shoulders. "Yeah, I guess. Still, it stings a bit."

The second-class disciple remained quiet, his gaze shifting from Wang Jun to me.

"Kai," he blurted, his tone curious. "How about you? Care to spar?"

The challenge hung in the air, and I straightened, feeling the weight of his gaze.

"Me?" I asked. "You sure you want to take me on after that warm-up?"

Jian Feng's lips twitched into a faint smile. "I'm curious," he said. "Wang Jun's strength is impressive, but I'd like to see how you compare."

The other disciples murmured among themselves, their interest piqued. I glanced at Wang Jun, who gave me an encouraging nod.

"Well," I said, rolling my shoulders. "If you insist. But don't say I didn't warn you."

Despite my feigned reluctance, I was quite eager. This would be a good test, as well as a way of furthering my quest to learn the Combat Anticipation Array.

Wang Jun stepped out of the clearing, grinning through his sweat. "Go get him, Kai. Show him what Gentle Wind Village is made of!" he said, waving me forward with a casual gesture.

"Hmph! Fear not! I shall avenge you!" I declared dramatically, striding into the clearing with a flair that made the disciples chuckle.

"Please don't," Wang Jun muttered, shaking his head in mock exasperation. "Just fight already."

Jian Feng inclined his head slightly, amusement flickering in his eyes. "I'll give you the first three moves," he said, planting his staff firmly in the ground. "Take your best shot."

"Generous," I replied with a grin, stepping into the stance of the Heavenly Flame Mantra. My hands ignited with a faint red glow as heat surged through my body, gathering in my palms. "I appreciate the gesture."

The clearing grew quiet, the tension crackling like kindling in a fire.

I moved first, closing the distance in a single step and aiming a flaming strike at Jian Feng's midsection. He parried effortlessly, his staff intercepting my hand with a solid thwack.

Undeterred, I spun, bringing my other hand up in a fiery arc aimed at his shoulder. Again, his staff was there to meet me, the impact sending a jolt up my arm.

My third move was more calculated, a feint to the left before pivoting to strike low. For a moment, I thought I had him, but Jian Feng shifted his weight, his staff sweeping in to block me with almost insulting ease.

From there, we continued to exchange several strikes, garnering a feel for each other's range. Jian Feng was similar in size and speed to all the second-class disciples. And that gave me an opportunity; sparring with Tianyi, who moved faster than the eye could see, had given me more poise and confidence even against physically superior opponents.

"Hngh!"

I tucked my shoulder in, allowing a strike to my shoulder. But with the Iron Boar hide cloaked over me, the impact was muted.

He stepped back, resetting his stance. "Clean strikes," he said, his tone calm. "But why are you holding back?"

"Who says I am?" I replied lightly, though my grin faltered slightly.

Jian Feng tilted his head, his sharp gaze unwavering. "I saw your fight against Ping Hai. Those other techniques . . . the Rooted Banyan Stance, the Bamboo Reprisal Counter. Why aren't you using them?"

I clenched my fists, extinguishing the flames momentarily. "I can't," I admitted. "And even if I could, I wouldn't. Not without my mentor's permission. He's made it clear I need to focus on mastering this style first."

Jian Feng's brow furrowed, but he nodded. "I see. And yet, this style . . . it doesn't seem to suit you."

He wasn't wrong. The Heavenly Flame Mantra demanded aggression, constant pressure; everything that went against my instincts. Every move I made felt like swimming upstream, my body fighting against ingrained habits.

But I trusted Elder Ming's instructions. This was a test, a way to push past my limits and grow stronger. And if that meant taking a few hits or losing, so be it.

Jian Feng didn't wait long before pressing his advantage. His staff moved like a living thing, darting and striking with precision. I blocked some of his attacks, but others slipped through my defenses, landing sharp blows on my arms and legs.

THWACK!

CRACK!

The impact stung, but I gritted my teeth and stayed on my feet.

"Still holding back," Jian Feng muttered, his disappointment palpable. He shifted his stance, preparing for what I could tell would be a decisive strike.

Now or never.

A map of the clearing materialized in my mind's eye, the position of his weapon, every subtle shift in Jian Feng's stance, and even the snow underneath us. It was like a glowing path etched in that mental map, revealing the most likely arc of his attack.

I dodged his next attack, stepping inside his guard. As he adjusted, I refined the heat of the Heavenly Flame Mantra into a single, concentrated point at my fingertips. With a sharp jab, I struck his thigh, channeling the heat directly into the muscle.

Jian Feng's leg spasmed involuntarily, a reflexive jerk that made him stumble. His eyes widened in surprise as I seized the moment, unleashing a flurry of rapid blows.

The strikes landed with precision, each one forcing him further off-balance.

Just as he staggered, his defenses crumbling, I pulled back my fist, stopping inches from his chest. The heat radiated from my hand, but I didn't deliver the final blow.

"I've learned well," I said, letting the flames flicker out as I stepped back.

Jian Feng exhaled slowly, bowing his head. "You've won," he said, his voice humble. "I underestimated you. That was a mistake."

I snorted, crossing my arms. "You were using a staff you're not familiar with. Let's not pretend it was a fair fight."

The disciples clapped, their expressions a mix of admiration and amusement. Wang Jun was the loudest, cheering as if I'd just won a grand tournament. "That's our Kai!" he shouted, his grin wide enough to split his face.

I rubbed the back of my neck, feeling a flush rise to my cheeks. "All right, all right," I muttered. "Don't make it weird."

I looked at my quest, feeling a sense of accomplishment.

Quest: Beyond the Memory Palace
—Successfully evade or counter ten different attacks by predicting their trajectories using a simulated visual map in real time. (10/10)
—Land five precise hits on a moving opponent using openings simulated beforehand. (3/5)
—Use the Refinement Simulation Technique on an alchemical reaction mid-combat to create an advantage. (0/1)

Learning how to predict and visualize people's moves had done wonders for me. Soon, I'd complete this quest and hopefully learn the Combat Anticipation Array just like Feng Wu did. But one task still loomed: using the Refinement Simulation in combat. That was a hurdle I hadn't yet crossed, and I had a feeling it wouldn't be easy.

But I was progressing. And that's all that mattered.

CHAPTER THREE

A Thousand Flames, One Shell

The days passed with an ease that felt almost unfamiliar, a calm that belied the chaos we'd endured just a few months ago. The second-class disciples of the Verdant Lotus Sect had become a steady presence in the village, their teachings a quiet boon. Able-bodied adults and curious children alike flocked to their drills, learning not just self-defense techniques but the basics of cultivation. Lan-Yin and Wang Jun were instrumental, rallying even the most hesitant villagers with promises of strength and confidence that extended beyond the training grounds.

Of course, putting wooden swords and blunted spears into the hands of children and untrained adults came with its share of . . . *incidents*. It wasn't long before the disciples' roles expanded to include patching up the inevitable scrapes, bruises, and occasionally sprained wrists that came with enthusiastic but clumsy sparring sessions. But they weren't just warriors; they were healers too. Each carried a satchel at their hip, stocked with an assortment of medicinal goods. Powders to stave off infections, and small clay jars of salves for burns and sprains seemed to appear out of nowhere whenever someone stumbled too hard or swung their staff the wrong way. Their efficiency was remarkable, their hands moving with practiced ease as they mended the bumps and cuts of their trainees.

But they didn't stop there. The disciples insisted on teaching the basics of first aid alongside their combat drills. Bandaging a wound properly, recognizing signs of infection, and even knowing basic pressure points to stop bleeding—all of it was woven into their lessons.

As one disciple put it, "What good is strength if you don't know how to recover from its consequences?"

And then there was the wine.

I smirked to myself at the thought. Nearly every disciple carried a flask of medicinal wine in their satchels, ostensibly to disinfect wounds or ward off illnesses. I'd watched them dab it on cuts and scrapes with a flourish, the sharp, heady scent filling the air as they muttered about purification. It worked, sure.

But let's be honest—it wasn't just about healing.

"Medicinal wine," I muttered under my breath one day as a disciple poured a generous splash onto a scrape. "The cure for wounds, colds, and sobriety."

The disciples' patrols, meanwhile, ensured a sense of safety that allowed us to focus on developing the village.

For me, though, the calm was an illusion. My days were anything but restful.

I stood barefoot in the middle of a blazing circle, the heat from the coals beneath my feet radiating up my legs. The flames danced erratically, licking the air around me as I moved through the prescribed forms of the Dance of the Thousand Flames, a training method from Elder Ming's former sect.

I don't know what psychopath invented this, but they were a genius.

Sweat poured down my back despite the winter chill, the sharp contrast between fire and frost an ever-present reminder of the harshness of this training.

It wasn't just a dance; it was a *tribulation*. Every movement demanded precision, every shift of weight a gamble between balance and pain. My qi flowed through me in a protective sheath, mimicking the unpredictable flickers of the flames that surrounded me. Each step burned a lesson into my body: light on your feet, adapt, never stop moving. The flames were not just an obstacle but a teacher, their relentless heat honing my control.

"Form tighter!" Elder Ming's bark cut through the roaring fire. His tone was sharp, a lash against the sluggish edges of my focus.

I gritted my teeth and adjusted, pulling my arms closer to my body as I twisted through the next step. The flames surged at my hesitation, a stray ember brushing too close to my exposed skin. A quick burst of qi canceled it out before it could bite deeper. The heat was constant, oppressive, but I couldn't let it win. Each breath was a fight for control, and each heartbeat carried the weight of Elder Ming's unrelenting gaze.

"Faster, Kai! If your brain can't outpace your feet, you'll be ash before dawn!"

My limbs ached, my lungs burned, and my head pounded with the effort of channeling fire qi to combat the flames, all while maintaining the rapid footwork that kept me from getting scorched. It was more than a physical challenge—it was a mental one. The synchronization of mind and body had to be absolute, my focus sharp enough to pierce through the heat haze that threatened to cloud my thoughts.

But even through the haze, something stirred.

As my body adapted to the fire's relentless assault, something clicked. My movements grew lighter, and the coals felt less like an enemy and more like a partner in this grueling dance.

And then that familiar chime echoed in my mind.

> *You feel a surge of power coursing through your veins. Your muscles ripple and your bones creak with newfound strength.*
> *Your body has reached Qi Initiation Stage—Rank 1.*

About time!

"Enough!" Elder Ming's voice cracked through the air like a whip. I didn't hesitate. With a last leap, I broke free of the circle of flames, landing on the frost-kissed ground beyond. The winter chill slammed into me like a wall, the sudden contrast drawing a gasp from my lips.

Patting down the remaining embers that clung to my robes, I pulled on my outer garments with shaking hands, the cold biting into my sweat-soaked skin. My legs trembled slightly from the exertion, but there was a strange clarity in my mind, a quiet triumph that hummed beneath my exhaustion.

I clenched and unclenched my fist, feeling a sense of harmony with my body that I hadn't felt before.

With that, my overall cultivation rank rose to the second level of the Qi Initiation stage! My body was always lagging, but now all three categories have gone past the mortal realm.

Elder Ming approached, his expression unreadable as always. He crossed his arms, his gaze sweeping over me critically.

"You're improving," he said at last, his tone begrudgingly approving. "But don't let that go to your head. The flame is still far from mastered."

I exhaled, letting the weight of his words settle as I felt a dull ache in my muscles. But there was a flicker of pride within me. Pride that couldn't be denied.

"Still," I said, managing a small grin. "I've come a long way, haven't I? Feng Wu said it'd take me three or four years to get to the second rank of Qi Initiation. But here I am, not even a year later."

Elder Ming tilted his head slightly, his sharp eyes narrowing. "You think you're some kind of prodigy now?" he asked, his voice tinged with dry amusement.

"Well," I started, letting the grin widen, "I mean . . . maybe? Isn't that what this means?"

Without a word, Elder Ming crouched low and began drawing in the dirt with a nearby stick. He etched a short, straight line. "This is you when you started," he said. Then, just beside it, he drew a significantly longer line. "And this is you now."

I nodded, feeling a swell of pride at the visual.

But then, with deliberate slowness, Elder Ming drew another line—a ridiculously long one that stretched far past the first two, nearly to the edge of the training ground. "And this," he said, his tone dry as the winter air, "is my sworn brother. Back when we were children, years younger than you are now."

My grin fell. "You've got to be kidding me."

Elder Ming straightened, brushing dirt from his hands. "Comparisons are a dangerous thing, Kai. They can motivate you or crush you. And you're not the only one growing stronger."

I huffed, crossing my arms as I glared at the absurdly long line in the dirt. "All right, point taken. Even so, you have to admit I'm not doing so bad."

His expression softened, but only slightly. "You're doing well," he admitted, "but the path ahead is far longer than you realize. And others aren't standing still. You know that."

Feng Wu's voice echoed in my mind, a reminder of just how far I had yet to go.

At your current level, it would take about three or four years of rigorous cultivation to reach the second rank of the Qi Initiation stage.

Feng Wu had been at the fourth rank of Qi Initiation then. By now, he was likely at the fifth, or even breaking into the Essence Awakening stage, growing with the rising qi throughout the region. The same could be said for the rest of my friends in the Verdant Lotus.

And my enemies.

I clenched my fists, the triumph I'd felt moments ago giving way to a sharp determination. Elder Ming was right. I couldn't afford to grow complacent. This was progress, yes, but it was only a step on a path that stretched far beyond the horizon.

I glanced back at the faint glow of the coals in the training circle, its light flickering against the encroaching night. "I'll just have to keep moving," I muttered, more to myself than to Elder Ming. "No stopping, no settling. I'll catch up, no matter how far ahead they are."

Elder Ming gave a faint hum of approval. "Good. Now stop wasting energy talking and go recover. You'll need your strength for the next session."

I gave him a half-hearted glare but turned to leave, my mind already churning with plans for what came next.

But just as I said those words, another notification appeared.

> *Quest: Body Refinement (Breakthrough)*
> *—Take on the Black Tortoise's Tribulation.*
> *Accept? (Y/N)*

That was odd.

I tilted my head, trying to remember the last time the Heavenly Interface had given me an option to accept or decline a quest. I dove deep into my Memory Palace, looking through the small sapling, which congealed all my knowledge of the Heavenly Interface into one area.

Aside from my first contract, I don't think it ever did.

It was odd that the Interface hadn't given a quest for me to break *into* the Qi Initiation stage, but only when I arrived.

Hesitation gripped me. My eyes lingered on the notification, and for a moment, I thought about asking Elder Ming what he thought. His insight had guided me this far, after all.

But then I shook my head.

Since when have I ever been the sort to turn down a challenge?

Let it be known Kai Liu never turns down a quest!

The moment I confirmed, the world seemed to twist. A crushing weight slammed down on me, dragging me to my knees before I could even gasp. My elbows hit the frozen ground hard, the shock of impact rippling through my arms.

"What the—!?" I wheezed, my voice strained under the sudden pressure. My chest felt like it was caving in, my limbs trembling as though my pill furnace had been dropped on my back.

The frostbitten ground blurred beneath me as my vision wavered. Every breath was a battle, each inhalation shallow and painful. My qi flared instinctively, but even that felt sluggish, as if the energy within me was being smothered by an invisible force.

"Kai!" Elder Ming's voice cut through the haze. His presence loomed over me, but I couldn't lift my head to meet his gaze.

"What . . . is this?" I choked out, my body refusing to move.

> *Sub-quest accepted: The Black Tortoise's Tribulation*
> *Objective: Punch and leave a visible dent in the ancient Banyan tree outside of Gentle Wind Village while carrying the weight of the Black Tortoise shell.*
> *Conditions:*
> *The Black Tortoise shell is bound to you and cannot be removed until the challenge is complete.*
> *The shell is invisible and intangible to others.*
> *You must rely solely on your own strength to complete this challenge.*

Shell?

Can't be removed until the challenge is complete?

Just my luck.

I got myself into a comfortable position with Elder Ming's help. After laying me down on my back, I explained the situation to him.

Elder Ming crouched beside me, his hand hovering near my back without touching. His expression was calm, but his eyes held a flicker of something I couldn't quite place. Concern, maybe? Curiosity?

"Interesting," he muttered. "The Black Tortoise's Tribulation, you said?"

I barely managed a nod.

"Foolish boy," he said, though his tone lacked its usual bite. "You accepted a quest involving a celestial tribulation without knowing what it entails?"

"I didn't think it'd feel like this!" I hissed, my arms shaking as I tried to hold them up. The weight pressed down harder, pinning me in place. As though the weight of the Two-Star Pagoda Pill Furnace was bearing down on me. Perhaps this was why the quest was only presented to me now.

It was the bare minimum I needed to even survive.

Elder Ming sighed, standing to his full height. "Of course, you didn't. But now that you've started, there's no turning back. The tribulation has begun."

"Great," I muttered through gritted teeth. "Care to offer some . . . sage advice while I get crushed to death?"

"Endure," he said simply, folding his arms. "If you can't withstand the weight of this trial, you have no business advancing further. You're good at that, aren't you?"

"Endure," I echoed bitterly, my fingers digging into the frozen dirt. "Yeah, thanks for that profound wisdom."

The faintest smirk ghosted across his lips. "Good luck."

I didn't have the energy to glare at him. The weight wasn't just physical; it pressed against my mind, my spirit, as if testing every fiber of my being.

Fine. If this is a test, I'll pass it. I always do.

"But . . . is this normal? Even before the Interface? Have you ever heard of a tribulation like this?" I asked Elder Ming.

He stroked his chin thoughtfully, his sharp eyes narrowing as he stared at the space just above my shoulder, as though he could see the invisible weight crushing me.

"No," he admitted finally, his tone unusually grave. "This isn't normal. I've heard of tribulations, but they occur at far higher cultivation levels and are more . . . dramatic."

"Like the Spirit Ascension Stage?" I croaked out, each word escaping between shallow breaths.

He shook his head slowly. "No. Higher. At the Earthly Transcendence Stage." His words carried a weight of their own, sinking into me like stones.

I blinked through the haze of pain. "Earthly Transcendence?" The words felt foreign on my tongue, like an elusive legend pulled from the pages of Liang Feng's novels. My mind swirled, trying to reconcile this mythical stage with the crushing weight pinning me down. "That's . . . real?"

"Yes, though not here," Elder Ming said, his voice firm. "It's exceedingly rare even on the mainland. Only the most elite cultivators, like sect elders of top sects, have a chance of reaching it. And even then, the heavens view them as a threat to their authority."

"What happens?" I asked, the strain of the shell momentarily eclipsed by curiosity.

Elder Ming's gaze darkened. "The heavens respond with lightning tribulations. Bolts of celestial fury strike to obliterate those who dare to ascend. Survive, and you advance to the next stage. Fail, and you risk losing your cultivation or your life."

A shiver that had nothing to do with the cold ran down my spine. Lightning tribulations. I suppose this was better than that.

"But," Elder Ming continued, snapping me out of my spiraling thoughts, "that's not something you need to worry about. At the rate you're progressing, it would take centuries for you to even think about Earthly Transcendence."

"Centuries?" I groaned, though whether it was from his words or the unrelenting weight, I couldn't say. "You really know how to motivate a guy. What comes after that stage? Is there one?"

He snorted. "Motivation or not, you need to focus on surviving this tribulation first. Worrying about stages beyond your reach is a waste of time."

"But this—" I gritted my teeth, pushing against the crushing force to sit upright, channeling qi to reinforce my body and give me some breathing room. "This isn't normal, is it? You've never seen anything like it?"

"Never," Elder Ming said, and for the first time, there was a flicker of genuine uncertainty in his voice. "I've read about many tribulations, seen one with my own eyes. None of them were like this. Whatever this is . . . it's new."

His words settled over me like a second weight, one not from the shell but from the realization that I was in uncharted territory. Whatever this Black Tortoise's Tribulation was, it wasn't following the conventional rules of cultivation.

Elder Ming gave me a long, appraising look. "If you make it through this, Kai, it will change you."

"Yeah?" I gasped, managing a shaky smirk. "Hopefully not into ash."

He chuckled, a rare sound that somehow lightened the oppressive atmosphere. "That depends on how stubborn you are. Now, stop talking and focus."

I gritted my teeth, the crushing weight pressing against my chest as I tried to summon enough qi to stabilize myself. This wasn't just a burden; it was an all-encompassing trial, testing everything from my physical endurance to my willpower.

As if sensing my struggle, Elder Ming's voice broke through the haze. "This is going to take weeks," he said matter-of-factly, pacing around me. His sharp gaze lingered on my trembling arms, the sweat dripping onto the frozen ground. "You won't be able to train properly in anything else until you've adjusted to this weight. We'll pause training while you adjust."

"Weeks?" My voice cracked, more from disbelief than exertion. "Are you serious?"

"Very," Elder Ming replied, crossing his arms. "If you're able to complete it, you'll be far stronger. But until then . . ." He let the words hang, his silence heavy with implication.

I groaned, my face contorting in frustration. "This is going to ruin all my plans! I had progress to make, techniques to master, and now I'm going to spend weeks just trying to stand without looking like an idiot!"

"Consider it a lesson in humility."

Before I could retort, a soft knock interrupted us. The sound was almost polite, a stark contrast to the tension of the moment. Both Elder Ming and I turned toward the courtyard's entrance.

"Elder Ming, Kai," a familiar voice called out. Xiao Bao's silhouette appeared just beyond the threshold, his face still marked with crumbs of food. "There are people here to meet you."

CHAPTER FOUR

A New Face

The chill bit harder than usual that morning as I stood with Elder Ming, the crushing weight of the Black Tortoise shell pressing down on every joint and muscle. My breath misted in the cold air, and each exhale felt heavier than the last. I'd barely pulled myself upright after Xiao Bao's announcement.

When I saw them, my heart sank.

The group approaching wasn't Feng Wu or the Whispering Wind Sect disciples I'd been hoping for. Instead, it was a caravan of strangers; at least a dozen figures, many of them seedy-looking types who wouldn't have been out of place in the darker alleys of Crescent Bay City. A handful of carts and wagons creaked behind them, weighed down with items I couldn't make out from this distance. Leading them was a man with a sharp, angular face, dressed too well for a simple traveler but not quite polished enough to be a noble. His hair was slicked back, and even from afar, I could see the smirk curling his lips as he locked eyes with Elder Ming and me.

The kind of smirk that made my stomach churn.

"Great," I muttered under my breath, forcing my legs to move. The shell's weight bore down on me with every step, and I had to focus just to keep my qi flowing steadily enough to reinforce my body. My limbs screamed for relief, but I straightened my back and clenched my jaw, doing my best to appear composed.

Why now? I cursed silently. *Out of all the times to take on a tribulation, why did it have to be today?*

The strangers continued their approach, and as they drew closer, the leader's smirk widened. His confident gait and the rough demeanor of his companions—all of it screamed trouble. I braced myself, each step feeling like a gamble. By the time I reached the courtyard's edge, my legs were trembling beneath the weight of the shell, but I kept my chin up.

"Are you Kai Liu?" the man called out, his voice smooth but with an edge that set my nerves on fire. His sharp eyes flicked toward Elder Ming briefly before settling on me again. "And the Village Head?"

Elder Ming nodded, and I stopped a few paces from him, fighting the urge to lean on the gate for support. "That's me," I said, keeping my tone steady. "Who's asking?"

The man's smirk didn't falter. In fact, it deepened. Without warning, he moved.

Fast.

Too fast for me to react.

My body tensed instinctively, qi surging to respond. But the weight of the shell slowed me down, and I could only watch, frozen, as his hand darted toward me.

My heart jumped into my throat, panic flaring—

And then he pulled something from his pocket.

"Here," he said, holding it out with a flourish.

It was . . . a silk-wrapped box?

The man's movements were deliberate as he extended the box toward me and then bowed deeply. His smirk was gone, replaced by a respectful expression that looked almost out of place on his sharp features.

"I'm Liang Chen," he said, his tone calm and deferential. "A humble merchant. These men and the caravans you see behind me are my workers. We've come to offer our services to your village."

I blinked.

He straightened, gesturing toward the wagons behind him. "We bring supplies, tools, and goods for trade. The roads here aren't well-maintained, but word of Gentle Wind Village as your abode has spread. It's rare to find a village with such a promising reputation." He offered a small smile. "And I couldn't pass up the opportunity to establish connections with someone who made it to the finals of the Grand Alchemy Gauntlet."

For a moment, I just stared at him, my mind reeling. I'd prepared myself for a fight, for a bandit leader or ambitious rogue sect trying to claim the village's resources. Instead . . . he was just a merchant?

I glanced at Elder Ming, whose expression remained as unreadable as ever. Of course, he'd probably seen through this man's intentions the moment he laid eyes on him. Meanwhile, I stood there like an idiot, trying to process the sudden shift in tone.

Liang Chen cleared his throat, holding the silk-wrapped box out toward me again. "This is a gift," he said. "A token of goodwill. I hope it will convey the sincerity of our intentions."

With effort, I unclenched my jaw and forced a smile. "Uh . . . thanks," I said, taking the box with hands that trembled only partly from exertion. The weight of the shell made it feel heavier than it was, but I managed not to drop it.

Just as I took the silk-wrapped box from Liang Chen, a familiar, indignant voice erupted from behind me.

"You!"

I turned to see Huan, the representative of the Azure Silk Trading Company, storming out of the village gates with all the dramatic flair of someone personally wronged. His eyes darted between Liang Chen and me before landing squarely on Liang Chen. He pointed an accusing finger at him, his expression a mix of shock and derision.

"What are you doing here, Liang?" Huan demanded, his voice tinged with an almost theatrical outrage. "Haven't you caused me enough trouble already?"

I blinked, completely off guard. Huan was rarely this animated unless he was haggling prices or trying to sell off his more dubious wares.

Liang Chen, for his part, seemed entirely unfazed. In fact, he chuckled. "Good to see you too, Huan. It's been a while." His smirk returned, but it was lighter this time, almost playful. "Still running things under the Azure Silk Trading Company, I see?"

"You know each other?" I asked, glancing between them.

Huan turned to me with wide, pleading eyes that would've looked ridiculous on anyone else. "Kai, you wouldn't betray me, right? After everything I've done for this village? For you? I got your letter to the Verdant Lotus Sect in time! Surely you're not going to let *him* steal my business now!"

Liang Chen let out a hearty laugh. "Steal your business? Come now, Huan. I'm not here to compete with you." He turned back to me, his smirk softening. "Your company has a good eye for potential, though. I'll give them that. It seems we both recognized this village's promise."

Huan looked skeptical. "Then why are you here, exactly?"

Liang Chen gestured to one of his workers, who hurried over with a small crate in tow. "Allow me to demonstrate," he said, lifting the lid to reveal an assortment of tools: woodworking equipment, farming implements, and sturdy-looking building materials. "My company specializes in practical goods and infrastructure support. Tools to make daily life easier for your villagers. Building supplies for expansions. And, should you need it, access to our network for more specialized needs."

I raised an eyebrow. "Building materials?"

He nodded. "I go where the money goes. And while your village is small, it's growing. Word of the Verdant Lotus Sect's interest in this place wasn't exactly subtle." His gaze was shrewd, calculating. "Opportunities like this don't come often."

Before I could respond, he added, almost as an afterthought, "Of course, there was another reason I came here."

I stiffened slightly, still wary of his motives. "And what's that?"

Liang Chen's smirk widened. "I crossed paths with someone I believe you know. Feng Wu, his name was? I found him leaving Crescent Bay. He was traveling alone, so I offered him a ride in one of my carriages for escorting us with my bodyguards."

My eyes widened. "Feng Wu?"

As if on cue, one carriage parked near the back creaked open. A familiar figure stepped out.

"Kai!" Feng Wu called, waving as he strolled over, completely unfazed by the group of workers or the tension in the air. "Long time no see!"

Relief flooded through me, and I couldn't help but smile. "Feng Wu," I said, my voice lighter than it had been all morning. "You're back! I thought you were supposed to arrive with the second-class disciples."

"Ah, I had business to attend to. It relates to the Whispering Wind Sect, so remind me to update you on that later."

I nodded, though Feng Wu's words only deepened my curiosity. For now, there were more pressing matters.

Like the fact that every step I took felt like I was dragging an entire mountain with me.

The second-class disciple's eyes narrowed as he stepped closer, his grin fading slightly. "Kai, you look . . . off. Are you limping?"

I forced a chuckle, though it came out more like a wheeze. "Just a little . . . sore from training. Nothing to worry about."

With his brow furrowed, his sharp eyes scanned me more closely.

I waved him off, though it took every ounce of willpower to keep my arm steady. "I'll explain later," I said, trying to inject some finality into my tone. "For now, I need some rest. Thank you, Liang Chen. It was nice meeting you."

Without waiting for his response, I turned and began hobbling toward my shop.

My qi reserves, already strained from reinforcing my body during Elder Ming's training, were dangerously low. I'd been burning through them just to maintain the semblance of composure in front of Liang Chen and his caravan.

I didn't dare glance back.

By the time I reached my front door, I was running on fumes. My legs buckled the moment I crossed the threshold, and I collapsed against the wall with a ragged sigh. The shop was quiet, the familiar scent of herbs and faintly sweet incense wrapping around me like a balm. For the first time since morning, I allowed myself a moment to breathe.

"Kai?" Tianyi's soft, melodic voice drifted toward me. Her silhouette cast a massive shadow over me. "You've fallen. Are you okay?"

I opened my mouth to explain but stopped myself. Where would I even begin? Instead, I groaned and waved toward the back of the shop. "Just . . . carry me to the bed, please."

Tianyi blinked, clearly confused, but didn't argue. She walked around me, her delicate frame belying the strength she used to support my weight. With surprising ease, she hoisted me off the ground and guided me toward the bed in the back of the shop.

Halfway there, she paused and cocked her head. "Kai . . . did you get fatter? Preparing for winter?"

Despite the exhaustion, I couldn't help but snort. "No, it's not fat. It's the product of a tribulation."

"A tribulation? I see."

She didn't press further, though it was clear she didn't fully understand. I didn't blame her. I wasn't entirely sure I understood it myself. Once she set me down on the bed, I waved weakly toward the door. "Can you bring me some fresh snow from outside? Just melt it onto the pill furnace."

Tianyi nodded, darting outside without a word. I let out another sigh and closed my eyes, focusing on the faint wisps of qi I still had left. With a final sigh, I let go of my qi reinforcement, letting myself fully sink into the bed.

CRACK!

. . . Looks like I'll have to ask Li Wei to fix my bed.

For several minutes, I sat there in silence, cycling my energy inward, drawing what little I could from the environment using the Crimson Lotus Purification technique. The air was saturated with qi, thanks to Tianyi's Qi Haven skill, and I could feel it seeping into my pores like a balm for my frayed reserves. Slowly but surely, my reserves returned with every breath.

When I finally opened my eyes, I glanced toward the furnace. The snow Tianyi had brought was already melting, the reflection on the surface rippling slightly. As I leaned forward, I glimpsed my reflection—and the massive, Black Tortoise shell draped across my back.

It gleamed like polished obsidian, its surface smooth yet etched with faint, intricate patterns. I reached out to touch it, but my hand passed through as though it weren't even there.

"Tianyi," I called, my voice steady now. She moved closer, her wings stirring the air. "Can you see anything on my back?"

She tilted her head, studying me intently. "No. Why? Are you experiencing hallucinations because of this tribulation?"

I frowned, glancing at the reflection again. "I'm not hallucinating," I muttered, more to myself than her. "But this . . . tribulation's effects are stranger than I thought."

Tianyi didn't press further, though the concern in her gaze lingered. "If you're sure . . ."

"I'm sure. It's just . . . a lot to take in."

Tianyi's antenna-like strands twitched, but she nodded and stepped back.

I turned my focus back to the reflection on the furnace's surface. The tortoise shell shimmered faintly, almost alive with some inner energy, its intricate patterns shifting subtly when I blinked. My fingers itched to study it more closely, to analyze whatever this tribulation had brought upon me. But even thinking about it made my back feel heavier, like the shell could sense my curiosity and reminded me of its presence.

"By the way, where's Windy?"

"He went hunting," she said, her tone matter-of-fact as she dusted off a shelf near the furnace.

I groaned, leaning down on the bed as carefully as I could. "Of course, he did. I told him not to stray too far! We're in no position to be chasing him if he runs into trouble."

I focused my senses on our emotional link. It was faint. Only Tianyi could detect his location or communicate with him. Perhaps being infused with her energy from his time as an egg led to their bond?

Her glowing eyes blinked at me, wide and unassuming. "He's grown more confident. You should trust his instincts."

I sighed, sinking deeper into the creaking bed.

Tianyi, utterly unfazed, returned to dusting. Still, her words gnawed at me. Maybe she was right, but that didn't make it any easier to watch Windy put himself in danger, even if I knew he was more than capable. I suppose this was how Elder Ming felt dealing with me in the beginning.

I let out a long breath, shifting my focus back to the more immediate problem—the crushing weight on my back and the dire state of my qi reserves.

This wasn't sustainable. Judging by what I'm feeling, the shell must weigh at least two and a half shi. And from the looks of it, it applied itself evenly throughout my body.

If walking a few steps around the village was enough to drain me, how was I supposed to maintain the shop, handle the villagers' requests, or even keep up with my cultivation? Every task, no matter how minor, would demand an immense amount of qi just to function normally.

And if I was going to survive this tribulation, or even just make it through the next few days, I needed a plan.

The answer was obvious. Pills. Copious amounts of them.

The irony wasn't lost on me. Not that long ago, I'd lectured Lan-Yin and Wang Jun about the dangers of overreliance on pills.

I glanced toward the furnace. I'd need to refine something potent enough to replenish my reserves without completely depleting my stock. The villagers needed these pills too, and if I burned through everything for my sake, it would set us all back.

"Tianyi," I said, my voice breaking the silence. She turned, her glowing eyes locking onto me.

"Yes?"

"I need your help," I continued, pushing myself upright with a wince. "I'm going to focus on cultivating as much qi as possible, but I need someone to monitor the furnace. And maybe help me fetch ingredients from the storage."

She nodded, her antennae twitching slightly. "Understood."

"Thanks," I said, reaching under the table where I kept my personal stash of pills. My fingers brushed against the cool surface of the wooden box, and I carefully brought it down to the bed.

Inside, neatly aligned in rows, were several pills, each gleaming faintly in the light from the furnace. They were my best work; high-grade recovery pills I'd refined over the past month. I'd been saving them for emergencies, either for a battle or if someone was gravely injured.

Well, if this wasn't an emergency, I didn't know what was.

Tianyi hovered near the furnace, watching me with her usual detached curiosity.

The next step in surviving this tribulation started now.

As I picked up one pill, the faint warmth it radiated seeped into my fingertips, a promise of the energy it held. It was going to be hard. But if I could complete this, then the reward . . .

I let out a slow breath, preparing myself for the long night ahead.

"Time to see just how far I can push myself."

CHAPTER FIVE

The Lotus Blooms in Fire

The steam from the teapot spiraled upward, curling in delicate tendrils that caught the morning light. I poured carefully, the amber liquid filling the porcelain cups with a shaky flow, because of my unsteady hands. Across from me, Feng Wu tapped a single finger against the table, a small gesture of appreciation as he cradled his cup with both hands.

But the serenity didn't last.

"The Black Tortoise Tribulation?" Feng Wu's voice cut through the quiet, laced with disbelief. His brow furrowed as he leaned forward, his cup momentarily forgotten. "This isn't some joke, right?"

I nodded, setting the teapot down. "Nope. No joke."

"One of the four mythical beasts. I suppose your claims of being special aren't so wrong after all." He shook his head, clearly still trying to process it.

"Well, here I am," I said with a shrug, lifting my cup. My eyes were baggy, and my entire body hurt. Even sleeping was a challenge with this tribulation, and I ended up spending half of my night cycling my qi. "Don't know whether to call this a blessing or a curse."

Feng Wu didn't laugh. Instead, he sighed, rubbing his temple. "The Heavenly Interface keeps throwing surprises. The Verdant Lotus Sect has been studying its quirks, and we've already adjusted the curriculum to account for the way it speeds up growth. How to trigger certain quests, and how to complete them . . . It's made the younger disciples ambitious. Li Na and Han Wei especially. They're growing steadily."

"Ambitious, huh?" I leaned back, trying to picture the younger disciples clashing over who could outpace the other. "I bet they're eager to try their skills, but I hope they're not reckless. Or at least, I hope they've mastered bandaging their own scrapes. The only reason I refined my body this far was because of my hydrosol and other medicines."

Feng Wu raised a brow. "You think we'd let disciples train without the basics? Every Verdant Lotus disciple is taught first aid."

I snorted, setting my cup down. "Ah yes, I've seen it in action. You all carry medicinal wine in your satchels? So much for being a taoist."

He rolled his eyes, his tone laced with exasperation. "You work with medicines, Kai. You know it's rooted in practical application."

"Oh, I agree," I said, smirking. "But then why go out of your way to make it smell and taste good? I bet you add . . . let's see . . . maybe star anise?"

Feng Wu stiffened, just barely, and I grinned. "So I'm right?"

"It's a sect secret," he said firmly, though the faint twitch at the corner of his mouth betrayed his amusement.

"Sure it is," I teased. "It just seems like it's less about wounds and more about giving these taoists an excuse to drink. But Li Na and Han Wei, huh? Good. I'll look forward to sparring with them again."

"Speaking of sparring . . . Jian Feng. I heard you beat him."

I waved dismissively. "He wasn't at his best. He was using a staff, which was clearly unfamiliar to him. If it had been hand-to-hand or with a weapon he actually trained with, I wouldn't have."

Feng Wu smirked. "And yet you still won. Convenient that you neglected to mention the fact that you were holding back, too."

"What?" I blinked at him, surprised.

"Oh, don't play coy," Feng Wu said, leaning back with a knowing grin. "I heard you didn't use Rooted Banyan Stance or Bamboo Reprisal Counter, all because Elder Ming asked you not to show your hand."

I felt my face heat. "That's . . . different."

"Different? How so?"

"It's not chivalrous to flaunt that. I'm not arrogant enough to rub my opponent's face because I was holding back."

Feng Wu stifled a laugh. "Not arrogant, huh? I could've sworn you had a 'young master' persona you liked to whip out now and then. What happened to that?"

I glared at him, though my blush probably ruined the effect. "Could you just tell me about what happened to the Whispering Wind Sect? Weren't they supposed to come by now?"

Feng Wu's smile faded, and his posture straightened, the air between us turning heavy.

"They're delayed," he said, his voice quieter now. "Because of the Silent Moon."

My cup paused halfway to my lips. "What happened?"

Feng Wu exhaled, his expression grim. "There's been a serious conflict in the east. A territory dispute turned into something much bigger. One of the Silent Moon elders, the ones from the mainland; they attacked and injured Tian Zhan."

I almost dropped my cup. "Tian Zhan? Injured? But he's one of the Whispering Wind Sect's strongest!"

"That's exactly why this is so serious," Feng Wu said. "Tian Zhan was leading the effort, and now the Whispering Wind Sect is mobilizing for a larger conflict. Their candidate for Sect Leader being injured is no small matter. The Silent Moon Sect knew what they were doing."

I leaned back, the weight of his words sinking in. "So that's why they haven't sent anyone here yet. I'm thankful the Verdant Lotus Sect hasn't withdrawn its support; otherwise, we'd be in a much worse position."

Feng Wu nodded. "Now that the Sect Leader has come out of seclusion, things are stabilizing."

My head snapped up. "Sect Leader Shaotian Ye? He's . . . out?"

"Not just out, he's broken through to the Spirit Ascension stage."

I blinked, stunned. I'd almost forgotten that the Sect Leader had gone into seclusion months ago.

"Spirit Ascension . . ." I repeated numbly. "That's incredible. So he's as strong as the Wind Sage now?"

"Perhaps," Feng Wu agreed. "We have no way of confirming it. The ambient qi levels are rising everywhere, and breakthroughs among elders and sect leaders who've plateaued for decades are becoming more common. The balance of power is shifting."

I nodded slowly, my thoughts churning. The ramifications of such a change weren't small. But for now, I had to focus on what I could control—like surviving this tribulation.

Through the window, I caught sight of Tianyi and Windy outside. They were in the snow, Windy darting through the drifts while Tianyi's wings sparkled in the sunlight as she leapt and twisted in the air. What looked like playful antics was clearly training, the two of them honing their instincts and skills with every movement.

Despite Windy's lower cultivation level, his instincts were first-rate and allowed him to keep up against Tianyi in a way I never could.

The sunlight glinted off the snow outside, illuminating the sharp contrast between Tianyi's glittering wings and Windy's sleek, serpentine movements. She spun midair, her wings slicing through the crisp winter air with precision, while Windy whipped his tail in controlled arcs, carving small trenches into the snow. It was hard to tell if they were playing or sparring, but knowing those two, it was probably both.

I sipped my tea, savoring the warmth that seeped through the porcelain. Feng Wu followed my gaze, a faint smile tugging at his lips. "Tianyi's really something. That Qi Haven skill of hers . . . It's no wonder you've made so much progress lately."

I raised an eyebrow. "How do you know it wasn't a result of my heaven-defying talent?"

He rolled his eyes. "Fair. It's also one reason I came."

I leaned back slightly. "Ah, my genius has drawn you to this village, I see. Figured you'd learn more observing me than training at the sect?"

"PFFT!" He struggled to hold in his laughter. I didn't see what was so humorous. "No, I meant how long Tianyi's Qi Haven skill lingers. The sect is curious about the rate of growth."

My brows furrowed. "Study it how?"

Feng Wu reached into his robes and produced a slim talisman, its surface inscribed with delicate runes. "This is a qi-measuring talisman. It records the density and quality of qi in an area. I'll use it today and then repeat the process next month to compare. It's not very precise, though."

My fingers drummed lightly against the table as I stared at the talisman. I frowned as a strange unease coiled in my chest, and I struggled to pinpoint its source.

Perhaps it was the reminder of how Tianyi's abilities were now under scrutiny—not just by me, but by others.

Feng Wu looked up from the talisman, his gaze sharpening as he caught my expression.

"Kai," he said, his tone firm, "you don't need to worry. This information won't leave me. The Verdant Lotus Sect won't misuse it, on my honor."

His sincerity was apparent, but the knot in my chest didn't loosen. I wasn't so much worried about Feng Wu or even the Verdant Lotus Sect. It was the possibility of information spreading beyond their control, into hands that wouldn't hesitate to exploit Tianyi or the village.

"It's not that I don't trust you," I said slowly, choosing my words with care. "It's just . . . this kind of thing could easily draw the wrong attention. Tianyi's Qi Haven skill is . . . unique. If others find out, it won't be long before they come sniffing around."

"I understand. That's why I'm being discreet as possible. No one else is involved in this."

I raised an eyebrow. "How do you plan to compare this place to others? The whole province's qi levels are rising; it's not exactly subtle."

"That's the challenge," he admitted. "Gentle Wind Village is the first location I'm testing. After this, I'll repeat the experiment in areas with different influences—sect grounds, other villages, and places rumored to have high natural qi density. For now, I'll focus on here."

His explanation made sense, but it didn't entirely soothe my concerns. "And they sent you alone for this?"

Feng Wu grinned. "I volunteered. No one else was better suited. Besides . . ." He gestured toward the window, where Tianyi and Windy continued their strange, synchronized dance. "I wanted to see this for myself."

I couldn't help but chuckle. "You're a scholar now, huh? Sometimes, I forget you're not a martial sect. Most of what I've seen is that side; swords, fists, and a touch of alchemy."

Feng Wu laughed. "Fair. Alchemy's the closest you've seen to scholarship, I imagine. But the Verdant Lotus Sect values research as much as combat. Understanding how to adapt to the Heavenly Interface, the ambient qi changes—it's all part of staying ahead. Even our martial techniques are improving because of it."

He picked up the talisman again, turning it over in his hands. "I'll start with the measurement shortly. Once we have a baseline, I can work on mapping Tianyi's influence across the area. It'll take time, but it's worth it."

I nodded, my fingers tightening slightly around my cup. "Just . . . keep it safe. I don't want this place turning into a battleground because someone got greedy."

Feng Wu met my gaze, his expression serious. "I promise. No one will know unless it's absolutely necessary."

That eased the tension a little, though the knot in my chest didn't fully unravel. I forced a smile, trying to lighten the mood. "Well, since you're here, maybe you can teach me some of those scholarly techniques. I might need them if the Heavenly Interface keeps throwing tribulations at me."

As the warmth of the tea settled in, I set my cup down and glanced at Feng Wu. It was the perfect opportunity to bring up something that had been nagging at me for weeks.

"There's something I've been meaning to ask you," I started, keeping my tone casual.

"Oh?"

"It's about the Interface. Have you heard of . . . technique tokens?" I asked, watching his expression closely.

He blinked, tilting his head slightly. "Technique tokens? I've never heard of those before."

"Yeah, I've been getting them as quest rewards. The description says they can upgrade skills or techniques to the next level, even bypassing prerequisites. But . . ." I hesitated, tapping a finger against the table. "I've been too nervous to use them."

Feng Wu leaned forward, his attention now laser-focused on the floating tokens. "Bypassing prerequisites to develop a skill? That's . . . fascinating. Why haven't you tried them yet?"

I sighed, rubbing the back of my neck. "Because I don't fully understand how they work. The system doesn't exactly come with a manual, and Elder Ming couldn't give me much advice either. He didn't want to guide me on something he wasn't familiar with, which I get."

"That's fair," he admitted. "But it's still surprising you haven't experimented. Surely you've thought about which skills to use them on?"

"I have," I said, exhaling slowly. "In fact, I've considered using one on my cultivation method, the Crimson Lotus Purification technique. It's slow to gather energy, but it has a purification aspect that only allows pure qi into my dantian. Any impurities are filtered out, which makes my reserves more stable, although it's agonizingly slow. But . . . I'm not sure it would work."

Feng Wu's brow furrowed. "Why not?"

"No matter how much I cultivate it, it hasn't advanced. It's been stuck at level one. That's why I was thinking of using a token to force it to the next level. But what if it destabilizes everything? What if it messes with the purification process and leaves me with polluted qi or something?"

Feng Wu put a hand to his chin, deep in thought.

"I think I have an answer," he said after a moment. "Cultivation methods, especially ones with a purification aspect, are designed to be as precise as possible. Any deviation in the qi flow could cause serious problems. In fact, methods like that are probably never meant to evolve—they're already optimized for what they're supposed to do."

My stomach sank at his words. "You're saying it might not even be possible to upgrade it?"

"Not necessarily," Feng Wu said quickly. "But it would explain why it hasn't leveled up naturally. Most sects don't develop new cultivation methods for a reason; there's just too much risk involved. Even minor changes require decades of study and careful testing."

I nodded slowly, letting his explanation sink in. It made sense, but it didn't make the decision any easier. "So, if the token does work, it might bypass those risks entirely. Or it might just destroy everything."

"That's the gamble," Feng Wu said, his tone measured. "But if it works, it could completely change how you handle this tribulation, right? An upgraded cultivation method would make a dramatic difference. Besides, the Interface hasn't shown any sign of sabotaging someone before."

I looked at the screen, ruminating on my options. Feng Wu's logic was sound, but the risks still loomed large in my mind. If this went wrong, it wouldn't just be my cultivation that suffered—it could set me back in ways I couldn't afford.

Still, the idea of overcoming the Black Tortoise Tribulation with a stronger foundation was tempting. Very tempting.

"Let's see what happens," I murmured, raising the menu.

> *To which skill would you like to apply the Technique Token?*
> *Spiritual Herbalism—6 (. . .)*
> *Nature's Attunement—6 (. . .)*
> *Accelerated Reading—9 (. . .)*
> *Rooted Banyan Stance—4 (. . .)*
> *Crimson Lotus Purification—1 (. . .)*
> *Bamboo Reprisal Counter—1 (. . .)*
> *Memory Palace Technique—1 (. . .)*
> *Refinement Simulation Technique—1 (. . .)*
> *Heavenly Flame Mantra—1 (. . .)*

I glanced back at Feng Wu, and he looked at me with a reassuring nod. "All right," I muttered under my breath. "Here goes nothing."

> *Are you sure you want to use a Technique Token on Crimson Lotus Purification? This action is irreversible.*

The system's confirmation window hovered before me, clear and final. And then, I confirmed.

The world vanished.

A flood of sensation and knowledge slammed into my mind like a tidal wave. I gasped as an intense warmth blossomed inside my chest, spreading outward in rapid pulses.

For a split second, I couldn't feel my body at all, as though I'd been pulled out of myself and suspended in pure, unfiltered knowing.

Patterns. Rhythms. My mind swirled as diagrams and circuits of flowing qi painted themselves across my consciousness in vivid detail. I saw it—the Crimson Lotus Purification—as I'd never seen it before. Every delicate cycle of qi moving through my meridians unfolded before me with clarity so sharp it burned. The breathing technique shifted; its cadence altered slightly, elongating my inhales, and smoothing my exhales.

The Lotus grows in harmony with breath and blood.

A voice—or perhaps just an impression—whispered into my mind. I couldn't tell if it came from the system, from myself, or from the technique itself.

The flow of qi wasn't just a steady stream anymore; it was a carefully choreographed dance. I felt the change.

The purification process refined itself, no longer a slow, clunky effort but a precise weave of energy. The sluggish feeling I'd struggled with for so long vanished like a mirage.

New pathways etched themselves into my awareness. Subtle twists and loops within my meridians I hadn't realized were there before. I could adjust my qi flow on instinct now, nudging it into optimal patterns with a thought. It was as if someone had shown me a hidden map of my body, one I never knew existed.

I blinked, my vision refocusing on the table in front of me. My entire body felt weightless yet grounded, as though I'd shed an invisible layer of exhaustion. A faint trail of drool was sliding down my chin, and I hastily wiped it away before Feng Wu could notice.

He did.

"You . . . drooled," he said, a mixture of amusement and concern coloring his voice. "Are you okay? You blanked out for a moment."

I stared at him, still reeling. Words failed me for a long beat before I croaked out, "I think . . . I think it worked."

The system chimed softly, and a window appeared in front of me.

> *Crimson Lotus Purification has evolved to Vermilion*
> *Lotus Refinement—Level 1.*
> *Remaining Tokens: 1*

I swallowed hard, my hands trembling as I absorbed the words.

"What happened?" Feng Wu asked, leaning forward, his scholarly curiosity fully unleashed now.

I exhaled slowly, my breathing instinctively following the new rhythm etched into my mind. "It . . . changed. The Crimson Lotus Purification is gone; it evolved. It's faster and smoother than before! It feels like it was always meant to be like this."

Feng Wu's brows shot up. "It actually evolved? The system adjusted a cultivation method?" His voice wavered between shock and awe. "Kai, do you realize how unheard of this is? Cultivation methods are sacred because tampering with them is dangerous—impossible, even! But the system . . . it just—"

"I know," I muttered, my mind still buzzing from the knowledge. "It didn't just force a level-up; it improved it. Perfectly. The system knew how to do it."

Feng Wu rubbed his face, muttering something about needing to draft a report for his sect. I leaned back in my chair, staring at the ceiling, my thoughts a tangle of awe, disbelief, and rising hope.

If the Heavenly Interface could do this . . . if it could refine techniques to such perfection . . . then what else was it capable of?

I glanced over at the second-class disciple with a grin.

"I know what I have to do."

CHAPTER SIX

A Snake Dreams of the Sky

The snow stretched endlessly around Gentle Wind Village, a pristine white blanket interrupted only by Windy's sleek, coiled form. His scales, pale white with a faint blue sheen, blended with the frost, making him nearly invisible except for the glint of his narrowed blue eyes. He rested atop a snowdrift, watching as the villagers bustled about, their faces flushed with admiration as they glanced toward the center of the village.

Toward her.

Tianyi, with her shimmering wings folded behind her back, stood near the gathering of villagers, her human form a delicate contradiction of strength and fragility. She was radiant, ethereal, a figure straight out of their stories. To them, she was nothing short of miraculous.

And then there was him—Windy.

The snake.

The villagers spoke of her transformation in awed whispers, calling her a "miracle," a "blessing." But when their eyes turned to him, they softened with a condescension that cut deeper than the winter chill. He could hear their thoughts as clearly as if they'd been spoken aloud.

Kai's snake. His pet. Loyal, but nothing more.

Windy's tail lashed against the snow. His frustration simmered just beneath his smooth scales. He wasn't *just* a snake. He wasn't *just* anything. He was a predator, an apex creature who had proven his worth repeatedly, in battle and in loyalty. Yet the world seemed to value not his power, but Tianyi's newfound ability to mimic the ones they protected.

Why must I wear another skin to prove my worth? The thought hissed through his mind like venom. *A serpent does not need wings to fly.*

He coiled tighter, his body instinctively readying to strike, though there was no enemy before him.

Windy's gaze drifted toward the tree line at the village's edge, where the wilderness began. The forest loomed beyond it, dark and tangled. A place of danger that Kai and Tianyi had warned him to avoid. But there were paths he could take that skirted its edges, away from the constraints of the village, away from the pitying gazes.

With a flick of his tail, Windy slid from the snowdrift and began weaving his way toward the outskirts of the village. The snow parted easily for him, his movements fluid despite the bitter cold. His mind raced, each thought sharper than the chill biting at his body.

Let them call me what they will. I do not need their recognition. I'll prove my worth to myself.

As he neared the village boundary, a shadow fell across the snow in front of him. He stopped, his tongue flicking out instinctively to sense who had blocked his path. Tianyi's scent was unmistakable.

"Where are you going, Windy?" Her voice was gentle, yet it carried the weight of someone used to being heeded. She hovered slightly above the snow, her wings stirring the air in slow, deliberate motions. "Does Kai know?"

Windy curled defensively, his eyes narrowing. *I don't answer to you. Or anyone. I go where I please.*

Tianyi tilted her head, her antennae-like strands twitching thoughtfully. She wasn't angry, merely curious. "Then be safe," she said at last, her voice soft. "And come back before dinner."

He flicked his tail dismissively, though a small part of him—one he refused to acknowledge—felt a flicker of warmth at her words. *I don't need your concern.*

"And yet you have it," she replied, her smile faint but genuine. She turned back toward the village, her wings fluttering as she left him to his path.

Windy watched her go, his frustration bubbling anew. He didn't want her care or Kai's approval. He wanted—*needed*—to carve his own place, one that was irrefutable. With a determined flick of his tongue, he set off into the wilderness.

The cold bit harder as he ventured further from the village. The snow deepened, and the trees became sparse, their skeletal branches casting jagged shadows across the ground. Windy moved with purpose, his serpentine body undeterred by the terrain, though the chill gnawed at his strength.

The wind howled around him, carrying with it the faint scent of prey; small animals burrowed beneath the snow, their heartbeats faint but detectable. He ignored them. Hunting wasn't his goal, not today. Today was about freedom, about proving that he could survive, thrive, without the protection of Kai or the village.

The wilderness seemed endless, its silence broken only by the crunch of snow beneath him and the occasional creak of ice-laden branches. His spirit beast constitution kept him moving, but even it couldn't fully shield him from the raw force of winter. The cold seeped into him, a reminder of the natural order he sought to defy.

Survival isn't enough, he thought bitterly. *I need more. I need . . .*

The word eluded him, but the yearning it represented burned in his chest.

Several li into his journey, the snow thinned as Windy approached a slope. His tongue flicked out instinctively, sensing something unusual below. The air was warmer here, a strange anomaly in the heart of winter. A faint hiss echoed from beneath the snow, carrying the unmistakable cadence of his kin.

Curiosity, mingled with a twinge of disdain, guided his movements. Windy slithered down the incline, his body flowing effortlessly over the frozen terrain until he found a narrow fissure in the ground, partially obscured by snow. The warmth emanated stronger now, a telltale sign of life below. He hesitated only briefly before slipping inside, his sleek form navigating the dark passage with ease.

The chamber revealed itself gradually, the dim light filtering through cracks above. The air was thick, humid compared to the bitter cold outside. Snakes of varying sizes and colors were coiled together in sprawling masses, their bodies intertwined in a survivalist embrace against the winter's grip. The sight was both awe-inspiring and, to Windy, faintly repellent.

He paused at the edge of the gathering, his presence immediately noticed. Several heads lifted, forked tongues flickering in unison as they assessed him. They did not hiss in warning or challenge but observed him with quiet curiosity. Even among his own kind, his radiant scales and subtle qi aura marked him as different. Other.

Windy slithered farther into the chamber, weaving between the coils of others. They parted for him, more out of instinct than respect. He sensed their deference but felt no kinship.

These are my kind, he thought, glancing at the dull, earth-toned scales of the others. *Yet they are not my kin. They survive, but they do not strive.*

Larger snakes occupied the central space, their bulk ensuring dominance over the rest. Windy's gaze lingered on them, searching for any hint of spirit, of that spark of potential he knew so well from Tianyi and himself. But there were none. They were impressive in size and strength but stagnant.

Creatures content with existing, not evolving.

Is this what it means to be a snake? The thought struck him with surprising bitterness. *To survive winters in the dark, dreaming of nothing but the thaw?*

For the first time, Windy considered conversing with the others. It was an alien thought to him; he had never sought the company of his own kind before. The underground chamber was alive with low hisses and subtle movements, a language he understood intrinsically but had rarely used.

He coiled tightly, his tail flicking against the stone floor in thought. When he finally spoke, his voice was sharp and clear.

"Do you feel it?" he hissed, addressing no one and everyone. "The pull to something greater?"

Several heads turned toward him, their interest piqued but their responses hesitant. One particularly large serpent, its dark scales glinting faintly in the low light, shifted closer, its tongue flicking toward Windy.

"What greater thing?" the larger snake replied. "The sun will return. The thaw will come. This is our time to endure, not dream."

Windy's eyes narrowed, his tail flicking dismissively. "Endure? Is that all you desire? To wait, huddled in the dark? Strength is not found in waiting. It is forged in striving."

A ripple of unease moved through the chamber, the muted hisses rising and falling in response to his words. The larger snake regarded him with something between curiosity and annoyance.

"You speak as if you are above this," it said. "And yet, here you are. A serpent, like the rest of us."

Windy bristled but forced himself to remain composed. "I am here, but I will not stay. I have come to see my kind, but I will not linger in the shadows. I was not made to wait. I was made to rise."

The larger snake seemed unimpressed, its massive coils shifting as it settled back into the mass. The chamber quieted again, the others returning to their state of dormancy, content to ignore him.

He had his answer. These were his kind, but they were not his peers.

Windy settled reluctantly among the coiled masses, his sleek form weaving through the tangled bodies of the hibernating snakes. The warmth of the chamber was a stark contrast to the biting cold above, yet it offered no comfort. He coiled tightly in an isolated corner, his scales brushing against the rough stone floor as he began a slow, deliberate mantra, the words a rhythm in his mind.

A serpent does not need wings to fly. A serpent coils its way to the heavens.

> *Your dao is slowly forming.*

The thought echoed within him, steady and unyielding. It wasn't just a mantra; it was a truth, a declaration of his identity. Windy repeated it silently, letting it root itself in the core of his being. The disdain he felt for the rest of his kin lingered, but he forced himself to observe, to study. If he were to rise, he needed to understand the foundation he sought to transcend.

Time passed in an unmeasured haze. The movements of the snakes around him were subtle and infrequent—a slow shift here, a flicker of a tongue there. The air was thick with the scent of their presence. Windy's eyes narrowed as he watched the larger snakes dominate the warmer central spaces. Their size alone granted them privilege, but they lacked the spark, the drive, that separated the extraordinary from the ordinary.

They mistake size for strength, Windy thought, his tongue flicking disdainfully. *They mistake endurance for purpose.*

He adjusted his coils, his tail curling protectively around his core as his instincts remained alert. Despite the lethargy that gripped the chamber, danger lurked here, subtle but present. He was smaller than many of the snakes, but he knew his strength surpassed theirs. His spirit beast nature ensured it, but they wouldn't see that. To them, size was the only metric of power.

As if on cue, a shadow loomed over him. Windy's muscles tensed, his senses sharpening. A massive snake, its dull scales mottled with scars, slithered closer. Its movements were deliberate, predatory. Windy's tongue flicked out, tasting the intent in the air.

It was hungry.

Before the larger snake could strike, Windy moved. His sleek body darted to the side, the attack missing him by the width of a scale. He twisted around, his fangs bared in a warning display. The larger snake hesitated, its dull eyes blinking slowly as if processing the failed strike. It recoiled slightly, confused by the agility of its smaller target.

"You dare?" Windy hissed, his tone sharp. "Do you not see what I am?"

The larger snake regarded him for a moment longer, then slithered away without another attempt. It was too dim-witted to comprehend what had happened but instinctive enough to recognize a threat it didn't understand.

He glanced around, noting that the others had barely reacted. They had seen the exchange but dismissed it as irrelevant, their dull gazes returning to their own torpid existence.

These snakes were content to wallow in their lethargy, oblivious to the greater world beyond their narrow existence.

If strength was the only language they understood, then he would speak it fluently.

Slowly, deliberately, he began slithering toward the heart of the hibernaculum, where the largest snakes coiled in their arrogant complacency. The temperature was warmer here, the air heavy with the combined breath of the dominants. Their hulking forms lay piled on one another, motionless save for the occasional flick of a tail or shift of a massive coil.

Windy's movements were smooth, his scales glinting faintly in the dim light as he approached the nearest of them; the same one that tried to attack him. The serpent's size was intimidating, easily five times his length, its girth enough to crush a boar. It barely acknowledged him, assuming him to be no threat.

It was a mistake.

With a blur of motion, Windy struck. His fangs sank into the massive snake's neck with precision, injecting a burst of venom that stunned the creature. Before it could react, Windy twisted his body around its bulk, constricting with a force far beyond his size. The larger snake writhed, its movements sluggish and uncoordinated compared to Windy's honed techniques. It thrashed violently but failed to dislodge him. Within moments, it lay still, its dominance stripped away.

The other snakes stirred at the commotion, their dull eyes now fixed on Windy. Whispers rippled through the chamber, hisses of confusion and fear.

"He defeated One-Eye," one murmured.

"Impossible. He's too small," another said.

Windy ignored them, his focus already shifting to the next largest snake. This one was more alert, its forked tongue flicking rapidly as it regarded him warily. But caution was no substitute for skill. Windy darted forward, his movements a blur as he coiled around its head, forcing its jaws shut before delivering a series of rapid strikes to its vulnerable underbelly. The fight was over before it began.

The defeated snakes hissed in outrage, their voices rising in a cacophony of bitterness.

"As one predator falls, another rises," one murmured, its tone bitter and resigned. "The strongest of our kind was slain, and now he takes its place."

"That brute?" another spat, its tone laden with scorn. "He wasn't even a shadow of the power the last apex held. But alas, even that one's might meant nothing to the shadow in the forest."

Windy froze, his body coiling tighter as their words settled over him like a layer of frost. *Shadow?* The term pricked at his instincts, carrying a weight far beyond their grumbled disdain. He slithered closer to one of the defeated serpents, his tongue flicking out sharply, his aura a cold and unyielding demand for clarity.

"What shadow?" Windy's voice cut through their murmurs, sharp and deliberate. "Speak clearly. What are you talking about?"

The snake nearest to him recoiled, its battered pride and aching body reluctant to cooperate. But Windy's unwavering gaze bore into it, his coiled body radiating a silent but potent menace. Reluctantly, it answered, its voice trembling with a mix of fear and bitterness.

"There's something in the forest," it admitted, its tone low and halting. "A predator far greater than anything we've known. It came from the depths of the forest and killed the apex of this place. None of us dared to face it."

Another snake chimed in, its voice tinged with equal parts fear and resignation. "It claimed its territory in the forest, and now it looms over us, unseen but ever-present. We stay here because we have no choice."

Windy's tongue flicked again, tasting the truth in their words. His mind churned with the implications, the image of this shadowy predator painting itself vividly in his imagination. Whatever this creature was, it had already marked its dominance in blood, and now it lingered, unchallenged, just beyond the reach of these lesser beings.

His coils tensed further, a spark of challenge igniting within him. He slithered closer to the speaking snake, his voice cutting through the thick, humid air like a blade.

"You cower here, waiting for the next shadow to claim you," Windy hissed. "But I will not. Tell me everything you know about this predator."

The hisses of his kind grew quieter as Windy's demand lingered in the air, his presence casting a long shadow over the defeated serpents. Slowly, they spoke, their fragmented knowledge spilling forth like scattered embers, illuminating the shape of the danger that awaited.

> *Quest: Path of the Serpent*
> *—Discover the shadow and confirm its existence.*
> *—Overcome a predator that surpasses you in cultivation rank without relying solely on speed.*
> *—Protect your territory.*

Windy's tail flicked sharply as he dismissed the screen. The notion of protecting the hibernacula grated against his pride, but the challenge intrigued him. If this shadow had claimed dominance over the forest, then it was his duty to confront it.

He slithered toward the fissure, his body tense with anticipation. The forest loomed in his thoughts, its dangers a distant hum in the back of his mind. Kai and Tianyi's warnings echoed faintly, but he brushed them aside.

"This is not for them," he told himself, his tongue flicking out to taste the chilly air as he emerged from the underground chamber. "This is for me. My territory. My strength."

It was night now, and the snow greeted him once more, its chill biting but invigorating. Windy coiled briefly at the entrance to the fissure, his gaze fixed on the tree line in the distance. The forest awaited, its shadows deeper and darker than ever.

With a final flick of his tail, Windy darted forward, leaving the hibernaculum behind. He was done waiting. It was time to rise.

CHAPTER SEVEN

Burden of the Black Tortoise

I rubbed my temples, sitting cross-legged by the furnace, the faint hum of the Vermilion Lotus Refinement technique threading through my meridians like a calming melody. It had been a week since I upgraded the technique, and though it hadn't magically solved my problems, it had given me something invaluable.

Breathing room.

My qi reserves were still in a state of being perpetually drained, but at least now I didn't feel like I was drowning every moment of the day. With the Vermilion Lotus Refinement, my energy cycled more efficiently, letting me reclaim enough qi daily to function somewhat normally without burning through my stash of pills. Even the crushing weight of the Black Tortoise shell felt less oppressive, although perhaps I was just hallucinating.

The door creaked open, and Lan-Yin peeked her head inside. "Morning, Kai! Brought you breakfast!" she chimed, holding up a basket of steamed buns.

Behind her, Wang Jun trudged in, carrying a crate of supplies for the shop. "And here's the shipment from Azure Silk. You're welcome."

I gave them a tired smile before slipping into a bow with clasped hands. "This young master promises to repay this debt."

Lan-Yin set the basket on the counter and waved dismissively. "Don't mention it. You'd do the same for us. Besides, it's not every day we get to see you being so . . . slow and clunky."

"Wow, thanks for the reminder," I said dryly, taking a bun and biting into it. The warm, fluffy dough melted in my mouth, and for a moment, I forgot about the tribulation entirely.

Wang Jun dropped the crate with a thud, stretching his arms. "This is the last one, according to Huan." He eyed me critically. "You look a bit less like death today."

I gestured to the furnace, where the faint glow of refining heat pulsed softly. "Thank the Vermilion Lotus Refinement for that. It's not perfect, but it's keeping me functional."

It was invaluable. But knowing that, I had tried to use my last Technique Token to upgrade it once more, right after using one while I was with Feng Wu. If it was this good after one upgrade, then what would it become if I used another?

Unfortunately, the Heavenly Interface curbed my enthusiasm.

> *You do not have enough tokens to upgrade Vermilion Lotus Refinement.*

The three of us fell into a comfortable silence as they busied themselves with tidying the shop and checking inventory. I watched them work, a pang of gratitude settling in my chest. Over the past week, Lan-Yin and Wang Jun had practically moved in to help me. Between running errands, organizing shipments, and keeping the shop in order, they'd taken on more responsibility than I could have asked for. Even the other villages chipped in, having heard I wasn't able to move all that well.

I'd have to thank Li Wei later with a new set of energy-boosting elixirs for reinforcing all the furniture I had.

"Thanks, really," I whispered. "For everything."

Lan-Yin waved me off, pretending to be busy with a jar of herbs. "Don't get all sentimental on us, Kai. You'll ruin your mysterious, aloof alchemist vibe."

Wang Jun snorted. "Yeah, because that's what everyone thinks of when they see him. *'Mysterious.'*"

I chuckled, shaking my head. The banter was a welcome distraction, but beneath it, I could feel the steady changes in my body. The weight of the tortoise shell was still there, but I'd grown accustomed to it. My muscles didn't scream with every step anymore, and my balance had improved enough that I didn't stumble like a newborn foal whenever I stood up. I'd learn to stand on my bones, aligning my skeleton without relying on my muscles to keep me upright.

With my constant flow of pills alongside Tianyi's healing, I entered an unceasing state of destruction and rejuvenation. My body was rapidly adapting to the weight, many times faster than even I could anticipate.

It wasn't just my body, either. My mind had adapted, forced to work in tandem with the Vermilion Lotus Refinement technique to squeeze every ounce of efficiency from my qi.

> *Your Mind has advanced to Qi Initiation Realm—Rank 3.*

The constant strain of thinking, planning, and visualizing my energy flow, reducing the waste so I could go about my daily life, resulted in my mind reaching the next rank . . . This tribulation was showing results already.

"Hey," Lan-Yin said, snapping me out of my thoughts. "Are you even listening?"

I blinked, realizing she was holding up a small pouch. "Sorry, what?"

"This is for you," she said, tossing it onto the counter. "A little something from the villagers. They've all been worried about you, you know. Even if you told them you were just 'injured,' they've been talking nonstop about when our herbalist will be back in action."

I picked up the pouch, hearing the faint clinking of coins and small trinkets inside. Warmth spread through me, pushing aside the lingering weight of the shell. "Tell them it won't be too long. In fact,"

I stood up slowly, brushing off my robes and stretching my arms. With a deliberate motion, I clenched my fist, channeling just enough qi into my right arm to stabilize it, and then threw a punch into the air.

"I should be able to join you all for morning training today."

The motion was smooth, though I couldn't deny the sluggishness compared to my usual self.

Lan-Yin and Wang Jun stared at me, wide-eyed.

"You can move like that now?" She asked, her tone disbelieving.

I grinned, rolling my shoulder. "Barely. But I've learned a trick: Don't use qi to support everything at once. Focus it where it's needed. It's not perfect, feels like wading through mud, but it's enough to get by."

Wang Jun crossed his arms, raising an eyebrow. "Then why'd you let us do all the work of cleaning your shop for you?"

I shrugged, the picture of nonchalance. "I couldn't let your goodwill go to waste."

The two of them exchanged a glance, then in perfect synchronization, smacked me on the back of the head. But with my weight being multiplied, I barely even moved.

"Ow."

"Serves you right," Lan-Yin muttered.

I straightened, rubbing the back of my head. "Fair, fair. Anyway, I'll head out with you two. I've got to see Elder Ming and start training again."

Before I left, I stepped outside. The crisp air nipped at my face. Tianyi was perched on the edge of the roof, her wings shimmering faintly in the winter sun. She looked down at me, and then my friends, before nodding.

"I'm heading to Elder Ming's," I called up to her. "Can you keep an eye on things here?"

She leapt gracefully to the ground, her movements as fluid as a dancer's. Her glowing blue eyes studied me, and without a word, she reached out and placed her hand on my arm. A surge of qi flowed from her into me, refilling my reserves in an instant. It was a torrent, powerful and brimming with vitality, and I felt my fatigue melt away.

"Thanks," I said, genuinely grateful, though a frown tugged at my lips. "But... has Windy come back yet?"

Tianyi tilted her head slightly, her expression pensive. "He returns at night, but only briefly. By the time you wake, he's already gone again."

I sighed, pinching the bridge of my nose. "That serpent's going to be the end of me. What am I supposed to do with him?"

"You could forbid him," she suggested, though there was no conviction in her tone. She knew as well as I did that it wasn't that simple. He'd probably strangle me in my sleep if I tried.

I shook my head. "I could, but how would I enforce it? He's as stubborn as I am."

Tianyi offered a faint smile. "Then trust him."

I sighed again, though her words gave me a sliver of reassurance. "Just monitor things. Let me know if anything comes up."

She gave me a playful salute, her wings fluttering as she watched me leave.

Lan-Yin and Wang Jun were waiting for me by the shop's entrance, and together, we made our way through the village. A few of the Verdant Lotus Sect disciples dotted the streets, their jade-green robes a familiar sight now. They had settled comfortably into the village, their presence blending with the day-to-day. With their sect courtyard now built, Lan-Yin's teahouse wasn't as packed anymore. It was comforting to know that they were keeping watch over the village, day and night.

"Looks like they've made themselves at home," Wang Jun remarked, bowing his head to Jian Feng, who seemed to be part of the early-morning patrol. I waved to him with a smile.

With Feng Wu departing to measure the ambient qi of another area, Jian Feng was the leader of the second-class disciples. And he did his job well.

We reached Elder Ming's home just as the sun peeked fully over the horizon, casting long shadows across the frost-covered ground. His eyes, sharp as ever, immediately scanned me from head to toe, lingering on my movements as I approached.

"You look better than I expected," he admitted, his gaze narrowing. "Are you ready to resume training?"

I nodded. "I am. I haven't been idle. I've been visualizing the stances and practicing the Heavenly Flame Mantra in my Memory Palace, just as you told me."

"Good. Then let's not waste any time. Start your conditioning."

Wang Jun let out a resigned sigh, already rolling his shoulders in preparation. Meanwhile, Elder Ming turned to Lan-Yin and me. "You two, lighter exercises.

Lan-Yin, for obvious reasons," he said, nodding toward her visible baby bump, "and Kai, because you're still adjusting to the weight."

Lan-Yin gave me a sympathetic look as we spread out. I settled into a push-up position, already bracing myself for the strain. The moment I lowered myself to the ground, the familiar pressure of the Black Tortoise shell bore down on me like an invisible mountain.

"One. Two. Three . . ."

By the time I reached twenty, sweat was dripping down my face. At thirty, my arms trembled. At fifty, I collapsed, gasping for breath.

Lan-Yin, who was practicing slow and deliberate movements nearby, chuckled softly. "Looks like we're both carrying extra weight these days."

I managed a grin despite my exhaustion.

Elder Ming's voice cut through the air. "That's enough resting, Kai. Into the horse stance. Hold it until I say otherwise."

Groaning, I pushed myself upright and spread my feet into position, lowering my center of gravity. The stance burned my thighs almost immediately, but I gritted my teeth and bore through it. Elder Ming walked around me, occasionally nudging my arms or legs to adjust my posture.

"This is progress," he said after several minutes of silent observation. "You've adapted to the weight."

"Still doesn't make it any less frustrating." I muttered under my breath. I used to do this stance in my sleep, with how often I practiced it. But now, it was reduced to a mere fraction.

He ignored me. "You can begin practicing the Heavenly Flame Mantra again—but only the footwork and stances, maybe some non-contact sparring. Attempting the full Dance of a Thousand Flames in your condition would incinerate you."

I sighed, knowing he was right. "Got it."

As I transitioned into the foundational stances of the Heavenly Flame Mantra, I focused on drawing qi into my palms. The heat built, spreading across my skin like a slow burn. It was a delicate balance; too little qi and the flames would sputter out, too much and I'd exhaust my reserves in seconds.

The added weight of the shell made even the simplest movements a challenge. My steps were heavy, deliberate, and the strain forced me to concentrate on every shift of my balance. Every so often, I reminded myself to stand as efficiently as possible, letting some of my muscles relax, conserving stamina and qi wherever I could.

"Good," he said finally. "That's enough for now. Wang Jun, spar with Kai. Non-contact."

Wang Jun cracked his knuckles, a wide grin spreading across his face. "This should be fun."

I rolled my shoulders, trying to ignore the knot of apprehension in my chest. Wang Jun would be fast, far faster than I was in my current state. The only way I could keep up was to outthink him, using the weight of the shell to force myself into a new rhythm.

The first exchange came quickly. Wang Jun lunged, his movements fluid and precise. I barely had time to react, shifting my weight and pivoting to avoid his strike. My counterattack was slower, a sweeping kick meant to keep him at bay rather than land a hit.

He dodged easily, his grin widening. "You're going to have to do better than that."

I adjusted my strategy, funneling a small amount of qi into my legs to enhance my mobility. It wasn't enough to match his speed, but it gave me just enough to make it competitive. I feinted left, then stepped back, forcing him to overcommit to his next attack. As he recovered, I brought my arm up in a defensive motion, letting the momentum carry me into a counterstrike.

The weight of the shell forced every movement to be precise. There was no room for wasted energy, no margin for error. It felt like a game, one where I had to think two moves ahead just to keep up. Every strike Wang Jun threw demanded an efficient response, a single move to counter two of his.

By the time Elder Ming called for a break, my body was drenched in sweat and my qi reserves were dangerously low. Even though it was non-contact, it felt like I'd gone through a gauntlet. I dropped to one knee, gasping for air, but a faint sense of satisfaction lingered beneath the exhaustion.

"You're doing well despite your handicap," Elder Ming said with approval. "Rest. Continue to circulate your qi and bring your reserves back to acceptable levels before we repeat the process."

I nodded, collapsing cross-legged onto the frost-covered ground. The Vermilion Lotus Refinement technique hummed through my body, its steady rhythm soothing the chaos in my meridians. My breath was heavy, each exhale forming a cloud of vapor in the frigid air.

Wang Jun sat beside me, looking far too comfortable compared to my aching state. He stretched his arms overhead, letting out a satisfied groan. "You know, this feels pretty good," he said, a lopsided grin on his face. "For once, I'm the one in control during sparring. Usually, it's you pulling your punches to help me improve."

I snorted, too drained to fully engage in the banter. "Don't get used to it. Once this shell is off me, I'll make you regret every second you enjoyed this."

Lan-Yin chuckled from her spot, where she was practicing her footwork. "You two are like children."

Wang Jun grinned, unabashed. "What can I say? Watching Kai struggle is a rare treat."

I rolled my eyes, but a small smile tugged at my lips. "Enjoy it while it lasts. Honestly, I don't mind this as much as I thought I would."

He raised an eyebrow. "Really? You looked like you were dying five minutes ago."

"Sure, it's exhausting," I admitted. "But this extra weight forces me to think differently. Every movement has to be deliberate, efficient. I've already learned more from one sparring session than I might've in a week of regular practice."

Elder Ming, who had been observing from the side, nodded approvingly. "That's the right mindset. This tribulation is not just a trial of endurance but an opportunity for growth. Those who treat it as such come out of it stronger."

I felt a spark of pride at his words, despite the lingering fatigue. My mind drifted to the steady progress I had made over the past week; the adjustments I had learned, the insights I had gained. Every step forward brought me closer to the end of the Black Tortoise Tribulation, and I could feel the faintest glimmers of hope that I would complete it sooner than I had expected.

The thought buoyed me as I closed my eyes, letting the Vermilion Lotus Refinement technique soothe my aching body. Despite the weight on my shoulders, there was a lightness in my heart that hadn't been there before.

This was the path forward. Soon, I'd rise.

CHAPTER EIGHT

One Bamboo Shoot, a Thousand Possibilities

My voice rang out across the crisp morning air.
Today was the day.
"It's ready! It's ready!"

Tianyi, perched on the roof as usual, tilted her head curiously, her wings twitching in my direction.

Sliding the greenhouse door open, I stepped into the humid warmth, the scent of fresh vegetation wrapping around me like a comforting blanket. My gaze swept past rows of thriving herbs and hybrid plants until it landed on the star of the show: the Golden Bamboo shoot.

It was magnificent.

The bamboo shoot stood just shy of the greenhouse ceiling. Its golden surface shimmered faintly. Though it was still a shoot, its flesh tender and brimming with vitality, it radiated with qi.

"Insane growth for less than a month," I murmured, crouching beside the shoot. There was no doubt that infusing essences had to do with its extraordinary growth rate.

I reached out, running my fingers over the golden surface. Unlike the harder culms the bamboo would eventually grow into, the shoot was firm but pliable under my touch. The warmth of life thrummed through it, the energy almost tangible. The yang-based ingredients I'd planted, extracted and used as fuel for its growth, had clearly worked wonders.

This wasn't just a success. This was a triumph.

I revived an extinct species.

Pulling a small knife from my belt, I lined it up carefully against the base of the shoot. This would be my first harvest, and I wanted it to be perfect. But as I pressed the blade against the shoot, I felt the resistance immediately. Despite its tender appearance, the base was incredibly tough. The knife barely nicked the surface before slipping off entirely.

"Seriously?" I muttered, inspecting the blade and seeing the edge dulling before my eyes. "Wang Jun just had this sharpened. How is this even possible?"

Sitting back on my heels, I scratched my head, staring at the shoot in frustration. Exerting more force was impossible. Not with this knife, nor in my current state with the Black Tortoise Tribulation.

"Tianyi!" I called out, glancing toward the greenhouse entrance.

A moment later, she glided inside, her wings folding behind her. Her eyes flitted between me and the bamboo shoot. "What is it?"

"This," I said, gesturing to the shoot. "Can you . . . you know, slice it with your wings?"

"You want me to cut it for you?"

"Exactly. Just at the base, where it's the hardest. I'll handle the rest."

She nodded, stepping closer to inspect the bamboo. "Mark where I need to cut."

I took a step back, giving her space as she unfurled her wings. They shimmered with a faint, ethereal glow, the edges sharp enough to gleam like blades. She stepped forward, her movements deliberate and precise.

"Oh, and don't hit the other plants! Or the glass! It'll shatter."

She paused briefly, aligning herself with the marks I'd made. For a moment, her wings brightened.

The motion was fluid, almost artistic, as her wing sliced cleanly through the bamboo with a faint hum. The top portion of the stalk fell away, and I caught it just before it hit the glass.

Tianyi straightened, folding her wings back with a satisfied expression. "Done."

I knelt to inspect the cut, running my fingers along the edge where her wing had sliced through. It was flawless—smooth and precise, with not a single splinter or jagged edge. The remaining stalk hummed faintly, its golden surface undamaged and ready to grow anew. Even without using all the seeds, I'd be able to grow it once more. I'd just have to watch it to prevent it from encroaching upon the other plants in the greenhouse.

"Perfect," I said, looking up at her with a grin. "This young master won't forget the grace you've shown. Thanks."

She gave a faint smile, but the words that left her mouth threw me off guard.

"Such a trivial matter is hardly worth remembering."

"You're reading too much Liang Feng!" I said in disbelief. "That's not polite."

"My conduct is beyond reproach," she said ominously, hiding her face with her sleeve. I shook my head.

With the top portion of the bamboo safely in my hands, I set it gently on the workbench inside my shop. Now came the real challenge. Using a more heavy-duty knife from my tool kit, I set to work separating the culm into sections. The knife sliced through the upper portion cleanly, but as I worked my way toward the base, the resistance grew.

At just a glance, I could tell the shoot was brimming with vitality. But the base, the culm, was something else entirely. It felt more like a material, something meant to be worked into tools or furniture rather than consumed or refined.

Carefully, I sectioned the bamboo, setting aside the softer outer layers for testing. I ran my fingers over the inner segments, marveling at the slight warmth they emitted. Each piece seemed to vibrate faintly, as though it held a rhythm of its own, alive even after being harvested.

Tianyi leaned against the wall, her gaze fixed on me as I worked. "What do you plan to do with it?" she asked.

"Test it," I replied simply, holding up a thin outer strip of the bamboo. "I need to understand its essence before deciding how to use it. If the outer layer alone is this potent, who knows what the core holds?"

Placing the strip in my palm, I activated my Essence Extraction skill, channeling qi into the material. A faint golden glow emerged, coalescing into a single drop of shimmering liquid in my palm. It was small, almost disappointingly so, but the energy it radiated was undeniably potent. I carefully stored it in a glass vial, sealing it tightly before setting it aside.

"The essence is concentrated in the inner layers," I muttered, more to myself than to Tianyi. "This outer layer is strong, but it doesn't hold nearly as much energy as I expected."

I moved, already shifting my attention to the denser segments I'd set aside. The core pieces practically thrummed with life, their golden sheen more vivid than the outer layers. My instincts, and the subtle prompts from Nature's Attunement, told me these pieces were the true treasure.

With a steady hand, I placed a core segment on the workbench and began the extraction process again. This time, the resistance was palpable, the bamboo fighting against the pull of my qi. A bead of golden liquid formed in my palm, larger and brighter than the first. Its energy pulsed like a tiny heartbeat, almost alive in its intensity.

"Now we're talking," I murmured, carefully transferring the essence into a larger vial.

Tianyi watched in silence, her gaze sharp and analytical. "What's your plan for the rest of it?"

"Research," I said, straightening and wiping my brow. "The details from Guowei Wang were scarce. I need to find out its exact properties and potential. First, I'll test if it behaves like regular bamboo in alchemical recipes or if it's entirely unique."

"You're expecting the latter?"

"Probably," I admitted, gesturing to the vials of golden essence. "But there's no harm in covering the basics. I'll start with the fundamentals: see if it reacts to heat and flame like normal bamboo, if it burns cleanly, and whether it leaves any unique ash residue. This could be a catalyst, an amplifier, or even an entirely new base ingredient for pills or elixirs. But before I get ahead of myself, I'll isolate the core essence and run compatibility tests with other ingredients. If it clashes with common components, it might require a specific refinement method."

I set the piece down and moved to the next section, this one smaller but denser. As I shaved thin layers from it, Tianyi's eyes narrowed thoughtfully. "And the outer layers? They seemed weaker, but you didn't discard them."

"Never discard unless you're absolutely sure it's useless," I replied, holding up a sliver of the outer bamboo. "They may not have as much raw essence, but they might hold some other properties. I'll experiment with its tensile strength and how it channels qi. Maybe Wang Jun or Li Wei could have some use for it. I'm interested in seeing a mature Golden Bamboo, but that'll have to wait."

Figuring out how to use Golden Bamboo in pills was first. To uphold my end of the deal with the Whispering Wind and Verdant Lotus, I'd make sets of body refining pills, either with the Golden Bamboo or plants infused with its essence.

But I'd have to test them first! On myself!

"This is a sacrifice for the greater good! Testing such a rare material on myself . . . Who else could shoulder this burden?"

The idea of testing the Golden Bamboo's essence on myself was exhilarating. If it lived up to even half of my expectations, it could be a breakthrough for my body, which was exactly what I needed for the tribulation.

But I forced myself to temper my enthusiasm. There was no point in rushing and potentially wasting such a rare resource. The rest of the bamboo needed to be safely stored and studied.

"I'll finish this after morning training."

With care, I packed the sections into a sturdy wooden box and carried it to my bedroom. It wasn't much, but it would keep curious hands away for now. I had to go train.

I grabbed my cloak, slung it over my shoulders, and stepped out into the crisp morning air, bidding Tianyi farewell. The snow crunched underfoot as I made my way toward Elder Ming's house. The weight of the Black Tortoise Tribulation still pressed on me, but it was no longer the oppressive burden it had been a week ago. My steps were steady, though slower than normal, each one deliberate. The snow yielded easily beneath my boots, cushioning my movements.

As I approached the main path, I spotted Liang Chen standing near a wagon loaded with goods, explaining some of his offerings to the villagers. His sharp features and somewhat sly smile gave him the air of a seedy merchant, but he hadn't shown any tendency he was plotting to take over the village.

He noticed me and waved, his grin widening.

"Kai Liu." he called out, his voice warm despite the chill in the air. "Out and about so early? Eager to look at our wares?"

I chuckled, adjusting my cloak. "Not quite. Morning training calls. And you? What's the occasion?"

"Ah, the same as ever," he replied, gesturing to the wagon. "The usual supplies. Though I brought a few specialty items. Let me know if you're interested."

My gaze flicked to the rough-looking men accompanying him, their hardened faces and weathered clothes a stark contrast to the polished demeanor of most merchants I'd met.

Liang Chen followed my gaze and spoke before I could ask. "They're from Crescent Bay. People who've had a rough go of things. Some were living in poverty; others . . . well, let's just say they've seen the worst the city has to offer. Nobody wanted to hire them, but I figured I'd give them a chance. They're as hard-working as can be."

I studied the men more closely, their guarded expressions and quiet demeanor speaking volumes.

"You're more generous than you look. To be honest, I thought you were just another shrewd merchant the first time we met."

He laughed, clapping his hand to his chest. "A shrewd merchant? I take that as a compliment! But don't let the exterior fool you. Every good deal needs a little heart."

"Careful, Chen," a familiar voice interjected. Huan emerged from behind the wagon. "If you steal away my best customer, the patriarch will have my head! I'll haunt you in the afterlife!"

I couldn't help but laugh at the theatrics. "Relax, Huan. My loyalty is to you. But," I added, glancing at Liang Chen, "it's good to know my options."

Huan groaned, throwing his hands up dramatically. "Options, he says! The betrayal!"

"Competition breeds excellence," Liang Chen replied smoothly.

Shaking my head at their antics, I continued on my way. I rolled my shoulders, preparing myself for the day ahead.

The first thing I noticed as I entered the courtyard of Elder Ming's house was Wang Jun and Lan-Yin sitting on a rock, their breath misting in the chilly air. They were on break, sharing cups of tea.

But as I drew closer, I saw the way Wang Jun hovered near her, his hand resting lightly on the bench close to her, almost protectively.

It was subtle, but the warmth between them was palpable. The way Lan-Yin leaned slightly toward him when she spoke, the faint smile that tugged at her lips whenever he replied. His gaze flickered now and then to her baby bump, a mix of worry and pride clear in his expression. It was . . . sweet, in a way that made me roll my eyes internally.

I wasn't jealous! Nope.

"Morning, you two," I called out, breaking their bubble as I stepped into the courtyard. "Taking a break already? Slackers."

Lan-Yin glanced up, her cheeks pink from the cold—or maybe from embarrassment.

"We've been up since dawn, thank you very much," she retorted, but her tone lacked its usual sharpness. "What about you? Finally dragged yourself out of the greenhouse?"

"Hardly," I replied with a smirk, before nodding toward her and Wang Jun. "So, about this whole 'betrothed' thing. Are you two speeding up the wedding now that . . ." I trailed off, gesturing vaguely at her bump.

Wang Jun rubbed the back of his neck sheepishly. "We have little of a choice, do we? My parents nearly beat me black and blue when they found out. Said I was an embarrassment to the family name."

Lan-Yin snickered. "Meanwhile, my parents were just amused. They called it 'young love' and said it's about time."

"Typical," I said, crossing my arms and shaking my head in mock disappointment. "Both families will lose face. Two hot-blooded teens who can't even control themselves. What a scandal!"

She gave me a flat look, while Wang Jun tried to stifle a grin. "Keep talking, Kai," she warned, "and you'll be eating snow for lunch."

Elder Ming stepped out of the house, teapot in hand.

"Kai," he said gruffly, "stop gossiping and start warming up. Light sparring with Wang Jun after."

"Yes, Elder," I replied, bowing slightly before moving to the practice area. Lan-Yin waved me off with a smug grin.

I started with some basic stretches and footwork drills, easing my body into motion. The weight of the Black Tortoise Tribulation was still there, but it felt less like a mountain crushing me and more like a persistent, annoying burden. The human mind was truly adaptable.

By the time Elder Ming called me over, I was ready to go.

Wang Jun stepped onto the practice ground with me, rolling his shoulders. "Non-contact sparring again, right?"

"No, Kai needs to push himself further. His movements are smoother now, and it's time he gets back into full sparring. Nothing excessive, but enough to test his limits."

I grinned, the challenge sparking a flicker of excitement. "Perfect. Let's make this quick, Wang Jun. I have more important things waiting for me after this practice."

Wang Jun smirked, raising an eyebrow. "Big words for someone I had to help with chores because they couldn't even move last week."

My mind raced as I observed his posture, analyzing his likely moves. In narrowing it down, I expected three possibilities.

He moved.

True to form, Wang Jun led with a feint; a sharp jab toward my face, before dropping into a low sweeping kick aimed at my legs. I was ready. Pivoting on my back foot, I let his kick glide past, the momentum leaving him slightly off-balance. Seizing the opportunity, I launched a precise counterstrike, my fist landing lightly below his rib.

A notification flashed briefly in my mind.

Quest: Beyond the Memory Palace
—*Successfully evade or counter ten different attacks by predicting their trajectories using a simulated visual map in real time. (10/10)*
—*Land five precise hits on a moving opponent using openings simulated beforehand. (4/5)*
—*Use the Refinement Simulation Technique on an alchemical reaction mid-combat to create an advantage. (0/1)*

I couldn't suppress a grin. The tribulation might have slowed my body, but it had sharpened my mind. Every move felt deliberate, calculated; like a living embodiment of my Memory Palace Technique. The endless drills, the constant strain, and the enforced efficiency had transformed my combat style into something more methodical and refined, and it bled into my other quests as a result.

But Wang Jun wasn't about to make things easy. Using his superior reach and physical strength, he kept me at bay with a series of calculated strikes, forcing me to waste energy just staying out of his range. Clever bastard.

Every step felt heavier as I moved, the multiplied weight dragging at my legs like invisible chains. It was frustrating.

Why was I treating my weight as a weakness?

The thought clicked, sharp and immediate. If my body were heavier, why not use that to my advantage? Instead of fighting against it, I could turn it into a weapon.

"Elder Ming," I called, keeping my eyes on Wang Jun. "Permission to increase the intensity? I want to test something, but it's hard to do when we're both holding back."

Elder Ming's sharp gaze flicked between us, then he nodded. "Do it. But don't let it turn reckless."

Wang Jun cracked his knuckles, a wide grin spreading across his face. "You're on."

He lunged, his punch carrying the weight of his entire body. I braced, channeling qi into my arms to block. The impact sent me skidding back half a step despite my immense weight, a testament to his raw strength, honed through countless hours in the forge.

"That all you got?" I taunted, masking the sting in my arms.

He was already closing the gap for another strike. But I was ready. Drawing a deep breath, I funneled qi into my legs, focusing on the connection between my feet and the ground. As he launched his next attack, I lifted my leg high, casting a shadow over Wang Jun.

The fourth stance of the Twelve Harvest Moon. An identical axe kick to the one Ping Hai used against me, so long ago.

With my increased weight, the kick came down like a falling boulder. Wang Jun moved to block, his forearms raised instinctively.

"Ugh!"

But the sheer force drove him downward, his arms buckling under the impact. His knees hit the ground as he struggled to push back, but before he could recover, I stepped forward, my hand raised for a finishing blow.

My hand came down, grabbing his ear. I felt a sense of satisfaction at seeing my ploy work flawlessly.

"Victory goes to me, as always."

He opened his eyes, glaring at me as he rubbed his ear. "Hey! That hurt."

"Sorry," I said with a grin, offering him a hand to stand. "But you have to admit—losing to me while I'm still weighed down? That stings, doesn't it?"

Wang Jun shook his head, a reluctant smile tugging at his lips. "I'll give you this round. Next time, you won't land a single hit. I was just tired!"

"Excuses, excuses." I replied, already feeling the adrenaline fading as the weight of the Black Tortoise Tribulation settled back onto my shoulders. I helped Wang Jun to his feet and continued on with morning training.

CHAPTER NINE

Shadows Linger in the Light of Breakthrough

The morning sun hung high, its rays piercing through the frost-covered trees as training ended. I stood in the courtyard, drenched in sweat, steam rising in the cool air of winter.

My muscles ached, my breath came in labored gulps, but there was a strange vitality coursing through me.

Elder Ming walked up to me, leaning on his staff, his sharp eyes scanning my posture. "You've improved," he said, his tone measured. "It's not perfect, but it's enough."

I nodded, wiping sweat from my brow. "Enough to spar without collapsing, at least."

He snorted, one corner of his lips quirking upward. "Enough to finish this tribulation, perhaps."

I tilted my head, curiosity piqued. "What do you mean?"

He gestured toward the horizon, pointing toward the village outskirts. "The banyan tree," he said simply. "You've reached the point where you should be able to make a dent. One blow, correct? That's all it takes to break through."

My stomach tightened. Of course, I knew. The tree was ancient, its roots sprawling across the earth like a web of veins. It had been the focal point of the quest, a symbol of the tribulation's end. If I could dent the tree, I'd finish the tribulation and be free of this troublesome weight.

I clenched my fist. My fingers trembled slightly, though I wasn't sure why. The unease that stirred in my chest wasn't logical. I was stronger now, better prepared. This should have been a cause for celebration, not hesitation.

So why was I like this?

"I'll do it," I said, forcing a confident nod. "Soon."

His sharp gaze lingered on me for a moment before he nodded. "Good. We'll be able to return to refining the Heavenly Flame Mantra once you do so."

As I turned to leave, I caught Wang Jun and Lan-Yin lounging on the training grounds, their faces flushed from their respective drills. I waved to them. "I'll see you two later. Going to refine the Golden Bamboo. If I'm blessed by the heavens, I'll have some new pills for the both of you to try!"

"Good luck; don't blow yourself up!" Lan-Yin called out.

I couldn't help but whistle as I trudged home, my legs heavy but my spirits light.

Back at the shop, the familiar scent of herbs and parchment greeted me like an old friend. I glanced around, not seeing Tianyi anywhere. But from our bond, I could feel she was somewhere within the perimeter. Probably training or doing her own thing. I shook my head, focusing on the task at hand.

I stepped inside, my gaze immediately drawn to the bedroom. The pieces I had so painstakingly cut and prepared sat in a box.

"This is it," I murmured, running a hand over the smooth surface of a bamboo segment. "Time to experiment."

Hours later, the world outside had dissolved into darkness. The soft glow of lantern light filled the shop, casting long shadows across the walls. My hands moved with practiced precision, grinding, mixing, and heating ingredients. The first attempt had been . . . less than successful.

I winced, glancing at the charred remnants of one failed batch still smoldering in a corner. "Guess I should note never to combine Golden Bamboo with Sunfire Blade Grass without stabilizing agents."

A sharp cough escaped my throat, the lingering effects of accidental poisoning still scratching at my lungs. I'd underestimated the potency of the essence, and the resulting fumes had nearly knocked me unconscious. Luckily, Tianyi had been nearby to pull me out of the shop before I joined the ancestors.

But now, after countless missteps and moments of inspiration, I held success in my hands.

The pill was small but perfect, its surface smooth and glistening like polished amber. It radiated a faint golden light, the energy within it palpable even without direct contact.

I leaned back in my chair, exhaustion washing over me in waves. My fingers trembled as I held the pill up to the light, admiring the way it seemed to capture and reflect the lantern's glow.

The Golden Bamboo had lived up to its reputation, though not without testing every ounce of my patience and skill. The process had pushed me to my limits, forcing me to adapt and innovate in ways I hadn't anticipated.

> *Spiritual Herbalism has reached level 7.*

I set the pill down carefully, thinking of my next move.

"Hm . . . Golden Pill of Radiance?" I muttered aloud, turning the vial in my hand. "No, too pompous. Maybe something simpler. Bamboo Essence Core? Nah, sounds like something you'd find on the discount shelf."

I drummed my fingers on the table, racking my brain for inspiration. The pill glistened under the lantern light, its golden sheen almost mocking me.

Every name I thought of sounded either overly dramatic or utterly forgettable. "This is harder than actually making the pill," I muttered, rubbing my temples.

At that moment, Tianyi stepped into the room with the top of her hair covered in snow, her wings folding neatly behind her. She glanced at the mess I'd made: ash stains, shattered vials, and a faint scorch mark on the ceiling.

"You made it," she said.

I nodded, gesturing at the pill. "Yeah, but now I'm stuck. What do I even call this thing? Everything I come up with either sounds ridiculous or like something someone else already named."

Tianyi hummed for a moment. She stepped closer, studying the pill for a moment before speaking. "Golden Drop."

I blinked. "Golden Drop?"

She nodded, her expression calm. "It's simple. Easy to remember. And it describes what it is."

I stared at her, then back at the pill. "Golden Drop, huh?" I turned the name over in my mind. It was straightforward, maybe a little plain, but it rolled off the tongue nicely. And there was a certain elegance in its simplicity.

"You know what?" I said, smiling. "It works. Let's go with Golden Drop."

I picked up the pill, holding it between my thumb and forefinger as I turned to her. "Guess that makes you the co-creator of this masterpiece. I'll make sure to share the glory with you when I reveal it to the world."

"Your generosity knows no bounds."

I chuckled, popping the pill into my mouth without hesitation. The moment it touched my tongue, a warm, golden energy coursed through me, spreading like sunlight breaking through a foggy morning.

I crossed my legs, closing my eyes as I focused on the surge of power. The Vermilion Lotus Refinement technique hummed to life, guiding the energy through my meridians with a newfound ease. But this energy was unlike anything I had experienced before. It wasn't just replenishing my qi reserves. It was weaving into my body, permeating my muscles and bones.

So this was the difference between a regular pill and a body refinement pill.

Each inhale drew the energy deeper, and the technique's purification process accelerated to match the intensity of the pill. The essence of the Golden Drop worked in harmony with the Vermilion Lotus Refinement, amplifying the speed and efficiency of purification beyond what I thought possible.

Was it extremely compatible with my physique?

My entire being felt alive, vibrant, as though every cell had been ignited with a golden flame.

Time slipped away unnoticed. Minutes? Hours? I couldn't tell. My focus remained sharp, every ounce of my will dedicated to controlling the flow of energy. It was strong, surpassing the potency of my share of the beast core elixir. The impurities within my body, which I thought I had already dealt with, surged to the surface with alarming potency.

The first breakthrough came with a crackling sensation that rippled through my muscles. My body surged with strength as the refinement reached its peak.

> *Body has advanced to Qi Initiation Realm—Rank 2.*

The notification was almost secondary to the sensation itself. My physical form felt more robust, like steel tempered through countless hammer blows. The weight of the Black Tortoise shell, which pervaded every movement, felt less of a burden than before. But the energy didn't stop there; it pushed further, deeper into my dantian.

The Vermilion Lotus Refinement roared, a crimson flower blooming within the swirling currents of qi. As my reserves expanded, the energy condensed and purified with startling efficiency. I felt the threshold looming, the line between one stage and the next. After all the pills I consumed to keep myself afloat during the tribulation, the Golden Drop was the last component I needed to achieve breakthrough.

And with a final surge, I crossed it.

> *Qi has advanced to Essence Awakening Realm—Rank 1.*

The difference was immediate and profound. My dantian pulsed with a newfound depth.

But then, the inevitable came.

A wave of black sludge erupted from my pores, the impurities expelled by the pill's purification. The stench hit me like a brick wall—a putrid, acrid scent that made my stomach churn.

I gagged, covering my nose with my sleeve.

"Not again . . ."

I opened my eyes, only to see the horrifying extent of the mess. Thick black sludge coated the floor around me, steaming faintly in the lantern light. It seeped into the cracks of the wood, staining the planks with its foul residue.

My jaw dropped. "No, no, no! This is going to stain everything!"

Scrambling to my feet, I nearly slipped on the viscous sludge. My robes were ruined, sticky with the tar-like substance. I stumbled to grab a rag, only to realize the futility of cleaning this mess with mere cloth.

"Tianyi!" I called out, half-panicked. "Get a bucket. Or ten! This is a disaster!"

Silence.

I paused, wiping the sweat—and sludge—off my forehead with a sleeve that was already beyond saving. Reaching out with my senses, I tried to locate Tianyi through our bond. There was no panic, no urgency in her emotions. Just calm focus, tinged with curiosity.

But she wasn't nearby. In fact, she was far; much farther than I'd expected her to be at this hour. What was she doing? My brows furrowed, but with no distress from her end, I decided against calling her back.

"Great," I muttered, grabbing an old bucket from the corner. "Looks like this disaster is mine to deal with."

With a sigh, I set to work. The black sludge had already dried in patches, its pungent stench thickening the air.

"Where'd I put that soap from Bai Hua . . . There it is!"

Every scrub with the rag felt like a battle against some malevolent entity that had decided my shop floor was its ultimate resting place. The wood creaked under the strain of my efforts, and I muttered a silent apology to the floorboards.

Hours passed. The first hints of dawn crept through the windows, painting the walls with a pale golden light. My muscles burned from the constant scrubbing, yet my energy remained strangely unflagging. I hadn't slept—not even a minute—but I didn't feel tired. If anything, I felt . . . alive.

Body refinement must've done more than I thought, I mused, rinsing the rag in murky water. Yet even with my enhanced stamina powering my efforts, the smell lingered like a stubborn ghost, refusing to leave no matter how much soap I used.

A knock at the door jolted me from my thoughts. I stood, groaning slightly as I stretched my back and trudged over to answer it. Jian Feng stood there, his green sect robes immaculate as always, a stark contrast to my sludge-covered, sweat-drenched self.

"Kai—"

Jian Feng paused, his sharp eyes taking in my appearance and the faint acrid smell wafting out of the shop. His nose scrunched up ever so slightly before he quickly smoothed his expression, likely out of etiquette.

I'd never live this down. *He's going to tell the rest of the disciples, and I'll lose face. They'll start addressing me as Stinky Kai, Master of the Olfactory Arts. Or the Pungent Prodigy. Or—*

"Kai," he said, inclining his head slightly and breaking me out of my spiraling thoughts. "There's something urgent you need to see."

I leaned against the doorframe, trying not to groan too loudly. "Can it wait? This stain's going to be permanent if I leave it."

He shook his head, his expression grave. "No. This is not something to delay."

The urgency in his tone made my heart skip a beat. I hesitated for a moment, then nodded, stepping back inside to grab a fresh cloak. As I moved, I glanced over my shoulder.

"Tianyi—" I started, but stopped short, remembering she wasn't nearby. My bond with her still pulsed with calm focus, reassuring me she wasn't in any immediate danger. But why was she so far from the shop this early?

Jian Feng's gaze followed mine, but he said nothing, his posture patient yet firm.

"I'll come. Just give me a minute to wash off and change."

After I put on one of my old robes and the Iron Boar cloak, the second-class disciple spun on his heel, his steps brisk as I followed him down the frost-laden path. The cold air was refreshing after the stifling mess I'd been dealing with, but the unease in my chest only grew as we approached the village outskirts.

"What's this about?" I asked, quickening my pace to match his.

Jian Feng's expression remained neutral, but the slight tension in his posture betrayed the gravity of the situation. "You'll see soon enough," he said, his voice steady but clipped. "I suggest you prepare yourself."

Not ominous at all.

My gut churned as we passed through the village, the frosty morning air biting at my face. The early-morning light was weak, struggling to push back the dimness that clung to the village like a shroud. Frost coated the ground in a thin layer of silver, crunching faintly beneath our boots as Jian Feng led me toward the outskirts. The air was frosty enough to bite, but it was the quiet—the heavy, uneasy silence—that made my skin crawl.

Most of the villagers were still asleep, their homes dark save for the occasional flicker of lantern light. Even the usual sounds of livestock stirring or carts creaking were absent, leaving the air thick with an eerie stillness.

I caught sight of Elder Ming standing at the center. His face was a mask of grim contemplation as he spoke to several Verdant Lotus Sect disciples. They were gathered in a tight circle and spoke in low, hurried tones, their breaths visible in the cold. Lanterns swayed in their hands, casting shifting light over the ground.

But it wasn't him or the disciples that drew my attention.

It was the massive corpse sprawled out in the snow.

I stopped in my tracks, my breath catching in my throat.

My breath hitched. The beast was unlike anything I'd ever seen. Its fur was jet-black, its stripes so faint they were barely visible. Even in death, it exuded an aura of power, its muscular frame taut and imposing. The sheer size was reminiscent of the Wind Serpents that attacked Qingmu.

"What . . . what is this?" I asked, my voice barely above a whisper.

Jian Feng stopped beside me, folding his arms. "A black tiger," he said. "A spirit beast of considerable strength. They are rare, even in the deepest forests. This one . . ." He gestured to the tiger's lifeless form. "This one is larger than any I've ever heard of. Probably the leader of its pack."

I stepped closer, the scent of blood and decay sharp in the air. My eyes were drawn to the gaping wound in its side—three deep claw marks that had torn through muscle and exposed the rib cage. Blood had frozen in jagged streaks around the injury, the snow beneath it stained a dark crimson.

"This killed it?" I murmured, crouching to examine the wounds.

Jian Feng nodded grimly. "It was found just beyond the outskirts of the forest, already dead when our patrols came upon it. To think something could drive a beast like this from its depths and leave it like this . . ." He trailed off, his expression dark.

Elder Ming's voice carried over. "There have been no sightings of a beast of this size or caliber in this area since I became Village Head," he said. "Such a creature would not leave the forest lightly, nor would it fall so easily. Whatever did this forced it out of its domain and killed it without mercy."

If something powerful enough to kill a black tiger had entered the outskirts of the forest, it meant danger was closer to the village than anyone was prepared for.

My eyes drifted back to the claw marks. They were brutal, precise—far too similar to the ones I'd seen before. My hand unconsciously brushed the edge of my Iron Boar cloak, the memory of the Iron Claw Sect's discovery flashing through my mind. The markings matched exactly.

There was a predator in the shadows.

The connections clicked in my mind like pieces of a puzzle, and a chill ran down my spine. Before I could voice my thoughts, the crowd parted, and Tianyi appeared, her face pale and her wings fluttering in agitation. Her usual calm was replaced by a visible worry that made my chest tighten.

"Kai," she said, her voice steady but strained. "Windy didn't return last night."

The blood drained from my face. "What?"

She nodded, her expression grim. "I went looking for him. I found a den of snakes. They told me he had left . . . to challenge a 'shadow' in the forest."

My heart skipped a beat. Windy. The reckless, stubborn serpent had gone into the forest alone, knowing full well the dangers that lurked within.

I didn't hesitate. Turning sharply, I started toward the forest. The icy air stung my face, but I barely noticed. My heart pounded, and my mind raced.

"Kai!" Jian Feng called after me. "What are you doing?"

"To bring him back," I said over my shoulder, my voice hard. "Whatever's in that forest, it's not taking him from me."

Tianyi fell into step beside me, her wings folding tightly against her back.

CHAPTER TEN

A Matter of Trust

Jian Feng stood in my path, his green robes pristine against the frost-covered ground. The soft glow of dawn lit his face, making his expression seem carved from stone. He said nothing at first, just held my gaze with that infuriating calm that only someone confident in their authority could manage.

"Move," I said, my voice sharp, barely holding back the anger bubbling under my skin. I clenched my fists, nails biting into my palms. "I don't have time for this."

Jian Feng didn't flinch. "And what do you intend to do?"

"Get Windy," I snapped. "What else?"

His lips thinned, and he folded his arms, his posture blocking the path as effectively as any gate. "And then what? March into the forest alone, without a plan, against an unknown threat? Do you have any idea what's out there?"

"I don't care!" The words came out louder than I had intended. "Windy's out there, Jian Feng. Alone. Hurt, maybe worse. I will not sit here while—"

"You will." His voice cut through mine like a blade, low and firm, with no room for argument. "Because your recklessness will cost more than just yourself. Do you think this is about your pet alone?"

I bristled at his wording. Windy wasn't *just* a pet. He was my friend. A companion that I treasured. "What's that supposed to mean?"

"It means you have responsibilities that extend beyond your personal attachments," he said evenly. "Your role as an alchemist is invaluable, Kai. Not just to the village but to the Verdant Lotus Sect and the Whispering Wind Sect. You asked for our help to protect this place, to secure its future. Now you're willing to throw that away because you're too emotional to see the bigger picture?"

My chest heaved, and I stepped closer, glaring at him. "So what? I'm supposed to twiddle my thumbs while—"

"You're supposed to trust us," he interrupted, his tone like ice. "We've already sent three disciples to scout the forest. They'll find out what happened. Isn't that why we're here? To act as the shield for this village while you focus on what only you can do?"

I opened my mouth to argue, but the words caught in my throat. He was right, and I hated him for it. My shoulders sagged slightly, the fire in my chest giving way to a smoldering guilt. "I . . . I just can't stand sitting here," I muttered, my voice quieter now. "Windy's family."

His posture softened slightly, but his gaze remained unyielding. "And the village is counting on you, Kai. Don't let your emotions blind you to your responsibilities."

I exhaled heavily, my anger fading into a deep, gnawing frustration. "Fine," I said through gritted teeth. "But what am I supposed to do in the meantime? It's not like the ones scouting the forest know Windy's gone. What are you going to do about that?"

He didn't respond immediately, his eyes briefly scanning my face before he stepped aside. "Trust. And wait."

Before I could respond, Tianyi's voice cut through the air. "Then I'll go."

Both Jian Feng and I turned toward her. She stood a few paces away, her wings tucked neatly behind her, her expression calm.

"No," I said immediately. "It's too dangerous."

Tianyi tilted her head, her gaze steady. "And yet, you were willing to go."

"That's different!"

"Why?"

"Because—" I faltered, unable to find the right words. "Because you don't have to. I'll find another way."

She shook her head, a faint smile tugging at her lips. "Kai, I am not bound like you are. I act as I choose, and I choose to find Windy."

Jian Feng frowned but didn't speak, clearly uncertain how to respond to her autonomy. Tianyi glanced at him, her tone blunt. "You have no authority over me, so there is no reason to object."

He hesitated, then inclined his head stiffly. "Do as you wish."

Her gaze returned to me, softening slightly. "Do not worry, Kai. I am stronger than they are. There is no need for concern."

I opened my mouth to argue, to stop her, but the words wouldn't come. She turned without another word, her wings unfurling slightly as she moved toward the forest.

"Tianyi!" I called after her, my voice tinged with desperation.

She paused, looking over her shoulder.

"Trust, Kai. Isn't that what you just agreed to?"

And with that, she disappeared into the shadowy expanse of the trees, leaving me standing there, hollow and unsure.

The group dispersed, the Verdant Lotus Sect disciples murmuring among themselves as they discussed what to do with the tiger's massive carcass. Jian Feng's voice rose briefly, directing a few of them to set up a perimeter while others prepared to move the body. The tension in the air lingered, but the urgency of their tasks took precedence over the uneasy silence.

Elder Ming stood beside me, his expression inscrutable as he watched the scene unfold. He turned to me, his feet crunching against the frost-covered ground as he gestured for me to follow.

"Come, Kai," he said simply. His tone was calm, measured, but there was a weight to it that made it hard to refuse.

I nodded, forcing my legs to move as I followed him back toward the village. The path was quiet, save for the soft crunch of snow beneath our boots. I kept glancing over my shoulder, as if Tianyi might suddenly reappear or the forest itself would yield some answer to the questions clawing at my mind. But the trees stood silent, indifferent to my unease.

Elder Ming didn't speak until we reached the shop. He paused at the threshold, his sharp eyes scanning the interior. "It's been some time since I last stepped inside your shop," he remarked, his voice tinged with a faint nostalgia.

I managed a thin smile, stepping inside and gesturing for him to follow. "Not much has changed," I said, though my voice sounded distant even to my own ears. "It's still . . . a work in progress."

Elder Ming hummed in response, his gaze lingering on the shelves of herbs and vials. I busied myself with fetching tea, my hands moving on autopilot as I set the kettle on the stove. The motions felt stiff, disconnected, as if I were watching someone else go through the motions.

When the tea was ready, I poured a cup and handed it to him. Elder Ming accepted it with a nod, his expression thoughtful as he sipped the steaming brew. I returned to the counter, my hands instinctively reaching for the inventory ledger. If I could just focus on something—anything—it might stop my mind from spinning.

But my hands trembled as I flipped through the pages, the ink blurring before my eyes. I tried to focus on the rows of ingredients, to calculate how many batches of pills I could produce with the current stock. But the numbers swam in my mind, and my thoughts kept drifting back to Windy, to Tianyi, to the *shadow* in the forest.

A soft clink brought my attention back to the present. Elder Ming had set his cup down on the counter, his gaze fixed on me. "Your hands are shaking," he breathed.

I looked down, startled to find that he was right. My fingers twitched against the edge of the ledger, and I clenched them into fists, trying to steady myself. "It's nothing," I muttered. "Just . . . tired."

He didn't respond immediately, his piercing eyes studying me in a way that made me feel like he could see right through every excuse I could muster. Finally, he straightened and stood up.

"Come with me," he said, his tone leaving no room for argument.

"Where?" I asked, though I was already moving to follow him.

"To the training grounds," he replied. "The morning drills are starting soon."

I hesitated. The thought of facing Wang Jun and Lan-Yin in my current state made my chest tighten. But the alternative—staying here, trapped in my head—felt even worse. I nodded, grabbing my cloak from the wall. "All right."

Elder Ming said nothing more as we stepped back out into the crisp morning air. The sun had risen higher now, casting long shadows across the village as we made our way toward the training grounds. My mind buzzed with restless energy, but the rhythmic crunch of Elder Ming's steps beside me kept me grounded, pulling me forward one step at a time.

The familiar sight of his courtyard brought a strange sense of relief.

Wang Jun was already in the center of the training grounds, stretching. His breath hung in the morning air, faint wisps dissolving into the frost-laden sky. When he spotted us, he raised a hand in greeting, though his usual enthusiasm seemed dampened.

"Morning, Elder Ming. Kai," he said, his voice quieter than normal. "Lan-Yin's resting today. She's been feeling nauseous."

I nodded vaguely, the gesture more reflex than acknowledgment. My thoughts were already elsewhere, a whirlwind of concern and frustration that left little room for anything else. Elder Ming gave his usual curt nod, his gaze sweeping over Wang Jun before settling on me.

"Warm up," he instructed. "We'll move to sparring once you're ready."

Without a word, I moved toward the practice area, my body falling into the rhythm of drills almost automatically. The familiar steps of footwork and strikes came to me easily, my muscles working through the motions; like they had been etched into my bones.

But my mind . . . my mind was somewhere else.

Even as my feet pivoted and my fists struck the air, I couldn't stop thinking about Windy. About Tianyi. About trust.

"Get ready for sparring," Elder Ming said.

Jian Feng's words echoed in my head, his sharp reminder of my obligations clashing with the gnawing need to act. He wasn't wrong. The stakes were too high to throw everything away in a reckless bid to save one life, no matter how much it mattered to me. But it burned knowing that I was seen as an asset first, a partner second.

Is this what trust feels like? I thought bitterly. *Counting on others to do what I can't because they believe I have to be preserved for something bigger?*

Wang Jun lunged, his fist aiming for my jaw. My head tilted to the side just in time, his knuckles grazing past. I pivoted, twisting into a counterstrike. My fist connected with his ribs—not hard enough to injure, but enough to knock the air from his lungs.

He stumbled, coughing. "Kai, what the hell?" he gasped, backing away to catch his breath. "You're moving like—are you even paying attention?"

I blinked, the haze in my mind momentarily lifting as his words registered. Paying attention?

My arms hung loosely at my sides, still poised for another strike, but my hands trembled.

"Kai!" Wang Jun snapped, his voice sharper now. "What's going on with you?"

I blinked again, my eyes focusing on him for what felt like the first time. He was staring at me, his expression a mix of irritation and concern. Behind him, Elder Ming's sharp gaze bore into me, his arms folded across his chest.

"I . . ." I started, but the words caught in my throat. What was going on? I glanced down at my hands, the faint tremor betraying the storm inside me. My fists clenched instinctively, the tension grounding me just enough to mutter, "Sorry."

Wang Jun straightened, his brow furrowed. "Sorry? Kai, you're sparring like you're possessed. You're faster. Stronger. What's going on?"

Faster. Stronger. The words struck something in my mind, pulling up the events of the previous night.

"I . . ." I exhaled slowly, lowering my hands. "I broke through. Last night. My body advanced to the second stage of Qi Initiation and my qi to the Essence Awakening stage. Made a new pill with the Golden Bamboo."

Wang Jun's eyes widened. "What? That's—wait, what? That's insane!" He grinned, the admiration returning to his face. "Congrats, Kai! No wonder you're moving like this."

But his enthusiasm didn't stir anything in me. My chest still felt heavy; my thoughts still spiraled. I glanced at Elder Ming, who stepped closer, his eyes narrowing slightly as he studied me.

"Your movements are sharper," he said, his tone measured. "More precise. This refinement has honed you well. But . . ." His gaze softened, just a fraction. "Your mind is elsewhere."

Wang Jun tilted his head, clearly still trying to piece together my erratic behavior. "What's going on? You just had a breakthrough. You should be—" He stopped, noticing the tension in my expression. His tone softened. "Kai, seriously, what's eating at you?"

I sighed, running a hand through my hair. The weight of the situation pressed down on me like a millstone, and I could feel Elder Ming's expectant gaze lingering. I wasn't sure I wanted to drag Wang Jun into this, but keeping him in the dark felt unfair.

"It's . . . complicated," I said at first, trying to organize my thoughts. "Something happened on the outskirts this morning. A . . . spirit beast. A black tiger—dead."

Wang Jun's eyes widened. "*Tigers?* They don't come up this close to the village."

"That's the question," I muttered. "It wasn't just dead. Something killed it, something strong enough to drive it out of its territory and leave it in pieces. And it's just like what happened to the Iron Boar in Qingmu."

Wang Jun's expression darkened as the weight of my words sank in.

"Windy's gone. Left to challenge something in the forest, something the snakes called 'the shadow.' Jian Feng wouldn't let me go look. Says I'm too valuable to send in there. And now Tianyi's out there looking for him." My fists clenched again as I continued to babble on. "She wouldn't listen. She just—"

"Went," Wang Jun finished, his tone sympathetic. "You've got your hands full. Sorry to hear about that."

I shook my head, the frustration bubbling back up. "And here I am, stuck sparring while she's out there. It feels . . . wrong."

"Of course it does," he said, his voice firm. "You're worried about them, Kai. Who wouldn't be? You have every right to be frustrated. If Lan-Yin were out there, I would've been out before the first word came out of your mouth. Nobody would've been able to stop me."

"Enough," Elder Ming interjected, his voice cutting through the tension like a blade. His gaze shifted between us, calm but unyielding. "Wang Jun, your loyalty to Kai is admirable, but don't fan his emotions unnecessarily. He doesn't need validation of his anger—he needs perspective."

Wang Jun frowned but nodded reluctantly. Elder Ming's attention shifted back to me. "The Verdant Lotus Sect has already dispatched scouts. This is their domain, and they're equipped to handle the forest. Your frustration is understandable, but it changes nothing about what needs to be done."

"That doesn't make it easier," I said, my voice quieter now. "It doesn't make it easier to trust them when Tianyi is out there alone. Who knows where Windy is?"

Wang Jun's lips twitched into a small smile, and he clapped a hand on my shoulder. "Hey, Kai. Don't forget why Tianyi stopped coming to these morning practices."

I glanced at him, confused. "What does that have to do with anything?"

"She stopped because she kept beating us so easily," Wang Jun said, grinning. "Think about it. If she could trounce me, Lan-Yin, and even you without breaking a sweat, then whatever's out there should be more worried about her than the other way around."

I blinked, his words slowly sinking in. A faint, reluctant smile tugged at my lips. "She always had a knack for showing us up."

"Exactly," Wang Jun said. "And look, if Tianyi and the scouts don't return by tonight, I'll go with you. We'll find them together."

I stared at him, the offer hitting harder than I expected. For a moment, the knot in my chest loosened just enough for me to breathe. "Thanks, Wang Jun," I whispered. "That . . . means a lot."

He shrugged, his grin softening. "That's what friends are for, right?"

Elder Ming didn't say anything, but his expression had shifted ever so slightly, the faintest hint of approval in his sharp eyes.

As the sparring session ended, I sat on the edge of the courtyard, gazing toward the direction of the forest. The faint rustle of the trees carried on the wind, distant yet persistent. I closed my eyes, my mind quieting for the first time all morning.

"Just be safe." The breeze carried my words away. "Both of you."

CHAPTER ELEVEN

The Forest Holds Its Breath

Windy slithered low against the ground, his pale scales brushing over the brittle, frost-touched grass. His tongue flicked out, catching the faint coppery tang of blood on the frigid wind.

The trail had been easy to follow at first, with crushed undergrowth and faint, unnatural disturbances in the air that only his sharp senses could detect. But as the hours wore on, the path grew colder, the figure moving with an eerie precision that left barely a trace behind. Yet, the serpent was determined. His coiled patience kept him moving, silent and watchful.

The hooded figure moved further than Windy had ever dared. Away from Kai. Away from Tianyi. It was only by pure chance that he caught sight of the elusive shadow that terrified the den of snakes. After days of traversing the forest, going deeper with every passing day, he found it.

His instincts screamed of danger, but the spirit beast wouldn't give up such an opportunity.

The figure was no ordinary prey, but neither was Windy an ordinary snake.

The battle had unfolded just ahead of him, in a clearing where frost clung stubbornly to the ground. Perched high in a tree, Windy wrapped himself around a branch, his pale scales blending with the icy bark as he watched. The massive tiger prowled into view first, its jet-black fur bristling with tension, its movements graceful yet predatory. It seemed angry, emitting a low growl that made his scales stand on end. It was a formidable foe; one he would be hard-pressed to defeat.

And the shadow *moved*.

The ragged cloth draped over its frame shifted unnaturally with each step, and its feet were gnarled and cracked.

The tiger lunged without hesitation, its roar splitting the silence. It was swift, deadly, its claws glinting in the dark as it swiped at the figure. But the hooded man did not dodge. The claws sank into the man's arm, but he pushed forward with no reaction to the pain, his bare hand lashing out with terrifying speed.

Ignoring the attack in favor of delivering a counterblow.

Windy's eyes narrowed.

Fingers, pale and claw-like, raked across the tiger's side. The force of the blow was staggering; three deep gashes appeared in the beast's flesh, muscle tearing apart as if it were paper. Blood sprayed in an arc, splattering the frost-kissed ground in dark streaks.

The tiger howled in pain, staggering back, its massive frame trembling from the sheer ferocity of the strike. The man's movements were precise, deliberate, and far too fluid, as if the edges of his body blurred with each step. He stood motionless for a moment, his hand dripping with blood.

The serpent's tongue flicked again, catching the sharp metallic tang in the air. He observed the tiger's swift retreat, the beast limping heavily into the undergrowth. It was still alive, but just barely. Its steps were slow, dragging, leaving a trail of blood in its wake.

Windy had waited, watched. He had expected the hooded figure to pursue the wounded tiger. That would have been the logical move. Injure the prey, track it, finish it. That was how Windy himself hunted tougher creatures; paralyze them with venom, then follow until their strength left them entirely.

But this was different. The hooded figure didn't move immediately. Instead, it lingered in the clearing, lowering itself onto its knees. Thin, ragged cloth clung to its frame, barely shielding it from the cold.

Immortals feel the cold, don't they? Windy thought, tilting his head. He could remember Kai layering on his maroon robes during the chillier nights. But this figure . . . it did not shiver. It knelt like a statue in the clearing, its movements unnervingly still. For a second, he thought it was just too injured to give chase.

Then it spoke.

The words were low, guttural, and wrong. Windy didn't understand them, but he didn't need to. The forest seemed to hold its breath, and the air grew heavier, laden with something vile and tainted. The sound was like a blade dragging across bone, reverberating with a malevolence that made Windy's instincts flare with alarm.

The way it prostrated itself before the tiger's bloodied trail spoke of something darker, more twisted. Windy could feel the impure essence seeping into the ground around it, poisoning the frost-kissed earth.

His instincts screamed at him to leave—to abandon this hunt and return to the safety of Kai and Tianyi's presence. But he couldn't. The hooded figure's actions were a threat to them, to *everything*.

The figure rose slowly. Windy slithered after it, careful to stay far enough that its shadowy form wouldn't sense him. It repeated the process for a couple of hours at a staggered but deliberate pace, leaving behind bloodstained footprints that glistened darkly in the weak moonlight.

It bleeds. Just like them.

The realization settled like a cold, steadying weight in Windy's mind. The shadow, for all its unnatural power, was not invincible. The tiger's strike had landed, and the droplets of blood that trailed in its wake were proof.

He couldn't fight it head-on. The figure was far stronger than he was, even wounded. But strength alone didn't guarantee victory. A snake never fought like a brute. It fought with precision, cunning, and patience.

This was his chance.

The hooded figure moved to the far side of the clearing, its steps silent despite the frost-covered ground. It paused, crouching again, and resumed its eerie ritual. The guttural, rasping words spilled forth once more, each syllable carrying an unsettling resonance. The figure's bloodied hand traced patterns in the frost, leaving streaks of crimson that shimmered faintly in the dim light.

From his vantage point in the treetops, Windy's coils tightened. His tongue flicked, tasting the air for any hint of a shift in the figure's focus. Nothing. The hooded figure seemed entirely consumed by its dark purpose, oblivious to the serpent watching from above.

Windy's intuition screamed at him to wait, to bide his time. The figure was powerful, far beyond anything he had encountered before. But the blood-streaked footprints trailing from its fight with the tiger reminded him of its vulnerability.

The shadow bleeds. It could be hurt.

And hurt things could be killed.

The figure's voice rose, the guttural tones growing more fervent. The tainted essence radiating from it was almost suffocating now, curling through the air like an invisible toxin. His instincts urged him once again to retreat, to slither back into the safety of the trees and return home. But if he fled now, the shadow would continue.

It would find Kai. It would find Tianyi.

I wanted to kill this monster for my pride, but now I fight so they'll never face it.

With a flick of his tail, Windy launched himself from the branch. His lithe body sliced through the air, silent and swift, his target clear—the figure's unguarded back. His fangs glinted in the faint light, venom ready to inject at the first bite.

For a heartbeat, it appeared he would land his mark. The hooded figure remained crouched, its focus entirely on its ritual.

Then, impossibly fast, it turned.

Windy's momentum carried him forward, but the figure's hand lashed out with unnatural speed. Fingers of iron clamped around his neck, halting his strike midair. The force of the grip made his scales crackle under the pressure. Windy writhed, his tail lashing instinctively, but the hold was unyielding.

The hooded figure stood, lifting the serpent effortlessly. Its hood tilted slightly, as though examining him.

Loose strands of unkempt, greasy hair fell across a lined forehead, their ashen color blending with the ragged shadows of the hood.

The man's skin was weathered and uneven, as though it had been both scorched by the sun and bitten by frost. His lips, cracked and pale, peeled back to reveal yellowed teeth, jagged, as if they had been filed down by years of grinding. His breath carried the stench of decay.

But it was his eyes that froze the serpent in place, even as he struggled. They were not the eyes of an immortal, sharp and calculating, but the eyes of a wild beast.

"So," it muttered, its voice low and dripping with disdain, "you've been following me."

Windy's tail coiled, striking out, but the figure barely flinched. Its grip tightened, and the serpent's vision blurred as the pressure threatened to crush his windpipe.

"I sensed you hours ago," the figure growled, its tone shifting to a sharp, simmering rage. "And yet, you chose now to reveal yourself. Interrupting me."

He knew the grip would kill him if he didn't act now. Summoning every ounce of his remaining strength, he funneled his qi into his tail. The air around him shimmered faintly as the energy coalesced, sharpening his strike.

With a fierce lash, his tail snapped forward, aiming directly at the figure's face. The blow connected with a sickening crack, catching the figure in its eye.

The figure recoiled with a hiss, its grip loosening just enough for Windy to twist free. He dropped to the ground, his body coiling defensively as he retreated several paces. His tongue flicked rapidly, assessing his opponent.

The figure staggered, one hand clutching its face.

"You insolent wretch!" the figure hissed, its voice trembling. Its movements were jerky now, like a marionette driven by rage. "How dare you interrupt! How dare you *defile* this sacred moment?"

It straightened, holding its wounded side as it staggered to the opposite edge of the clearing. Despite the obvious signs of pain, its grip on its ritual was unwavering.

The figure began chanting, its voice a guttural rasp, the words laced with a twisted reverence. "Great one, hear me! Forgive your unworthy servant! But I will make it right, oh divine one! This infidel's blood will quench your thirst. This unclean, profane creature will serve!"

Windy remained still, his body low to the ground. His mind raced. The figure's reaction had been too quick, too deliberate. It hadn't been caught off guard at all.

This wasn't a failed ambush.

It was a trap.

The realization settled in Windy's mind like a shard of ice. He had walked into the figure's game, and now he was its prey.

Tianyi moved silently through the dense forest, her steps light and deliberate as her sharp eyes scanned the undergrowth. The trail she followed was faint. Windy had always been a master of stealth, and she realized this time, he didn't want to be found.

Her lips pressed into a thin line. Windy's subtlety was both a gift and a curse. She admired it, respected it, but now it felt like an impenetrable veil keeping her from him. She pressed on, her senses sharp, her antennae-like strands twitching faintly to detect the smallest vibrations in the air.

The forest was unnervingly still.

It was wrong.

This silence reminded her of . . . something.

Memories, faint and fragmented, surfaced unbidden.

Before Kai. Before Windy.

A time when she was nothing more than a fragile creature, flitting through endless trees under an endless sky. The forests then had always been alive with sound—birds chittering, beasts moving, the hum of the wind as it carried the scents of the earth.

But not now.

She unfolded her wings, the glowing blue edges spreading wide. With a sharp leap, she propelled herself into the canopy, gliding effortlessly between branches. The world below blurred as she moved with purpose, the wind rushing against her skin.

The two strands falling down her face twitched again, sensing the subtlest of disturbances. There; a faint rustle, too deliberate to be wind. She veered toward it, her wings angling to catch the light breeze.

She landed softly on a sturdy branch, crouching as her sharp gaze scanned the shadows below. Her antennae flicked, homing in on the faint movement ahead. It was quick, almost imperceptible, but it was there.

"Windy . . ." she murmured under her breath, her voice low and calm. She doubted he would respond. He wouldn't unless he wanted to.

Still, she moved closer, her wings pulling her effortlessly from branch to branch.

Why are you hiding?

The question lingered in her mind, but she didn't stop. Her movements grew faster, her focus sharper, as she pursued the fleeting traces. The trail wasn't growing colder; it was changing. More erratic.

And the forest remained silent.

Her antennae twitched violently, catching something.

An aura, faint but impure. Her wings shifted instinctively, angling her to glide low, just above the forest floor, as she followed the faint disturbance.

Ahead, she caught the barest flicker of motion. It wasn't Windy.

The metallic tang of blood hung thick in the air now, growing stronger with each step. She slowed further, her wings folding partially to minimize the faint hum they emitted. Her sharp eyes caught the glow of a lantern, flickering weakly against the shadows of the forest. She moved closer, crouching low to avoid detection.

Her mouth pressed into a thin line as the scene came into view.

Three figures lay scattered across the forest floor, motionless and broken. The robes of the Verdant Lotus Sect hung from their forms, torn and bloodied. One disciple was crumpled against a tree, his head bent at an unnatural angle. Another lay face down in a pool of crimson, a trail of smeared blood leading to him as if he had tried to crawl away. The third was slumped against the remains of a shattered lantern, the faint light casting an eerie glow over his lifeless face.

Tianyi's stomach twisted as recognition dawned. These were the disciples. The ones sent ahead to scout.

Her eyes narrowed, scanning the clearing for the source of the slaughter. Her antennae quivered again, drawing her attention to the center of the carnage.

There, kneeling amid the carnage, was a person.

No, not a person. Not entirely.

Their form was like the one described by the den of snakes. A shadow. They were covered in a robe, its edges frayed and tattered.

The figure knelt, its hood obscuring its face, though long, loose strands of hair clung to its angular features. Its body was unnaturally still, save for its hands, which moved with eerie precision. It dragged one of the lifeless disciples closer, arranging the body with care, as though laying it to rest. But the intention was far from reverent.

She watched the figure shift to another body, rolling it to its back and dragging it to form a crude triangle with the others. Her sharp eyes caught something glinting in the figure's hand.

A seed, black as pitch, pulsating faintly like a diseased heart.

The figure leaned forward, burying the seed in the center of the triangle. Its clawed hands dug into the blood-soaked earth with fervor, smearing its palms with a mix of dirt and gore. It chanted again, the guttural, raspy words sending ripples of unease through the clearing.

Tianyi didn't need to understand the words to feel their intent. The air thickened, curling with malevolent qi as the seed absorbed the blood pooling beneath it. The forest seemed to recoil, its silence growing more oppressive.

A moment passed. Then another.

The ground where the seed was buried pulsed faintly, like the rhythm of a beating heart. The blood around the triangle of corpses glowed faintly, drawn toward the seed in thin, crimson tendrils.

The figure raised its bloodied hands high, its chant reaching a fever pitch. "May your bloom feed on the unworthy! May your roots drink deep of their essence! Let this offering strengthen your dominion!"

Tianyi's sharp gaze fixed on the ground as the soil erupted.

A dark vine, thorny and grotesque, burst from the earth, writhing as though alive. The vine twisted upward, its movement jerky and unnatural, until it unfurled a flower at its peak.

Her antennae pulsed violently, detecting the vile essence radiating from the flower. It was not natural. It was wrong.

The figure knelt again, its clawed hands gripping the base of the bloom as if in worship.

Tianyi's stomach churned. She had seen enough. This was not her goal. Her goal was to find Windy.

But before she could retreat, the figure froze mid-chant. Slowly, almost deliberately, it turned its head toward her. The hood shifted just enough to reveal a pale, feminine face streaked with dried blood. Their eyes, wild and sunken, locked onto hers with a predatory gleam.

A sickly smile stretched across her cracked lips, and her voice shifted to a low rasp as she rose to her feet.

"Ah, another offering," she murmured, gaze gleaming with manic fervor. "The Heavenly Demon provides bountifully indeed."

CHAPTER TWELVE

A Butterfly Against the Shadow

The hooded woman's claws ripped through the air with feral precision, each swipe carrying enough force to shatter the trunks of nearby trees. Snow exploded in every direction as her strikes gouged deep into the ground, but none found their mark. Tianyi flitted just out of reach, her movements too quick, too light, too unpredictable.

To anyone watching, the fight might have seemed like a mismatched dance; the raw power and relentless fury of the beast-like woman clashing against the unyielding grace of a winged dancer.

Tianyi's wings shimmered faintly in the dim light, catching the morning light as she darted between the branches. Her movements weren't simply fast; they were alien, erratic, her sharp turns and sudden dives defying the rhythm of a conventional fight. The shadow snarled in frustration, claws carving empty arcs through the frost-chilled air.

She's powerful, Tianyi thought, her antennae twitching faintly as they detected the faint pulses of malevolent qi radiating outward like ripples in a poisoned lake. *Too powerful.*

The shadow's qi made her exoskeleton prickle, her body instinctively recoiling from the unnatural energy. But no matter how strong the enemy was, she couldn't strike what she couldn't touch.

The woman lunged again, clawed hand crashing into the trunk of a tree as Tianyi twisted midair, her wings propelling her upward in a graceful arc. She leapt higher, using a branch as a springboard, and landed lightly on the outstretched arm before she could react. Her delicate frame balanced perfectly atop the exposed limb, and for a heartbeat, their gazes locked.

One calm, almost serene; another wild and furious.

THWACK!

Then she kicked the shadow squarely in the face.

The blow sent her opponent's head snapping back with a sickening crack, and Tianyi flipped off her arm, landing softly in the snow a few paces away. The hooded woman staggered but recovered easily despite the force of the blow.

"You think you're clever?" Her voice was a venomous rasp, muffled slightly as she wiped blood from her nose. "Let's see how you handle this."

With a swift, jerking motion, she reached into the triangle of Verdant Lotus Sect disciples' bodies, clawed hand plunging into the chest of one corpse. Tianyi's antennae twitched violently at the act, but she didn't falter, her sharp eyes narrowing as she tracked her opponent's every move.

The woman turned back to her, clutching a satchel now torn open from the speed of her movement. As she lunged forward, the satchel ripped fully, and glass bottles tumbled out, shattering against Tianyi's head, wings, and the snow beneath her.

A sharp, acrid scent filled the air as different liquids splashed across her frame, soaking into her skin and into the gaps between her joints.

She licked her lips experimentally, tasting the faint bitterness of alcohol. Confusion flickered across her face.

What is this supposed to—

A lantern flew toward her, its weak flame flickering precariously. Tianyi moved to dodge it instinctively, her wings flaring, but the flame ignited the alcohol as soon as it hit the ground near her.

And all she knew was *heat*.

Pain seared through her as the flames licked at her wings and body, the acrid smell of burning alcohol mingling with the icy air.

Tianyi's instincts screamed, and she folded her wings tightly against her back, dropping into the snow. She rolled desperately, the freezing surface biting into her skin but extinguishing the flames. Smoke and steam rose around her as she pushed herself upright, her breath coming in quick gasps.

But the maneuver left her vulnerable.

The hooded woman was on her before she could fully regain her footing. Her clawed hand descended, and Tianyi barely raised her arm in defense. The impact sent a jolt of pain through her body as the malevolent qi surged into her, biting and writhing like a living thing.

Fissures spread across her arm, delicate and jagged like fractures in glass. She staggered back, clutching the injured limb as a sharp, pulsing pain radiated outward from the wound.

The woman straightened, her grin jagged and triumphant as she advanced on her winged adversary. "You're not so untouchable now, are you?" she sneered, claws flexing in anticipation.

Her antennae drooped, exhaustion and pain settling over her. Her wings trembled faintly, still slick with alcohol that hadn't fully evaporated, droplets sliding down her face and neck.

SHLURP!

Tianyi's tongue moved instinctually to collect the alcohol dripping down her skin. Her eyes burned faintly, not just from the residual flames but from the fumes clinging to her. She couldn't even blink, her focus locked on the hooded woman as she prowled closer.

Her body felt strange—warm, unsteady, and sluggish. A tingling heat spread through her veins, and her mind buzzed faintly, as if she were on the verge of something she couldn't quite grasp. She licked her lips again.

What is this feeling?

The shadow lunged, its claws slicing toward her with terrifying precision. Tianyi moved on instinct, wings flaring as she dove to the side. But her timing was off. Too slow, too deliberate. The woman's claws grazed her shoulder, leaving faint lines that burned with residual qi.

She laughed, a high-pitched, grating noise.

Her antennae twitched, but instead of despair, a strange clarity settled over her. The warmth spreading through her body wasn't a weakness; it was something else she could use. She drew in a shaky breath, her wings folding tightly against her back as she crouched low.

The hooded woman smirked, mistaking her stillness for submission. She rushed forward again, claws gleaming with malevolent energy.

But just as she closed in, Tianyi vanished.

A blur of motion to her right, then left.

Tianyi reappeared behind her, foot slamming into the back of the shadow's knee with enough force to drop her momentarily. She roared, spinning to swipe at her, but Tianyi was already gone, darting upward into the branches.

Her movements had changed. They weren't the sharp, rapid bursts of speed she had used before. Now they were unpredictable, a mix of slow, deliberate shifts and sudden, explosive strikes. The rhythm disoriented the hooded woman, her attacks cutting through empty air as Tianyi evaded by a mere hair's breadth.

This is my chance.

She landed softly in the snow, her sharp eyes tracking his every move. Her wings hummed faintly as she darted forward, striking again and again. Her movements were like a dance, weaving through attacks, landing precise blows that chipped away at her opponent's strength.

The hooded woman snarled, blood dripping from her mouth as she staggered back. Her movements grew slower, her strikes less precise.

Infusing her wings with more qi than before, she dipped low to the ground and *pushed.*

Sharpened to their utmost, her wings sank deep into the hooded figure's torso.

She coughed violently, blood splattering the snow.

For a moment, Tianyi thought it was over. The malevolent qi that had surrounded her moments ago was fading, dissipating like smoke carried away by the wind.

Tianyi's breaths came sharp and shallow, each one a reminder of how close she had come to being overwhelmed.

But then the air around her opponent shifted.

It wasn't the gradual quiet of death settling in. No, this was something else—something wrong. The snow beneath the woman's broken form darkened as her claws dug deep, tearing into the earth. Her body convulsed violently, back arching as though she were a marionette pulled by invisible strings. A rasping, guttural sound clawed its way out of her throat, rising into an unnatural chant that made the air itself feel heavier.

"Heavenly Demon, grant me strength! Your servant offers all!"

She took a cautious step back, her sharp eyes narrowing as she assessed the change.

Despite the gaping wound in her chest, the hooded woman rose.

The movement was jerky, unnatural; limbs spasming as though resisting the sheer will that forced them to move. Blood spilled freely from injuries, steaming as it hit the cold ground, yet she stood upright, her frame trembling with unnatural vigor.

She wasn't healing. The wound across her torso remained, a deep, gaping slash that should have rendered her immobile, if not dead.

Her skin was ashen, and her movements unsteady, yet her eyes burned with a manic light.

It wasn't life. It was a grotesque semblance of it, fueled by desperation and blind devotion.

Tianyi had seen something like this before, deep in the wilds. The death throes of a cornered animal, its body surging with impossible strength as it fought against the inevitable. A rabbit that bit clean through a predator's paw, a bird that kept flying even after its wings were torn. This was no different. An echo of that primal instinct, amplified a hundredfold by feverish faith.

Claws lashed out, faster than before, slicing through the air with a ferocity that made her wings hum as she barely evaded the strike. Tianyi flipped backward, her feet barely brushing the snow as she retreated to gain space. But the hooded woman was relentless.

"Your mortal strength means *nothing*!" she roared, voice fraying at the edges, cracking like brittle ice. "The Heavenly Demon guides me! I am more than flesh! I am *purpose*!"

Her strikes came in a whirlwind, each one faster, stronger, more precise. The snow churned beneath her feet as she surged forward, her movements no longer hindered by pain or injury. Tianyi dodged on instinct, her body weaving and twisting to stay ahead. The warmth that had overtaken her moments ago had largely faded away.

But the sheer speed of the attacks pushed her to her limits. Her claws grazed her wing, the malevolent qi biting into the delicate structure like acid. Pain flared through her, sharp and searing, but she forced herself to stay focused.

She had to end this.

Tianyi's antennae twitched faintly, sensing a subtle shift in the rhythm of battle. The shadow's movements, while faster and stronger, had grown erratic—wild swings that left small openings in her defense. It wasn't much, but it was enough.

Taking a deep breath, she narrowed her focus, funneling every ounce of her remaining energy into her wings. They glowed faintly in the moonlight, the edges sharpening into blades of shimmering blue. She darted forward, her movements slower, more deliberate, but precise.

The hooded woman lunged, claws arcing toward her throat. Tianyi twisted midair, her wings slicing upward with a graceful, lethal sweep.

Her strike landed.

The shimmering edge of her wings cleaved fully through the shadow's torso. The blow sent a shockwave through the clearing, snow exploding outward as the body jerked violently. For a moment, she stood frozen, claws twitching, chant faltering into a gurgling gasp.

Then, with an unnatural groan, she collapsed.

The forest fell silent once more. Tianyi landed softly, her wings folding against her back as she stood over the lifeless form. Her breaths were ragged, her body trembling, but she forced herself to stay upright.

Tianyi steadied herself, her breaths slowing. That warmth—still faint, still inexplicable—lingered within her chest. It wasn't the searing heat of the flames or the fiery rush of qi coursing through her wings. No, it was something calmer, yet steady. It had carried her through the fight, grounding her when her instincts screamed to flee.

What was that? she thought, her antennae twitching faintly. It reminded her of the moments in practice when she had flowed with unpredictability, where precision didn't matter as much as feeling. But this . . . this wasn't skill. This was something deeper.

The memory of her erratic, unpredictable movements, how they seemed to confuse the hooded woman, surfaced in her mind. Was it the warmth that had guided her, loosening her form, her approach?

The thought was absurd, yet it stuck with her. She shook her head, dismissing it for now. There were more pressing matters to attend to.

Tianyi stood amid the carnage, her sharp eyes scanning the broken remains of the clearing. The bodies of the Verdant Lotus Sect disciples lay motionless, their blood staining the snow like dark petals scattered across an icy canvas. She could see the remnants of their struggle—the gouged earth, the shattered lanterns, the signs of desperation etched into the ground.

Grimly, she clutched her injured arm. The cracks in her exoskeleton shimmered faintly in the morning light. It pulsed beneath her skin, a festering corruption that sent sharp stabs of pain radiating through her limb. She winced, her lips pressing into a thin line as she focused her energy.

Tianyi closed her eyes, taking a deep breath. Her qi flowed, soft and steady at first, then growing stronger as she directed it toward her wounded arm. The pure energy swirled around the cracks, pushing against the invasive qi that writhed within her. She gritted her teeth, her body trembling with the effort.

The corrupted qi resisted, coiling like a living thing as it clung to her, refusing to be displaced. But Tianyi pressed harder, forcing her own energy to envelop it, isolate it, and begin breaking it apart. Beads of sweat formed on her brow as the effort drained her reserves, each pulse of her qi weakening her further.

Finally, the malevolent energy dissipated, retreating like a shadow burned away by sunlight. The cracks in her exoskeleton remained, raw and tender, but the vile presence within them had diminished. The pain subsided to a dull ache, and she exhaled shakily, lowering her arm.

"Windy," she murmured to herself, her voice soft and hoarse. "Please be safe."

She straightened, forcing herself to stand tall despite the weariness that pressed down on her. The forest around her was eerily silent, the stillness almost suffocating. Her antennae twitched again, searching for any trace of her friend.

CHAPTER THIRTEEN

To Coil and Strike

How long had it been?

Windy hissed low, his pale scales disappearing against the frost-covered ground as he slithered through the snow. The sting of failure gnawed at him, sharper than the icy wind. His ambush had failed, leaving his body battered and his pride in tatters. The best he could do was slither around, avoiding the man's attacks with evasive movements.

Behind him, heavy footsteps crushed the snow. His instincts screamed to flee, to vanish into the safety of the deeper woods.

But he didn't.

The serpent wanted to ask himself why, but deep down, he already knew the reason.

Cold bit into him, numbing his pain, but it was a double-edged sword. Snow sapped his strength, and he couldn't linger here long.

The hooded man's voice rasped through the quiet. "Hiding, little snake? I'll tear you out by your fangs."

The serpent burrowed into the snow, leaving faint tracks leading one way, then doubled back silently. His pale form weaved through the frost like a phantom, coiling beneath another drift. His tongue flicked again, tasting the air. The man's injured arm hung stiffly at his side, the deep gash still raw despite his lack of reaction to the wound.

That's the weakness. That's where I strike.

With a burst of motion, Windy launched himself from the snow. His tail whipped forward, qi sharpening its edge as it cracked like a whip toward the man's wounded arm.

The hooded man spun faster than Windy expected, his glowing eyes flaring with anticipation. His injured arm shot up to block, but the tail strike landed, splintering bone further. Without giving the slightest regard to his wound, the shadow raised his working arm for an attack.

The man's claws lashed out in a vicious arc, and Windy twisted desperately, his body contorting midair. He evaded the worst of it, but the claws grazed his tail, sending him spinning into the snowbank. Pain flared, sharp, as crimson streaked the frost where he landed.

It was terribly difficult to deal with someone who was driven by madness to kill the other person without caring about their own life, regardless of the martial art's level.

Windy hissed, coiling defensively. His mind raced. *He's too strong. Too fast. I can't match him head-on. Cunning alone won't save me.*

A memory flickered in his mind—Tianyi's erratic movements in battle, her unpredictable rhythm that seemed to defy logic. She hadn't abandoned her butterfly instincts; she'd transformed them into something more.

Windy's coils tightened beneath the snow as realization dawned.

> *Your dao is slowly forming.*

The hooded man tore through the snowbank, following the serpent's false trail, his claws ripping into roots and frost alike. Windy waited, silent, until the man turned his back.

This time, he moved differently. Not just a predator, but something more. Something deadly.

Windy slithered low through the snow. The cold bit deep into his body once more, but he welcomed the sharpness; it kept him present, grounded. Each movement was measured as the hooded man's enraged roars echoed through the forest. Snow churned, branches cracked, and the oppressive weight of malevolent qi bore down on the clearing like a smothering fog.

His tongue flicked, tasting the air. Blood, decay, anger. But Windy's own qi was dangerously low, flickering like the last embers of a dying flame. The fight had gone on for too long.

He slithered beneath a snowbank, his body coiling tightly. Pain flared in his tail, where the man's claws had torn through his scales, but he didn't let it distract him.

This ends now. One way or another.

The hooded man staggered into the clearing, his movements wild, erratic. Snow caked his bloodied claws, steam rising from his cracked lips.

Moments of clarity broke through Windy's haze of exhaustion. The serpent's way had always been stealth, patience, and precision. Yet now he saw the need for something more. The image of Tianyi, darting unpredictably through the air, weaving her butterfly instincts into a dance that transcended logic, flickered in his mind.

Adapt, he realized. *The serpent waits, but it can also strike from angles unseen.*

Snow churned as he moved in sudden, erratic bursts. He used low-hanging branches to disappear and reappear. He coiled around loose snowbanks, his pale body merging with the frost to confuse the man's senses. Each feint pushed the hooded man closer to blind rage.

The man's claws tore through a snowbank with terrifying force, scattering white powder into the air. "You slippery little—!" His words were cut off as Windy darted past him, a blur of motion that left only the faintest trace in the snow.

Each feint drained Windy's qi further. His breathing grew labored, his scales dulled. He had to finish it now.

The hooded man's eyes flared with malevolent light. He paused suddenly, his wild thrashing replaced with calculated stillness. Windy froze, his tongue tasting the shift.

A trap.

The man feigned an opening, his injured left arm hanging loosely. Windy hesitated for a fraction of a second but knew he had no choice. He struck.

The moment his tail lashed out, the man twisted, his claws slicing through the air with blinding speed.

Time seemed to slow. Windy's body coiled instinctively, his mind racing. And then, an image.

Kai, deflecting a blow with an effortless motion, redirecting its force.

The serpent didn't think. He acted.

As the man's claw descended, his body moved in a flowing, wavelike motion. He didn't meet the strike head-on but shifted just enough to guide the attack past him. The force of the man's blow struck empty air, his balance faltering as he stumbled forward.

Now.

Windy twisted, his body coiling upward like a whip. His tail lashed around the man's arms, tightening with brutal precision. His fangs sank deep into the man's neck, injecting every drop of venom stored within him.

The hooded man roared in fury, sinking his teeth down into his serpentine body. He tore into Windy's scales with a brutal ferocity that sent waves of agony coursing through the serpent's body. Each strike bit deeper, shredding flesh and muscle, and with every tear, the man's corrupt qi seeped into Windy's wounds like a toxic fog. The invasive energy burned, spreading through his veins and coiling around his core like a living parasite.

Windy hissed in agony, his body trembling under the relentless assault, but his coils only tightened.

A serpent doesn't have to fight head-on.

The venom worked quickly, coursing through the man's veins like liquid fire. His movements grew weaker, his snarls fading into ragged breaths. Still, Windy didn't loosen his grip. He couldn't. If he let go, it would all be over.

It waits in silence, coils its prey, and leaves nothing but bones.

The man collapsed to his knees, his claws falling limp at his sides. His body convulsed once, twice, before finally going still.

Windy uncoiled slowly, his battered body trembling with exhaustion. He slithered back, his vision swimming, but he refused to fall. He raised his head, tasting the air one last time.

The malevolent qi that had tainted the clearing was gone. The suffocating presence that had hung over the forest like a storm cloud had dissipated, leaving only the faint metallic tang of blood on the wind.

Windy collapsed into the snow, his body coiling instinctively as pain radiated through him. His scales, once pristine and shimmering, were now marred with blood, torn in jagged lines where the hooded man's attacks had struck. His breath came in shallow gasps, each exhalation a faint wisp of steam that dissipated into the frost-laden air.

The world blurred around him. The snow seemed colder now, not a numbing reprieve but a creeping chill that threatened to steal his remaining strength. He could feel his life slipping away, his qi reserves drained to nothing, his venom depleted.

Yet, in the stillness, a strange peace settled over him.

I did it, he thought, his tongue flicking weakly. *I protected them. Even if I end here, Tianyi and Kai will be safe.*

The sound of a faint chime cut through the quiet, the Interface's notification resonating in his mind.

> *Quest: Path of the Serpent has been completed.*
> *You completed the quest with additional challenges.*
> *Your efforts do not go unnoticed.*

Windy hissed faintly, amused despite himself. *What good are rewards if I'm not around to claim them?*

The thought gnawed at him as his vision blurred, but there was no bitterness. Just the quiet satisfaction that came from knowing he had done what he set out to do.

His vision dimmed, and he let himself sink deeper into the snow, his thoughts drifting to the ones he fought to protect. Tianyi's sharp wit and the subtle grace with which she fought. Kai's unyielding determination, his fumbling kindness. They would go on.

And that was enough.

Just as his consciousness slipped away entirely, a faint voice pierced the haze. "Windy? Are you still alive?"

The serpent groaned internally. Of all the moments for Tianyi to arrive, why now? He was at death's door, bloodied and broken, and yet the thought of her seeing him like this sent a surge of embarrassment through him.

He uncoiled painfully, lifting his head with a hiss that was meant to sound defiant but came out pitifully weak.

Of course I am.

Tianyi stepped into view, her antennae twitching faintly as she scanned the clearing. Her usually flawless appearance was disheveled—her hair singed at the edges, her robes charred and torn in places. The faint scent of smoke clung to her, and the fissures along the exoskeleton of her arm gleamed faintly in the moonlight, showing signs of corruption.

Windy narrowed his eyes, his sharp gaze taking in the signs of battle. *The shadow. You . . . fought one too?* he asked, his voice quieter now.

Her wings folded tightly against her back as she knelt beside him. "Yes. But we'll talk about that later. You're hurt."

He hissed faintly, trying to shift away. *I'll be fine.*

Tianyi didn't respond. She placed her hand gently on his scales, and a soft pulse of qi radiated from her palm. Warmth spread through his battered body, washing over the deep wounds and malignant qi.

The pain dulled, then faded, as her energy worked its way through him. For the first time since the fight began, he could breathe without agony clawing at his chest.

As the tension in his body eased, his vision dimmed again, this time with a strange sense of relief.

"Let's go home." Tianyi said softly, her voice steady despite her own injuries.

Windy felt her arms lift him gently, cradling his weakened form. He let himself relax, the fight finally over, the weight of survival no longer his alone to bear.

And for once, as darkness claimed him, he felt safe.

I paced the edge of the forest, the frost crunching beneath my boots as the winter wind bit into my skin. The chill seeped through my robes, but I couldn't bring myself to retreat to the warmth of the house. Not when they were still out there.

The tree line loomed, a silent wall of shadows and snow. I stared into the darkness, searching for any sign; anything to prove that Jian Feng's words weren't baseless, that trusting the Verdant Lotus Sect hadn't been a mistake. The waiting gnawed at me, an itch under my skin I couldn't scratch.

Trust. Believe in the sect. Let them handle it.

Jian Feng's voice echoed in my mind, but the words felt hollow now. How could I sit idly by while they risked everything?

I crossed my arms, gripping the fabric of my sleeves tightly to steady my trembling hands. Every passing moment felt heavier, the silence pressing down on me. The shadows beneath the trees shifted, but it was only the wind stirring the branches.

Still nothing.

My breath hung in the air as faint wisps of steam, dissolving into the cold. I felt the weight of the winter evening pressing against me, the fading light casting long, creeping shadows over the snow.

A flicker, faint and fleeting, brushed the edge of my consciousness. I froze. The bond I shared with Tianyi stirred, weak but unmistakable. Her presence faint and frayed but alive. A wave of exhaustion, worry, and relief flooded through me.

"Tianyi," I whispered, the word barely leaving my lips before my body moved.

I bolted toward the forest, my boots slipping on the icy ground as I pushed through the underbrush. The sharp sting of branches scraping my face didn't register; my focus was on that faint connection growing stronger with every step.

"Tianyi!" I called out, my voice cutting through the air.

The faint hum of her wings answered first, a sound that made my chest tighten. I broke through the thick brush, the snow crunching underfoot, and finally saw them.

She stood at the edge of the forest, her wings folded tightly against her back. Her figure was small and fragile-looking, but her posture was steady. In her arms was Windy, his pale scales dulled and marred with streaks of blood.

"It's me!" I shouted, my breath catching as I reached them. "Are you—what happened?"

She met my gaze, her antennae twitching faintly. Her face was pale, her features drawn with exhaustion, but her grip on Windy was firm despite the fissures along her forearm.

"We're alive," she said simply, her voice steady but quiet. "But the shadows . . . They attacked us."

My heart sank. "There were? How many?"

She nodded, her expression grim. "Two. The Verdant Lotus Sect's disciples . . . the immortals . . . they died."

Her words hit like a physical blow. I stared at her, my mind racing to process what she was saying. The Verdant Lotus Sect had sent three second-class disciples, and they were gone? The realization settled heavily in my chest. This was far worse than any of us had anticipated.

"What about Windy?" I asked, my voice barely above a whisper.

Tianyi looked down at the battered serpent in her arms. "He fought against a shadow. But it's strong. Too strong. He held his ground until I found him."

My gaze fell on Windy's motionless form. His once-pristine scales were torn and bloodied, his breaths shallow and uneven. The sight of him like this made my stomach twist.

I clenched my fists, forcing myself to steady my breathing. "We need to get him inside. Both of you. You're hurt."

The wind bit my face, but I barely felt it. My thoughts churned as I reached out, carrying her like a priceless vase, fearing a single misstep would shatter her delicate form.

Whatever this was, it wasn't just an isolated threat anymore. The Verdant Lotus Sect had been decimated. This was only the beginning.

I glanced back at the forest one last time, the tree line standing silent and unyielding against the darkening sky.

"Let's get home," I said finally, my voice low. "We'll figure this out. Together."

CHAPTER FOURTEEN

A Bloody Return

The shop was cold, its silence pressing against me as I carried them inside. Windy's body, once sleek and pristine, hung limp in Tianyi's arms, streaked with blood and torn scales. Underneath the faint glow of the furnace, his injuries became clearer—and more horrific. Entire sections of his flesh were exposed, his pale scales cracked and jagged. I could see faint quivers beneath the open wounds, the muscles twitching weakly as though fighting a battle of their own.

My stomach churned. I forced myself to breathe, to stay steady. Panic wouldn't save him.

My mind turned inward, reaching into the repository of knowledge I'd painstakingly cultivated over the years. Recipes, techniques, theories—all stored, all ready.

What's the best I can make? What can I use now?

Lines of ingredients arranged themselves, forming pathways of reactions and counter-reactions. I could almost feel the potential, the weight of a hundred choices and their outcomes pressing against me.

One recipe stood out. The Purifying Basin Solution. I'd read about it in the Million Book Pavilion during my quest to refine a hundred recipes, its formula etched into my mind. It was potent, thorough. But it required Verdant Amberroot, an ingredient I didn't have.

I frowned, my thoughts racing. Could it work without the Amberroot? Its primary purpose was stabilization, keeping the solution from overwhelming the injured body.

Substitute. There has to be something I can use instead.

I lowered him onto the counter as gently as I could, biting the inside of my cheek to stay focused. My hands trembled as I reached for a clean basin. The faint coppery scent of blood mixed with the lingering aroma of herbs in the shop, creating a nauseating contrast.

"Rinse first," I whispered, grabbing a bucket and hurrying outside to scoop up fresh snow. The icy chill stung my fingers, grounding me, though it did little to ease the tightness in my chest.

Back inside, I set the bucket near the furnace, stoking its flame with practiced precision. The Refinement Simulation Technique sparked to life, ghostly projections overlaying the furnace's interior. It felt automatic, my mind barely registering the glowing matrix of heat distribution and water conversion.

As the snow melted into warm water, I brought the basin closer, careful not to disturb Windy. "This will help," I murmured, more to myself than him. My voice wavered, betraying the fear I couldn't shake.

The moment I poured the water over his scales, a faint hiss echoed; not from Windy, but from his wounds. My heart sank. A dark, oily residue bubbled to the surface, writhing as though alive. The edges of his wounds pulsed faintly, the corrupted qi resisting even the warm water.

Tianyi stepped closer, her antennae twitching. "I tried," she said softly, her voice trembling. "My healing wasn't enough. It doesn't work well against it. Only slows."

"I know," I said, forcing calm into my tone. "You did well. You saved him."

I turned back to the shelves, scanning for the strongest herbs I had to substitute for the Verdant Amberroot. My fingers hovered over the Golden Bamboo essence, but I hesitated.

Too intense. It could push him over the edge.

I dashed into the greenhouse and grabbed the Jadeleaf Lily instead, its soft green petals glowing faintly under the moonlight.

I moved with practiced efficiency, stripping the petals and grinding them into a paste. My mind raced as the Refinement Simulation Technique spun to life again, showing me potential reactions. Each step shimmered in my mind, but I still felt the weight of uncertainty pressing against my ribs.

As I worked, Yin Si, a shadowy blur against the wall, descended silently. She moved with urgency, her thin legs weaving fine strands of silk in precise, almost frantic patterns.

"She wants to help," Tianyi said softly, her voice a thread in the quiet room.

I glanced over my shoulder. The spider's movements were swift, her delicate webs already wrapping around Tianyi's injured arm. A wave of gratitude welled up in me, but I focused on my task.

The mixture took shape, a potent purifying concoction. "This has to work," I muttered, distilling the paste into the basin with precision. The water glowed faintly, the dark residue bubbling more violently as the liquid took on purifying properties.

Windy twitched weakly as I lifted him into the basin. His body slipped under, but I kept his head propped above the water's surface, careful not to let him drown.

His pale form floated almost lifelessly, his breathing shallow, but the glow of the concoction pushed back against the corrupted qi.

"Hold on," I whispered, gripping the basin's edge tightly.

I observed him for several minutes, tracking every change. I breathed a sigh of relief; it seemed the mixture was dispelling some of the malignant qi, as slow as it was.

Tianyi moved beside me, her injured arm cradled against her chest. Yin Si was gone just as quickly as she had appeared. But she left Tianyi's arm covered tightly with silk thread. My gaze flicked to her briefly, catching the jagged cracks along her exoskeleton.

"Your arm," I said quietly, breaking the silence.

"From the shadow," she replied, though her voice lacked strength. "They are slow, but allowing one attack leads to this."

I grabbed another clean cloth, soaking it in the same medicinal mixture. "What happened out there?"

She hesitated, her wings shifting faintly. "The shadow . . . They were chanting something. Doing something to the bodies. They planted a seed."

My pulse quickened, but I forced my hands to stay steady. "What did they say?" I said, my voice low.

"I . . ." She hesitated, her antennae curling slightly. "I don't want to. It doesn't make me feel good."

"Please, Tianyi. We need to learn who they're behind."

After a moment of indecision, she relented. ". . . She kept saying, '*Praise the Heavenly Demon.*'" Her words were hesitant, each syllable dripping with unease.

The air seemed to shift, the phrase lingering unnaturally. There was something wrong with those words, something deeper than fear. It clawed at the edges of my mind, like a shadow slithering through unseen cracks.

I hurriedly soaked the cloth in the leftover mixture, squeezing out the excess before pressing it gently against the silk threads wrapped around Tianyi's arm. My fingers trembled as I worked, the motions automatic but weighed by the sight of her injuries. The threads glistened faintly as they absorbed the concoction, swelling slightly. The glow of the liquid seemed to seep into the silk, a faint pulse radiating across the threads.

Tianyi's wings fluttered faintly, and her posture relaxed. The tension in her shoulders eased, her antennae lifting slightly. The pain must have dulled; her sharp exoskeletal features no longer seemed as rigid with strain.

"Is it working?" I asked, though I could already see the answer.

She nodded, her voice soft. "It's better."

Relief swept through me, but it was quickly replaced by guilt. Without thinking, I leaned forward and wrapped my arms around her, pulling her into a tight hug. She stiffened at first, then let out a faint sigh, her arms resting awkwardly at her sides.

"I'm sorry," I whispered, my voice breaking. "I'm sorry for leaving you alone out there. For trusting them. For letting you fend for yourselves."

Her head tilted slightly, her expression unchanging as she looked at me. "There's nothing to apologize for," she said bluntly. "I chose to go. Windy did too. You didn't make us."

"But I should've stopped you," I said, pulling back slightly to look at her. "I should've been there. I should've—"

"You can't change what happened. And you weren't wrong to trust the sect disciples. They were capable. Just not enough."

Her bluntness cut through the storm of my thoughts, but the weight in my chest didn't lift. I glanced at Windy, his pale form floating weakly in the basin. My hands curled into fists, and for a moment, I let the guilt overwhelm me.

"You almost died. Both of you. And I let it happen."

Tianyi tilted her head, her antennae twitching faintly. "You didn't let anything happen. You're here now. Fixing it."

Her words struck a chord, but they didn't absolve me. My vision blurred as I stared at Windy. "I was indecisive. I stayed here, trying to believe Jian Feng's words. I should've trusted my instincts."

"You didn't know what would happen," she said simply. "Neither did we. You are not perfect, Kai."

Her honesty was both grounding and painful. My shoulders sagged, the weight of the day pressing down on me. For the first time since I'd carried Windy into the shop, I let myself feel fear, anger, and overwhelming guilt. A few tears slipped down my cheeks before I could stop them.

"I won't let it happen again," I said, my voice firm despite the quiver. "I won't leave you in danger. Ever again."

Tianyi didn't reply immediately. Instead, she rested her uninjured hand on my arm, her touch light but steady.

The danger wasn't over—not with whatever this "Heavenly Demon" was. If I was going to protect them, I couldn't let myself drown in guilt.

I turned my focus back to Windy and Tianyi, channeling every ounce of determination I had into their recovery. There was no room for anything else.

"Tianyi," I whispered, keeping my voice calm. "You've done more than enough for today. You need to rest."

Her antennae tilted, and her unfocused gaze met mine, stubbornness flickering faintly in her expression. "I don't need—"

"You do," I interrupted gently. "Please trust me. Rest."

She hesitated for a moment, her gaze lingering on me as if assessing whether I truly meant it. Finally, she nodded, albeit reluctantly, and shifted closer. Without another word, she laid herself down, her movements stiff as her head settled lightly on my lap. Her wings folded against her back, and though her eyes didn't close, they lost their sharpness, becoming distant. Her body went limp, her breathing slowed, and a strange stillness settled over her.

I sat there for a long time, observing her and Windy. The room was quiet, with the faint crackle of the furnace the only sound as the minutes stretched into hours. My gaze flicked between the two of them, the weight of the day pressing down on me in ways I couldn't ignore.

And yet . . . I didn't feel tired.

That realization crept in gradually, like a thought half-formed before taking shape. I should've been exhausted after staying awake this long, completing morning training, and keeping my body infused with qi to withstand the tribulation throughout the day.

But my body didn't ache. My movements didn't feel sluggish or strained. Even my reserves weren't as drained as they should be. I flexed my fingers experimentally, marveling at how steady they felt.

The transition from every rank in the mortal realm was like a gradual climb up a staircase. But going up a rank in the Qi Initiation stage had been significant, like leaping a flight of stairs. If I kept going at this rate, the tribulation would be mitigated within two more breakthroughs. I'd be able to move as though I weren't moving with triple my body weight.

A thought struck me. I closed my eyes and turned my focus inward, toward the energy coursing through my body. On top of my breakthrough in my body, my qi going from the peak of the Qi Initiation stage to the beginning of the Essence Awakening stage was like night and day.

The noise of the world around me faded into a faint hum, leaving only the quiet pulse of my qi. It coursed through me like a river, steady and deep, but as I concentrated, I realized something was different.

In my mind's eye, I visualized my dantian. It had always been a source of strength, growing larger as my qi reserves expanded. But now, it had changed. The orb seemed smaller, almost as though it had shrunk slightly since my last breakthrough. Yet, despite the decrease in size, it felt denser, heavier, as though it carried the weight of something far greater than before.

I frowned, focusing more intently. My reserves weren't diminished; if anything, they had increased. But this denser, more concentrated form of qi was . . . efficient. Each pulse felt sharper, more deliberate, like a blade honed to its absolute peak.

That's how I'd been withstanding the tribulation all day. My body, strengthened by the breakthrough, endured most of the additional weight without expending as much qi. And my reserves, though denser, seemed to stretch further, making every bit of effort more sustainable.

I was getting stronger. Rapidly. Too rapidly.

I opened my eyes, staring down at my hands. They didn't tremble now, despite everything. My body felt alive in a way it never had before, humming with potential. This wasn't normal—even with the province experiencing growth like never before. Most cultivators spent months, even years, consolidating their breakthroughs. Yet here I was, ascending in leaps and bounds as though something—or someone—was pushing me forward.

My gaze drifted to the Interface, its presence a constant but quiet hum in the back of my mind. It didn't feel intrusive, but I couldn't shake the sensation that it was guiding me, nudging me along a path I couldn't yet see.

"Preparing me for something," I muttered under my breath, the words barely audible in the quiet room. Whatever it was, it couldn't be good.

I clenched my fists, my knuckles whitening. This was too fast. Too much. But it wasn't a blessing I could afford to question. Not when I needed this strength to protect Windy, Tianyi, and the village.

My thoughts shifted to the Verdant Lotus Sect. I thought of Jian Feng's words earlier, his calm, unyielding confidence that they would handle everything. I had trusted them, believing their strength and experience would keep us safe. And yet their scouting team had perished.

Trust didn't mean blind obedience. Elder Ming's voice echoed in my mind, telling me to rely on the Verdant Lotus Sect, to believe in their capability. But tonight had made one thing painfully clear: they weren't infallible. I couldn't afford to follow blindly anymore. Not when lives hung in the balance.

I looked at Tianyi, her fragile figure resting against me, and at Windy, his pale form still soaking in the basin.

Carefully, I shifted, laying Tianyi down on a clean cushion beside me. Her antennae twitched faintly, but she didn't wake. Windy's breathing had steadied, his body no longer trembling with the strain of the corrupted qi.

I reached for a dry cloth, gently lifting Windy from the basin and patting him dry. His scales, though still marred with faint cracks and remnants of malignant qi, had regained some of their luster. I set him down in a makeshift nest of soft cloths, ensuring his head was propped up slightly.

Standing, I took a deep breath, letting the cool air of the shop steady me. The moment of rest was over. There was still much to do, and the Verdant Lotus Sect needed to know what had happened.

CHAPTER FIFTEEN

Hidden Currents Surge

Tianyi flitted ahead, her movements sharp and deliberate, her antennae twitching as she retraced her footsteps. Behind me, the seventeen disciples of the Verdant Lotus Sect followed, their presence a mix of stoic determination and a tension that hung in the air like a held breath.

At the front of their group, Jian Feng moved with speed and precision that belied the turmoil etched on his face. His usual air of confidence was gone, replaced by something raw, something broken. His jaw was set, his eyes fixed ahead as if avoiding any risk of meeting mine. His stride carried urgency, but there was no denying the weight of his steps.

I tried not to focus too much on him, but it was impossible not to notice the tightness in his shoulders, the faint tremor in his hands when he adjusted the hilt of his blade. The memory of my earlier anger toward him burned in my chest, sour and bitter. I had blamed him—yelled at him, even—for stopping me from running into the forest after my companions. At the time, his refusal had felt like arrogance, like a misplaced sense of control over the situation.

Now, as I watched him push forward, faster than the rest of his disciples could comfortably follow, I realized the truth. Jian Feng wasn't infallible. I'd placed him on a pedestal, much like the older disciples, as people wiser and smarter than I was. But he'd been reeling, his world knocked off-balance by the news of his comrades' deaths.

Guilt gnawed at me, but there was no time to dwell on it. The pace he set was grueling, faster than I would have liked given the lingering weight of the tribulation on my body. My strengthened frame and newly increased qi reserves kept me moving, but I couldn't ignore the sharp pull on my energy reserves. Every step required a touch of qi to counteract the oppressive weight I still bore, and though it wasn't unbearable, it added up quickly.

Tianyi slowed briefly, glancing back at me. Her eyes narrowed in concern, but she didn't speak. She didn't have to. I nodded at her, a silent assurance that I could keep up. Her antennae twitched, and she turned back to lead the way.

The disciples murmured faintly behind me, their voices hushed but laced with unease. I caught snippets of their conversation.

Three second-class disciples dead. The first incident of this magnitude in years. *If I had never asked them to protect the village, then maybe . . .*

The air grew heavier as we neared the clearing. Tianyi paused, hovering above the snow, her wings folding tightly against her back. She tilted her head, her antennae twitching as if confirming something unseen. Without a word, she gestured forward, leading us into the site of the battle.

The first thing I noticed was the silence. It was absolute, oppressive, like the forest itself was holding its breath. Then the smell hit me; blood, heavy and metallic, mixed with something acrid and wrong.

Jian Feng froze as the scene came into view. The three disciples lay sprawled across the snow, their bodies twisted unnaturally. Their robes, once pristine and marked with the insignia of the Verdant Lotus Sect, were shredded and stained with dark streaks of blood. But it wasn't just the sight of their injuries that made my stomach turn.

It was the flower.

At the center of the clearing, surrounded by the broken forms of the disciples, was something I could barely bring myself to name. It was shaped like a flower—or at least, some grotesque parody of one. Its petals were fleshy and raw, glistening in the faint light like exposed muscle. Dark, vein-like tendrils snaked along its body, pulsing faintly as if carrying some vile lifeblood. The veins extended outward, creeping across the snow like roots seeking sustenance. They touched the disciples' bodies, and where they did, the decay was undeniable. Flesh sagged, clothing frayed, and even their once-pristine weapons seemed dulled.

The petals of the flower quivered slightly, as if breathing, and with every faint movement, a pulse of malevolent energy twisted the air around it. It pressed against my senses, slithering like an unseen fog.

It was feeding. Slowly but surely, it was absorbing everything: their blood, flesh, and even the very fabric of their robes. One of the disciples' sashes had disintegrated entirely, leaving frayed threads that dissolved into nothingness the longer I stared.

I forced myself to look away, focusing instead on the faces of the fallen disciples. My chest tightened, the breath hitching in my throat as I recognized them.

I had known them—not well, but enough. These weren't just faceless warriors who came and went from the village. They had patrolled our streets. Protected the people. Zhao Yun had taught the children simple self-defense techniques, his patience endless. Ning Xue... I barely knew her. She had passed through as the patrol late at night, offering a polite nod or an occasional comment about the weather. Nothing memorable, nothing profound. She was just there, another face in the village's rhythm, part of the fabric of everyday life.

And now, she was gone.

Their faces were unrecognizable, twisted in agony, their features distorted by whatever dark energy had claimed them.

This was my first time seeing the dead. Not the peaceful kind, where age had taken its toll. Not like my parents, who were taken by illness. This was violent, sudden, wrong.

I tried to swallow, but my throat felt dry. A numbness settled over me, broken only by the faint tremble in my hands as I clenched my fists at my sides. My mind tried to process it, to reconcile the smiling faces I remembered with the grotesque reality before me.

Jian Feng's voice shattered the silence, raw and trembling. "Zhao Yun," he whispered, his knees buckling as he dropped beside the nearest body. His hand hovered above the disciple's torn shoulder, trembling as if afraid to touch. "Ning Xue. Hua Cheng..."

Each name was a blow, punctuated by the grief in his voice. The other disciples stood in stunned silence, their expressions frozen in varying degrees of shock and horror. They didn't speak, didn't move. They simply stared at the scene before them, the unshakable foundation of their faith in the sect cracking under the weight of what they saw.

Jian Feng knelt beside the nearest body, his trembling hand hovering over the torn shoulder of Zhao Yun. His lips parted as if to speak, but no words came. The weight of the loss seemed to press him into the snow, his shoulders sagging under an invisible burden. His eyes closed for a moment, his breath hitching as he fought to steady himself.

He clenched his jaw, struggling to speak.

"What... what is this?" he demanded, his voice a mix of anger and desperation.

I wanted to say something, anything, but the words stuck in my throat. My gaze was drawn back to the flower, its grotesque form a stark reminder of how little I understood. Its energy clawed at my senses, invasive and wrong, but beneath the revulsion, there was something more—an echo of the phrase Tianyi had repeated.

Praise the Heavenly Demon.

The phrase hung in my mind, heavy and unrelenting, like a storm cloud that wouldn't disperse. There was something sinister about it, something that clawed at the edges of my thoughts and refused to let go. I turned back to the grotesque flower, my gaze lingering on the pulsing veins that snaked outward. The way they latched onto the fallen disciples, siphoning their essence... it wasn't just wrong.

It was familiar.

I racked my brain, my thoughts spinning through the tangled web of everything I'd read, seen, and experienced. *Why* did this seem familiar? Why did this grotesque flower, this abomination, feel like something I should know?

And then it hit me.

"The Grand Alchemy Gauntlet," I whispered, my voice barely audible.

Jian Feng turned sharply, his grief momentarily pushed aside by the urgency in my tone. "What did you say?"

I didn't answer immediately. My mind had already latched onto the memory, dragging it into the light. The preliminaries, where I'd been tested on my knowledge of herbs and ingredients. There had been one I couldn't identify, no matter how hard I tried. Its withered, grotesque form had stood out even among the rarest specimens. Zhi Ruo's voice came to mind.

Ah, yes. That . . . that would be a—

"Bloodsoul Bloom. That's the flower."

The resemblance was undeniable, though the one I'd seen in the Gauntlet had been a dried husk compared to this monstrous thing.

"What do you know about it?" Jian Feng pressed, his voice tight with urgency.

"It's . . . it's from the Gauntlet," I said finally, the words tasting bitter on my tongue. "The one I saw was dried, withered. They don't grow like normal herbs. They subsist on blood. They were found in the territory of demonic cultivators—to siphon life force and qi, to fuel their rituals."

I saw Jian Feng's expression shift. The devastation in his eyes gave way to something colder, sharper. Fear, anger, realization.

The second-class disciple's jaw tightened, his knuckles pale as his hand hovered over his blade. His grief was momentarily eclipsed by something else—a rising urgency, a flickering rage barely contained beneath the surface.

"We need to destroy it," he said, his voice sharp and commanding. "If what you say is true, this abomination can't be allowed to remain."

"Wait," I interjected, my voice steady but firm. Jian Feng turned toward me, his expression darkening, but I pressed on. "Destroying it won't help us understand it. We need to study it to figure out how to counter it. If this flower was planted here intentionally, destroying it now means losing a chance to learn its purpose."

"And if it spreads?" he snapped. "If its roots burrow into the earth, if it takes hold of the forest? You think you can outpace that kind of corruption with your experiments?"

His words stung, but I forced myself to stay calm. "It hasn't spread beyond what it's already claimed," I said. "Not yet. Look around you. It's feeding off the bodies and the ground here, but it's contained. If we handle it carefully, I can keep it that way."

Jian Feng's eyes narrowed, his frustration clear, but I saw the hesitation in his stance.

"You're saying you can contain this thing? That you can learn something the sect can't?"

"No," I said simply. "It's because I'm the closest alchemist you have. The sect is days away, and we don't even know if they've dealt with something like this before. But I've studied plants for a lifetime. I know their patterns, how to isolate them. Let me handle this."

He opened his mouth to argue, but his words faltered. For a moment, I saw the exhaustion in his eyes, the weight of the losses he'd borne. "Fine," he said finally, his voice low and taut. "But if it shows even a hint of spreading, we burn it. Understood?"

"Understood," I said.

The disciples shifted uneasily, their gazes darting between me and the flower as though expecting it to lash out at any moment. They carefully approached the bodies of their fallen comrades, their movements deliberate and reverent. With blades glowing faintly with qi, they cut away the grotesque veins latched onto the corpses. The tendrils recoiled slightly, releasing their grip with an unsettling wet sound before falling limp.

I turned to Tianyi. "Do you remember anything about the person you fought? Did they have anything on their person?"

She hesitated, her antennae twitching as she glanced at the fallen disciples. "I didn't check; I was focused on getting Windy and myself out."

"Then we need to search them," I said, gesturing toward the hooded figure's body. "If they had more seeds or anything else, we need to know."

Jian Feng gave a terse nod, motioning for two disciples to join us. Together, we approached the corpse.

The figure's body lay in two halves, its dark robes soaked in blood that had turned the snow beneath them into a blackened slush. Its hood had slipped back, exposing a grotesque visage.

The face that greeted us was inhumanly unsettling. It was a woman—or what had once been one. Her disheveled hair clung to her scalp in patches, strands tangled with dried blood. The corners of her cracked lips curled unnaturally, as though frozen in a fractured smile.

Tianyi pointed to a satchel at her side, its strap barely hanging onto her shoulder. One disciple hesitated, then carefully cut the strap and opened the bag. Inside were several small, dark seeds, their surfaces veined with the same sinister pattern as the Bloodsoul Bloom.

Jian Feng's expression darkened further as he inspected them. "We'll send these back to the sect immediately," he said. "They need to know what we're dealing with."

"And I'll keep the live sample," I added, gesturing toward the flower. "I need it to figure out how to counter whatever this is."

He turned to his disciples, barking orders. "Cut the flower carefully, roots and all. Pack it securely. Five of you will escort the bodies, the flower, and the seeds back to the village."

The disciples moved with grim efficiency, their movements precise as they worked to separate the grotesque veins from the bodies. I couldn't bring myself to watch for long, my gaze drifting instead to the darkened forest beyond.

"There's still one more," Tianyi said, her voice quiet but insistent. "The one Windy fought. It's further in."

Jian Feng straightened, his expression sharpening. "Lead the way."

We followed Tianyi deeper into the forest, the tension mounting with every step.

She trekked several li into the heart of the wilderness. My fists clenched. Hard enough to draw blood.

After dispatching the monster that had killed three disciples, she continued to press on.

The thought sent a shiver down my spine. This deep into the forest, the air was different. Heavier. The trees loomed taller, their gnarled branches twisting into shapes that blocked the faint light of the moon.

They had been alone, fighting an opponent strong enough to push them this far, while I had been pacing the edge of the forest like a helpless fool.

Tianyi moved ahead, her wings folded tightly against her back, her antennae twitching as she scanned for the location of the battle. Despite her confident pace, there was tension in her posture, a stiffness that hadn't been there before. She knew the way, but I could tell even she wasn't comfortable being here.

The Verdant Lotus Sect disciples followed in silence, their expressions grim and their hands hovering near their weapons. Jian Feng remained at the front of the group.

Tianyi slowed, her wings fluttering faintly as she tilted her head. "We're close," she breathed.

Her words sent a ripple of tension through the group. I focused ahead, the faint outlines of a clearing becoming visible through the dense trees. She paused at the edge, her antennae twitching rapidly as she scanned the area.

When we stepped into the clearing, Tianyi froze.

I stiffened, watching her gaze sweep the clearing.

"It's not here," she said, her voice trembling slightly.

Jian Feng was beside her in an instant. "What do you mean, 'not here'?" he demanded, his voice sharp.

"The body. It's . . . gone."

CHAPTER SIXTEEN

A Flower That Feeds on Death

The day passed by like a blur, each moment blending into the next as I stood among the villagers and Verdant Lotus Sect disciples. Their decision to halt further excursions into the forest was met with heavy silence, the weight of the fallen disciples pressing down on everyone like a suffocating shroud. No one argued. Even Elder Ming, upon hearing the news, had only nodded gravely, his usual calm replaced by a somber stillness.

The village mirrored his mood. Conversations were hushed, movements subdued. It wasn't fear, exactly; it was grief, and something more insidious. A creeping awareness that the forest had changed, that we were no longer safe.

Now, back home, I stood in the quiet shop, my focus narrowing to the task before me. Tianyi and Windy were resting, their breathing steady but their conditions still far from healthy. I couldn't allow myself to linger on their injuries or the sense of helplessness that crept in whenever I looked at them. There was no time for doubt.

The Bloodsoul Bloom sat contained in a reinforced vessel on my workbench, its grotesque form quivering faintly.

I took a deep breath, steadying my hands as I prepared my tools. This was dangerous, possibly reckless, but I couldn't wait for the sect's response. If this flower was a harbinger of more to come, then understanding it was the only way to protect the village and everyone I cared about.

I closed my eyes, entering my mindscape, perusing the Memory Palace for an iota of information regarding the plant in my studies. But aside from Zhi Ruo's brief mention, nothing was there. But if I had to guess, it was from the same era as the Golden Bamboo; maybe even older.

My hands hovered over the reinforced vessel. I hesitated, my gut warning me to stop, but I pushed the doubt aside. Plant Whisperer. It had served me well before. Surely, the skill would reveal something now.

I exhaled slowly, centering myself. My fingers brushed the edge of the vessel, and I reached out, extending a thread of connection to the bloom.

The reaction was immediate.

The world around me seemed to blur, the shop melting away into an oppressive void. It was as if I were staring into an endless abyss, the air thick and suffocating. My connection didn't meet the usual serene flow of a plant's essence. Instead, it collided with something jagged, chaotic—a swirling storm of death and decay.

A wave of dread crashed over me, unlike anything I'd felt before. It wasn't just fear; it was primal terror, as if I were gazing at something that shouldn't exist. Shadows danced at the edges of my vision, and a low, keening sound reverberated in my mind. It wasn't a voice, not exactly, but the sensation was clear.

Doom.

Impending, unrelenting, inevitable doom.

I gasped and yanked my hand back as though burnt, severing the connection. My heart raced, my breaths coming in short, shallow bursts. The shop reappeared around me, its quiet warmth a jarring contrast to the suffocating void I'd just experienced. Windy and Tianyi were still sleeping a small distance away, undisturbed by my reaction.

The Bloodsoul Bloom quivered faintly in its vessel, unchanged. Yet, its malevolence seemed stronger, as if it had fed off my brief attempt to commune with it.

My hands trembled as I gripped the edge of the workbench to steady myself.

"What are you?" I whispered.

I didn't have an answer, but one thing was clear: this wasn't a plant in any conventional sense. Its essence didn't nurture or grow. It consumed. Fed on death. Every instinct I had screamed that it didn't belong in this world.

But I needed to find out more.

Reviewing the brief experience, it was certainly a yin-aligned plant. Its energy was cold, dark, and stagnant. Yet, something about it felt wrong, distorted. Yin qi itself wasn't inherently harmful; an imbalance could wreak havoc, much like an overabundance of yang qi, but it typically manifested in ways that promoted tranquility, rest, or even renewal.

This was different. It was aggressive, almost predatory. It didn't soothe or slow; it devoured. I couldn't help but compare it to the Moonlit Grace Lily, a serene yin-aligned plant that radiated calm and grew gently under moonlight. The Bloodsoul Bloom was its antithesis; chaotic and unnatural.

I leaned closer, studying the bloom's grotesque physical form. The fleshy petals pulsed faintly, as if alive. The vein-like tendrils along its surface quivered intermittently, giving the impression of something waiting, dormant yet insidious. Its roots coiled tightly within the vessel, refusing to extend or interact with anything around them.

If it truly thrived on death, I needed to test that theory.

I reached for a hybrid astragalus plant from my collection. A contrast to the bloom's oppressive nature. Carefully, I placed it near the Bloodsoul Bloom, watching for any reaction.

Nothing.

The Bloodsoul Bloom remained inert, its tendrils still and uninterested. The astragalus continued to sit unaffected by the ominous presence beside it. I frowned, removing the plant and pacing the room as I tried to puzzle through the bloom's nature.

It was feeding on something. It had to be. The flower in the forest had clearly absorbed the vitality of the disciples and even the essence of their robes.

I glanced toward the far corner of the shop, where shadows pooled. The faint glimmer of silken threads caught my eye, and I grimaced. Yin Si's handiwork. Webbed bundles of tiny corpses were nestled there—rats and small animals Windy used to prey on before his absence from home had left them untouched, piling up in neglected corners.

It was unpleasant, but it was also a lead.

I murmured an apology under my breath for disturbing Yin Si's stash, carefully extracting a webbed-up rat corpse from the tangle. The weight of it in my hand was unsettling, the little body stiff and lifeless, but it was exactly what I needed.

Back at the workbench, I placed the corpse near the Bloodsoul Bloom. For a moment, nothing happened. Then, as I leaned closer, I noticed the faintest stir.

The veins running along the bloom's surface pulsed faintly, the rhythm irregular but unmistakable. Slowly, one of the tendrils extended outward, its motion unnaturally deliberate. It crept toward the rat corpse, pausing mere centimeters away, as if testing the air around it.

My breath caught as the tendril twitched once, twice, before darting forward and latching onto the corpse. A low, keening sound filled the air, barely audible but enough to send a chill down my spine.

I stepped back, resisting the urge to sever the connection immediately. Instead, I forced myself to observe. The tendril pulsed as it fed, the motion hypnotic and grotesque. Already lifeless, the rat's body shriveled further, its form collapsing in on itself as the bloom drew whatever essence remained.

The rat's already-decayed body collapsed inward, its form reduced to an ashen husk. I noted every detail, my mind racing to piece together the implications.

The tendril withdrew once its feeding was complete, curling back toward the bloom's base. It pulsed faintly, as though sated, before becoming still once more. My chest tightened as I observed the faint traces of malevolent qi emanating from it, growing more pronounced after its macabre feast.

I needed more data.

Turning to my pill furnace, I carefully separated a small piece of the bloom, its flesh slightly sticky and exuding a faint, acrid smell. The fragment quivered unnervingly in my hand as I placed it into the furnace. I adjusted the heat with painstaking precision, my Refinement Simulation Technique overlaying projected reactions and temperature gradients over the furnace's surface.

The bloom's fragment burned, releasing a dense, black smoke that spiraled upward. I leaned back, watching as the fumes shifted unnaturally, almost writhing in the air. The acrid scent thickened, accompanied by a faint metallic tang. My stomach churned as the smoke curled into strange patterns before dissipating.

Ash remained, its color an unnatural deep crimson, flecked with black. I collected the residue carefully, placing it into a small vial for later analysis.

The bloom resisted conventional alchemical reactions. Most herbs, when burned, would leave identifiable traits in their smoke—earthy, sweet, bitter. This was none of those. It was alien; its properties were incomprehensible through normal means.

"Now, let's see if I can extract its essence . . ."

I separated another piece from the live sample. Normally, drawing essence from plants was straightforward, a pull and flow, as though coaxing sap from a tree. But as I focused on the Bloodsoul Bloom, I realized this was going to be anything but simple.

The moment I extended my qi, it was as if I had touched a live wire. The bloom resisted fiercely, its essence jagged and uncooperative. Most plants yielded to my pull, except for certain ones with exceptional strength bearing some resistance, like the Golden Bamboo. This, however, felt entirely different. It wasn't like extracting from a plant at all. It was closer to siphoning from something alive—a living being with a will of its own.

I hesitated, the weight of that realization pressing against my thoughts. The skill allowed me to extract from both plants and metals, but I'd never tested its limits since my preparation for the Gauntlet. I hadn't touched Master Li Tao's teachings in weeks because of the sheer number of tasks I had to keep up with.

The process of learning to extract the essence from metals had been grueling, requiring weeks of effort and countless failures. Yet here I was, confronted with something that blurred the line between plant and . . . something else.

There was no better time to test myself.

Steeling my resolve, I pushed forward, pulling harder with my qi. The bloom's resistance was palpable, the process a grueling tug-of-war. My entire focus narrowed to the connection, every fiber of my being attuned to the intricate battle of wills. The bloom's essence was fighting. For every thread of qi I extended, the plant pushed back with a chaotic, almost predatory force.

Sweat beaded on my forehead as I poured more energy into the extraction. Unlike metals, which had required sheer force and will, this felt nuanced. It wasn't about overpowering the bloom but maneuvering around its chaotic energy, finding gaps in its resistance, and weaving through them. The process, while grueling, was less foreign than working with metals had been. Perhaps because at its core it still kept some similarity to plants.

Finally, the resistance broke. A tendril of dark essence peeled away, its motion sluggish and reluctant as it separated from the bloom. I guided it carefully, condensing it into a single droplet that hung in the air, pulsing faintly with an eerie rhythm.

The essence settled into a reinforced vial with a soft hiss, the liquid thick and viscous. It shimmered faintly, the color shifting between deep crimson and black as though alive.

> *Spiritual Herbalism has reached level 8.*

I exhaled sharply, wiping the sweat from my brow. The level increase was a slight relief, but it didn't offset the unease curling in my gut. The essence carried the same malevolence as the bloom itself, amplified in its concentrated form. I sealed the vial tightly, ensuring it wouldn't spill or interact with anything.

For now, I wouldn't test it further. This was a discovery I needed to tread carefully with. Yet the fact I'd extracted it at all gave me a glimmer of hope.

I set the vial aside, the bloom fragment now shriveled and lifeless.

Finally, I prepared myself for the most dangerous experiment yet. My qi.

I hesitated, my gaze fixed on the demonic plant. Infusing qi into plants was typically a harmonious process, a way to amplify their natural properties, strengthen their essence, and speed up their growth. It was a technique rooted in balance, nurturing the plant's inherent nature. But this was no ordinary plant. The usual certainty that infusing qi would bring benefit was nowhere to be found.

Instead, doubt gnawed at me. Would my qi strengthen its already warped nature? Could it evolve into something even more dangerous? Yet, I needed answers. I needed to see if this plant could change; if it had stages of growth, hidden layers of power that could reveal more about its origins. Despite the risk, I knew this was the only path forward. For better or worse, I needed to learn.

Taking a deep breath, I placed my hand just above the plant, creating a connection with the bloom. I kept the flow steady and controlled, testing its reaction.

At first, nothing happened. The bloom quivered faintly, as it had before, but then—

It writhed.

The tendrils along its surface flared outward, pulsating erratically. The petals twisted, curling inward before unfurling violently. A low, keening sound filled the air, louder than before, as though the plant was protesting.

Suddenly, the bloom collapsed. Its petals withered rapidly, darkening and shriveling as though my qi had poisoned it. The tendrils recoiled, retreating into the vessel before falling limp. Within moments, the entire plant was lifeless, its once-malevolent presence reduced to nothing more than a shriveled husk.

I stumbled back, staring in disbelief. My breathing was ragged, my chest tight with both relief and confusion. What had just happened?

My qi hadn't purified or strengthened it. It had *killed* it.

I sank into the chair by the workbench, my mind racing. Was it the nature of my qi? My wood affinity, perhaps? Or my fire affinity? Both elements were known for their cleansing properties, but this reaction felt . . . different. It wasn't just cleansing. It was a rejection.

I noted everything carefully in my encyclopedia, every detail of the experiment. It was crucial; the Bloodsoul Bloom could be counteracted, perhaps even neutralized. But the implications of why it reacted this way to my qi would take time to unravel.

For now, I stared at the lifeless bloom, a mix of triumph and unease settling over me. I was closer to understanding it, but the more I learned, the more questions arose.

"I need a break."

I glanced over at Tianyi and Windy, seeing them resting peacefully together. It was the longest I'd ever seen her rest. The butterfly-turned-human held the basin containing Windy carefully, cradling his head so he stayed afloat. My face twisted, remembering how close I was to losing them.

They should never have faced something like this alone.

I stepped outside, the evening air biting against my skin as the door creaked shut behind me. The hours had slipped away unnoticed, consumed entirely by my experiments. The sky was now streaked with deep purples and grays, the horizon barely holding onto the remnants of daylight. The village felt quieter than usual.

I leaned against the greenhouse, letting out a slow breath. My stomach grumbled faintly, a sharp reminder that I hadn't eaten since morning. I ignored it. The lingering unease from the experiments made the idea of food unappealing. Instead, I allowed myself this moment of stillness, my mind sorting through the discoveries of the day.

The Bloodsoul Bloom was unlike anything I'd ever encountered. Malevolent, predatory, and unnatural in every way. It consumed, destroyed, and now, I'd learned, it could be countered—killed, even. But how? What had my qi done to it that had such a drastic effect?

I tilted my head back, staring at the darkening sky. The weight of responsibility pressed harder against my shoulders. Every answer seemed to open another door of questions, each more daunting than the last. But for now, I had a lead.

The faint sound of hoofbeats broke my train of thought. I straightened, my gaze snapping toward the outskirts of the village. A single rider approached, their horse galloping hard, its breaths visible. The jingling of bells marked the man as a messenger. Something urgent.

I didn't hesitate. Pushing off the wall, I bolted toward the village square, meeting the rider as they pulled up sharply. The man was hunched over, his face pale and slick with sweat. He barely kept his seat as the horse stamped and snorted beneath him.

"Are you all right?" I asked, steadying the reins and holding the horse still.

The man shook his head, his voice hoarse and ragged. "Verdant Lotus . . . I need . . . I must speak with them."

"Calm down," I said, trying to steady his breathing. "They're still in the village. What's the message?"

He clutched his chest, gasping as though the words themselves pained him. "The—the Silent Moon . . . they—"

An icy dread coiled in my stomach as I heard his words.

CHAPTER SEVENTEEN

When the Snow Runs Red

The wind howled through the mountains, a mournful wail that carried snow in thick, blinding waves. The Silent Moon Sect stood cloaked in winter's grip. White drifts covered the once-pristine stone pathways, and the ornate carvings of moonlit motifs on the buildings were barely discernible beneath layers of frost. The sect felt subdued, muffled by the storm's relentless assault.

Xu Ziqing's boots crunched against the snow as he made his way along the outer wall, his hand resting on the hilt of his sword. He had taken this patrol shift himself, dismissing the junior disciples who were clearly more interested in the warmth of the barracks than their duties. While understandable, it grated on him. Laxity had no place in the Jianghu, least of all now, when the air itself felt thick with unease.

The wind tugged at his robes, and he adjusted his hood, squinting into the swirling snow. The storm played tricks on the eyes; shadows flitted at the edges of his vision, shapes that vanished the moment he focused. The sentries nearby chatted in hushed tones, their laughter carrying over the storm's din. They huddled close to a brazier, their weapons discarded nearby; a dangerous negligence that twisted the stern second-class disciple's stomach.

His hand tightened on his sword hilt.

A blade is useless if left sheathed. A mind dulled by complacency cannot sense danger until it's too late.

Yet, even as he chastised the sentries silently, he couldn't deny the weariness that had settled over the sect. The mounting tension between the mainland elders and Sect Leader Jun had taken its toll, fracturing trust and sapping morale. Their growing impatience for war with the Whispering Wind Sect, combined with the dwindling supply of beast cores, had left the sect in a precarious position. They were not unified; they were brittle, and Xu Ziqing feared they would shatter under the weight of their own ambition.

His thoughts drifted to the confined elders—those that served the sect their whole lives—now reduced to prisoners within their own home. Their protests against Sect Leader Jun's ascent to power had been silenced with confinement, an act kept secret to maintain the illusion of strength. But illusion was all it was. The sect's foundation was crumbling, and he felt it with every strained conversation, every hollow order barked by those scrambling to keep control.

Xu Ziqing paused, his sharp eyes scanning the storm-laden horizon. A flicker of movement caught his attention.

A faint, fleeting shadow.

He narrowed his eyes, but the snow seemed to swallow it whole, leaving nothing but white emptiness. The sentries, oblivious, continued their conversation, the glow of the brazier casting fleeting warmth over their flushed faces.

He opened his mouth to call out to them, but the words died in his throat. A strange sensation gripped him, an icy weight settling in his chest. It wasn't the cold—it was something far deeper. Instinct.

Something's coming.

The wind howled louder, almost masking the faint crunch of snow that didn't belong to him or the sentries. Xu Ziqing's fingers tightened around his sword.

The crunching of snow grew louder, though the sentries seemed deaf to it, their laughter continuing unchecked. The second-class disciple's grip on his sword tightened as his eyes scanned the shifting whiteness beyond the sect's walls.

A voice interrupted his focus. "Brother Xu," came a call from behind him. He spun, his narrowed gaze falling on a second-class disciple hurrying toward him, his robes whipping in the storm. The man gave a small bow, though his expression was strained, as if reluctant to be there.

"What is it?" Xu Ziqing asked, his tone curt but controlled.

"The Sect Leader has summoned you," the disciple replied, brushing snow from his sleeves. "He wishes to discuss . . . the elders' latest demands."

His jaw tightened. He did not need to ask what the demands entailed. The mainland elders were growing bolder, their frustrations boiling over into open contempt for Sect Leader Jun's authority. Another fruitless debate awaited him, no doubt.

"And you?" he asked, his eyes narrowing further. "You will take my place?"

The disciple nodded, though his reluctance was evident. "Yes, Senior Brother. I'll ensure the sentries remain vigilant."

Xu Ziqing's gaze shifted to the sentries gathered around the brazier. Their postures were slouched, their weapons abandoned in favor of warmth. His expression hardened.

"See that you do," he said sharply, his voice cutting through the storm like a blade. "This storm may obscure the horizon, but it also blinds us to threats. Stay alert. Do not let your guard falter for even a moment."

The second-class disciple winced at the harshness in his brother's tone. "Brother Xu, there's no need to be so . . . tense. It's just a storm. Nothing can approach in weather like this."

Xu Ziqing's glare silenced him.

"Complacency is the first step toward death," he said coldly. Then, with a last glance at the sentries, he turned on his heel and stalked away, snow crunching beneath his boots.

As he disappeared into the storm, the second-class disciple sighed, shaking his head. "Uptight as ever," he muttered, his voice barely audible over the wind.

One sentry smirked, leaning closer to the fire. "He's always like that. A real kiss-ass to Sect Leader Jun. Probably thinks it'll get him somewhere."

"Right," another chimed in, laughing. "The man wouldn't know how to relax if his life depended on it. Bet he's still tapping that sword hilt of his while talking to the Sect Leader."

Their laughter mingled with the crackle of the brazier, a fleeting moment of levity in the storm's relentless grip.

But the laughter died as swiftly as it had begun.

The first sentry froze, his eyes widening as he turned toward the storm. "Did you hear that?" he asked, his voice trembling.

"Hear what?" another asked, his tone dismissive.

For a moment, there was only silence. Then, the faintest sound reached them—a wet, crunching noise, different from the wind or snow. "There," he whispered, gripping his spear tighter. "Listen."

This time, both sentries went still.

The second sentry's hand moved to his horn, the brass glinting in the brazier's light. "Should I—" Shadows emerged from the storm, hooded figures moving with eerie precision. They were upon the sentries in moments, their strikes swift and merciless. The second sentry managed half a breath before lifting the horn to his lips. The note that emerged was cut short, becoming a wet gurgle as sharpened claws found their mark. The horn clattered against stone, its warning lost to the storm.

The storm swallowed the scene once more, leaving only the red-stained snow as evidence of what had transpired.

Within the stone walls, the storm's howling was reduced to a muted roar, a distant reminder of the world outside.

Elder Wei leaned against the table, his left hand clutching his side where a bandage peeked out beneath his robes. The wound—inflicted by Whispering Wind Sect's prodigious first-class disciple, Tian Zhan—throbbed persistently, a stark reminder of the growing strength of the locals. His face twisted in irritation as he readjusted his posture, masking the pain with a practiced sneer.

"An insect stung me," Wei spat, breaking the silence. "A first-class disciple, they say. I would hardly call him that; his power surpassed that of an elder of this sect. Yet, the fact remains—he landed a blow. That should never have been possible."

Elder Fang, seated across the room, was meticulously sharpening a jade hairpin. He didn't look up as he replied, his tone calm but edged with concern. "A troubling development. If even their disciples have reached such heights, we cannot afford to continue underestimating them."

Elder Xun scoffed, crossing his arms over his broad chest, his scars illuminated by the faint glow of enchanted lanterns. "Troubling? It's infuriating. These backwater cultivators scrape the bottom of the barrel for qi, and yet they keep pace with us? It's absurd."

"They don't scrape," Fang interjected, finally meeting Xun's gaze. "They refine. Their methods are born of necessity, honed over generations to make the most of the ambient qi and lack thereof. Efficiency born of scarcity. Meanwhile, our cultivation methods squander resources on the mainland without the thought of efficiency."

The comment struck a chord. Wei's scowl deepened, his fingers tightening on the edge of the table.

Cheng, the eldest among them, sat in contemplative silence, stroking his beard. "Luck favors the prepared. And the Whispering Wind Sect is preparing for war, whether or not we like it. Each delay strengthens them."

Fang's lips pressed into a thin line. "Which is why I've said it before: Sect Leader Jun's hesitance is a liability. He basks in his newfound power, oblivious to the narrowing window of opportunity. If we do not act decisively—"

"You mean to usurp him," Wei interrupted, his voice sharp. "Spare the pretense, Fang. You've danced around the idea long enough."

Xun barked a laugh, the sound grating against the tense air. "About time someone said it. Jun is a fool, clinging to scraps of control while we do the real work. Without us, the Silent Moon would crumble."

Cheng raised a hand. "Jun is a fool," he conceded, "but he is also useful. Removing him prematurely could destabilize the sect. We would inherit chaos, not control."

"And what do you propose, then? Another round of groveling to this puppet leader while we stagnate?"

"No," Cheng replied evenly. "We push him to act. Force his hand. The Whispering Wind Sect must fall, and Jun must be made to lead the charge. His ambition blinds him to our manipulation—let him think it was his idea."

The room fell silent, each elder weighing Cheng's words. Fang resumed sharpening his jade hairpin, his motions precise and deliberate. "And if he refuses?"

Cheng's expression darkened, his tone like iron. "Then we remind him why he needs us. And if that fails . . ." He let the unspoken threat hang in the air, a promise that none doubted he could keep.

Within the chamber, the cold quiet was suddenly shattered by a deep, resonant boom. Screams echoed faintly, footsteps converging rapidly on their location. Elder Wei's hand instinctively shot to his sword, its surface inscribed with glowing jade patterns that shimmered faintly even in the dim light.

The doors to the elders' quarters burst open, the sound reverberating like a thunderclap. A wave of biting cold rushed in, carrying with it the metallic tang of blood and something far worse—a suffocating, malevolent aura that clung to the air like oil.

Figures stepped through the threshold, their forms cloaked in ragged, bloodstained robes. The aura around them crackled with dark energy, twisting the air and casting long, grotesque shadows across the stone floor.

"Demonic cultivators," Cheng growled, his voice low and steady despite the tension rippling through his body. "What business do you have here?"

They didn't answer. The cultists moved with a predatory grace, spreading out in an almost coordinated formation, their jagged weapons gleaming ominously. Their silence was unnerving, broken only by the faint sound of their boots scraping against stone.

Elder Xun wasted no time. He slammed his foot against the ground, and a massive ball and chain materialized in a burst of crimson qi, the links rattling as it coiled around him like a serpent. "I'll handle this filth," he snarled, swinging the weapon in a wide arc. The heavy ball struck the floor with a deafening crash, leaving a deep gouge in the stone.

One cultist darted forward, their movements unnaturally fast, but Xun was faster. The ball shot out, its trajectory erratic yet controlled, smashing into the cultist with bone-crushing force. The figure crumpled, its body folding in on itself like brittle paper.

"Too easy," Xun muttered, a smirk forming—until the cultist's body convulsed. With a guttural cry, the fallen figure rose again, their broken limbs twisting unnaturally as it lunged forward, undeterred by its injuries.

"Praise the Heavenly Demon!" the cultist screeched, their voice distorted and filled with unholy fervor.

The words sent a shiver down the elders' spines. Wei stepped forward, his sword flashing like lightning as he skewered the cultist through the chest. The jade inscriptions flared brilliantly, releasing a burst of qi that disintegrated the figure into ash.

"They're not staying down," Fang said coldly, his spear spinning in his hand as he stepped to Xun's side. His movements were precise, almost surgical, as he thrust forward, dispatching another cultist with an upward strike that pierced through their skull. Yet even as the body fell, another cultist stepped over it, their movements eerily synchronized.

It was clearly an unrefined attack. There was no sophisticated martial art clear within their attacks. There were no flashy techniques or feints to fool the opponent.

Just like the movements of a wild beast—swing, smash, break.

Wei snarled, the veins in his temple bulging as he channeled his qi into the blade. "Then we make sure they can't get back up!"

Cheng joined the fray with a flick of his wrist, conjuring a shimmering barrier of translucent light that surged outward, slowing the cultists' advance. His illusionary techniques distorted their perception, causing some to lash out at phantom foes while others stumbled into one another. "Hold them back!" Cheng barked.

Another cultist lunged at Xun, their jagged blade slicing through the air. He caught the weapon mid-swing with his bare hand, his immense strength crushing the blade with ease. With a roar, he drove his fist into the cultist's chest, shattering ribs and piercing flesh. Blood spattered across the stone floor, but the cultist didn't fall. Instead, they grabbed Xun's wrist with inhuman strength, their lips curling into a manic grin.

"Praise the Heavenly Demon," they rasped, their voice filled with malice.

The cultist's body convulsed violently, their grip tightening as a burst of dark energy erupted from their chest. Xun stumbled back, his face twisted in pain as the corrosive force seared into his flesh. Blood seeped from the wound on his arm, blackened at the edges, as though the injury itself was tainted by the cultist's malevolent qi.

Wei surged forward, his sword spinning in a furious arc to intercept another cultist who was already closing in on the wounded elder. The jade inscriptions on the spear flared once more, releasing a wave of concentrated energy that tore through the cultist and sent their mangled body flying into the wall.

But even as the cultist crumpled to the floor, lifeless, two more surged forward, their weapons raised. Wei gritted his teeth, slamming the hilt of his sword into the ground and releasing a shockwave of qi that sent them staggering. "We need to regroup!" he barked, glancing back toward the others.

Xun, however, was struggling to recover. The initial injury had slowed him, and that momentary weakness seemed to have emboldened the cultists. They converged on him like a pack of ravenous beasts, their movements erratic yet eerily coordinated. Xun swung his ball and chain in wide arcs, smashing into the first wave and sending bodies flying, but the cultists pressed forward relentlessly, ignoring their injuries.

"Get back!" he roared, his voice filled with fury as he slammed the ball into the floor, creating a massive crater that cracked the stone beneath their feet. Several cultists were thrown off-balance, but it wasn't enough. One darted in from his blind spot, their blade cutting into his side. Another followed, their weapon finding purchase in his leg. The injuries piled up, each one sapping more of his strength.

"No!" Fang shouted, his spear darting toward the mass of cultists to create space. But even as the weapon struck true, impaling one of the attackers, it barely slowed the others. The cultists seemed impervious to pain, their focus singular and unwavering.

Xun let out a guttural roar, his qi surging in a last-ditch effort to push them back. The ball and chain spun faster, tearing through the cultists closest to him, but the momentum was short-lived. One cultist leapt onto his back, driving their blade into his shoulder. Another slammed into his chest, forcing him to the ground.

The others swarmed him, their weapons and claws tearing into his flesh with sickening ferocity. Blood sprayed across the chamber, the metallic scent filling the air as Xun's roars of defiance turned into gurgled gasps.

His immense strength, his indomitable will—it all meant nothing against the sheer number of enemies willing to sacrifice themselves to bring him down.

By the time the cultists pulled back, Xun's body was barely recognizable, torn apart in a frenzy of violence. The remaining elders stared in horror, their faces pale and their breaths shallow. They were no strangers to death, but this . . . this was something else. Something monstrous.

Cheng's voice trembled as he spoke, his composure cracking under the weight of the scene before him. "They're . . . animals."

Before anyone could respond, one of the cultists stepped forward, their hood falling back to reveal a gaunt, pale face etched with deep scars. They moved with deliberate purpose, reaching down to Xun's shredded remains. Their hand delved into the bloodied folds of his robe, emerging moments later with a ring glinting faintly in the dim light.

Wei's eyes widened in recognition. "The storage ring!" he hissed, his grip tightening on his spear. "What are they—?"

The cultist didn't hesitate. They placed the ring against their palm and released a surge of dark qi, forcibly breaking the protective seals. Items spilled onto the floor in a chaotic heap—artifacts, talismans, vials of rare elixirs. The cultist ignored most of it, their attention singularly focused.

Then they found it.

A small vial, its crystalline surface shimmering faintly. Within it, an amber liquid glowed softly, radiating an unmistakable aura of vitality and purity.

"The Phoenix Tears," Fang whispered, his voice barely audible over the sound of the cultists' fervent murmurs. His face turned ashen as the realization struck him. "They *know*."

The hooded figure held the vial aloft, their scarred lips curling into a twisted grin.

"Praise the Heavenly Demon," they intoned, their voice resonating with chilling reverence. Around them, the other cultists echoed the chant, their fervor reaching a fever pitch.

CHAPTER EIGHTEEN

Praise the Heavenly Demon, Shatter the Moon

Xu Ziqing's boots crunched against the icy debris scattered across the once-pristine pathways. The faint moonlit carvings, symbols of the sect's pride and history, lay buried beneath layers of frost and ruin. Bodies—friends, comrades, disciples he had trained alongside—littered the ground, their lifeless forms twisted and broken. The sect, once an unshakable fortress, now stood as a graveyard.

The storm howled like a dirge, its mournful wails carrying the echoes of screams and clashes still fresh in Xu Ziqing's ears. He forced himself to keep moving, his hand gripping the hilt of his blade tightly enough that his knuckles turned white. Each step felt heavier than the last, each crunch of snow a painful reminder of the fallen.

The ground beneath his feet trembled, and he flinched instinctively as an explosion shattered the oppressive silence. The central hall, once the heart of the sect, collapsed in a fiery cascade of rubble, sending shards of wood and stone spraying outward. Xu Ziqing's jaw tightened as his gaze swept the chaos. Amid the destruction, figures darted through the wreckage.

The mainland elders.

They were running.

Xu Ziqing's breath hitched as he spotted the dark tide surging behind them. Shadows moved with feral precision, a tide of hooded figures that devoured everything in their path. Weapons glinted in the flickering light, and their eerie silence was more unsettling than any battle cry. They swarmed forward like predators with nothing but death in their wake.

Among the fleeing elders, a figure stumbled.

"Elder Fang?"

The once-mighty cultivator, a man Xu Ziqing had feared, now moved with a desperate limp. His leg dragged awkwardly behind him, blood staining the snow in uneven streaks. Fang's face, always a mask of controlled arrogance, was contorted in pain and desperation. He pushed forward, his every step a struggle as the shadows closed in.

"Wait!" Fang's voice rang out, trembling with fear and anger. "Help me!"

Wei and Cheng, the other two mainland elders, were just ahead. They turned at the sound of his voice, their eyes meeting his for a moment. Xu Ziqing couldn't hear their reply. If there was one. But their actions spoke louder than words.

Neither elder slowed. Neither offered a hand. They simply turned and continued running, their forms disappearing into the storm.

The betrayal was written plainly across Fang's face. For a fleeting moment, disbelief and fury warred in his expression. His lips parted as though to shout again, but no words came. Instead, his eyes hardened, his grip on his weapon tightening as he stopped and turned to face the oncoming horde. His shoulders squared, though his body trembled from exertion and pain.

Xu Ziqing couldn't look away. Fang, the man who had once brought him and Ping Hai to their knees with sheer killing intent, now stood alone against the tide. It should have been a moment of defiance, a last stand worthy of legend. But what he saw in Fang's eyes wasn't courage.

It was fear.

Elder Fang planted his spear into the snow with a deliberate motion, the weapon glowing with a cold, pale light as he channeled his qi into it. The storm seemed to part around him, the snowflakes slowing as though held in suspended animation.

With a guttural roar, the elder swung the weapon in a wide arc, releasing a wave of qi that ripped through the oncoming horde. The front line of cultists disintegrated, their forms collapsing into ash and ichor that stained the snow black. For an instant, the battlefield fell eerily silent, save for the faint hum of Fang's spear.

Xu Ziqing's breath caught. This was the power that had made Elder Fang a figure of awe and terror—a force so overwhelming that it put him among the ranks of sect leaders. But even as the wave of destruction faded, the shadows pressed forward. The cultists stepped over the remains of their fallen with a single-minded determination.

Fang swung his spear again, the tip carving through the air with an audible crack. Another cultist fell, their body torn apart by the elder's precision strike. Yet, as the tide surged closer, their tactics shifted. Instead of attacking directly, the cultists lunged at his weapon, grabbing at the spear's shaft with clawed hands. Fang's strikes became slower, his movements more labored as each swing was met with resistance.

"Get off!" he snarled, his voice raw with desperation. He shook his spear violently, dislodging the cultists clinging to it, but their numbers were too great. Each moment he spent shaking them off allowed more to close the distance.

Fang staggered, his injured leg buckling under the strain. His breaths came in ragged gasps, the frost clinging to his lips as he struggled to keep his footing. Blood seeped through the torn fabric of his robes, staining the snow beneath him in vivid crimson.

Xu Ziqing's stomach churned. Even now, the man's immense power was undeniable, yet it wasn't enough. The cultists were unrelenting, their lack of fear and disregard for their own lives rendering Fang's attacks increasingly futile. One grabbed the shaft of his spear, then another, slowing its momentum just enough for a blade to slice through his side. Fang roared in pain, pulling back and impaling his attacker, but the opening had already been created.

They swarmed him.

"Ah! *AHHHHH!*"

Blades and claws tore into his flesh, ripping through muscle and sinew with sickening ease. Fang's screams echoed across the battlefield, a sound that clawed at Xu Ziqing's resolve.

The snow turned dark and heavy with blood, the storm carrying the metallic scent through the air.

And then, silence.

The cultists straightened, their forms dark and alien against the snow. One of them bent down, retrieving a ring from the corpse.

Xu Ziqing's heart pounded as his mind raced. He forced himself to move, sprinting through the wreckage with renewed urgency. His knuckles ached from how tightly he gripped his sword, but he didn't care. The mainland elders were gone. The sect was in ruins. If he didn't act now, there would be nothing left to save.

His gaze darted across the battlefield, locking onto a familiar figure huddled against the remnants of a crumbled pavilion.

"Ming Yuan!"

The young man flinched, his sword trembling in his grip. His usually confident expression was replaced by wide, hollow eyes. He didn't respond, his focus fixed on the blood-streaked snow beneath him.

Xu Ziqing reached him in a few quick strides and grabbed his shoulder, shaking him firmly. "Ming Yuan, look at me!"

The disciple blinked, his gaze snapping to Xu Ziqing's face. "S-Senior Brother Xu . . . I—I can't—"

"There's no time for this!" Xu Ziqing snapped, his voice cutting through the storm. "We're going to free the elders. Without them, we have no chance."

Yuan Ming's face twisted in confusion. "The elders? But . . . Sect Leader Jun—he wouldn't—"

"To hell with Jun's orders! If we don't act now, there won't be a sect left to protect. Do you understand me?"

Yuan Ming hesitated, his breathing shallow and uneven. Xu Ziqing gripped his shoulder tighter, his voice softening slightly. "The sect needs you. Get up."

The younger disciple swallowed hard, nodding shakily. "A-All right. I'm with you."

"Good." Xu Ziqing hauled him to his feet, sparing only a moment to steady him before setting off at a sprint. "We'll gather anyone we see along the way."

As they moved through the ruins of the sect, his eyes scanned the wreckage for other survivors. By the time they reached the elders' quarters, they had gathered a dozen disciples. A few of the senior disciples split up in order to gather more people. Most bore injuries or expressions of raw fear, but they followed.

The elders' quarters were cold and dark, the heavy doors sealed but unguarded. Xu Ziqing drew his blade, the metal glinting faintly in the dim light. Tradition dictated that these elders remain confined for opposing Sect Leader Jun's rise to power. But tradition had no place here. Not now.

He smashed the hilt of his sword against the lock of the first door, the echo reverberating through the corridor. With a loud crack, the mechanism gave way, and the door creaked open to reveal an elder seated on a worn mat. His eyes, once sharp and commanding, were wide with disbelief.

"Disciple Xu?" the elder asked. "What madness is this? What's happening outside?"

"The sect is under siege," Xu Ziqing said, his tone clipped and urgent. "There's no time to explain. The disciples need help."

The elder rose slowly, his movements stiff from confinement. "By the heavens . . ." he murmured. "I heard the sounds but thought—" His words faltered as he met Xu Ziqing's gaze. "The Silent Moon is being attacked? By whom?"

"Monsters."

The elder's jaw tightened. "Then let's not waste any more time."

Xu Ziqing nodded sharply and moved to the next door. The other disciples did the same, freeing the confined elders and explaining the situation.

When the last elder joined them, the group stood in tense silence for a moment. Though gaunt and weathered, their presence carried a weight that reminded Xu Ziqing of the Silent Moon's former glory. These were not broken men; they were leaders who had been waiting for the chance to prove their worth again.

"We move now," he said firmly, leading the group into the storm.

Xu Ziqing's pace quickened as he neared the destroyed dining hall. Inside, the heavy air was thick with the scent of stale blood and lingering smoke. Scattered tables and benches were overturned, and the dim light from a half-burnt lantern cast long, flickering shadows across the walls.

At the far corner of the room, a familiar figure sat slumped against the wall—Ping Hai. His hulking frame, which usually radiated confidence, was curled in on itself. His head was buried in his arms, and his shoulders trembled. Around him, a handful of third-class disciples sat in silence, their eyes wide with shock.

"Ping Hai!" Xu Ziqing barked, striding across the room.

The large disciple flinched, his head snapping up. His face was pale, his eyes red-rimmed and unfocused. "S-Senior Brother . . ." he stammered, his voice barely audible.

"Get up," Xu Ziqing said sharply, gripping the front of Ping Hai's robes and hauling him to his feet. "We don't have time for this."

"I—" His voice broke. He looked away, his hands trembling. "I'm not ready for this, Senior Brother. I can't . . ."

Xu Ziqing shook him once, hard. "None of us were ready for this!" he snapped. "But hiding here won't save anyone. Look around you."

Ping Hai's gaze flicked to the younger disciples huddled nearby. Slowly, the trembling in his hands subsided. He swallowed hard and gave a faint nod.

"What do you need me to do?" he asked, his voice steadier now.

Xu Ziqing released him and stepped back. "Find the injured and anyone still alive. Escort them to Crescent Bay City and call for reinforcements. The elders and I will hold the line."

Ping Hai hesitated, his eyes searching the second-class disciple's face. "You should come with us, Senior Brother. You're more—"

"No." His tone left no room for argument. "My place is here. The elders and I will buy you time to retreat."

"Senior Brother . . ." Ping Hai's voice wavered, but Xu Ziqing cut him off with a sharp glare.

"This is an order."

". . . Understood."

Xu Ziqing turned to the other disciples in the hall, his voice rising to command their attention. "All of you, listen! Follow Ping Hai and retreat to Crescent Bay City. Help him find the injured and the stragglers. Do not stop until you're safe."

The faint crunch of snow under hurried footsteps drew his attention, and he turned to see the disciples who had split off earlier converging toward him. Behind them came dozens more—a scattered, disheveled group.

"Senior Brother Xu!" one of the returning disciples called out, his voice strained but resolute. "We found more!"

Most were third-class disciples. Among them were a few second-class disciples, their faces hardened but their eyes betraying the same fear that gripped everyone present.

"Form up!" Xu Ziqing barked, his voice carrying above the howling wind.

The group obeyed with a mix of hesitation and urgency, clustering together for warmth and reassurance. The elders moved to the front of the formation, their presence a steadying force amid the chaos. Xu Ziqing's sharp eyes tracked the movements of each disciple, assessing their state. Some stood firm, their grips tight on their weapons, while others faltered, their gazes fixed on the ground as though afraid to meet his.

Ping Hai stepped forward, his large frame now carrying an air of purpose despite the earlier faltering. "Senior Brother," he said quietly, "there are more out there, but we don't have time to find them all."

Xu Ziqing nodded grimly. "Then we focus on saving those who are here."

He turned back to the gathered disciples. "Listen carefully!" His voice cut through the storm, sharp and commanding. "The third-class disciples will retreat immediately, led by Ping Hai. Second-class disciples—those of you willing to protect them—join him. Get to Crescent Bay City. Find reinforcements. The rest of us will stay and hold the line."

Each order Xu Ziqing barked was a tether to sanity, a way to keep moving forward when every instinct screamed to stop, to hide, to grieve. The disciples looked to him with wide, fearful eyes, and he forced himself to meet their gazes, knowing he had to be the pillar they needed, even if his own foundation was cracking.

The announcement sparked murmurs within the group. Some third-class disciples immediately shifted toward Ping Hai, relief mingling with guilt on their faces. Among the second-class disciples, a clear divide emerged. Half moved to join the retreating group, their expressions a mixture of shame and fear. The others remained rooted, their jaws set with grim determination.

Xu Ziqing scanned their faces. Those who stepped back were avoiding his gaze, their shoulders hunched under the weight of unspoken words. He couldn't bring himself to judge them. Fear was a powerful force. One he himself had struggled against.

"Go," Xu Ziqing said quietly, his voice losing some of its sharp edge. "Protect them. That's your duty now."

The departing disciples nodded, their steps hurried as they moved away. Ping Hai led them, his voice rising above the wind as he barked orders to keep the group organized. Xu Ziqing watched them go, a knot forming in his chest.

He turned back to the remaining disciples and elders, their number now halved. Those who stayed exchanged glances, their expressions tight with resolve. They had seen the carnage firsthand, had felt the oppressive fear of the cultists' presence. Yet they stood.

The group pressed forward in tense silence, their collective dread palpable as they navigated the battered sect grounds. The path ahead was clear—marked by a trail of carnage. Lifeless bodies lay strewn across the snow, their blood soaking into the ground.

Xu Ziqing led the way, his blade drawn, its cold steel catching the faint light of the storm. The elders moved to the front, their forms imposing despite the wear of confinement. Behind them, the first-class disciples held steady, their weapons raised, and their faces set in grim determination. The second-class disciples flanked the group, their steps uneven as they cast nervous glances at the wreckage around them.

The wind howled, carrying with it the faint metallic tang of blood and the acrid stench of smoke. Xu Ziqing's grip on his sword tightened as they neared the central courtyard. The remnants of their attackers stood there; twenty figures cloaked in black, their presence as unnatural as the storm that raged around them. They moved with an eerie stillness, as though the wind itself bent around them in deference. At their center, the gaunt figure worked with deliberate precision, an incense burner in his hands releasing thick, pungent smoke that mingled with the swirling snow.

The Silent Moon forces halted as one. Xu Ziqing felt his breath catch, his legs refusing to move forward. Even though they outnumbered the hooded figures, it was as though an invisible wall had risen before them, a barrier of raw fear that sapped their strength and resolve. His chest tightened, his pulse hammering in his ears as he stared at the figures ahead. The memories of Elder Fang's death flashed before his eyes: his raw screams, the blood-soaked snow, the cultists' unrelenting advance even in the face of death.

We can't win. Not against that.

Around him, the disciples faltered. Their gazes darted between the cultists and the ground, some unable to look forward at all. Their breathing came in uneven gasps, their hands trembling as they clutched their weapons. The elders, though more composed, seemed uneasy as well.

But there was a difference. The elders didn't have the same hollow look of terror in their eyes. They hadn't been there to witness the carnage firsthand. They hadn't seen Elder Fang's final stand or the initial assault that carved through their defenses with ease.

Xu Ziqing couldn't even muster anger. No righteous fury, no defiant rage—just cold, unrelenting fear.

The hooded figures, for their part, paid no attention to the Silent Moon forces. Their leader continued the ritual, the blood-red pill glowing faintly as it was consumed by the flames. The serpentine mist that emerged writhed and coiled with unnatural purpose, its crimson-and-black form cutting through the air like a living thing. The cultists watched in reverence, their heads bowed, their stillness unnerving.

The Silent Moon forces remained frozen, their formation breaking as disciples hesitated or stepped back. Xu Ziqing's breath quickened. His grip on his sword tightened, his knuckles aching, but he couldn't bring himself to step forward.

Suddenly, a figure moved. One elder, his sword drawn and his face twisted with anger and grief, broke from the formation. Without hesitation, he strode forward, his blade glinting as he raised it high. "For the Silent Moon!" he bellowed, his voice cracking as he charged.

"No!" Xu Ziqing's voice tore from his throat, raw with panic. But it was too late.

The elder's sword descended with a resounding slash, carving into the nearest cultist's turned back. The force of the blow split flesh and bone, sending dark blood spraying across the snow. For a fleeting moment, the elder's attack seemed victorious.

But the cultist barely reacted. He turned slowly, his expression one of annoyance rather than pain. The injury on his shoulder bled freely, yet he moved as though it didn't exist. His hand shot out, gripping the elder by the neck with inhuman strength.

The elder gasped, his blade falling from his grasp as he struggled against the iron grip. He slashed wildly with his free hand, but the cultist didn't so much as flinch. His voice, low and guttural, cut through the storm. "Profane infidel," he sneered. "You are unworthy of life. Death is the only end for those who oppose the cult."

The Silent Moon forces watched in horror, their terror solidifying into stone. Xu Ziqing's heart pounded in his chest, every instinct screaming at him to move, to help—but he couldn't. His legs wouldn't obey, his fear anchoring him to the ground.

With a sickening crunch, the cultist crushed the elder's neck, silencing his gasps. His lifeless body fell to the snow, his face frozen in a mixture of shock and pain. The sound of his death echoed across the battlefield, a final, hollow punctuation to the sect's despair.

The disciples flinched as the cultists who stepped forward prepared to advance. Their leader's voice cut through the tension, sharp and commanding. "*Enough*. There is no time to spend indulging these remnants. Our mission is clear, and we must gather the Phoenix Tears at all costs."

The advancing cultists froze, then knelt, smashing their foreheads to the bloodied snow.

"Forgive this lowly servant, Envoy!" they shouted, their voices hollow yet fervent. They remained motionless, even as blood pooled beneath them, a self-inflicted penance for their disobedience.

The Envoy turned, his scarred face staring solemnly at the Silent Moon forces.

"You will die soon enough," he said, his tone dripping with disdain. "But your existence is meaningless to us now. Do not mistake this reprieve for mercy."

The serpentine mist twisted, forming a path deeper into the storm. The cultists rose, their movements synchronized and precise. They disappeared into the snow, their retreat leaving only silence in their wake.

Xu Ziqing's legs finally gave out, and he sank to his knees, his breath coming in shallow, ragged gasps. Around him, the Silent Moon forces stood rooted, their fear palpable even as the storm swallowed the cultists' figures. For a moment, none dared speak or move.

The sect was in ruins. Their victory was no victory at all—just the hollow aftermath of terror.

CHAPTER NINETEEN

A Lesson in Silence

"The Silent Moon was destroyed overnight?!"

Jian Feng's hands slammed onto the table with enough force to rattle the teacups set along its edges. His face was pale, his eyes bloodshot, and his breathing uneven. It was clear he hadn't slept for quite some time.

The messenger flinched, pulling his fur-lined cloak tighter around his shoulders. His face was lined with exhaustion, and his voice trembled as he answered. "Y-Yes. The details are scattered, but the sect grounds were overrun. Several survivors reached Crescent Bay to deliver the news."

I gripped the edge of the table, my knuckles white as a chill ran down my spine. The Silent Moon Sect was supposed to be the second strongest sect in the region; and that was *before* they added those four elders. That they could be overrun overnight was hard to process.

"They were wiped out in a single night?" Elder Ming asked, his tone measured, though his furrowed brow betrayed his concern.

The messenger nodded grimly. "Their attackers . . . It's likely demonic cultivators. The survivors who made it to Crescent Bay reported injuries bearing signs of corruption."

"Corruption," I echoed softly, my mind flashing back to the Tianyi and Windy's injuries.

"This isn't an isolated incident," Jian Feng said, his voice cutting through the room. He gestured toward the map spread across the table. "Look at this. Crescent Bay here. Iron Claw Sect to the northwest. Silent Moon in the east. And now, two of them were spotted near Gentle Wind Village. They're everywhere."

"But why?" Wang Jun asked, his voice unusually quiet. He exchanged a glance with Lan-Yin, whose brows were furrowed in thought. "Why attack sects and villages scattered so far apart?"

It was a good question, one I didn't have an answer to. If they were trying to gain territory, they wouldn't spread themselves so thin. If it was resources, the attacks seemed too destructive. And if it was vengeance . . . what could they possibly be avenging?

I hesitated, then spoke. "What else do we know about the attack on the Silent Moon? Did anyone find out why they were attacked?"

The messenger shook his head. "No other news has come from the sect or Crescent Bay. Whatever their motive, it's still unclear."

My thoughts turned to Xu Ziqing, Ping Hai, and the other Silent Moon disciples I'd met during the Gauntlet. I didn't like them—far from it. But hearing this news felt like a blow to the chest. They were still people. Still human. And now, they were likely gone.

Jian Feng turned to the messenger. "Relay this as well: Gentle Wind Village was attacked. The creatures involved called themselves demonic cultivators and referred to the Heavenly Demon. We're gathering what we've learned and will send it to the sect."

I exhaled slowly, trying to steady my nerves. "I'll write everything I've learned from my experiments with the Bloodsoul Bloom. If the sect can disseminate this information, it might help others prepare."

Jian Feng gave a tight nod. "Good idea."

I retrieved a blank piece of paper and wrote, summarizing the bloom's properties, its feeding habits, and its resistance to conventional alchemical reactions. The memory of its malevolence still lingered in my mind, and my fingers trembled slightly as I worked. When I finished, I sealed the scroll and handed it to the messenger.

"You'll need to deliver this to the Verdant Lotus Sect," I said. "They'll know what to do."

The man accepted it with a nod but looked hesitant. "I still have to relay this news to other villages and sects along the way. I don't know if I'll make it to the Verdant Lotus quickly."

Jian Feng sighed, rubbing his temples. "We'll send someone else from the village. Thank you for your service."

As the messenger prepared to leave, I hesitated, a thought gnawing at the back of my mind. "Wait."

He turned, his brow furrowed. I dug into my satchel, pulling out the energy-boosting potions I'd been meaning to give Li Wei. They were crude, but they worked well enough in a pinch. "Take these. They'll help keep your stamina up."

The messenger's eyes widened slightly as he accepted them. "Thank you, young master."

I shook my head. "No need for that. Just avoid any roads that take you into the forests. If these demonic cultivators are hiding anywhere, it's there."

"I'll keep that in mind," he said with a faint smile, his voice softening. "Thank you for your work here."

As the messenger mounted his horse and rode off into the encroaching twilight, I turned back to the table where Elder Ming, Lan-Yin, Wang Jun, and Jian Feng still stood.

"We need to think about what happens next," I said, breaking the tense silence.

"We can't stay here forever," Lan-Yin said quietly. "If this village becomes a target again . . ."

I nodded grimly. "Should we evacuate to Crescent Bay?"

Jian Feng shook his head. "It's not feasible. Moving an entire village would require enormous resources and days of planning. The villagers aren't as fast as cultivators, and we'd be vulnerable to attack during the journey."

I swallowed hard, trying to push down the rising sense of helplessness. The thought of staying in the village while knowing the threat was still out there felt suffocating.

Elder Ming folded his arms, his calm voice cutting through the tension. "Then we stay and prepare. We cannot afford to let panic rule our actions. The village must remain strong, no matter the circumstances."

Everyone fell silent, the gravity of our situation sinking in. We were essentially trapped. Any move we made carried risks that could lead to an even greater disaster. And so, for now, we could do nothing but wait.

But I couldn't stay idle. Waiting felt like surrender.

"I need air," I muttered, pushing away from the table. I didn't wait for a response, striding toward the door as the wind beckoned me outside.

The night air bit my skin, but the sharpness helped clear my head. My thoughts churned like the storm clouds overhead, and I clenched my fists tightly. I glanced upward, half-expecting the Interface to display some new task or hint, but it remained frustratingly quiet.

"You're giving me all these rewards," I murmured, my voice low and bitter. "Making me grow faster than everyone else. You want me to be something. Fine. Then give me something now. Again."

The words hung in the air, swallowed by the stony silence. My chest tightened with frustration. Whatever power controlled the Interface, it remained as cryptic as ever.

I turned and made my way home, each step feeling heavier than the last. The faint light from within spilled onto the snow, and I pushed open the door to find Tianyi awake. She sat by the basin, her expression tender as she cradled Windy's head above the water. His small body floated weakly, his breathing shallow but steady.

"You're back."

I nodded, unable to keep the tension from my voice. "How is he?"

"He's stable. For now," she said softly, brushing a hand gently over Windy's pale scales. "But the corruption . . . it lingers."

I clenched my fists, guilt and helplessness swirling within me. Windy had nearly died, and here I was, grasping at straws for a solution in the sky.

No. I had to find it myself.

My gaze drifted to the shelf where the Golden Bamboo essence sat. The faint golden hue of the vial seemed to pulse as I approached.

I've been putting this off for too long.

I grabbed it, turning toward a nearby ginger plant. Placing the essence atop its soil, I focused, channeling a trickle of qi into the connection.

The change was immediate. The ginger plant shuddered, its leaves straightening as its color deepened to a vibrant green. The essence suffused it, infusing the plant with strength and vitality. It looked healthier than I'd ever seen, its energy radiating in soft waves.

> *Quest: Mastery of Spiritual Plant Cultivation has been completed.*
> *Due to your status as Interface Manipulator, rewards have been adjusted accordingly.*

> *Spiritual Herbalism has reached level 9.*

> *Reward calculation completed.*
> *Your reward will put you in a trance-like state. Proceed?*

When my senses returned, I found myself standing in a room that felt eerily familiar. The air was cold, the space dimly lit by an undefined light source. The landmarks were vague—stone walls with cracks that seemed to shift when I wasn't looking, a featureless wooden desk in the center, and empty bookshelves lining the walls.

I turned, and my stomach tightened. I knew this room. It was the same one I had stood in when I received the quest to create the healing hydrosol.

A faint hum broke the silence, and the robed figure appeared. This time, however, I didn't freeze. I knew now that I wasn't corporeal in this state.

The figure moved with precision, its faceless features giving nothing away as it stepped to a cauldron at the center of the room. The hum grew louder, a low vibration that resonated in my chest as three orbs of swirling essence materialized in the figure's hands. Each glowed faintly—one vivid green, another deep red, and the last ethereal blue.

The figure placed the first orb into the cauldron with simmering water. The moment it hit the liquid inside, a soft light erupted, casting shifting patterns across the room. The figure extended its palm over the cauldron, infusing it with qi. I watched intently, noting the rhythm and precision of the infusion.

The second orb followed, its red hue mixing with the green, creating a strange, unstable swirl of colors. Again, the figure infused its qi, the energy spiraling down from its palm into the cauldron. The process repeated with the blue orb, the final addition creating a harmonious glow.

The figure stepped back, its robed arms rising slightly as the cauldron's light dimmed. When the glow subsided, a small vial appeared in its hand, filled with an elixir that shimmered in all three colors.

I frowned, watching as the figure held the vial for a moment before placing it aside and turning back to the cauldron. This time, it began a new process. Different plants materialized around the figure, their forms hazy yet distinct. It was hard to recognize them, as though they were being intentionally obscured from me. The figure reached for one, pressing its palm against its base.

The plant quivered, then released a stream of essence. This one was orange, and as it separated, the plant wilted, its energy siphoned completely. The figure moved to another plant, repeating the process, but the essence this time was pale yellow.

I leaned closer, my mind racing as I tried to piece together what was happening.

It's not about the ingredients. It's about the essences. But why was he using a different set?

The figure repeated the process, extracting essences of varying colors. When it moved to the cauldron, it went through the same steps as before: placing each orb in the liquid, infusing qi at precise intervals, and creating another shimmering elixir. This time, however, the colors were different—orange, yellow, and green—but the end product glowed with a similar vibrancy.

I watched, my brows furrowing deeper as the figure continued its repetitive, precise cycle. Three essences, always three. Different colors, different sources, but the process and the result were eerily consistent. The elixir shimmered with the same faint glow, no matter what combination was used.

It didn't make sense. Alchemy was as much about the specific properties of ingredients as it was about the *process* of refinement. Yet here, it was as though the figure was saying the what didn't matter as much as the why.

"Is this about ratios?" I muttered, half to myself. The figure didn't respond. It moved with the same deliberate fluidity, extracting essence from yet another plant. This one produced a deep violet glow, starkly different from the orange and yellow before it.

I stepped closer, my frustration bubbling over. "All right, I get it. Three essences. Fine. But what are you trying to show me? Why not just explain it? Can you even talk?"

The figure froze mid-motion. Slowly, it turned toward me, its faceless visage somehow conveying an almost palpable exasperation. It raised one gloved finger to where its lips would have been—if it had a mouth—and mimicked a shushing motion.

I blinked, momentarily caught off guard. "Are you seriously telling me to be quiet? You've dragged me into some surreal alchemical fever dream and expect me to figure it all out without a single word of explanation? This is ridiculous!"

The figure turned away, completely ignoring me, and resumed its work. It placed the latest extracted essence into the cauldron, infused its qi at the same precise intervals as before, and retrieved yet another shimmering vial.

My hands clenched into fists. "Fine. Don't talk. I'll figure it out on my own," I muttered, stepping even closer to observe the reactions within the cauldron. If I weren't corporeal, my eyebrows would've been singed off by my sheer proximity to the boiling cauldron.

As the figure worked, the subtle patterns in the concoction began to stand out. The first essence caused a gentle ripple to spread across the liquid—a calming, unifying motion that reminded me of the initial steps in balancing volatile ingredients in a recipe. Harmonization.

The second essence produced a faint glow, accompanied by wisps of steam that rose from the cauldron. It was cleansing, purging impurities from the mixture. Purification.

The third essence caused the liquid to thicken slightly, the glow intensifying as the concoction stabilized. Its consistency grew stronger, more cohesive, as though preparing to hold up under pressure. Fortification.

I leaned back, the pieces clicking together in my mind. I watched as it repeated the process, with the same reactions taking place. Did it mean that as long as the essences fulfilled the role of purification, harmonization, and fortification that the elixir would work?

"Three stages," I murmured aloud. "Harmonization, purification, fortification. That's the pattern."

The figure paused mid-motion, its head tilting slightly as though acknowledging my realization. Then, with what could only be described as an exaggerated sigh, it set the latest vial aside and folded its arms.

"Was that so hard to show me without all the theatrics?" I snapped, my irritation bubbling over. "You could've just said, 'Hey, look for the three stages.' But no, you had to be all cryptic about it."

The figure raised a hand and waved dismissively, as though brushing off my complaints. My annoyance surged. "Don't you wave me off! I'm the one doing all the work here—"

Before I could finish, the world around me dissolved into light, the dim room and robed figure vanishing in an instant. My body jolted as I snapped back to reality, my hand still resting on the table. Not even a second had passed in real time.

The abrupt return left me momentarily disoriented. I blinked, glancing around the workshop. Everything was as I'd left it—Tianyi still tending to Windy, the faint glow of the furnace casting warm light across the room.

Tianyi looked up from the basin, her antennae twitching as she studied me. "What's wrong?" she asked softly.

"Nothing. Just . . . got a quest reward."

Her expression didn't change. "And?"

"And I don't know what to make of it," I admitted, letting out a long sigh. "It's . . . complicated."

"Complicated? How?"

I hesitated, then relented. "It's about an elixir. Or rather, how to make one. The Interface showed me . . . well, someone—or something—did. The process was strange. It kept using different essences, but the method and results stayed the same. But they didn't explain anything about how it . . ."

As I said it, the clearer the picture became. I paused, letting myself sink into the realization of what the recipe was for.

She tilted her head. "Did you figure something out?"

I glanced toward Windy, his small body barely moving as he floated in the basin. "A purifying elixir," I said, the pieces clicking together as I spoke. "Three essences. The first harmonizes the mixture, balancing everything out. The second purifies it. The third fortifies it, making it strong."

Infusing qi wasn't just a random step. It was deliberate, purposeful. My qi had withered the Bloodsoul Bloom—corruption couldn't stand against it, for whatever reason. The elixir was a weapon, a way to cleanse and strengthen. Maybe Windy didn't have to endure this any longer.

Perhaps the Interface was listening closer to my desires than I thought it was.

I turned back to the shelf, grabbing the essences I'd prepared earlier. My hands trembled slightly, but I forced myself to stay focused. Harmonization, purification, fortification. I repeated the steps in my mind like a mantra, grounding myself in their rhythm.

CHAPTER TWENTY

Harmonize, Purify, Fortify

I set the three vials of extracted essences on the table beside my pill furnace. These weren't my rarest or most expensive essences, but they were potent enough to test my theory.

If this worked, I'd be able to cure Windy.

I took a deep breath, steadying myself. Extracted essences were volatile by nature, their concentrated energy unpredictable. Using more than one or two in a single recipe had always felt reckless—an invitation for disaster. But the figure's method from the trance-like vision had been clear: it wasn't about the ingredients themselves but their roles in the process.

Harmonization. Purification. Fortification.

I reached for the green vial of Reishi mushroom, the essence inside swirling like liquid jade. Harmonization. This one would set the foundation.

With a practiced hand, I poured the essence into the furnace, the liquid releasing a faint hiss as it met the heated interior. I placed my palm over the furnace's edge and channeled a steady stream of my qi into it, mimicking the figure's rhythm. The chaotic swirl of green essence slowed, settling into a gentle rotation.

So far, so good.

Next was the pale yellow vial: astralagus essence. Its contents shimmered like liquid sunlight, a stark contrast to the green. Purification. As I added it to the furnace, the mixture hissed and roiled, the green and yellow colliding in a chaotic swirl of energy. Once again, I infused my energy into it.

Instantly, the turbulence eased, the colors beginning to blend into a muted chartreuse. I let out a slow breath. It felt as though the essences were acknowledging my qi, cooperating rather than resisting.

The amber vial came last, and I smiled faintly upon remembering Jingyu Lian's usage of it in the Gauntlet. Female ginseng. Fortification and amplification. The essence inside was thick, almost syrup-like, its energy dense and potent. This was the most crucial stage, strengthening the elixir to ensure Windy's body could withstand the purification process. As I poured it into the furnace, the mixture reacted violently, bubbling and emitting a sharp, acrid scent.

I didn't panic. My palm remained steady over the furnace as I infused another pulse of qi, this one stronger than before. The bubbling slowed, the amber hue melding with the concoction until it took on a pearlescent glow.

White.

The elixir was turning white.

I frowned, my mind racing. The figure's elixirs had been pale, almost translucent, but not this vivid. Was I doing something wrong? Doubt crept in, threatening to undermine my confidence. But my Refinement Simulation Technique didn't seem to show anything going wrong.

I let out a slow breath, steadying myself. Maybe this wasn't a mistake. Maybe the elixir's color reflected my qi's purity, amplifying the concoction beyond what the figure had shown. I had to trust my instincts, trust the process.

The furnace hummed faintly as the mixture stabilized, its white glow intensifying with each passing moment. I continued to channel my qi in steady intervals, watching as the energy within the furnace seemed to dance in harmony. The once-chaotic blend now moved with purpose, each color complementing the other until they became one.

When the glow faded, I removed my palm and leaned over the furnace. The air was thick with the scent of herbs and energy, a heady mix that filled the room. I reached for a ladle and carefully extracted the elixir, now pristine, milky white, and poured it into a small vial, warm to the touch.

I held the vial up to the light, marveling at its clarity. This was unlike anything I'd ever created.

I stared at the vial, the faint pulse of the elixir resonating in my hand. The process was complete, but the real test was still ahead. Turning, I glanced at Windy, still floating weakly in the basin of purifying solution. His breathing was shallow, and the dark spots of corruption along his scaled body seemed as stark as ever against his pale, luminous white.

This had to work. It *had* to.

I approached slowly, kneeling beside the basin as I set the vial carefully on the floor. "All right, Windy," I murmured, my voice barely above a whisper. "Let's see if this helps."

With delicate hands, I lifted him from the basin, his small body limp in my palms. The corruption had sunk deep; the dark patches were rough, almost like burns, radiating a faint, malevolent aura that made my skin crawl. I grabbed a cloth and patted him dry, trying to be as gentle as possible.

"Hold on, buddy," I said, my throat tightening.

I uncorked the vial, the faintest hiss escaping as the elixir met the air. My heart pounded as I dipped the tip of a finger into the liquid, drawing out a single, glistening drop. Hovering it above the largest patch of corruption on his side, I hesitated. What if this harmed him instead? What if—

No. I shook my head. *Trust the process.*

The drop fell.

The reaction was immediate. A soft, almost imperceptible sizzling sound rose as the elixir made contact with the wound. I froze, watching intently. The dark energy around the patch seemed to writhe, resisting the elixir's influence for a moment before being forced outward. The blackness dissipated like smoke, leaving the area beneath it brighter, healthier.

It worked.

A breath I didn't realize I was holding escaped me. I dipped my finger into the vial again, drawing out another drop, then another, applying them to the next patch and the next. Each time, the elixir expelled the corruption, leaving behind unblemished scales. The sizzling sound was less pronounced now, the process smoother as the malignant energy was pushed out of Windy's body.

But I stopped before emptying the vial. As much as I wanted to rid him of every trace, I couldn't risk destabilizing him by using too much at once. The elixir was potent—*too* potent, perhaps—and his slight frame was already weak.

I turned to the basin still filled with the purifying solution. If I incorporated the elixir into the solution, it might sustain its effects over time, allowing his body to recover more naturally. Activating my Refinement Simulation Technique, I hovered the vial above the basin and let a single drop fall.

The solution rippled faintly, but there was no violent reaction, no sign of instability. Encouraged, I added three more drops, watching as the solution took on a faint opalescent hue. The energy within it seemed to shift, harmonizing with the elixir almost seamlessly. This was working.

Gently, I placed Windy back into the basin. He stirred weakly as the liquid enveloped him, his breathing shallow at first, then gradually deepening. I watched as his small chest rose and fell, each breath steadier than the last. The dark patches that remained seemed to fade slightly, their edges softening as the solution did its work.

Relief crashed over me like a wave, my knees buckling as I slumped to the floor. I pressed my hands against the cold ground, my head bowed as I let out a shaky exhale. "Thank you," I whispered to the silence around me, though in my heart, I was addressing both the faceless figure and the Interface itself.

It didn't respond. It never did. But for once, I didn't mind.

I turned to Tianyi, who had been sitting silently in the corner, her wings folded tightly against her back. She met my gaze, her expression unreadable but her antennae twitching faintly in what I recognized as concern.

"Your turn," I said, standing on unsteady legs.

She hesitated but nodded, unwrapping the bandages that covered her forearms. The sight made my stomach twist—deep fissures ran along her pale, segmented skin, tinged with the same malevolent energy that had afflicted Windy. Her natural healing abilities had slowed the corruption's spread, but it was clear they weren't enough.

I drew another drop of the elixir from the vial and placed it carefully on the worst of her wounds. The reaction was immediate but less pronounced than with Windy. The corruption recoiled, retreating under the elixir's influence, but it didn't fully dissipate. I applied another drop, then another, until the blackness faded entirely from that spot.

Tianyi's antennae twitched, her blue-tinged eyes watching the elixir's effects with a mixture of hope and hesitation. When the corruption receded, leaving the wound clean but raw, she tilted her head slightly, her voice soft as she broke the silence. "It . . . doesn't hurt as much anymore."

I nodded, relief washing over me. "It's working, but your injuries are as deep as Windy's. We'll need to treat them carefully, a little at a time."

Her wings fluttered faintly, and she looked down at the fissures lining her arms. "This . . . elixir. Could it work against them? The ones who spread this darkness?"

I straightened, the thought sparking in my mind. She had a point. If this elixir could purify corruption from Windy and her wounds, what effect would it have on the demonic cultivators? The Bloodsoul Bloom had reacted violently to the infusion of qi—what would it do in the presence of this?

"It's possible," I admitted, my gaze shifting to the vial in my hand. "Their techniques rely on malevolent energy. If this elixir disrupts it . . ."

Tianyi nodded, her expression grim. "It could be a weapon."

The thought was both exhilarating and terrifying. This was no ordinary healing solution—it was something more. But I'd need to test it further, refine the formula, and see how it interacted in different conditions.

"I'm going to spend the rest of the afternoon experimenting," I said, my resolve hardening. "We need to understand what this elixir can do—not just for healing but for defense."

Tianyi folded her wings tightly against her back. "I'll stay with Windy," she mumbled. "He's . . . resting better."

I glanced at the basin, where Windy floated in the faintly glowing solution. His breathing was steady now, his coiled body no longer trembling. My chest tightened with a mix of relief and determination.

The first rays of dawn were still hours away, and the village was cloaked in a deep, pre-dawn stillness. The air was crisp, biting against my skin as I adjusted the Iron Boar cloak around my shoulders.

I stood before the banyan tree, its massive trunk a dark silhouette against the faint starlight. The ground beneath my feet was firm, dusted with frost, and the chill seeped through my boots as I stared up at the towering symbol of endurance, the inspiration of my signature defensive technique. My breath came in slow, measured puffs of steam.

This was supposed to be simple. Hit the tree, leave a dent, and complete the Black Tortoise Tribulation sub-quest. Yet, my fist remained frozen midair.

Why don't I want to finish this?

The question gnawed at the edges of my mind. Every other quest I had completed had brought a rush of satisfaction, a tangible reward that propelled me further down the path of cultivation. But this one . . . This quest was different.

I lowered my fist, my eyes narrowing as I considered the weight pressing down on me. This quest hadn't just been about endurance or strength; it had taught me efficiency. The weight forced every movement to count, every step to conserve energy. It had pushed me to refine my martial techniques and to grow stronger, not just in body or mind, but in my control of qi.

> *You completed the quest with additional challenges.*
> *Your efforts do not go unnoticed.*

The Interface had rewarded me handsomely for going beyond in the past. It wasn't just about completing the task; it was about mastering the principle behind it. If I finished the quest now, the weight would vanish, and with it, the unique opportunity to push myself further.

My fingers curled into a tight fist, and then I lowered it.

"Not yet," I muttered.

The banyan tree stood silent. I turned on my heel, the crunch of frost beneath my boots the only sound as I made my way back to the village.

The stars above seemed to glimmer faintly, as though in approval. Or maybe that was just my imagination.

When I entered Elder Ming's courtyard, the darkness had barely lifted. The familiar scent of incense and chilly morning air greeted me as I stepped onto the training grounds. Elder Ming was already there, his posture as still as the stone statues lining the path, his gaze sweeping over me as I approached.

"You're early," he remarked, his tone neutral.

I nodded, rolling my shoulders beneath the cloak. "I thought it best to make use of the time. Stopped by the banyan outside of the village."

His eyes narrowed slightly. "And the quest? Did you complete it?"

I hesitated, then shook my head. "No."

Elder Ming's brows rose ever so slightly, a faint note of surprise breaking through his calm demeanor. "Why not?"

I met his gaze, my voice steady. "Because completing it now would be short-sighted. The weight has been more than a test; it's been a tool. It's forced me to refine my movements, to adapt. If I finish the quest now, I'll lose that chance to grow further."

His expression shifted. At first, from one of surprise, then to one of deep thought. Then the faintest hint of a smile formed on his lips. He nodded slowly. ". . . Wise. Many cultivators are so focused on immediate gains that they miss the deeper opportunities presented to them. You've seen beyond the surface of this trial, further than I did. That is commendable."

A comfortable silence spread between us, but Elder Ming quickly broke it with two words.

"I apologize."

I turned my head in surprise. "What for?"

He truly looked his age as he exhaled slowly, the morning mist curling around his lips. "For misjudging the situation," he said, his voice carrying a rare solemnity. "You were right to stop Tianyi from going into the forest alone."

I blinked, surprised. He wasn't the type to hand out apologies lightly. If anything, he had always been a firm believer in taking responsibility without dwelling on past mistakes.

"You don't need to apologize," I said, shaking my head. "In a normal situation, you and the Verdant Lotus Sect would've been right. If this were just another bandit attack or some rogue beast problem, caution would've been unnecessary. But this . . ." My gaze drifted to the distant trees, the lingering shadow of what had happened still heavy in my chest. "This isn't normal."

Elder Ming remained silent.

I let out a slow breath. "When I was younger, I thought that the right choice was to trust those wiser and stronger than me. To follow their guidance because they knew better. And for a long time, that was true. But if I keep thinking that way, if I assume every problem has a tried-and-true solution, then I'll never be able to act when things don't fit into a neat pattern."

My fingers clenched around the edge of my cloak. "The Silent Moon Sect was wiped out overnight. Demonic cultivators are moving in ways no one understands. The old ways of thinking, the way we're used to approaching threats . . . they aren't enough anymore. That's why I want to delay the tribulation. I'll make sure I've gained everything I can before I do. I want to move like how I did before—no, even faster. Without using qi to keep my movements."

He folded his arms, his expression contemplative. "Then let's test that resolve. The Dance of a Thousand Flames—do you believe you can execute it properly now, even with the weight you carry?"

I nodded without hesitation. "I need to. If I'm going to grow stronger, I can't avoid difficult challenges."

Elder Ming's smile widened.

He moved to the edge of the training grounds, where a modest pile of charcoal sat waiting, untouched for weeks. With a practiced hand, he reached for the flint and steel resting nearby. Sparks danced in the air before catching on the kindling beneath the charcoal. A flicker of orange light bloomed, small at first, but quickly growing.

The flames licked hungrily at the wood, and within moments, the charcoal glowed, its surface crackling as embers spread like veins of molten fire. The heat radiated outward, a wave of intensity that made the cold evening air feel like a distant memory.

"Very well. Let's begin."

CHAPTER TWENTY-ONE

Tipsy Wings

Everything blended together in a blur of training, cultivation, and stolen moments of sleep. My body ached in ways I hadn't thought possible, but I could feel the difference—the growth. Each day, I pushed myself further than I ever had before. And each morning, I woke up feeling a little less broken than I should have.

I had my suspicions. No matter how many times I told Tianyi not to use her healing on me while I slept, I had a sneaking feeling she ignored me. She tried to play it off with her usual innocent expression, her antennae twitching slightly whenever I brought it up, but I knew better. I'd wake up with a deep warmth in my muscles, the kind that came from more than just natural recovery.

Honestly, it was infuriating and humbling. Without her, I'd still be crawling out of bed like a half-crushed insect, even with my newfound power from the Golden Drop Elixir. I was able to produce a batch and distributed it among the Verdant Lotus disciples but kept a few for myself to supplement my growth. Thanks to her, I was recovering twice as fast, my muscles knitting back stronger each time they tore under the weight without overreliance on pills.

Windy, however, hadn't stirred. He floated in his basin, his breathing steady but shallow. The corruption was gone, thanks to the Essence Purifying Elixir, but his body needed time to repair itself. Every day, I checked on him, hoping for some sign of improvement, but nothing yet. All I could do was monitor his condition and wait.

I mulled over the problem as I continued my training, each step accompanied by the rhythmic crunch of snow beneath my boots. It would've been nice if the Verdant Lotus had given us more information, but they'd been silent. No response from the sect since we sent out a messenger to hand over the seeds of the Bloodsoul Bloom, all I knew about it, and the bodies of their second-class disciples and the demonic cultivator who killed them.

I couldn't afford to let this stagnation continue, nor could I afford to stand here and wait.

Communication and support were all tied to forces beyond my control—and I hated that.

The only thing I could control was myself. My training. My skills. Preparing potions for any situation. The Interface hadn't given me any new quests recently, but that didn't mean I couldn't push myself further. I just needed to be smart about it.

"Use the Refinement Simulation Technique on an alchemical reaction mid-combat," I muttered, repeating the vague requirement of the quest for the Combat Anticipation Array. I'd been gnawing at that puzzle for days now. How could I leverage alchemical reactions while fighting? It wasn't as though I could carry a pill furnace into battle.

With a frustrated sigh, I shook the thought aside. If the answer wasn't coming to me, then I'd focus on what I could solve. My other skills—Rooted Banyan Stance, and the Heavenly Flame Mantra—had all seen steady progress, but I needed to push them further.

Accelerated Reading was stuck, no thanks to the lack of books in the village. The Million Books Pavilion had been a treasure trove I hadn't fully appreciated. Now, I was left grasping for scraps of knowledge, kicking myself for not copying more texts while I had the chance.

Rooted Banyan Stance was a different story. With Elder Ming's permission, I'd been working on it in isolation, holding the stance for extended periods to fulfill the prerequisite for upgrading it to the next stage. It wasn't enough to simply maintain the form; I'd started experimenting with imperfect stances, mimicking real battle scenarios.

Every time I sparred with Wang Jun, I remembered the fights with Wei Long and Ping Hai. The times I couldn't execute the stance perfectly had left me vulnerable. But the experimentation was paying off. I'd noticed that even when I couldn't maintain the stance's integrity, my body still kept a density and hardness that seemed unnatural.

That got me thinking: could the Rooted Banyan Stance become more than just a defensive technique? If I could harness its power offensively, combining my immovable foundation with the explosive strength of the Heavenly Flame Mantra, it might just change the way I fought entirely. The problem, of course, was timing. The stance required me to stay rooted, immobile, a major disadvantage in battle if misused. Finding the right balance between stillness and motion was a challenge I was determined to overcome.

I closed my eyes, letting the idea take form in my mind. A vivid image of Wei Long loomed, his towering frame as imposing as ever. His fists had been like battering rams, each swing carrying enough force to shatter stone. If I could make the Rooted Banyan Stance work offensively against someone like him, it would be proof that this idea wasn't just a fleeting fantasy.

I sank into the stance, my legs rooted firmly to the ground, my left hand extended, and pictured Wei Long charging, his massive fist cutting through the air toward me. With a slow exhale, I grounded myself, then visualized the counter.

ROOTED BANYAN STANCE!

My lead hand snapped back as I shifted my weight, pulling all the force from my rooted position into a single explosive punch with my right. The motion wasn't fluid—it didn't need to be. I didn't strike with brute strength alone but concentrated power, focused entirely on one point.

Not a real strike, I reminded myself, but the placement of where his fist should meet mine. The visualization sharpened as I imagined the moment of impact: my strength against his, amplified by the stance's immovable nature.

For a brief second, I stilled completely, my muscles tensed as if waiting for the outcome to reveal itself.

". . . Perhaps this is something that only works in actual combat," I muttered, my voice low as I straightened from the stance.

It was impossible to know if it would've worked. Wei Long had been the strongest opponent I'd ever faced, his raw power unmatched. But this wasn't about matching strength for strength. It was about precision. Just like how Tianyi did, overwhelming him with pinpoint strikes rather than meeting him head-on.

I continued to test out my theory, with varying outcomes. The closer I was to the horse stance, the more I could root myself in place.

> *Rooted Banyan Stance has reached level 6.*

By the time I finished training for the evening, my body felt like a lead weight, but I still had one last task. I trudged toward my greenhouse, inspecting the rows of plants nestled under frost-covered glass. My garden outside was faring worse, the winter chill slowing growth to a crawl.

As I tended the plants, my mind wandered to the dwindling supplies. No matter how carefully I rationed the herbs and essences, it wouldn't be enough. I needed to expand the greenhouse—or find an alternative source of materials entirely. That would be another challenge for another day.

The cold prickled my skin, and I caught sight of Tianyi in the distance. She was practicing again, now that her wounds had mostly healed, unimpeded by the corrupting energy. Her silhouette was illuminated by the pale moonlight, and her wings shimmered faintly as she twisted and turned.

I watched for a moment, curiosity gnawing at me. Her movements were elegant but offbeat, almost out of rhythm. It wasn't like anything I'd seen her do before, and for Tianyi—who usually moved with insect-like precision—it was odd.

Unable to contain myself, I walked over. "What are you doing?"

She froze midstep, her antennae twitching as she glanced at me. "Practicing," she said simply.

"Practicing what?"

She sighed, lowering her hands. "During the fight with that demonic cultivator . . . I felt something. A burst of energy, warmth. It gave me the strength I needed to fight back. I've been trying to recreate it."

My brow furrowed. "A burst of energy? Like enlightenment?"

She shook her head. "What does that mean?"

I tried to verbalize how it felt. I'd experienced it. Against Ping Hai, it had been crucial in helping me coalesce my training of the Bamboo Reprisal Counter into something beyond just technique.

I closed my eyes, letting the memory of that fight resurface.

"It's . . . hard to describe," I intoned. "It wasn't like figuring out a new technique or executing a plan. It was like . . ." I exhaled, trying to piece it together. "If my body, my thoughts—everything—ceased to exist except for that single moment. When I fought Ping Hai, I didn't think about countering. I didn't analyze his stance, his trajectory, his force. My body already knew what to do. It wasn't just reaction or instinct. It was . . . like I was moving in perfect rhythm with the world itself."

I met her gaze. "It was like stepping into a river and letting it carry me forward. No resistance, no force. Just flow."

Her brows furrowed slightly, and I could tell she was considering my words. "Elder Ming has described that to me. He said it's like dancing."

I blinked, the comparison catching me off guard. "Dancing?"

"Yes. But I don't think that's what it felt like. I already do that whenever I fight," she replied.

I sighed. I forgot she was a genius.

She spoke, continuing to explain her conundrum. "This was different. The shadow, she . . . she did something. Threw bottles at me. Some broke. She threw one of those things. A lantern. And then I was on fire."

I froze. "Wait. *She lit you on fire?*"

She nodded, her gaze dropping. "At first, it hurt. But after I stopped burning, it felt . . . different. My vision blurred, my balance was off. But it was like I was floating. Like I was dancing on clouds."

My thoughts churned as I tried to piece together her words. Fire? Warmth? Floating? "You're saying being on fire helped?"

"Yes," she whispered. "But only after the burning stopped."

I opened my mouth to argue, then closed it. The mental image of Tianyi alight with flames wasn't one I wanted to dwell on, but her words gnawed at me. There had to be more to this. Something I was missing.

"You said she threw bottles at you. Did any of the liquid get on you? Or . . . in your mouth?"

She blinked, her antennae twitching in thought. "Yes. There was alcohol. Why?"

My eyes narrowed as a theory took shape. "Have you ingested any alcohol since . . . well, since you turned human?"

"No, I haven't."

A grin tugged at my lips despite myself. "That might be the key. You're a butterfly, but now you're human. Maybe alcohol interacts with your body differently now, or their medicinal wine comprises some special ingredient. It might've triggered whatever that burst of energy was. Let's test it."

Tianyi's antennae stilled, her blue-tinged eyes widening. "You want me to drink alcohol?"

I nodded. "Not a lot. Just enough to see if it triggers the same reaction."

She hesitated, her wings fluttering slightly. "And if it doesn't? Will you light me on fire?"

"Why in the *heavens* would I do that?! Just—ugh, let me see if I still have Master Qiang's rice wine . . ."

I went inside and collected a bottle. Handing it over to her, I watched as she gingerly picked up the bottle and put it to her lips.

GLUG!

GLUG!

"Hey, not that much!"

I stepped forward to snatch the bottle away from her, but before I could even get close, Tianyi leaned backward.

Her foot connected squarely with my face, sending me stumbling back into the snow with a muffled groan.

My head snapped back, and I froze.

Tianyi swayed unsteadily, the bottle dangling from her hand, but her expression stopped me cold. Her usual calm, detached demeanor was gone, replaced by a glare so sharp it could've cut through steel. Her cheeks were flushed, her antennae twitching erratically, and for the first time since she had turned human, she looked genuinely, undeniably furious.

"You stupid idiot!" she snapped, her voice uncharacteristically loud. "Why are you trying to take things from me?!"

I blinked, caught completely off guard. "I was just—wait, what?"

Before I could gather my wits, she darted forward, her movements faster and more erratic than I'd ever seen.

Instinct kicked in. I dropped into the Rooted Banyan Stance, bracing myself just as her foot lashed out again. Her kick landed on my shoulder with a thunderous impact. But before I could counter or even process her next move, she hooked her leg around me, using the momentum to swing herself upward and deliver a sharp elbow straight to the side of my head.

Pain exploded in my skull, and my vision blurred. The world tilted as my legs buckled, and I hit the ground hard, the breath knocked out of me. I tried to scramble to my feet, but my body refused to cooperate, my limbs sluggish and unresponsive.

I looked up, dazed, just in time to see Tianyi standing over me, her fist raised. For a moment, I thought she might actually finish me off.

"Tianyi—wait, stop!" I croaked, too weak to move.

Her fist came down.

But instead of a devastating blow, it landed lightly on my chest, more of a push than a punch. I stared up at her, confused, as her shoulders shook. She sank to her knees beside me, her wings drooping as tears welled up in her glowing blue eyes.

"You're such a stupid, stupid idiot," she muttered, her voice cracking. "Always blaming yourself. For me. For Windy. For everything. It's not your fault."

Her voice, once muffled by her hands, rose again, a tangle of slurred words and hiccupping sobs. "You . . . you think it's all your fault, don't you? That Windy is . . . is . . ." She trailed off, sniffing loudly before continuing, her antennae twitching erratically. "He's not gone, you idiot! He's just . . . just sleeping. He's tired. Because . . . because he's strong, and you . . . you need to stop being stupid!"

I blinked, still sprawled on the snow, wondering what in the heavens had possessed me to hand her the bottle in the first place. My head throbbed, my ribs ached, and now the same person who'd knocked me down was crying on top of me, calling me stupid between gasping hiccups.

"Tianyi," I started cautiously, trying to sit up. "I get it. I messed up. But can you—"

She jabbed a finger into my chest, cutting me off. "No! You don't get it!" Her voice rose in pitch, her eyes glassy and tear-filled. "You think . . . you think everything's your fault! But you're wrong! It's not! And you . . . you need to stop blaming yourself, okay?!"

Her words came out in a rush, barely coherent, and I found myself too stunned to argue. Before I could respond, she sniffled again, wiping at her face with her sleeve as fresh tears spilled over.

"And Windy . . . poor Windy . . ." Her voice broke, and she let out a shaky sob. "He's hurt because of me. I should've protected him. But you . . . you keep blaming yourself. Why? Why would you do that, Kai?"

I sighed, finally pushing myself up on one elbow. "Because I was the one who—"

"Don't you dare try to shut me up!" she wailed, glaring at me through her tears. "I'm not done! You're . . . you're so stupid! And you think . . . you think you can fix everything, but you can't, Kai! You need me! You need Windy! And . . . and we need you too, you idiot!"

This was going to be a long night—and an even longer headache in the morning.

CHAPTER TWENTY-TWO

The Drunken Dao

The morning after was just as troublesome as the night before.

Tianyi knelt before me, her antennae twitching in what I could only assume was mortification. Her head was pressed firmly to the ground, her wings folded tightly against her back. The sheen of her black hair caught the faint morning light as she kowtowed before me.

"For my transgressions last night, I shall carve the word 'shame' into my wings and leap into a pit of flames to atone . . ."

"Stop!" I raised both hands before rubbing my head, still aching from the blows she landed on me. "First of all, there's no need for that. Second . . . where did you even learn to say things like that?"

Tianyi blinked, tilting her head in genuine confusion. "The books in Elder Ming's house. Am I not using the phrase properly?"

I groaned, rubbing my temples as I recalled the novels. There *was* a scene in the Storm Sage Chronicles like that. They'd been full of dramatic oaths and over-the-top declarations, and apparently, Tianyi had taken them to heart. "No, Tianyi. Nobody actually disembowels themselves over an accident."

She sat back on her knees, her wings drooping slightly. "Oh. But . . . I was so disrespectful. Surely, I must—"

"You have to stop overreacting and let me get a word in." I sighed, glancing at the empty rice wine bottle still sitting on the counter. "Besides, we have bigger things to talk about. Do you remember anything about last night?"

"I . . . bits and pieces. I remember drinking the rice wine—" She paused, looking away. "—and then everything gets . . . hazy. I recall moving, fighting, but . . . it was different. Less clear. Less . . . me."

I nodded, unsurprised. "You drank enough rice wine to fell an ox. I'm amazed you remember anything at all."

Tianyi's gaze dropped, her hands twisting nervously in her lap. "Did I . . . hurt you?"

I rubbed the faint bruise on my jaw, the memory of her drunken rampage still fresh in my mind. "You tried. But that's not what I'm worried about." I leaned forward, fixing her with a serious look. "Tianyi, your fighting style changed completely. You went from your usual style to something . . . wild. Almost like a brawler."

Her wings twitched, and she tilted her head in confusion. "A brawler?"

"Unrefined. Reactive. It wasn't controlled in the way you usually fight, but it was . . . effective. You were faster, more aggressive, and your strikes had more impact, but they lacked precision."

"That doesn't sound like me at all."

"It wasn't. At least, not the you I'm used to seeing. But it might not be a bad thing." I hesitated, weighing my next words. "Whatever happened last night, the alcohol seemed to change the way you fight. If we can figure out how to control that, it might give you an edge in combat."

Her eyes widened slightly. "You're saying I should drink more alcohol?"

"No! Not exactly," I groaned, realizing how dangerous that suggestion sounded. "What I'm saying is that we need to understand *why* the alcohol affected you that way. It's not just a matter of drinking; there's something deeper going on here. Maybe it's tied to your transformation into a human or how your body processes substances like alcohol now. We'll go bring this up with Elder Ming."

"But . . ."

She glanced over at Windy.

Tianyi hesitated, her blue-tinged eyes flickering with uncertainty as she glanced at Windy, still floating in the basin. His breathing had steadied, his scales had regained their luster, and the faint traces of corruption had finally disappeared. But he remained unconscious, his form eerily still despite the visible improvements.

"I don't want to leave him," she admitted softly, her antennae drooping slightly.

"Nothing will happen to him," I reassured her firmly. "Yin Si will be here. She can keep watch."

At the mention of the spider, Tianyi lifted her head. A faint skittering noise echoed from the shadows, and sure enough, Yin Si emerged, her multiple eyes gleaming in the dim morning light. There was a brief pause—a silent conversation I wasn't privy to—before the spider moved closer to Windy's basin, her posture almost protective. A thin strand of silk trailed behind her, securing the area like a silent barrier.

With one last glance at Windy, she followed me out of the shop and into the morning air.

The village was quieter than usual, the early dawn casting long shadows over the snow-dusted paths. Despite the stillness, the tension in the air was palpable. Disciples patrolled the village perimeter, their movements sharp and vigilant. Their pouches, once standard issue, now carried the Essence Purifying elixirs I had created. It was a subtle but necessary change—one that might save their lives if demonic cultivators attacked.

I let my gaze linger on the pouches as we walked. Jian Feng had insisted the disciples carry them after I revealed what the bloom could do. At the time, I had agreed without hesitation. But now, as I felt the empty space where my supply should have been, I realized the problem—I was running out of essences, and plants to extract them from.

We needed more.

For the village's safety, for the disciples' survival, and for whatever larger threat lay beyond the mountains. The Silent Moon had fallen overnight. If that wasn't a warning, I didn't know what was.

By the time we reached Elder Ming's home, Wang Jun and Lan-Yin were already there, their postures straightening at the sight of Tianyi.

"Tianyi?" Lan-Yin blinked in surprise. "Are you well enough to be out?"

"I am fine," she said simply, her wings folding behind her. "Kai has healed me."

"We might have found a way for her to grow stronger," I explained. "We wanted Elder Ming's insight."

At the mention of his name, Elder Ming stepped forward from the shade. His gaze was calm yet expectant as he looked between us. "Explain."

I summarized the events of the previous night—Tianyi's sudden burst of strength, the change in her fighting style, and the connection to alcohol. He listened in silence, his expression unreadable, before nodding slowly.

"An interesting theory," he murmured. "We must test it."

He turned his gaze to Wang Jun and me. "You two will spar against her."

I flexed my fingers, already feeling the weight of the coming challenge. We stood together, a short distance away from Tianyi. She had always been fast, but last night had proven she could be something else entirely. Something untethered. If that was the case, then we needed to see just how far this transformation could go.

Elder Ming raised his hand. "Begin."

Wang Jun charged, hammer swinging down hard. Tianyi didn't flinch. She watched, unmoving, until the instant his weapon neared her face.

Then, she was gone.

A blur of motion—too fast to track.

She reappeared low, sweeping Wang Jun's legs out from under him. He barely caught himself, but before he could react, her foot snapped up, striking his ribs with pinpoint precision. He staggered back, breath knocked from his lungs.

I moved in at the first opportunity, my palm alight with the Heavenly Flame Mantra.

She twisted around my strike, her balance effortless. A sharp kick drove into my side, perfectly timed to my momentum, sending me skidding back. She was noticeably better than before.

Had she improved in a few days? Or had that battle awakened something in her?

"Enough." Elder Ming raised his hand.

Wang Jun recovered, his grip tightening around his hammer as he adjusted his stance. "And I thought I was going to catch up . . ."

Tianyi landed lightly on her feet, her wings fluttering once before folding against her back. Unlike last night, there was no erratic wildness in her movements. She was completely in control, calculating and precise.

I clenched my fists. How had she ended up so badly injured in the first place? If she was this strong now, just how terrifying had the demonic cultivators been to leave her in such a state?

Elder Ming disappeared into his home for a moment, and when he returned, he held a small ceramic cup filled with clear liquid. He extended it toward Tianyi.

"Rice wine," he stated simply. "Not as strong as Master Qiang's, but still potent enough."

I frowned, rubbing the faint ache on my jaw from last night's chaos. "Elder Ming, I don't know if that's a good idea. Perhaps we should start her off with—"

"That was because she consumed an unfiltered, high-proof concoction. That blacksmith doesn't know the first thing about subtlety. This is a far weaker mixture, properly distilled. The effects will be different."

Wang Jun scratched his head. "I would defend Master Qiang here, but . . . Elder Ming's right. He's always liked his spirits strong. Even I can't have more than a cup or two."

Tianyi glanced at me, then back at the cup, her antennae twitching slightly. Without further hesitation, she took it from Elder Ming's hands and brought it to her lips. Her throat bobbed as she downed the contents in one go, her expression unreadable as she lowered the cup.

Elder Ming nodded approvingly. "Good. Now, resume the spar. Let's see if we can observe any changes."

Wang Jun and I exchanged a brief look before taking our positions. Tianyi stood opposite us, her wings still and folded neatly against her back. For a few moments, nothing seemed different. She bounced lightly on the balls of her feet, shifting into a familiar stance.

Then she moved.

Wang Jun barely had time to react before Tianyi struck. Her fist connected with his stomach in a precise, almost surgical strike, and he crumpled immediately, his body folding over her extended knuckles before he hit the ground hard. The breath rushed out of him in a single pained gasp.

I stiffened.

She turned to me next, her blue-tinged eyes locking onto mine with a sharpness I hadn't seen before. Then, she advanced.

Her movements were different now—not just fast, but invasive. She was closing the distance deliberately, forcing me into close-quarters combat, an area I usually avoided in favor of mid-range strikes. I pivoted, throwing a quick palm strike, but she ducked beneath it, her body swaying in a way that made her movements unpredictable.

I tried again, this time adjusting my timing, but she twisted at the last second, my attack grazing harmlessly past her shoulder. Before I could react, she drove her foot forward in a sweeping kick, catching me right at the ankles.

My balance faltered, and I was falling.

I caught myself with one arm, barely stopping my full weight from crashing down. But the Black Tortoise Tribulation made this a losing battle—my body was heavier than before, each motion requiring more effort than I was used to. Even with qi reinforcing my limbs, the strain was immense.

Tianyi didn't hesitate. She shifted, her foot already moving to land another strike while I was still vulnerable.

But before she could follow through, Wang Jun lunged in, his hammer swinging low. Tianyi snapped her head toward him just in time, leaping back as his weapon slammed into the ground where she had been standing a heartbeat ago.

The brief opening gave me a chance to roll back to my feet, my stance immediately shifting back into readiness. Tianyi exhaled sharply, her gaze flicking between us before she swayed slightly in place, her posture looser than before.

"Enough," Elder Ming called, stepping forward. "The spar is over."

We all froze in place. Tianyi tilted her head slightly, her antennae twitching as she turned toward Elder Ming.

"Can you understand me?" he asked evenly.

For a moment, I worried if she'd attack in a drunken rampage. The Village Head wouldn't survive an attack from the uncontrolled strike of a drunk spirit beast at the Essence Awakening stage.

She blinked and then nodded, though her movements were slightly sluggish. A moment later, she swayed again, catching herself just before stumbling.

Elder Ming studied Tianyi carefully, his sharp eyes narrowing slightly as she steadied herself. The slight unsteadiness was noticeable, but not nearly as bad as last night's uncontrolled rampage.

"Sit," he commanded, gesturing toward where he was sitting. "Drink some water."

Tianyi obeyed, moving to the bench and accepting the cup Wang Jun handed her.

Elder Ming stroked his beard, exhaling through his nose. "I have seen this before."

I blinked. "You have?"

He nodded. "A constitution like hers. I once witnessed a cultivator in a tournament who possessed something similar—what is often called a drunken fighter's constitution."

I let out a sharp laugh. "That's a real thing?"

"Indeed. It is rare, but not unheard of. Though, in Tianyi's case, her transformation into a human may have altered it in ways I cannot predict."

Tianyi's antennae twitched as she lowered the cup of water. "Drunken . . . fighter?"

Elder Ming nodded. "It is a unique constitution that allows one to fight with unpredictable movements when under the effects of alcohol. The more they drink, the more erratic—and dangerous—they become. But it is a double-edged sword."

I frowned. "Double-edged how?"

He leaned forward slightly, his gaze unwavering. "The tournament fighter I witnessed had full control over his abilities because his alcohol was specially refined—it granted him strength and clarity in battle. However, the nature of this constitution is unstable. The effects are not linear. The more alcohol one consumes, the more unpredictable their movements become. But with that unpredictability comes a loss of precision. What you saw just now is a controlled state. But if she were to drink more . . ."

I glanced at Tianyi. She was still swaying slightly, her posture much looser than usual, but her gaze was sharp, focused. This was nothing like the chaos of last night.

She bit her lip, her wings twitching slightly. "So . . . it's not just random?"

"No." Elder Ming's voice was firm. "Your instincts adjust. You fight differently, relying on reactions rather than conscious thought. Against an opponent who has never faced such a style, it is overwhelming. But to a prepared opponent . . . it becomes a liability."

Wang Jun rubbed his chin. "Meaning if she drinks too much, she won't just lose control—she'll be easier to read."

"Exactly," Elder Ming said. "A skilled opponent would recognize the shift and adjust their strategy accordingly. The key to mastering this constitution is not in drinking more, but in knowing how much to drink. It is not a simple power—it requires discipline."

Tianyi was quiet for a long moment, her fingers tightening around the ceramic cup. "Then . . . I should avoid drinking?"

Elder Ming shook his head. "Not necessarily. It is a tool, one that can be sharpened like any other skill. But you must know when to use it. And when to stop."

I crossed my arms. "So what you're saying is that Tianyi has a new ability, but if she abuses it, she'll be just as likely to get herself killed."

"Cultivation itself is full of double-edged swords," Elder Ming pointed out. "She is not an exception to the rule."

I let out a slow breath. It made sense, but it was still hard to wrap my head around. A fighting style that relied on alcohol . . . it sounded absurd. But I had just witnessed it firsthand. And the implications . . .

I turned to Tianyi. "How do you feel right now?"

She tilted her head slightly. "Strange. But . . . clearer than before. Not like last night. Closer to what I felt when I fought against the shadow."

"That's because this time, you drank a controlled amount," Elder Ming said. "Your instincts sharpened, but your mind remained intact. If you continue training with it, you may learn how to balance the two."

Tianyi was silent for a long time. Then she exhaled softly. ". . . I see."

She frowned, her antennae twitching slightly. "If I train this ability, will it strengthen me?"

Elder Ming nodded, his expression measured. "Yes. It will undoubtedly become a powerful skill once you learn to harness it."

Tianyi absorbed his words in silence, her wings shifting slightly. She looked down at the empty cup in her hands, her fingers pressing lightly against the ceramic.

"Then I will learn."

There was no hesitation in her voice. No bravado. Just quiet determination.

For some reason, that made me feel lighter.

As heavy as everything felt right now—the endless list of things I needed to do, the uncertainty of what lay ahead—I wasn't alone in this.

Tianyi was training to become stronger. Wang Jun, Lan-Yin, and everybody in the village too. Even the disciples carried the elixirs I had made, a quiet reminder that they trusted my alchemy to protect them, preparing and learning about the threat around us.

It was easy to feel like I had to do everything myself, to bear the burden of every crisis. But that wasn't true, was it?

I exhaled slowly, the tension in my chest loosening just a little.

I didn't have to do this alone.

CHAPTER TWENTY-THREE

Between Hunger and Preparation

"Sorry, Xiao Bao," I said, shaking my head. "I'm out of mint. I thought I had enough, but I went through it faster than expected. Tell your mother I'll have more in a few days, but I need time to grow a new batch."

The boy's face scrunched up, clearly disappointed, but he nodded. "Okay, I'll tell her!" Then he turned and ran out of the shop, disappearing into the crisp winter morning.

I sighed, leaning against the counter, my fingers tapping against the worn wood. This was happening more and more.

Despite the latent qi in the village making my garden flourish beyond normal standards, it still wasn't enough to keep up with my consumption rate. Herbs that used to last me months now barely made it past a few weeks. Between refining pills, making salves, and distributing them among my friends, my stock had thinned far too quickly.

And that was only the common ingredients.

The Golden Bamboo was the one exception, its growth rate incredible—so long as I provided it with yang essence. The sturdy, radiant stalks thrived in the enhanced qi, stretching higher by the day. But even that was a problem. My supply of yang essence was running dangerously low. If I didn't gather more soon, the bamboo would go inert.

I rubbed my temple. I needed more herbs. More resources. More time.

If we were going to survive the winter, if we were going to defend ourselves against whatever was looming over us, we needed more than just luck. We needed stability.

I felt a pang of hunger and looked down at my stomach. Perhaps it was thanks to my body reaching the Qi Initiation stage, but I didn't need to eat as often anymore. Food still nourished me, but the raw need for it had dulled, replaced by the steady flow of qi within my body.

It was the same with sleep. I still rested, but exhaustion didn't grip me like it once did. Before, a day of labor in the shop or a night spent refining pills would leave me sluggish and aching the next morning. Now, I could go longer, push further, and recover faster. The Black Tortoise Tribulation had hardened my body, and cultivation had reshaped it into something . . . different.

Still, hunger hadn't disappeared entirely. It was just more of an afterthought, something I only noticed when I stopped moving long enough to pay attention.

And right now, I noticed it.

I exhaled, running a hand through my hair. *I should grab something to eat.* With that in mind, I went down to the village in search of food. Past the square, and into the docks.

The coastline was quieter than usual.

Once-flowing water turned into jagged sheets of ice, the sea frozen over in large patches. Normally bustling, the docks had now slowed to a crawl as anglers adjusted to the seasonal shift. Despite that, a sizable pile of fresh fish still sat on the wooden planks, their scales glistening under the pale morning light.

The villagers haggled and exchanged coin. Winter may have slowed things down, but it hadn't stopped them.

I spotted Tie Niu near the edge of the dock, standing beside a pile of neatly arranged nets. He was an older fisherman, one of the few who had been doing this long before I was even born. His hands were calloused, his face lined with age, but his posture was firm, his movements steady as he pulled in the last of his morning catch.

"Three carp, please," I said as I approached, glancing at the fish still flopping weakly in his nets.

Tie Niu grinned, nodding as he reached down to grab them. "Good timing. Just pulled these in before you arrived. You know, for a while, I thought we'd be out of luck this winter. Ice makes fishing a nightmare."

I looked at the considerable pile of fish still being sorted. "Doesn't look like you're having much trouble."

The old fisherman chuckled, lifting one of his nets. "That's thanks to this."

I raised an eyebrow. "Your net?"

He nodded, tapping the intricate knots along the rope. "It's different now. That ol' Interface taught me a new way to tie it—better tension, stronger hold, and it lets me pull in more fish at once. And that's not all."

Tie Niu leaned in slightly, his voice lowering as if sharing a secret. "I can feel where the fish are now. When they gather under the ice, I know where to cast the net."

I blinked. "You gained a skill?"

He grinned, pulling up a section of the net, displaying the smooth, tight weaving of the rope. "That's what I'm saying! Took me decades to learn how to fish properly, but after one o' those quests, I learned a technique I never would've dreamed of. I even started catching fish under the ice before anyone else did. It'll keep my family fed through the worst of the winter."

I exhaled, shaking my head in amusement. "So what, you uncovered the Dao of Fishing?"

Tie Niu laughed heartily, slapping his knee. "You joke, but maybe! The Interface works in mysterious ways. All I know is that I'm grateful. It's making life a little easier—just in time for the coldest months."

I nodded, taking the wrapped carp from his hands. "Good. We're going to need all the help we can get."

Tie Niu's grin faded slightly as he studied me. "That why you're down here? Looking for supplies?"

"That's part of it," I admitted. "Even I'm running out of herbs for the garden. I also wanted to see if the merchants had any news. Still no word from the city?"

He shook his head, expression darkening. "Not a whisper. No shipments, no travelers, no letters. The trade routes are dead silent."

That wasn't good.

I exhaled slowly, shifting the fish in my hands. "Thank you. Stay safe."

"You too, Kai. Take care o' yourself!"

As I walked back up the docks, my mind churned through the implications.

No supplies from the city. No word from the merchants. My herbs were dwindling faster than I could replace them.

I had options. I just needed to figure out the best one before the situation got worse.

After quickly reaching home, I set the carp down on the counter, rolled my shoulders, and considered my next steps.

If I wanted to keep up with demand, I had to experiment with Golden Bamboo-infused hybrids. The idea had been stewing in the back of my mind; using the bamboo's powerful yang properties to enhance the growth and medicinal effects of other plants.

If it worked, I could create fast-growing herbs that were both potent and sustainable. But the problem was choosing the right ones.

Golden Bamboo wasn't limitless. Every stalk I infused would take a toll on my already dwindling supply of yang essence. If I wasted even a few batches on poor candidates, I'd be left with nothing but inert stalks and a list of regrets.

I sighed, rubbing my chin. Which ones would be most viable?

Rice could benefit from faster growth, but would it be fast *enough?* Lettuce and amaranth were other prospects, but they came with their own pros and cons to consider.

I'd have to test them one by one. But first . . . food.

I lifted the lid of my Two-Star Pagoda Pill Furnace. The cauldron pulsed with faint, refined energy, a far cry from the battered pots I used to cook with.

I smirked. If the high-and-mighty alchemists from the great sects saw me using a pill furnace to cook fish, they'd probably faint on the spot.

But why waste good tools? This furnace was leagues above anything I'd used before, and it could regulate heat far more precisely than an open flame. If I could brew elixirs in it, I could damn well cook a decent meal too.

I cleaned the carp quickly, filleting the meat with precise cuts before placing it into the heated furnace. A touch of qi adjusted the temperature, keeping the heat at an optimal level as the fish sizzled.

A handful of crushed herbs went into the pot, the aroma rising as they blended into a fragrant broth. With a few more adjustments, the liquid took on a rich golden hue.

Within minutes, the dish was perfect.

I ladled a portion into a bowl, setting it down carefully before preparing another; this one with more broth and no fish.

Right on cue, Tianyi stepped into the room.

She paused, her antennae twitching slightly as she inhaled the scent of the meal. Her gaze flickered to the fish, then to the broth. She made no move toward the meat.

I wasn't surprised. Despite gaining a human form, she still had no interest in eating flesh. She could eat fruit, drink tea, and sip on medicinal concoctions without issue, but meat never appealed to her.

I slid the bowl of broth toward her. "Here."

She nodded in thanks, settling down beside me as she took a careful sip.

For a while, we ate in silence. The warm broth settled in my stomach, taking the edge off my hunger. Across from me, Tianyi dipped her fingers into the bowl, scooping up small sips like she was more familiar with drinking nectar than handling a spoon.

Her gaze flickered toward Windy.

He remained still in the basin, his injuries gone, the scars faint reminders of the battle he had endured. His breathing was steady, his body no longer trembling.

But he still hadn't woken up.

Tianyi lowered her hand, the last drop of broth slipping from her fingers. "He's healing."

"I know."

She turned to me, her eyes sharp. "But will he wake?"

I hesitated. I didn't know.

Everything pointed toward yes. His body had fully recovered. His qi was stable. The corruption had been purged. By all logic, he should wake up any day now.

And yet . . .

I clenched my jaw, shoving the thought aside. "He will."

Tianyi studied me, her antennae twitching slightly. But she said nothing more, simply turning back toward Windy and staying by his side.

I set my empty bowl down. I couldn't stay idle.

Tonight, I needed to work.

If I wanted my hybrid plants to be viable, I had to test them now.

The flickering candlelight cast shifting shadows across the worn pages of the ledger, the faint scratch of ink against parchment the only sound filling the dimly lit room.

Across from the desk, the messenger shrank under the blind man's eyes.

"It is bold of the magistrate," the bookseller murmured, his fingers idly tracing the spine of a book, his sightless eyes fixed ahead. "To come here again, demanding my help."

The messenger swallowed hard, glancing at the door as if gauging the possibility of escape. "The magistrate would not make such a request lightly," he said, seeming to struggle to keep his voice steady.

He tilted his head slightly, as if considering the words. "No? I seem to recall a similar conversation recently. What happened to the great crisis of the Silent Moon Sect? The magistrate was certain that those elders were a threat. Now they're gone. And yet, here you are, with a new problem."

The messenger hesitated, shifting on his feet. "The elders were a threat. But they are nothing compared to what we face now."

"And how is that my problem?" His fingers drummed lightly against the surface of the desk. "The magistrate should take this matter to the sects, not waste his time sending errand boys to disturb an old man."

"We are already reaching out to the sects," the messenger insisted, his desperation showing. "But this is bigger than any one group. The demonic cultivator sightings are increasing. It's only a matter of time before Crescent Bay City is struck. We need—"

The man never got to finish his sentence.

He felt a shift in the air.

The bookseller had not moved. His expression remained serene, his fingers still resting lightly atop the book. And yet, an unmistakable pressure settled into the space between them, suffocating in its silence.

The messenger trembled. A warning.

And a promise.

"I will say this once," the blind man murmured. *"Leave."*

The messenger stumbled back, his breath coming in short, rapid bursts. But he had just enough courage left to stammer, "I will return. The city will need you soon, whether or not you admit it."

With that, he turned and all but fled from the shop, his boots thudding against the wooden floor as he disappeared into the streets.

The pressure vanished the moment he was gone.

The bookseller let out a long sigh. His fingers, which had remained steady throughout the conversation, twitched slightly.

He was tired.

Once, he had believed he would be left in peace.

That the weight of his past would remain buried beneath the dust of forgotten records, lost among the ink-stained ledgers and brittle parchment that lined his shop.

He had been foolish to believe it.

No matter how far one ran, no matter how deeply one buried themselves in the quiet corners of the world—the Jianghu always called.

And it did not care if one wished to answer.

He rose with deliberate slowness, his hands moving automatically to straighten the desk, smoothing the edge of an already-perfectly aligned scroll. A habit. A meaningless act of control.

Then, with a resigned sigh, he turned and made his way toward the back of the shop.

The air was cooler here, where the scent of ink and parchment faded, replaced by the faintest trace of old metal and lacquered wood. Shelves of untouched tomes stood in neat rows, their contents undisturbed for years. Beyond them, tucked beneath a forgotten counter, a box waited.

He knelt before it, running his fingers lightly across its surface. Dust clung to the lacquered wood, the once-polished sheen dulled by time.

For a long moment, he did nothing.

Then, with a quiet click, he undid the latch and lifted the lid.

Twin hook swords lay within.

Slightly curved, their edges still gleamed beneath the dim candlelight. Small bells dangled from the hilts, their delicate chimes long since silenced by dust and time.

His fingers hovered over them. He did not touch them.

It would be so easy.

The magistrate would not give up. That much was certain. And soon, when reason and pleading failed, they would threaten him.

And yet, even now, staring down at the weapons of his past, he felt . . . nothing.

No pull. No desire.

Just exhaustion.

With a slow, deliberate motion, he closed the lid. The latch clicked back into place, sealing the past where it belonged.

He rose to his feet, dusting off his robes. Then, to himself, he muttered.

"It has been a long time since I left the city."

His sightless gaze turned toward the doorway, where the wind whistled softly through the cracks in the wood.

Perhaps it was time for a change.

CHAPTER TWENTY-FOUR

Millet and Martial Fusion

"Behold!"

I extended my hands dramatically, presenting the small clay jar before me. The morning light caught the rim, casting a faint sheen over the golden grains nestled inside.

Lan-Yin and Wang Jun exchanged a glance, unimpressed. Their gazes flicked to the jar, then back to me, waiting for an explanation.

"Is this like that red rice you made before?" Lan-Yin finally asked. "That was pretty tasty, actually. The Verdant Lotus disciples loved it."

"Sort of," I said, barely containing my grin. "But this is different. Last night, after much deliberation, testing, and research, I finally settled on millet as the prime candidate for a hybrid crop."

"Millet?" Wang Jun frowned. "Why millet?"

"Because," I said, tapping the jar, "it grows quickly, it doesn't require as much attention as rice, and it's already a staple crop here. But more importantly, I infused it with something special."

"Special?"

I nodded. "Golden Bamboo. I extracted its essence and infused it into these seeds."

That caught their attention. Wang Jun's posture straightened, and Lan-Yin's eyes gleamed with intrigue.

"Golden Bamboo is incredibly rich in yang energy," I explained. "So its properties, like rapid growth, resilience, and body-enhancement of those who consume it, would apply to it. In theory, this millet should not only grow much faster than normal, but it should also be resistant to the winter cold. The yang energy should give it just enough warmth to survive the frost."

A beat of silence.

Then, Wang Jun exhaled through his nose. "You're telling me you made a spirit millet?"

I grinned. "Essentially, yes."

Lan-Yin picked up the jar, tilting it slightly to watch the golden grains shift inside. "And you think it'll work?"

"I won't know for sure until we plant it," I admitted. "Which is why I'm going to plant it in my greenhouse. But my space is limited, and I need to see how it performs in different conditions." I glanced between them. "Would you two be willing to plant some in your gardens? I also plan to distribute some to other families to test its viability on a larger scale."

Wang Jun shrugged. "I don't see why not. My mother will probably appreciate it more than I will."

Lan-Yin hummed in thought before nodding. "If it can grow in winter and help people, it's worth testing."

I clapped my hands together. "Perfect! I knew I could count on you both. Such wisdom, such foresight! Truly, I am a man of remarkable generosity and vision!"

Wang Jun rolled his eyes. "You're really proud of yourself, aren't you?"

As we walked outside of the Soaring Swallow to show off my newest invention to the rest of Gentle Wind Village, the reaction was immediate.

When word spread that I had cultivated a crop that might grow through winter, the villagers gathered in the square with hopeful curiosity. Their fields lay dormant, their food stores rationed for the cold months ahead, and the idea of a winter harvest—no matter how small—was enough to bring a spark of excitement.

"If this millet works," one of the elders murmured, "we won't have to rely so much on stored grains."

"Even if it only grows a little," another added, "it's better than nothing."

Elder Wen, one of the more experienced farmers, stepped forward, eyeing the jar in my hands. He studied the grains with an expert's eye before finally speaking.

"The idea is sound," he said. "But the fields need time to rest. We just finished harvesting. Even if the grains grow, the soil might not be ready."

I nodded. "I understand. Ideally, we'd rotate the crops to prevent exhausting the land. Give one field a season to recover while another is planted. But with the winter being longer than expected, and no supplies coming in, I figured this would tide us over."

Wang Jun furrowed his brow. "Rotate?"

Ah, right. He wasn't as familiar with crop rotation as I was.

"Hmm . . . If you keep hammering the same piece of metal without letting it rest, right? It becomes brittle and weak. The land is the same. If we use the same field for every harvest, the soil loses its strength. That's why farmers let fields rest for a season before planting again."

Understanding dawned on his face. "Ah. So if we keep planting in the same spot, the soil gets weaker?"

"Exactly."

Elder Wen nodded approvingly. "You've done your reading."

"I try," I said with a humble bow. "But I was hoping we could test the millet in a smaller section at least."

Instead of answering, Elder Wen knelt, reaching past the layer of snow and into the soil. When he withdrew his hand, his fingers were coated in dark, rich earth.

He frowned. "Perhaps we won't have to worry about it right now."

"Why?"

"This soil . . . it shouldn't be this rich so soon after the last harvest. It should be weaker, drained from months of growing crops. And yet . . ." He crumbled a bit between his fingers. "It's full of vitality. Almost like it's been resting for years."

A realization dawned on me, sending a quiet thrill through my thoughts. The ambient qi in the village. It wasn't just helping cultivation. It was enhancing the environment too.

"Then we should try planting," I said. "If the soil is this fertile, it might support a winter crop after all."

Elder Wen nodded slowly. "It's worth a shot. I'll oversee a test plot. If your millet grows as you claim, we'll know soon enough."

The village square buzzed with renewed energy as Elder Wen relayed instructions to the other farmers. A test plot would be established near the outskirts, where the soil had been least disturbed, ensuring the experiment wouldn't interfere with their main fields.

I handed out small pouches of golden millet to each volunteer, careful to portion it out evenly. The seeds gleamed faintly in the light, a subtle sheen of yang energy lingering around them. Even those who knew nothing of alchemy or qi could sense something unusual about them.

As the village began its quiet preparations for the millet experiment, I took a deep breath, letting the crisp winter air fill my lungs.

This was good. This was progress.

But I had one more stop to make.

The newly built courtyard for the sect disciples stood as a testament to the sect artisans' craftsmanship and Li Wei's talent. The wooden beams were sturdy, the roofing flawless, and the courtyard itself had been arranged with both practicality and aesthetics in mind. It blended seamlessly with the natural surroundings, a subtle but undeniable improvement to the village.

I paused for a moment, admiring the work before knocking on the door.

Jian Feng answered, looking as tired as I expected. His usual composed demeanor was intact, but there was a heaviness to him that hadn't been there when he first arrived. Losing three disciples in the forest had left its mark.

"You're here early," he said, stepping aside to let me in.

"Sorry for intruding, but I really do need your help."

He gave a dry chuckle, leading me to the courtyard. "Of course, of course."

There was only so much I could learn from fighting Lan-Yin and Wang Jun. I needed training partners who can actually push me. Tianyi matched that description. But she couldn't hold back—her nature as a spirit beast made every fight an all-or-nothing exchange. The most she could compromise was not bisecting me with her lethal moves. But these disciples? They had control. They could lower themselves to my level, force me to refine my techniques without completely overwhelming me.

A few disciples remained in the courtyard. Most were patrolling or helping in the village. The ones here were training or meditating.

Jian Feng stepped back, motioning toward the open space. "Three free moves," he said. "Use them wisely."

I didn't waste time.

A controlled pulse of Heavenly Flame Mantra ignited along my palm—not enough to leave lasting damage, but enough to make each strike painful if it landed. I launched forward, striking with precise bursts of flame, each attack carefully measured.

Jian Feng deflected my first two strikes with ease, his movements fluid, effortless. The third strike came closer, a feint leading into a real attack, but he still evaded, twisting just enough to avoid the hit before countering with a swift palm strike to my chest.

I barely deflected it, skidding back a step.

Even while holding back, he was leagues ahead. Our first spar from back then wasn't indicative of our true abilities. Although it was easy to say I was handicapped with the Black Tortoise Tribulation, it was hard to say whether I could beat him even without being weighed down. A lifetime of martial training wasn't that easy to overcome, even with the advantage of the Heavenly Interface.

Thinking otherwise was arrogant; the equivalent of me looking down on the Jianghu.

He stepped on my foot, stopping my momentum and drawing me forward as his fist stopped right in front of my face.

On a sharp exhale, I rolled my shoulders. "I yield. I learned well."

Jian Feng tilted his head. "Satisfied?"

"For now," I said. "But I want to try something else in the next round."

He crossed his arms. "What is it?"

I hesitated. "I don't know if it'll work if I tell you beforehand."

His eyes narrowed slightly, but after a moment, he nodded. "All right. Let's see what you've got."

The watching disciples murmured among themselves, curiosity piqued. I reached for my satchel, tightening the strap as I adjusted my stance.

The quest's requirement to learn the Combat Anticipation Array echoed in my mind.

> —*Use the Refinement Simulation Technique on an alchemical reaction mid-combat to create an advantage. (0/1)*

I had struggled to make sense of it before. But now, after days of reflection, I understood.

The quest hadn't been asking anything new of me. It reminded me of something I didn't use properly.

If I had used this during the battle with Wei Long, could I have changed the outcome? Could I have tipped the scales before I needed Tian Zhan to rescue us?

I had made a mistake—one I wouldn't make again.

The spar began.

This time, I wasn't just Kai the martial artist, nor Kai the alchemist.

For the first time, I would fight as both.

Jian Feng's stance remained steady, his expression unreadable as he studied me. The other disciples were silent, their curiosity clear.

What was I planning?

I reached into my satchel and pulled out a small vial, rolling it between my fingers. The liquid inside sloshed slightly, dark and viscous.

Jian Feng's eyes narrowed. "The Ambrosia of Radiant Dawn?"

I smiled. His memory was sharp, to remember my using potions to enhance myself against Ping Hai.

"Nope."

Before he could question me further, I threw the vial down at his feet.

The glass shattered with a soft crack, releasing a dark liquid that quickly pooled on the courtyard floor. Jian Feng glanced at it, wary, but I gave him no time to think.

I lunged.

Flame flickered around my palm, controlled and sharp, striking toward his midsection. Jian Feng sidestepped, his movement swift and effortless. His foot touched the liquid for barely a second before he twisted away.

Not enough time.

I pressed forward, driving him into an exchange of strikes. The familiar wall of experience met me head-on. No matter how fast I moved, no matter how much I refined my techniques, Jian Feng's responses were effortless, built on years of dedicated training. Even with the Black Tortoise Tribulation weighing me down, the gap between us was undeniable.

But that was fine.

Because I wasn't trying to beat him head-on.

I reached into my satchel again, retrieving a second vial. I let it slip from my fingers.

This time, as it fell, I activated the Refinement Simulation Technique.

A burst of understanding filled my mind.

The first vial, nightshade flowers and dried wood fungus, blended into an oil that clung to surfaces.

The second vial; ginger essence, volatile and reactive.

By themselves, harmless. But together?

My mind visualized the interaction before it even occurred.

The instant the ginger essence met the first mixture, the conflicting natures clashed. A thick, acrid smoke erupted from the impact point, curling into the air in a dense, choking cloud.

I withdrew just before it occurred.

Jian Feng was a moment too late.

He emerged from the smoke coughing, his stance momentarily unsteady. His eyes were squeezed shut, reflexively protecting themselves from the irritants in the air.

Opportunity.

I surged forward, weaving through the dissipating cloud. My leg swept out, catching his ankle just as he adjusted his footing. He tried to recover, his instincts still razor-sharp, but the moment of disorientation made the difference.

I pressed my palm forward, stopping just short of his chest.

Silence.

Jian Feng coughed once more, rubbing his eyes as he blinked rapidly. He exhaled through his nose, clearing out the last traces of the smoke, before glancing at the palm inches from his ribs.

Then he let out a soft chuckle.

"I yield," he admitted.

I lowered my hand, stepping back as the smoke fully dissipated. The gathered disciples murmured among themselves, processing what had just happened.

"Clever," Jian Feng continued, rubbing his jaw. "You're using potions to create an advantage mid-battle. Alchemical combat."

I nodded, panting. The Refinement Simulation Technique was more than just a tool for the furnace—it could be a tool for battle. I had been limiting myself, seeing alchemy and combat as separate disciplines. But they weren't. Hadn't the final round of the Grand Alchemy Gauntlet been proof?

Whether through pills to enhance my reserves or concoctions to tilt a fight in my favor, alchemy was another weapon in my arsenal.

I just had to wield it properly.

> *Quest: Beyond the Memory Palace has been completed.*
> *Due to your status as Interface Manipulator,*
> *your rewards will be adjusted accordingly.*

CHAPTER TWENTY-FIVE

Awakenings

The quest reward was relatively simple. Contrary to receiving a new skill, it just adjusted my current one.

> *Refinement Simulation Technique (Level 1): A technique that enhances both alchemical refinement and combat adaptability by simulating complex processes in real time. Originally developed for alchemy, it predicts how ingredients will interact based on past experiences, allowing precise adjustments mid-refinement. This principle extends to martial combat, enabling the user to anticipate an opponent's actions by analyzing past encounters and reacting with a reflexive counter tailored to the situation.*

All this time, I had been treating the Memory Palace Technique and Refinement Simulation Technique as separate entities—one for storing and reviewing information and the other for predicting alchemical interactions. But if this new skill allowed me to simulate martial exchanges as well, didn't that mean it wasn't an isolated ability?

They were intertwined.

The Memory Palace was the foundation. Storage, organization, and retrieval of information. The foundation for everything else. Its power wasn't just in perfect recall but in how quickly it could sift through vast amounts of data, retrieving whatever I needed at a moment's notice.

The Refinement Simulation built upon that. It wasn't just prediction; it was a specialized application of the stored knowledge, focusing on real-time interactions, whether alchemical or martial.

It made sense now. The Memory Palace's basic simulation abilities were rudimentary, visualizing a simple object, recalling past events and simulating them within my mind. But the moment it branched into something more focused, it enhanced the ability to actively process information rather than just retrieve it.

If this were true, then wouldn't upgrading the Memory Palace Technique improve everything that came from it? Wouldn't it refine the Refinement Simulation Technique as well?

Like a murky stream becoming purified after the source itself is cleaned.

I grabbed two more vials from my shelf, rolling them between my fingers before tossing them outside my house. One after the other, they shattered against the ground, releasing their contents in twin bursts of liquid.

I felt it unfolding in my mind before it happened. A ripple of predictions formed, outlining not just the effects of the concoction, but its range and impact on the surroundings.

The splattered mixture darkened the ground, spreading outward in a predictable pattern, its fumes dispersing at a controlled rate. I knew, down to the second, how long it would linger.

I let out a low whistle. "That's a neat trick."

But it didn't end there.

Out of curiosity, I turned my gaze toward Tianyi. She was in the distance, moving through one of her routines, her body a blur of sharp, efficient motion.

The technique activated again.

It pulled from my existing knowledge of her fights, overlaying patterns based on what I had seen before. Her movements, her attack sequences, the way she shifted between strikes—it was all cataloged, replayed, and analyzed in real time.

She was predictable.

A small chuckle escaped me. Not that Tianyi was lacking skill—it was just that she was incredibly efficient in her attacks, meaning she repeated the same movements often.

But . . . what did that really mean for me?

I exhaled, shaking my head with a wry smile. Prediction meant nothing if I couldn't react fast enough.

Even knowing exactly what she was going to do wouldn't save me if I lacked the speed to counter it in time. Right now, if we fought, I'd see the hit coming—but I'd still get struck three times over before I could capitalize on it.

This wasn't an invincible technique.

But it was a boon. Honing my instincts with the experience I accumulated, it'd only become more effective the longer I trained and the more I learned.

Despite my satisfaction, a part of me remained restless.

With enough time and effort, I would become strong. My entire skill set was built around long-term growth, refining my abilities bit by bit until I reached the peak of my potential. But being strong in the future wasn't enough.

I needed to be strong now.

I tempered my impatience, reminding myself that I was doing everything I could. I was empowering myself and my friends, giving us every advantage possible. Yet, there was always that nagging temptation in the back of my mind—the desire to find a shortcut, to grasp at a way to leap forward in power within a brief period.

My eyes flickered to the tightly sealed container in my storage, where the extracted Bloodsoul Bloom essence sat untouched.

I refused to use it in medicine—it was too dangerous. The risk of corruption, of unforeseen consequences, was too high. But as an alchemist, I couldn't ignore its properties forever. If I didn't intend to ingest it, then I needed to learn how to break it down, to strip it of its instability and weaponize it.

Just as that thought passed through my mind, a faint sound reached my ears.

A shuffle.

I stilled.

At first, I thought I had imagined it. But then it came again. A slow, dragging slither, followed by the unmistakable sound of a soft hiss.

My breath caught. My head snapped toward the area where Windy had been recovering.

He was awake.

For the first time in what felt like an eternity, Windy stirred, shifting sluggishly as his blue-tinged eyes blinked open. A rasping exhale left his body, his tongue flickering weakly from between his fangs.

My stomach lurched.

"Windy?" My voice came out unsteady, disbelieving. "You're awake?"

His gaze turned toward me slowly, clouded and unfocused. His body trembled slightly, his movements sluggish, as though he was still half-trapped in whatever state he had been in for so long.

Relief crashed over me in waves. Before I could think, I crossed the space between us and carefully scooped him into my arms.

"Hold on—Tianyi!" I called, my voice carrying through the house. "Tianyi, he's awake!"

I pressed Windy close to my chest, feeling the familiar coolness of his scales against my skin. "You're all right," I murmured, barely registering the way my voice wavered. "You're all right."

There was no response, but after a moment, he shifted slightly. His small head pressed against me, rubbing against my robes with a slow, deliberate motion.

I mistook it for affection at first.

Then he did it again. And again.

His rubbing grew more aggressive, to where I winced, shifting uncomfortably under the persistent pressure. "Windy—ow, stop that, you're—"

Then I saw it.

A section of his scales flaked away, peeling from his body.

My breath hitched as understanding dawned. "You're shedding."

Windy didn't slow down. If anything, he pressed harder, using my body as the main surface to rid himself of the old, damaged layer of his scales. I sucked in a breath, trying to bear the discomfort as the process continued. The sight was both unsettling and mesmerizing—large sheets of dull, faded scales sloughing off to reveal fresh, pristine layers underneath.

Tianyi arrived just as his molting finished. She froze in the doorway, her antennae twitching as she took in the sight before her. Then, without hesitation, she joined me, her hands carefully supporting Windy as the last remnants of his old skin peeled away.

When it was over, he was still for a moment, his breathing even and steady. His form, once frail and battered, was whole again. The scars remained—faint, silvery marks scattered across his pristine white scales—but his body no longer trembled with weakness.

Relief overwhelmed me all over again.

I hugged him tighter. "You're okay."

Tianyi didn't hesitate to follow suit. She wrapped her arms around him, pressing her forehead lightly against his scaled body.

For a long moment, the three of us remained like that.

Then, just as I was about to pull away, a soft chime echoed in my mind.

> *You have deepened your bond with the Spirit Beast Windy.*

I stiffened.

And then—

Something else flooded through me.

A sensation. A vague, foreign emotion, threading through my and Tianyi's feelings of relief and joy.

It wasn't coming from me.

It was coming from Windy.

And the emotion was . . .

Embarrassment.

I blinked, my arms still loosely wrapped around him.

Windy had gone completely still, and if I didn't know any better, I would've thought he was pretending to be dead. Tianyi pulled back slightly, tilting her head in confusion as she noticed the same strange energy radiating from him.

Slowly, I eased back, adjusting my grip so I could look at him properly. His scales were flawless now, his injuries long gone, his body moving with a newfound ease. His eyes, no longer clouded, gleamed with unmistakable intelligence as he stared up at me.

Then, without warning, he abruptly wriggled free from my arms, slipping onto the floor and coiling up tightly, his tail curling in a way that screamed flustered.

Tianyi and I exchanged glances.

". . . Windy?" I tried.

He refused to look at me.

A huff of air left him, and his tail flicked with barely contained mortification.

I blinked again before realization set in, and suddenly, I couldn't hold back my laughter.

"Don't worry, this young master forgives you for using him as a rubbing surfa—"

Windy's response was immediate. His tail snapped up and smacked me clean across the face.

The forge crackled with warmth as Wang Jun examined the serpent closely.

"He was in bad shape, but he looks . . . pretty good. Only a few scars, here and there."

"Yeah, well," I said, adjusting my grip. "That was after days in a coma, with Tianyi and me treating him every day. That would revive someone even from the dead."

Windy lifted his head with pride, flicking his tongue at Wang Jun in greeting. He seemed more . . . docile. He wasn't the most social animal, and he held himself with a hint of pride. But it looked as though the serpent had mellowed out.

Tianyi, however, was still unwilling to let him out of her sight. I caught her hovering slightly, her antennae twitching every time Windy moved even a little. She had always been lax, but right now, she was like a protective mother.

Though, judging by his status, he didn't need any protecting.

Name: Windy
Race: Wind Serpent (Aberrant)
Affinity: Wood and Metal
Cultivation Rank: Qi Initiation Stage—Rank 5
Special Abilities
Tail Whip: Delivers a swift and powerful tail strike infused with qi.
Paralyzing Venom: Injects venom that temporarily paralyzes the target.
Moonlight Empowerment: Gains increased power and vitality under the moonlight.
Predator's Insight: Perceive the most efficient paths to a lethal strike.
Illusory Motion Technique: A movement technique that creates afterimages and subtle distortions in your wake.

> *Bond Level: 3 (Close Companion)*—*Windy has formed a deep bond with you, displaying loyalty and commitment to your shared journey. His abilities may strengthen in response to your connection, and he will be more attuned to your emotions and needs. Additional abilities or enhancements may become available as your bond continues to grow.*

Two new skills, along with an increase in his cultivation rank.

Had Windy also experienced a bout of enlightenment during his battle against the demonic cultivators?

The thought made my grip tighten slightly. Every day, my abilities evolved. But my companions weren't falling behind. They were keeping pace, pushing their own boundaries just as I was.

I turned my gaze to Tianyi. Sure enough, when I pulled up her status, her own newly minted skill stood out.

> *Name: Tianyi*
> *Race: Mystical Butterfly*
> *Affinity: Wood*
> *Cultivation Rank: Essence Awakening Stage—Rank 1*
> *Special Abilities:*
> *Qi Haven: Transforms frequented areas into concentrated qi zones, boosting recovery and cultivation efficiency for those within its boundaries.*
> *Moonlight Empowerment: Gains increased power and vitality under the moonlight.*
> *Qi Siphon: Can absorb small amounts of qi from its surroundings to sustain itself.*
> *Qi Transfer: Can imbue living beings with energy by transferring its qi, providing a small boost to those who receive it.*
> *Qi Infusion: Infuse your body with qi, strengthening and making it faster.*
> *Drunken Constitution: A constitution that enhances one's ability to fight while intoxicated.*
>
> *Bond Level: 3 (Close Companion)*—*Tianyi has formed a deep bond with you, displaying loyalty and commitment to your shared journey. Her abilities may strengthen in response to your connection, and she will be more attuned to your emotions and needs. Additional abilities or enhancements may become available as your bond continues to grow.*

Wang Jun leaned back, folding his arms. "So, what now? You gonna announce it to the village?"

I shook my head. "Nope. Just thought you'd like to see for yourself. I'll show him off to the others later."

His lips twitched as he set his hammer down and killed the flame of the forge. "Well, I gotta admit, this is definitely worth celebrating."

I grinned, picking Windy up and letting him rest along my shoulders. "Then let's celebrate properly. At the Soaring Swallow!"

"Let's go!"

We had barely stepped out of the forge when Tianyi suddenly stilled. Her antennae twitched, and her wings fluttered slightly, as if sensing something.

I turned to follow her gaze.

Beyond the village outskirts, a group of figures emerged from the mist.

Even though the sky remained clear, winter's breath had thickened the air and made it hard to see. But as they drew closer, their outlines sharpened—thirty or so figures, moving steadily toward the village.

Immediately, I tensed.

"Who are they?"

I wasn't the only one. Wang Jun's stance shifted subtly, his fingers curling into fists. Windy's eyes narrowed into slits, watching the group intently from my shoulder.

But the tension eased slightly as I took in their movements.

They weren't advancing like enemies.

No aggression, no disciplined march. Their pace was weary, some figures leaning on others for support. Even from here, I could make out the distinct weight of exhaustion in their gait.

Refugees? Travelers?

Then I spotted him.

A familiar figure near the front.

Recognition struck like a hammer to the chest. My grip tightened on Windy, who flicked his tongue as if sensing my unease.

I exhaled slowly, steadying myself.

It seemed our quiet celebration would have to wait.

CHAPTER TWENTY-SIX

Walls That Do Not Protect

Their movements were too sluggish, their bodies hunched from exhaustion rather than battle readiness. These weren't bandits or wandering cultivators looking for trouble.

Still, caution was necessary.

I turned to Wang Jun. "Go get Elder Ming. Let him know what's happening."

He hesitated, gaze flicking between me and the approaching figures, then nodded and sprinted off. My attention shifted to Tianyi and Windy, both watching intently.

"You two stay here," I ordered, though I had a feeling Tianyi wouldn't listen if things went south. Windy flicked his tongue, his blue eyes narrowing slightly, but he didn't argue.

Several of the Verdant Lotus disciples on patrol had already begun moving, their sharp awareness proving itself as they stepped in to assess the situation. Among them was Jian Feng, one of the second-class disciples. He met my gaze as I approached, his posture rigid, hand resting lightly on his weapon.

"They're refugees," Jian Feng said before I could ask. "From Crescent Bay City."

I blinked, taken aback. "Crescent Bay? What happened?"

A man at the front of the group took a step forward. He was older, possibly in his forties, his face lined with fatigue. A crude bandage obscured one of his eyes, his posture unsteady but determined.

"We belong to the districts beyond the city wall," he said, his voice rough, likely from dehydration or strain. "The ones outside the protection of Crescent Bay's core. We've been facing attacks from demonic cultivators."

A cold weight settled in my gut. "Demonic cultivators?"

He nodded. "They come in waves. Unpredictable. Some nights, nothing. On other nights, whole families disappear. We tried to resist, but . . ." he gestured behind him to the ragged group. "We're not warriors. The city guards have abandoned us. They're moving inward to defend the wealthier districts, leaving us to fend for ourselves."

A murmur passed through the disciples, their expressions darkening.

"What about the sects?" I asked. "Crescent Bay has several. Why aren't they helping?"

The man let out a short, bitter laugh. "Some do. Some don't. The attacks are scattered, random. The sects only move when a pattern emerges, and since there isn't one, they're hesitant to commit forces to defend us." His gaze hardened. "Some just don't think we're worth saving."

My jaw clenched. This wasn't the first time I'd heard of sects prioritizing strategic interests over people's lives, but it still made my blood boil.

"But why come here?" I asked, trying to wrap my head around it. "Qingmu is much closer. Why didn't you seek refuge there?"

Before the man could respond, Elder Ming arrived with Wang Jun. The Village Head took in the scene quickly, his sharp gaze sweeping over the refugees. He didn't speak immediately, simply listening as the man explained further.

"We did go to Qingmu," the refugee admitted. "But they could only take so many. The most injured and weak were prioritized, and the rest of us were told to move on. We had nowhere else to go."

Elder Ming's expression remained unreadable. "Were you attacked on your way here?"

"No," the man shook his head. "We've been fortunate. The weather and lack of supplies have been our biggest threat."

Then, with great effort, he bowed, pressing his forehead to the cold earth. "Please . . . let us stay here. We do not know how much longer we can keep going."

I looked at the group again, really looked at them. I had been so focused on their words that I hadn't fully taken in their condition. Exhaustion lined every face, their bodies trembling from hunger and exposure. Some had makeshift bandages covering injuries that should have been treated long ago. Others clutched at their children, shielding them as best as they could from the bitter cold.

They had nowhere else to go.

All eyes turned to Elder Ming. The Village Head.

He exhaled slowly. Then he nodded. "Come inside. You will be fed and treated. We will discuss your stay after you have recovered."

The collective sigh of relief was almost palpable.

The Soaring Swallow Teahouse hadn't been this crowded since the Verdant Lotus disciples first arrived.

Refugees filled nearly every available seat, their weary bodies slumped over steaming bowls of rice porridge. Some sat in silence, too exhausted to speak, while others murmured quietly among themselves, their voices tinged with lingering fear and uncertainty. Outside, several villagers and disciples helped move their carts of supplies, moving whatever meager belongings they had brought with them. The air was thick with the scent of hot food and the low hum of conversation, but beneath it all lay a weight that pressed against my chest.

This would put an immense strain on our resources.

I knew that. Elder Ming knew that. Everyone in the village knew that.

But what were we supposed to do? Turn them away? Send them back into the cold, with no certainty of shelter or safety? The villages beyond ours were even more remote, and the closest sect—Narrow Stone Peak—would not be much better than Crescent Bay itself.

Despite everything, though, there was something else that troubled me far more than the logistics of food and shelter.

He was seated quietly in the corner, hunched slightly over his bowl, eating in small, deliberate motions. He was old, perhaps older than I had initially thought. His robes, once fine, were now lined with wear and tear, stained with ink and dust.

I stepped forward, approaching him with measured steps. "Elder," I greeted, my voice careful, respectful. "It has been some time."

The blind man tilted his head slightly, as though studying me despite the absence of sight. Then, recognition flickered across his face, and he smiled.

"Ah . . . the young master who purchased many of Liang Feng's novels."

I let out a small laugh. I didn't think he'd actually recognize me. "It is. My name is Kai Liu."

"Ren Zhi, book merchant." the man introduced himself. "It seems fate has brought us to the same place once more."

I hesitated before asking, "Why did you leave Crescent Bay? You lived within the walls—you should have been safe."

The concept of an old, blind man enduring the winter cold to reach all the way here was astonishing. If they left behind the oldest and weakest refugees in Qingmu, then what did it spell for them if Ren Zhi wasn't included among their ranks?

The older man's smile faded slightly. "Nowhere is safe, young master. Not truly. The walls were protection, yes. But they were also a prison. As tensions rose and fear took hold, the people turned inward. Refugees were forced to the outskirts, and those who remained within the walls . . ." He shook his head. "They grew desperate. I left before the situation worsened. When the first group of refugees fled, I went with them."

I nodded slowly, absorbing his words. "You're safe here," I said firmly. "Elder Ming will not let you suffer. And though you may not know me, I'm a fairly decent herbalist. I'll do what I can to support you."

Ren Zhi was silent for a long moment. Then, he exhaled. "I apologize for not being of more use," he murmured. "As a bookseller, my skills will be of little help. But I will work hard to ensure I am not a burden."

I opened my mouth to reassure him, but before I could, another voice cut in. "That won't be necessary."

I turned, watching as Elder Ming stepped forward. His gaze met Ren Zhi's.

And then, to my utter shock, Elder Ming bowed.

"Venerable elder," he said, his voice calm yet deeply respectful. "Long time no see."

I turned to Ren Zhi, but he looked just as befuddled as I did.

His brow furrowed slightly.

"Who are you?" he asked, voice steady but laced with genuine confusion.

Elder Ming did not answer immediately. Instead, he exhaled, his expression unreadable. "You may not remember me, and that is fine. It has been many decades since our paths last crossed. But I am glad to see that you have found some peace."

Ren Zhi was silent for a long moment. Then, his head lifted just a fraction, and in a voice softer, almost distant, he murmured, "Shan Ming?"

The name sent a jolt through me.

I had only ever known him as Elder Ming or Village Head. Never by any other name.

But what stunned me even more was what came next.

Ren Zhi's fingers tapped lightly against the side of his bowl. "That boy . . . from the boat."

A quiet moment passed between them, a flicker of something old and unspoken stretching across the years.

I frowned. "Wait. How do you know each other?"

Elder Ming's gaze flickered toward me, his usual firm composure returning. "It is not my place to divulge," he said simply.

Ren Zhi, however, exhaled and gave a small nod. "We met on a boat," he said. "Traveling from the mainland to Tranquil Breeze Province. Our paths crossed briefly, then parted soon after."

His words were so unassuming, so casual, that for a moment, I nearly let them pass.

But then my mind caught up with the details.

"Wait—what part of the mainland did you come from?" I asked, my curiosity flaring to life. "What was it like? What was—"

"Enough," Elder Ming interrupted, his voice firm. "Let Elder . . . Ren Zhi rest. He must be tired from the journey."

But his voice faltered ever so slightly on the name, as though it was unfamiliar. As though he had known him by something else.

Ren Zhi merely smiled, shaking his head. "Nothing special. Nothing worth talking about. It bears more similarities to here than one might think."

I paused, watching him closely. There was something in his tone—not quite reluctance, but something close. He didn't want to speak further.

I sighed, relenting. It was impolite to bring up old memories if one didn't want to divulge. "Then, venerable elder, make yourself at home."

I stole a glance at Elder Ming, who had yet to look away from him.

Who exactly was this man? I thought he'd been peculiar; a blind bookseller that was the only one carrying Liang Feng's novels. But now . . .

I shook my head.

It wasn't my place. Despite my curiosity, everyone was privy to their secrets.

Leaving the Soaring Swallow, I returned to Wang Jun's forge to collect Windy and Tianyi.

I stepped outside, my breath misting in the evening air. Despite the warmth of the teahouse and the lingering confusion from my encounter with Ren Zhi and Elder Ming, the moment I was alone, my thoughts hardened, turning toward the reality of our situation.

Even with the hybrid millet we planted, even with Tie Niu's newfound Dao of Fishing, this wasn't sustainable.

How long before a person comes to me with an ailment I *can* treat, but without the needed herbs? What good was all my knowledge, all my formulas, if I lacked the raw materials to put them to use?

If I didn't do something, if I didn't find more before winter deepened its hold, then the next time someone came to me . . .

I might have *nothing* to give.

It was one thing to ration food, to cut portions and make every grain stretch. But herbs were another matter entirely. I could live on thin meals. The disciples could tighten their belts. But if I ran out of medicinal herbs, if I had nothing left to treat injuries and sickness, then the consequences would be irreversible.

That wasn't something I could allow.

I tightened my fists as I walked through the village, my steps leading me instinctively toward my shop. Inside, the scent of dried herbs filled the air, jars and pouches lining every available shelf. I moved with practiced precision, gathering the essentials—ginseng for strength, frost-lotus for fever relief, qi-restoring mushrooms, and as many wound-purifying salves as I could carry. I sorted them quickly, wrapping them in cloth before tucking them into my satchel.

But as I worked, my mind drifted toward what needed to be done next.

I would need to speak with Jian Feng. We had to return to the forest.

I wasn't blind to the dangers. The demonic cultivators might still be lurking, waiting for another opportunity to strike. But what choice did I have? The Verdant Lotus disciples had scouted the surrounding areas, but their focus had been on security, not resources. The forest held herbs I couldn't cultivate in my garden. If I wanted to keep treating the wounded, if I wanted to keep this village alive through the winter, then I needed to gather them myself.

A rustling sound broke my train of thought. I glanced up, spotting Windy slithering over the counter, his pale scales catching the dim light. Tianyi hovered nearby, watching me with an expression I couldn't quite place.

"You are troubled," Tianyi murmured.

I exhaled. "There's a lot to think about."

She tilted her head. "You plan to leave again."

It wasn't a question.

I hesitated, then nodded. "I have to. If I don't, people are going to die."

Windy flicked his tongue, his tail coiling loosely around my wrist.

Tianyi was silent for a long moment before she finally spoke again. "I will come with you."

I looked at her, then at Windy, considering. "I still need to talk to Jian Feng first. If the disciples can support us, we'll have a better chance."

With the supplies packed and my mind set, I slung the satchel over my shoulder and stepped back into the cold, heading toward the village square.

Things needed to change.

CHAPTER TWENTY-SEVEN

Blazing a Trail

Jian Feng took my words with an ease that unsettled me.
    I had expected resistance—perhaps some mild challenge, or at least the usual back-and-forth that came with dealing with a second-class disciple of his caliber. Instead, he merely nodded, accepting my plan with a quiet deference that felt . . . off.

Had he always been like this? Or was it something else?

I studied him out of the corner of my eye as we walked. Was it losing his comrades? The burden of leading his remaining disciples? Or had something shifted in the way he saw me?

I didn't have an answer. And right now, I had more important things to focus on.

The first foraging mission had been easy enough to organize. Three teams—one scouting, one gathering, and one maintaining the camp and processing what we gathered.

My team took the lead.

It included Jian Feng, Windy, Tianyi, and three other disciples from Verdant Lotus—each one specializing in speed and stealth, their movements trained for quick assessments of terrain and hidden threats. We were the eyes of the expedition, meant to identify rich resource areas and determine whether they were safe to harvest.

Tianyi's sensitivity to qi fluctuations, Windy's instincts as a predator, and the disciples' honed senses made us well-suited for the task. My role was simple; find the best foraging areas, as I was the most familiar with the forest. The others ensured we weren't walking into a den of hidden threats.

And so far, it was working.

I moved through the undergrowth, weaving between frost-dusted foliage with measured steps. Every so often, I paused, running my fingers over a plant's leaves, assessing its vitality, before plucking the most mature specimens and storing them away.

My storage ring was proving invaluable.

If I had been limited to a basket or even a satchel, we would have been forced to make multiple trips back to camp. But with my ring, I could store everything efficiently, allowing me to pick with precision.

Still, not every find could be taken immediately. Some herbs grew in difficult terrain or required careful extraction to retain their potency. Those, I marked down in a small ledger, noting the location so the second team could retrieve them later.

Behind me, Windy and Tianyi moved independently, their roles clear.

The lack of major predators in the region had led to an unusual abundance of smaller animals; rabbits, hares, bamboo rodents, and even small birds. It was a natural consequence of balance being disrupted.

Windy wasted no time. His body coiled, then snapped forward like a released bowstring, sinking his fangs into the neck of an unsuspecting hare. The poor creature barely had time to react before it went limp.

I grimaced as he lifted his prize, tail flicking with satisfaction.

". . . Do you have to eat snakes too?" I muttered, watching as he dispatched a smaller serpent with just as much enthusiasm.

Windy flicked his tongue in response. Despite our closer bond, it wasn't at a level where I could understand him. Thankfully, I had a translator.

Tianyi raised her head from where she was. "He said a snake that does not grow stronger has no place in this world."

I sighed. Great. Existential snake philosophy.

Tianyi had taken to catching birds, her movements eerily precise. She didn't kill them outright—just disabled them with a sudden, sharp gust of wind from her wings, leaving them stunned for easy collection.

Between the two of them, our food supplies were building at a rapid pace.

Once we had marked enough areas for the second team to scour more thoroughly, we doubled back, retracing our steps to where the main group had set up camp.

Jian Feng examined the process. As we handed off our notes and let the gatherers take over, I caught him studying me with something close to . . . admiration.

"You're surprisingly efficient," he said. "Even our trained disciples aren't this precise when identifying viable growth areas."

I scoffed, rubbing some lingering dirt off my hands. "What, you thought I'd just grab whatever looked the shiniest?"

Jian Feng didn't answer immediately. Instead, he glanced at the gathered herbs being sorted. Even in winter, our haul was substantial—likely double what anyone would expect this season.

"The environment is shifting," he murmured. "More life, more vitality."

I nodded. "The ambient qi is affecting everything. The land, the plants, even the soil. It's why the fields were still rich after the last harvest."

The second-class disciple exhaled. "I don't know if that's a blessing or a warning."

Neither did I. But for now, it was helping. That was enough.

As I adjusted my satchel, preparing for another scouting round, he suddenly spoke again.

"That signal vial you gave the disciples," he said. "It was clever."

I glanced back at him. "It's basic alchemy."

He shook his head. "No, it's practical. You didn't just think of an escape route; you designed a way to make sure teams can communicate at a distance without needing messengers. Dark smoke that lingers just long enough to be seen, but not long enough to give enemies a clear trail."

I shrugged. "It's the least I could do with what I've learned from Verdant Lotus."

Jian Feng hummed, watching as the second group of disciples dispersed into the forest. "You're wasted as just an alchemist."

I arched a brow. "And?"

A smirk tugged at the corner of his lips. "Nothing. Just an observation."

I rolled my eyes, but a small part of me acknowledged the truth behind his words.

I wasn't just an alchemist anymore.

And judging by the way everyone was looking at me now . . .

I wasn't just another villager either.

A few hours passed, and we had surveyed a large area with this strategy—efficiently, methodically, and most importantly, without incident.

The stillness of the forest had lessened, but it remained eerie. There were more sounds now, the rustling of leaves, the occasional distant cry of a bird, even the scurrying of small animals emboldened by the lack of natural predators. But it was unnatural in a different way—like something lurking just beneath the surface, unseen but present.

I knew deep down that there had to be demonic cultivators nearby. The body of the one Windy fought had disappeared without a trace, and I doubted that was a coincidence. Someone had taken it. But whether they were watching us now or lying low, I couldn't be certain.

Still, the expedition had been a success. No losses, no injuries, no signs of immediate danger. That was enough for now.

We gathered at the established base camp, sorting through the supplies we had collected. The second team had done well in following up on the marked locations, their packs overflowing with herbs and foraged plants.

I split the resources between myself and the disciples, ensuring that each of them carried a portion. They were well versed in preparing medicines and herb preservation, a necessity for their sect's training, so I had no concerns about their ability to handle their share.

As we began our journey back to the village, I mentally cataloged our haul, already considering the next steps. Even with all these materials, I wouldn't have everything I needed.

That meant I had work to do.

The night passed in a quiet hum of thought and motion.

I sat cross-legged in my shop, surrounded by freshly sorted herbs, my fingers tracing over parchment as I mapped out combinations, permutations, and potential hybrids.

Not every herb I gathered could be used as-is. Some were missing their key complementary ingredients. Others needed to be refined before they reached full potency. And a few, while useful on their own, had the potential to be something far greater if combined correctly.

I welcomed the challenge.

This was what alchemy was meant to be. Not just memorizing recipes but understanding each ingredient, finding the balance between its properties, and seeing what could be drawn out with the right process.

Each step forward in this field was a step toward independence.

I adjusted a cluster of ginseng roots, my mind weaving through possibilities. If I infused them with the right essence, could I create something that provided long-term stamina rather than just temporary bursts of energy? What about the frost-lotus; could I refine its cold-resistant properties into something usable beyond medicine?

A faint hum in my mind, like a soft ripple through a still pond.

> *Nature's Attunement has reached level 7.*

A slow smile spread across my face.

Progress.

Coals beneath my feet hissed, shifting as I lightly stepped across them.

I heard the ring of fire surrounding me roar as it flickered, the heat curling around my skin, testing me. My movements had long since settled into something of a natural rhythm—instinctual.

I was close.

Each step burned, but it was no longer just endurance keeping me steady.

Force and fluidity.

Elder Ming's words echoed in my mind, cryptic at first, but growing clearer with each repetition.

I had never thought of dancing as anything more than an art. Yet, the deeper I went into the Dance of a Thousand Flames, the more I understood.

It began with my feet. No longer merely enduring the pain, they were feeling the heat, anticipating the movement of the coals, finding the moments of cool relief amid the fire. My soles became like eyes, guiding me forward with every shift, every flicker of movement.

A breath. A pivot. A step.

The rigid control I had always held over my movements loosened. The familiar weight of Rooted Banyan Stance, the instinctual pull of Bamboo Reprisal Counter—they were strong, reliable. But they weren't made for this.

Wood resisted. It endured. It held its ground.

But fire?

Fire didn't wait. Fire didn't plant itself in place. It moved, it flowed, it devoured and rebirthed itself in the same breath.

My body trembled as I realized the depth of what Elder Ming had been trying to teach me.

My defenses weren't just a style I relied on—they were a habit I couldn't shake. Even in my most fluid moments, I carried tension. A readiness to resist. To stand firm. But the Heavenly Flame Mantra demanded something different.

Surrender.

Not weakness. Not submission. But a release of the tension I had spent the beginning of my martial journey cultivating.

I stepped forward again, not bracing for the pain, but moving with it. My body flowed, weaving through the heat, no longer trying to conquer it but accepting it as part of the dance.

The flames flickered—then bent.

For the first time since the training had begun, they didn't resist me. They followed me, coiling around my limbs in a ghostly wisp before dissipating entirely.

The ring of fire around me collapsed in an instant.

A sharp breath left me as I landed on solid ground, the last embers extinguishing at my feet.

A moment of silence.

Then—

Your Body has reached Qi Initiation Stage—Rank 2.
Heavenly Flame Mantra has reached level 2.

A pulse of warmth flooded my limbs, settling deep within my core. The weight of the Black Tortoise Tribulation lessened—only slightly, but noticeably so.

I exhaled, steadying myself, feeling the lingering heat curling at the edges of my awareness.

Elder Ming studied me for a long moment before nodding. "You've reached the next level."

It was a statement of fact more than it was a question.

I wiped the sweat from my brow, still catching my breath. "That was . . . different."

"It had to be," he said. "You were shackled to your foundation. The Rooted Banyan Stance is formidable, but it is not suited for fire. It teaches control, stability. Those are strengths—but here, they became a hindrance."

I nodded slowly. "I get it now. The balance between tension and looseness . . . It wasn't something I could just think my way into. I had to feel it."

A quiet hum of approval. "Good. This will make your learning of the Heavenly Flame Mantra even faster."

"I want to learn it!"

Wang Jun, who had been watching from the sidelines, strode forward with barely contained excitement. "That looked incredible. If I can learn something like that, I—"

Before either of us could stop him, he hopped onto the extinguished pile of coals, kicking up a small puff of ash.

A loud yelp echoed through the courtyard.

Wang Jun launched himself off the coals, landing far away with a furious curse, frantically shaking his foot. "They're still hot! How'd you stay on these while they were still on fire?"

Elder Ming sighed, rubbing his temple. "Because unlike Kai, you did not move."

I held back a laugh, watching as Wang Jun glared at the remains of the coal bed like it had betrayed him.

"That," he muttered, pointing at the training ground, "was not worth it."

Despite myself, I grinned. "You'll get there one day."

"One day?" He shot me a glare. "Forget that. If I'm learning a technique, it's going to be one that doesn't set me on fire."

Elder Ming let the moment settle before speaking again. "Now that you've grasped the basics, it's time for the next stage of your training."

I stretched my arms, still feeling the warmth lingering in my limbs. "Next stage?"

He nodded and then gestured toward Wang Jun. "He's been helping me prepare for this."

The blacksmith perked up at that, rubbing his singed foot with a handful of fresh snow. "That's right. You'll thank me later."

I highly doubted that.

Elder Ming motioned for us to follow. We moved toward the storage shed behind his house, where he pulled open the doors to reveal a collection of weapons resting inside.

Swords. Spears. Axes. Iron-tipped staffs.

I blinked. "... Are we preparing for war?"

"Not yet," Elder Ming said, "but as you advance in cultivation, you will inevitably face a variety of opponents at once. And they won't all be unarmed."

I frowned, glancing at the weapons. "I thought this training was about my body and technique. What does this have to do with that?"

"You must learn how to defend against weapons," Elder Ming said simply. "You are at a stage where avoiding them is no longer an option."

I hesitated. "But I don't use weapons. I gave up on training the staff a long time ago."

Elder Ming arched a brow. "And you think your opponents will care?"

... Fair point.

He stepped forward and picked up a long spear, its wooden shaft polished smooth, the steel tip gleaming in the morning light.

"Made them all battle-ready, just for you! They're about as sharp and balanced as can be." Wang Jun said with pride. In truth, I'd rather he made them blunt instead.

I tensed. "Shouldn't we start with the less dangerous ones? Like the staff?"

Elder Ming ignored me.

Then he lunged.

I barely had time to react before the spear shot toward me. I twisted to the side, narrowly avoiding the thrust, only for him to pivot the weapon and bring the shaft around in a sweeping arc.

I ducked, cursing. "Wait! Are we just starting like this? No warning?"

"You should always assume your opponent won't wait for you to be ready," Elder Ming said calmly, stepping forward again.

I scrambled back. "That's a very convenient philosophy when *you* have the weapon!"

Another thrust. Another dodge.

The tip of the spear whistled past my ear, close enough that I felt the wind from it. Because of the limitations of my Refinement Simulation Technique, predicting his moves was difficult. I hadn't much experience with armed opponents.

"Kai," he said between strikes, "you've learned how to move with fire. Now, learn how to move with your opponent's intent."

He shifted his grip, switching from a thrust to a feint, then swung the spear in a sharp downward motion.

I twisted, barely avoiding the strike, but my balance was off.

Elder Ming capitalized instantly.

The shaft of the spear swept my legs out from under me.

I crashed to the ground with a grunt.

Wang Jun laughed. "Wow. That was fast."

I groaned, staring at the sky.

Stronger cultivation, better techniques, deeper understanding of combat—*why did all of it just mean getting beaten up faster?!*

Elder Ming placed the butt of the spear against the ground, looking down at me. "Again."

I exhaled sharply, rolling to my feet.

"Of course," I muttered. But despite my complaints, I stood up.

"Let's go!"

CHAPTER TWENTY-EIGHT

He Who Cultivates the Earth, Cultivates Strength

The village had adapted faster than I expected.
It had only been a few days since the refugees arrived, yet Gentle Wind Village had already found a rhythm; one that made their presence feel less like a disruption and more like an inevitable expansion.

People adjusted, shifted, and filled in the gaps where they could. The village had no choice but to make room. And against all odds, it was working.

Liang Chen, the merchant who had arrived just before the refugees, was already struggling after being cut off from his usual supply network. I had assumed he'd be hesitant about investing too much in the village's future, considering his situation. But he had thrown himself into the efforts with surprising enthusiasm.

"It's not like I can move my wares elsewhere," he had muttered when I'd asked about it. "Might as well make myself useful."

And useful he had been.

With Li Wei and the artisans that had remained behind, Liang Chen spearheaded the construction of temporary housing, using what little building materials he had left from previous shipments. But even with those, the reality was simple: We would need more supplies.

That was where the foraging expeditions had given an unexpected benefit.

While we scouted for herbs and food, Liang Chen's workers had cut down trees near the outskirts of the forest, ensuring not to venture too deep. The wood would build new homes; a necessary step, as keeping so many people in the Soaring Swallow was unsustainable. Li Wei and Wang Jun worked night and day to create the other required building materials, but they seemed to relish the work, honing themselves and growing with every challenge.

The teahouse had already stretched beyond its limit, but Lan-Yin persevered. Despite her condition, she could still work and cook, albeit at a limited pace than before. I chipped in where I could, providing small elixirs to boost stamina and encourage recovery.

Not to be outdone, Huan had made efforts to contribute, though his resources were more limited. He specialized in herbs and spices, not lumber or stone. Still, that was something.

But perhaps the biggest enigma of them all was Elder Ren Zhi.

The blind bookseller, who I had assumed would be limited in his ability to help, had instead become a central figure in the village.

Not through labor.

Through stories.

Every afternoon, without fail, he gathered the village children and wove tale after tale, his voice steady and mesmerizing. His words painted vivid pictures of ancient battles, wandering heroes, cunning tricksters, and legendary cultivators, drawing his audience in with every twist and turn.

But he didn't stop at words.

With careful, practiced movements, he drew illustrations onto a small scroll, sketching figures and landscapes onto the cart that carried his bookmaking materials. Though he couldn't see the finished product, the precision of his strokes made it clear he knew what he was doing.

The children were hooked. And so were some adults.

I stood at a distance one afternoon, watching the group huddle around him. The laughter, the awed gasps, the whispers of anticipation as he unraveled another legend. It was a kind of magic that had nothing to do with cultivation. Directly, at least.

During times like this, when survival was uncertain, morale was everything.

And in a way, his contributions were more valuable than anything he could have done with his hands. Farmwork, construction—those things were important, but they only sustained the body.

He sustained the spirit.

I exhaled, crossing my arms as I leaned against the outer wall of my shop, watching the scene unfold from afar.

Even now, there was something about him I couldn't quite place. His demeanor, his past familiarity with Elder Ming, the way his presence carried more weight than his outward frailty suggested.

There was a story behind him.

And his way of storytelling . . .

"It's like . . ."

I dismissed the thought with a wave of my hand. I had better things to do than obsess over an old man's past. My garden still needed tending, and there was a mountain of herbs from the last foraging trip waiting for me. My stock's been depleted ever since I used a chunk to treat the villagers.

Then, without warning, I sidestepped—just in time to avoid a shard of ice that whizzed past my head.

I blinked, looking down at the splintered ice where it had embedded itself in the packed snow.

Windy and Tianyi.

Sure enough, a short distance away, I spotted them sparring. Now that Windy had fully recovered, he had wasted no time testing himself against Tianyi. The two clashed in a flurry of motion, Windy's lithe form darting through the snow while she darted upward, taking advantage of her ability to fly.

But despite that, Windy was holding his own.

I narrowed my eyes, watching carefully.

Tianyi launched a quick, precise strike—one that, under normal circumstances, should have landed. But Windy wasn't there.

For a moment, it looked as though her attack passed clean through him.

I blinked again. No, it wasn't a mirage. It was the way he moved. He used the snow to obscure his form and create subtle visual distortions. His serpentine body weaved through the frost-laden ground in a way that made it almost impossible to tell where he actually was. The white of his scales, the way the snow kicked up around him—it made Tianyi's attacks whiff at the last moment.

She let out a frustrated hum, her antennae twitching as she adjusted her stance, trying to account for his erratic movements. Windy, for his part, remained eerily calm, his tongue flicking out, waiting for her to overcommit.

He had grown stronger.

I watched for a moment longer, trying to understand the mechanics behind it, but it wasn't something I could grasp so easily.

Filing the observation away for later, I cleared my throat. "Take the fight further out unless you want the greenhouse to be missing a few glass panes."

They didn't respond verbally but complied, pushing themselves further away toward the open fields.

Shaking my head, I continued back into my shop, where the scent of dried herbs and fresh soil greeted me.

The gathered herbs lay artfully arranged on the workbench, separated by type and potency. I had already transplanted some into small clay pots, each one part of an ongoing experiment in hybridization. If I wanted to stretch our resources, I had to get creative.

There was no sense in using rare, potent ingredients for everything. Sometimes, the best medicines came from the simplest sources.

I recalled Elder Wei Lian's words during the Grand Alchemy Gauntlet, where he showed Jian Duan the full potential of pyrite. I repeated it in my head like a mantra, engraving it into the way I approached my current situation.

There are no useless ingredients. Only useless alchemists.

The more I worked, the more I realized how true it was. Even the most ordinary herbs could produce powerful effects if handled correctly.

And with the myriad of abilities and tools I had now, my understanding of what was possible became limitless.

I set my notes aside and reached for something unusual—a handful of brightly colored bamboo seeds.

They weren't Golden Bamboo.

Ever since I had worked with Golden Bamboo essence, a thought had been sitting in the back of my mind. What if I applied the same principles to ordinary bamboo? Could I push its growth beyond natural limits?

I decided to test it.

Stepping outside, I moved to a safe distance away from the shop. If this went wrong, I didn't want it anywhere near my storage ring full of volatile herbs.

I held up a single bamboo seed, given a measured amount of kudzu root essence. Known for its rapid, aggressive growth properties, often seen as a nuisance plant that could overtake entire fields if left unchecked, there were plenty from our expedition.

Next, I took out a vial of water processed with deer antler velvet. It was relatively scarce, but Huan was willing to part with a jar of the stuff at a discount.

I carefully let a single drop land on the seed.

Then, I tossed it.

The instant it hit the ground, the change was immediate.

A sharp crack split the air as the seed burst open, and before my eyes, a stalk of bamboo shot up from the earth, growing to nearly its full height within seconds.

I took a step back, observing the impossibly rapid growth. The stalk stood tall and firm, its deep-green surface gleaming under the winter sun. It wasn't as potent as Golden Bamboo, but it was far more efficient to cultivate.

My mind was already racing with applications.

Housing materials—this could help with building materials; all it'd need is Li Wei and Liang Chen processing the bamboo for use.

Reinforcement for buildings—with a few modifications, I could make them even sturdier than standard wood.

Weaponization? If I could enhance the growth process, could I grow bamboo as an attack? An instantaneous growth beneath an opponent, a spear of bamboo stabbing from below before they even realized it.

Something clicked.

Spiritual Herbalism has reached level 10.
Your skill has reached the qualifications to evolve to the next stage,
Herbal Sage Alchemy.

> *Herbal Sage Alchemy enhances your two abilities and grants you a third one.*
>
> *Essence Extraction—You can extract the spiritual essence of plants, beasts, and metals for the creation of pills and elixirs. You can further extract essences into its different properties.*
>
> *Spiritual Plant Cultivation—You can infuse plants with your qi to increase their potency, imbue them with new properties, or accelerate the growth of herbs, forcing them to mature quickly by flooding them with substantial amounts of qi.*
>
> *Alchemical Nexus—A formation requiring no physical carvings field that can grant greater stability, speed, or potency to the refinement process. In the absence of a pill furnace, it can act as a substitute, allowing for on-the-go refinement.*

The moment the knowledge settled, I felt the familiar rush of enlightenment. Everything I knew about alchemy, about herbalism—about cultivation itself—shifted into sharper focus, threading together like pieces of a grand formation I hadn't realized I was building all along.

For a long time, I had been waiting for this. The slow, meticulous journey from basic herbalism to alchemy. I had wondered why I never gained a skill like alchemy, but it seemed the Interface was waiting to give me an even bigger reward.

My skills had always leaned heavily on my understanding of plants, but now? I exhaled sharply, excitement bubbling beneath my skin.

Essence Extraction had evolved beyond simply pulling essence from materials. But according to the description, I could refine specific properties within those essences, separating them further into their most potent aspects. Before, extracting a fire-aligned essence from a Sunfire Blade Grass meant simply taking its energy wholesale. But now? Maybe it was possible to extract just its heat-producing properties or isolate its qi-nourishing aspects. It was a level of control that would make my alchemical refinement infinitely more precise.

My mind spun with possibilities.

Then there was Spiritual Plant Cultivation.

I had already hybridized plants by infusing them with foreign qi, but now I could force their growth entirely, pushing them past natural limitations with a direct influx of qi. If Golden Bamboo had once taken days to reach full height, then perhaps now I could accelerate it within moments. If an herb needed a season to mature, did it mean I could bring it to fruition within hours? The implications were staggering.

But . . .

The Alchemical Nexus.

A formation that didn't require physical carvings. No intricate arrays drawn in sand, no painstaking etching onto parchment.

I tested it, raising my hand.

A soft glow flickered around my palm, and I watched in awe as faint, golden lines manifested in the air. Similar to the ones I'd seen Jingyu Lian and other alchemists use, but the symbols used were different. It didn't pertain to any standard alchemy formations I knew. But perhaps that was expected of the Interface, to revive lost arts or create new ones.

The symbols pulsed, shifting as my intent pressed into them. I could choose only one aspect—stability, acceleration, or potency. Each pathway was rigid, but that rigidity made it stable. No deviations, no unnecessary complexity.

I clenched my fist, dispersing the formation, but my heart raced with anticipation.

This would change everything.

My biggest weakness had always been my lack of practice in higher-level techniques. It was hard to practice alchemy formation outside of a structured environment without a mentor. The gap between me and trained sect disciples in alchemy had been in how seamlessly they could manipulate formations in their refinement process. I had made up for it with careful technique, intuition, and my Refinement Simulation Technique. But now, I finally had a way to bridge that gap.

A slow grin spread across my face.

Even the Bloodsoul Bloom . . .

I had worried about its volatility before. The idea of refining it had seemed like a distant goal, something I could attempt only after a long time of careful observation. But now, with the Alchemical Nexus and upgraded Essence Extraction at my disposal?

I could create a formation to stabilize it. I could control its refinement, what property I wanted to take.

For the first time, it felt possible.

Still, that was a thought for later. Right now, I had another test in mind.

I turned on my heel, striding toward the greenhouse.

Windy and Tianyi had long since finished their sparring match, and the fields beyond the village were quiet. They left for elsewhere, but I knew they weren't in any trouble. The moment I stepped inside the greenhouse, warmth enveloped me. The ambient qi within was thick, pulsing faintly between the rows of carefully cultivated herbs and experimental hybrids.

I scanned the plants, my fingers brushing over leaves and stems as I considered my options.

Which one would I test first?

The answer came quickly.

I stood at the newly planted patch of Golden Bamboo Millet. A cross between the resilient millet I had cultivated and the powerful energy of Golden Bamboo. If it worked, it would be a grain that could thrive even in the coldest winters while providing a slow, nourishing build-up of qi to those who consumed it.

Bending over slowly, I pressed my palm to the patch of soil.

CHAPTER TWENTY-NINE

In the Soil

I woke up face down in the dirt.

It wasn't exactly the most dignified way to start the day.

Groaning, I pushed myself up, spitting out a mouthful of soil. My body felt sluggish, my limbs leaden in a way that spoke of more than just stiffness. I'd passed out.

For a moment, panic flared through me. How long had I been out? I whipped my head toward the greenhouse door, spotting the faint glow of early dawn filtering through the gaps. The village was still quiet, no distant voices, no sounds of movement. Morning training hadn't started yet.

I exhaled in relief. Not that missing it would have killed me, but I could already hear Elder Ming's nagging in my head.

Still, this wasn't good. I was pushing myself too hard.

I ran a hand through my hair, forcing myself to take stock of my body. The exhaustion settled deep in my bones; the creeping kind that had been building up for days. My routine had been brutal: morning training, foraging, processing herbs, crafting medicine, assisting the refugees, experimenting with new alchemical techniques . . . Sleep had become an afterthought.

And last night? Last night, I had emptied the last of my reserves to fully mature the millet.

My gaze flickered to the patch of land before me, and my exhaustion vanished in an instant.

The Golden Bamboo-Millet hybrid stood tall, shimmering under the soft glow of dawn. Its stalks were thick and sturdy, the grains plump and golden, far more abundant than I had ever expected.

I crouched down, running my fingers along the stems. It worked.

I let out a breathless laugh.

"I actually did it. Holy shit!"

The yield was absurd. A single patch had produced double what the regular millet could—and it had done so overnight. No fertilizers, no special cultivation methods. Just qi-infused growth, forced into rapid maturity by my own hands.

I shook my head, grinning despite myself. "This is insane."

Of course, I couldn't afford to do this every time we needed food. The sheer amount of qi it had taken to mature just this patch from budding seeds had left me unconscious, which meant larger-scale applications were out of the question.

But that didn't matter.

Because this wasn't about food. This was about medicine.

If I could grow millet in a night, then what about high-grade herbs? What about rare herbs that normally took months or years? If I could force their growth—refine their properties faster—it would change everything.

The sheer potential of it sent a thrill through me.

But first things first.

I had a perfectly good batch of hybridized millet in front of me, and I wasn't about to let it go to waste.

Quickly, I grabbed a small sickle from my belt and began cutting the stalks, gathering them into neat bundles.

Within minutes, I had an armful of golden stalks. Carefully, I secured them in a cloth bundle, slinging them over my back before stepping out of the greenhouse.

As I stepped outside, I was immediately greeted by a familiar presence.

Tianyi, standing aloof with Yin Si perched on her shoulder. Windy was curled near her feet, his body lazily coiled but his gaze sharp and alert.

"You must really like the greenhouse; I've never seen you sleep there before."

I shook my head, adjusting the bundle of millet on my back. "Guess I do now."

"It's quite warm. The puddles on the floor are good when you're thirsty."

I turned toward my shop, already focused on what needed to be done next. Processing the millet would take time—threshing, winnowing, and grinding—but I wanted to get it done before training started. If I was lucky, I could prepare a few test portions and have it for breakfast.

I was halfway to the door when Windy slithered up to me and dropped something at my feet.

A dead snake.

I stared at it. Then at him. Then back at the limp, motionless serpent lying on the ground.

Tianyi piped up to act as a translator. "Windy hunted it."

I blinked. ". . . Okay?"

"He wanted to give it to you," she continued, as if it was the most natural thing in the world. "Since you slept early last night and didn't eat."

I looked at the snake. Then back at Windy, whose blue eyes met mine with unblinking intensity. Was this . . . generosity? Or dominance?

It was hard to tell with him. The gesture could just as easily mean *Here, I caught this for you, eat* as it could *I'm the superior predator. Accept my offering, weakling.*

Tianyi, ever the helpful translator, flicked her wings. "He insists that you must eat and rest."

Ah. That meant bossy generosity then.

I sighed, rubbing my temple. "Fine. I get it." I picked up the snake by the tail, giving it a shake. "Could you prepare it? I'll just deal with the millet first."

She perked up, her wings fluttering with approval. "I will. I've read how to do it in Storm Sage Chronicles."

I wasn't sure if that was reassuring or not. Did the series even have a scene where they gutted a snake? I shook my head and got to work.

The millet came first. I untied the bundle, laying the golden stalks out neatly before moving through the process. I rubbed the harvested grains between my hands, loosening the husks and separating the edible portions. A simple gust of air from Tianyi was enough to blow away the chaff, leaving behind clean, golden grains.

I scooped up the finished product and weighed it in my hands, still moist to the touch.

From just one patch, I had over twenty servings of millet.

That was ridiculous.

Just with its hybridization, this was already outpacing normal crops. But with my ability to accelerate its growth? I could create a near-endless supply of nutrient-rich food overnight if I had the qi.

I let out a slow breath. This is a significant change.

Of course, it was still unsustainable for large-scale production. The sheer amount of qi needed to grow a whole field of this stuff would drain me dry in an instant.

But in urgent cases—when medicine or food was desperately needed?

This was a miracle waiting to be used.

Satisfied, I set the millet aside and turned my attention to the snake.

Tianyi had already skinned and gutted it with meticulous precision, the flesh cleaned and expertly prepared.

I watched from the corner of my eye as she returned to Windy's side, my mind drifting.

They were so . . . casual about killing.

Windy, as a predator, had never hesitated when it came to hunting even his own kind. Tianyi, despite her delicate appearance, approached taking a life in the same way I'd ask her to separate grain from chaff. She only held back out of consideration for me.

I didn't hesitate to kill animals, but I still thought about it. And I always considered whether I'd be able to do so against a human.

Shaking the thought away, I finished processing the millet and moved to cook it. I portioned out the grains, rinsing them thoroughly before setting them in a pot of water over my pill furnace.

I sliced the snake meat into thin strips and threw it into the furnace alongside the millet.

The movements were automatic, my mind elsewhere as I stirred the pot and adjusted the flame. Within seconds, I had a bowl of millet stew with snake meat.

I was already considering my next steps—what I needed to do now that my alchemy skills had evolved, how this new level of control would change my approach. Perhaps I'd ask Jian Feng if they could coordinate with me.

I'd have to test the Alchemical Nexus properly, refining a batch of low-grade pills to see how much it truly improved speed, stability, and potency. Then, I needed to—

THUMP.

A sharp, insistent nudge against my hand pulled me out of my thoughts.

I blinked down at Windy, who had butted his head against my hand.

He hissed, a clear demand, pointing his tail at the bowl with a flicker of annoyance through our bond.

". . . Do you want some?"

Windy flicked his tongue.

Tianyi helpfully translated. "He says to stop thinking and eat."

I sighed, rolling my eyes as I picked up the bowl, fully prepared to tell Windy that my work takes precedence—that there were too many things to do, too many preparations to make, and that I couldn't waste a single moment.

But before the words could leave my mouth, I hesitated.

Was that really true?

For the first time in what felt like forever, there was no immediate crisis.

The village was somewhat stable. Refugees had shelter. Access to food was expanding with our foraging efforts and my experiments. There wasn't an urgent threat looming over my head.

It was . . . quiet.

A rare thing.

Slowly, I lowered the bowl back onto my lap and exhaled.

Windy and Tianyi were both watching me expectantly. Not impatiently, not nagging—just waiting.

"Maybe . . . just this once."

I settled back down and took a bite of the millet porridge, letting the warmth spread through my body. The grains were soft but firm, carrying an earthy sweetness I hadn't expected. The snake meat, lightly charred from the furnace's controlled heat, added a savory depth to the dish.

It was . . . good.

Better than usual.

I blinked, pausing between bites. "Tastes different."

"You are using a new ingredient. It is from your work. You must be proud."

I huffed a quiet laugh. She wasn't wrong.

But as I continued eating, a different realization settled over me.

When was the last time I just . . . ate?

Not shoving down a meal while planning my next move. Not absentmindedly chewing while skimming a book or running calculations in my head.

Just eating. Just being.

It felt strange. Foreign.

Like something I had forgotten how to do.

I finished the meal slowly, savoring each bite, and by the time I set the empty bowl aside, I felt . . . lighter. The exhaustion was still there, but it didn't weigh on me as much.

A moment of silence passed between us.

Then, I stood, picking up the bundle of processed millet grains I had set aside earlier.

"Let's share this with the village," I said. "We'll make a stew out of it."

Tianyi's antennae twitched with interest. "A feast?"

"A small one," I corrected. "A warm meal for everyone before morning training. Maybe I'll even ask Elder Ming for a day off."

Tianyi let out a small hum of amusement. "You would use your one day of rest to feed others? How magnanimous."

I snorted. Her influence from novels continued to shine through. "It's just how I operate. After all, my wealth knows no bounds! Some grain is hardly an act of charity for me."

Windy flicked his tail in satisfaction, as if this was exactly the outcome he had intended. With a laugh, I gathered the sack and exited the shop.

And for the first time in a while, as we stepped out into the quiet, pre-dawn village with our supplies in tow, I felt . . . content.

The Silent Moon Sect lay in ruins.

Bodies had already been cleared away—those they could recover, at least—but the scent of death lingered in the air, thick and cloying.

He exhaled sharply, his grip tightening on the scroll in his hands.

What a mess.

The cultists had withdrawn, their assault swift and brutal, leaving behind nothing but devastation. Dozens injured or dead. The Silent Moon Sect, once feared, once respected, was disgraced and broken. Whether they would stand the test of time . . .

Xu Ziqing gritted his teeth.

That was a question he dared not answer.

He turned toward the collapsed outer wall, where a handful of surviving disciples worked in silence, their movements slow, mechanical. Not a single one of them spoke. There was nothing to say.

The attack had stripped them bare, revealing just how fragile their foundation truly was. Sect Leader Jun's reckless ambition had alienated every potential ally. The tributes had run dry, their once-steady stream of resources cut off as a direct consequence of his actions. Without the backing of the four mainland elders, there was nothing left to mitigate the fallout.

And those elders? Gone. Killed or vanished into the wind the moment it was clear they would not emerge victorious.

Xu Ziqing exhaled sharply.

That was the problem with relying on outsiders. They had no loyalty to the cause, no reason to stay when the tides shifted against them. The moment things turned dire, they abandoned the sect without hesitation.

He wanted to blame them.

But he couldn't.

His fingers twitched at his sides, a faint tremor running through his hands. He clenched them into fists, willing the memory away, but it surfaced anyway.

The cultists.

You will die soon enough, but your existence is meaningless to us now. Do not mistake this reprieve for mercy.

Even now, the memory sent a chill crawling down his spine. That man—no, that thing—was something beyond human. The pressure he exuded was suffocating, a tide of malice so deep it had nearly drowned him on the spot. Xu Ziqing had always prided himself on his strength, his unwavering resolve, but when he stood before the shadows that overtook his home . . .

His body had refused to move.

He had felt the crushing weight of inevitability. Of death.

And yet, the leader had not struck them down. Hadn't even bothered with them, like the sect was beneath his notice. No, his interest had been elsewhere.

Phoenix Tears.

The words still echoed in his mind, spoken with a certainty that made his blood run cold.

That was what they had come for.

And the elders had it.

Xu Ziqing's jaw tightened. The two remaining elders had likely fled the moment they realized the cultists were after them. They weren't fools—they knew they couldn't win a direct confrontation. Instead, they had vanished into the cities, blending into the chaos of the common folk, using innocent lives as their shield.

That was why there had been so many attacks lately. It wasn't random. It wasn't indiscriminate slaughter.

The cultists were hunting.

And the mainland elders had led them straight into the capital, forcing them to sift through thousands of lives to find their prize.

Xu Ziqing ground his teeth.

The Silent Moon Sect had been nothing more than a stepping stone.

His grip on the scroll tightened, the parchment crinkling under the pressure. He had no illusions about where this left them. The sect was shattered. Their reputation, in tatters. Their leader, growing more erratic by the day. And with no external support, no reinforcements, no resources . . .

The barking of orders cut through the thick silence.

Xu Ziqing's eyes flickered toward Sect Leader Jun, who stood in the middle of the wreckage, his robes disheveled, his usually pristine sleeves wrinkled and out of place. His face was drawn tight with barely contained fury as he tried to force some semblance of order upon the sect.

"Move with purpose! We are not a pack of frightened dogs!" His voice cracked through the courtyard, but it lacked the commanding presence it once had. "You call yourselves disciples of the Silent Moon, but you cower and drag your feet like common beggars!"

His words were ignored.

The remaining disciples—those too wounded or too weary to have already fled—moved with slow, languid steps. Their faces were drawn with exhaustion, their eyes hollowed by sleepless nights and nightmares of dead comrades.

The fear of another attack had sunk too deep into their bones. They were not warriors anymore. They were survivors, barely clinging to what remained.

And Xu Ziqing could see it clearly.

Sect Leader Jun, for all his bluster, had already lost them.

The only one who still approached him was Ping Hai.

The bald, broad-shouldered third-class disciple who had once been a pillar of the outer ranks, a man of few words but undeniable presence. He walked with purpose, his fists clenched tightly at his sides as he stepped forward.

"Sect Leader," Ping Hai said, his voice steady but clipped.

Jun turned sharply, his irritation clear. "What?"

"I request permission to leave the sect," Ping Hai said. "There are reports of demonic cultivators in the far north. My hometown . . . It's vulnerable. The sect withdrew all forces to merge here, but that means—"

"You think I don't know what that means?" Sect Leader Jun snapped. His already frayed patience snapped, his face twisting with frustration. "Are you blaming me for withdrawing our forces from Pingyao?"

"No, Sect Leader. I would never!"

Jun stepped forward, his presence looming. "Then let me remind you, disciple. The sect is your home now. We are your home now. And you wish to abandon your home? To run away, after all it has given you?"

Ping Hai's fists tightened at his sides. The muscles in his jaw tensed, but he did not speak.

"You owe everything to the Silent Moon," Jun continued. "And in its darkest hour, you would desert it?"

Silence.

Xu Ziqing's lips thinned. He saw the flicker in Ping Hai's eyes. The way his breathing had changed, the way his stance shifted, was like a thread had been pulled too tight and was one breath away from snapping.

Ping Hai lowered his head, his voice quiet.

"No, Sect Leader. I apologize."

Jun scoffed, turning away as if the matter was settled, but the second-class disciple caught the way Ping Hai's hands trembled before he forced them still.

Xu Ziqing said nothing. He simply watched.

Day bled into night.

The Silent Moon was quieter than ever. The sect had always thrived under shadow, but now, it was like a graveyard.

Then, a figure stepped into the cold.

Ping Hai.

His hood was drawn, his movements careful, but they were not the movements of a man sneaking away. There was no hesitation in his steps, no second-guessing.

He had made his choice.

The moment his foot touched the threshold of the outer gate, a voice cut through the winter night.

"You're leaving."

Ping Hai stilled.

Xu Ziqing leaned against the outer wall of the sect, watching the snowfall settle over the ruined courtyard. His face was impassive as he stepped into the dim light of the illuminated path.

For a moment, neither of them moved.

Then, slowly, the third-class disciple turned. His expression was guarded, but his stance had already shifted—his center of gravity lower, his muscles tensed to prepare for a fight.

Xu Ziqing didn't move. He merely tilted his head slightly, regarding him.

"I understand," he said. His voice was quiet but steady. "If it were me, I would do the same."

Ping Hai's fingers twitched. He didn't drop his stance.

The senior disciple continued, his gaze steady. "I don't have a family. I never did. But I know what it's like to have something worth protecting." His lips curled, just slightly, bitter. "For me, it's the sect."

The third-class disciple's shoulders tightened.

"That's why I can't let you go."

A gust of wind howled through the ruins, carrying with it the weight of his words.

Ping Hai's eyes hardened, but his fist shook with every step he took.

He was prepared to fight, but there was hesitation, uncertainty.

"Senior Brother, I—"

He opened his mouth, but Xu Ziqing spoke first.

"That's why," he said, "I'll go with you."

Ping Hai blinked.

". . . What?"

"You heard me."

The third-class disciple stared, as if waiting for a trick, but his senior's expression didn't waver.

"But . . . why? You're risking a lot for this. Your position, your life . . . It would be easier for you to just stay here."

Xu Ziqing didn't answer immediately. He let the silence stretch, let his thoughts settle into something he could stomach.

Then, he remembered the feeling of his hands shaking.

The burning shame that coiled in his gut as the Silent Moon fell.

The realization that the sect was already in ruins before the cultists ever arrived—that all it took was a single push for everything to collapse.

And that he had done nothing.

He looked at Ping Hai, and for the first time in a long time, he decided not for the sect, not for survival, but for himself. For what he felt was right.

The bearded warrior reached out, clapping Ping Hai on the shoulder.

"I already told you, the sect is my everything." His voice was light, but his grip was firm. "And how can I let a sect brother walk to his death alone? You are part of the Silent Moon, and therefore, my responsibility."

The bald man swallowed. His hulking frame trembled in gratitude and relief for his senior's support.

He hesitated—only for a moment—then nodded.

"Let's go."

The snow crunched beneath their feet as they walked, the sound swallowed by the silence of the ruined sect behind them. He didn't look back, but he tilted his head upward.

The moon was full tonight. It cast a pale glow over the landscape, illuminating the wreckage of the Silent Moon Sect behind them.

A broken sect beneath an unbroken sky.

For years, the Silent Moon had been his home. Its teachings, his foundation. Its name, a legacy he had been raised to uphold. But now, as he stood beneath the very moon their sect was named after, he realized something.

The Silent Moon had already lost its way.

And yet, the moon above remained unchanged.

Perhaps if he followed this path—if he made this choice—there would still be something left to salvage. Not the sect as it was, but the ideals it had abandoned.

A part of him hoped that, in doing this, he could reclaim some of what had been lost.

The moonlight cast long shadows on the snow, but as Xu Ziqing took another step forward, he felt reassured by his decision.

No longer waiting.

No longer hesitating.

For the first time in a long time, he was moving toward something, rather than away.

CHAPTER THIRTY

Blood in the Thickets

The forest was quiet, but not unnaturally so. Birds chirped in the canopy, and the occasional rustle of small animals in the underbrush signaled that life still thrived here. Even the usual tension that accompanied these expeditions had lessened. With no incidents, our scouting party moved with a relaxed efficiency, spreading out slightly to cover more ground.

Jian Feng and the other Verdant Lotus disciples staked out a different section, their muted voices and occasional movement filtering through the trees. Windy slithered away, fixated on a nimble bamboo rat, and I could feel his patience running thin through our bond. Tianyi flitted ahead, her wings glinting in the morning light as she gave chase to a startled bird, momentarily drifting past the scouting perimeter. I let them go without concern. Both of them were sharp enough to retreat if danger loomed.

That left me with my task.

I exhaled, eyeing the Skyreach Flower perched precariously on a ledge above me. Normally, I would've marked it down for the second team to pick, but I had time. We've covered plenty of ground with our spread-out formation, and I'd have an easier time bringing it back with my storage ring due to how delicate it was.

Besides, scaling this ledge while bearing the weight of the Black Tortoise and without infusing my body with qi was bound to be a good exercise.

The bloom pulsed with a faint glow, its petals curling toward the sky like reaching hands. Carefully, I adjusted my grip and began climbing up.

Then, I heard it.

A ragged panting, shallow and faint.

I stilled. The usual forest noises quieted, but that breathing persisted. Unsteady. Pained.

Slowly, I turned to look down toward the source.

At the base of a large tree, partially obscured by thick roots and fallen leaves, lay a massive bear. No—not just a bear. A spirit beast. Its sheer size and the unique silver streaks running down its fur marked it as something beyond a normal animal. But what caught my attention wasn't its presence—it was its state.

Deep, jagged claw wounds tore through its shoulder, exposing raw flesh and bone. It was missing the right ear, and clearly on death's door.

The sight was sickeningly familiar, an echo of the Iron Boar and Black Tiger corpses. Wounds that hadn't been made by a natural predator.

My pulse quickened.

I opened my mouth to call for Jian Feng—

Goosebumps prickled my skin. A sudden, sharp dread seized me, cold and suffocating.

Move.

I didn't hesitate. Instinct overrode thought as I pushed off the ledge, dropping just as something—someone—sliced through the air where I had been standing moments before.

I hit the ground hard, creating a small crater where I landed before snapping my head up.

A pale, hooded figure loomed where I had stood moments before. His tattered robes hung loosely over a skeletal frame, his skin so pallid and thin it seemed nearly translucent beneath the dappled sunlight. His outstretched hand, frail as though it'd snap in a strong breeze, was buried deep into the cliffside—right where my neck should have been.

Cold eyes met mine.

Demonic cultivator.

My heart pounded as I backpedaled, forcing myself to keep my breathing steady.

"Jian Feng! Tianyi!" My voice cut through the trees as I retreated, opening my satchel to throw the vials for emergency signals.

Then, with unnatural speed, he lunged.

I twisted sharply, forcing my body into a sideways roll as his strike carved through the space I had occupied. My unclasped satchel fell to the floor, the strap destroyed, blackened where it was cut. I cursed. It'd take time for them to converge on my location without the emergency signal; and I needed every second I could get.

I couldn't afford to take a hit. Not even one. Windy's injuries, Tianyi's account of her battle, the festering corruption that had nearly consumed them both—a single strike would be lethal.

"Shit!" I ducked under another strike. Each was made with the intent to kill.

He was faster than me. That was the worst part. Even with qi reinforcing my muscles, his speed was greater. My instincts screamed at me to flee, but with him closing the distance so effortlessly, escape wasn't an option.

Instead, I kept a wide berth, making erratic movements, never giving him a straight path toward me. It was ugly. Unrefined. Unlike any other battle or spar I've had, where I could properly test my techniques, gauge my opponent, and adapt my approach. Here, there was no room for that. No space for drawn-out exchanges, for clever counters or refined stances.

This wasn't a fight. This was survival.

My feet pounded the earth as I maneuvered backward, ducking low, rolling when necessary, staying out of his immediate striking range. The slightest misstep would mean my death.

Still, he pressed forward, a specter of inevitability.

The terrain worked against me. A rocky outcrop jutted out behind me, narrowing my available space. I'd unknowingly backed myself into a corner.

His hand lifted, fingers curled in a claw-like shape, aiming for my chest.

My back hit the cliffside.

Trapped.

I had an instant to react. I couldn't block. I couldn't parry. If I tried to counter, I'd be dead before my strike landed.

His hand shot forward, an execution more than an attack. My mind screamed through every possibility, every technique, every scrap of knowledge I had, and came to one conclusion.

I planted myself in my most practiced technique.

ROOTED BANYAN STANCE!

The moment his strike shot forward, my entire body tensed, feet sinking into the ground, my core tightening like iron bands. But I left it imperfect; my right hand extended directly in the path of his attack.

My fist connected with his elbow just as his attacking arm was extending, the claw within moments of reaching my heart.

The impact, focused and powerful, violently redirected the trajectory of his attack. It became a glancing blow. Instead of piercing my chest, the claw ripped through my left shoulder, the force of the redirected momentum still carrying it through. A searing burn ripped through me. A sharp, wet crack sounded as flesh and muscle gave way beneath his unnatural strength.

"AHHHHHH!"

But—I was still alive.

The pain barely had time to register before a worse sensation took hold.

A deep, festering cold.

It seeped from the wound outward, spreading like ink through water. My qi buckled immediately, the flow disrupted as the corruption wormed its way in.

Demonic qi.

Agony lanced through my body as it burrowed into my veins, clawing its way deeper with every heartbeat. It was unlike any pain I had ever felt—cold, festering, like something foreign was gnawing at my very essence. My breath hitched as my vision blurred for a split second.

No.

I forced my mind to steady. My left arm was useless, but I still had one good hand.

With a roar, I activated the Heavenly Flame Mantra to its fullest. The air shimmered as raw heat surged through me, igniting at my palm with a brilliant red-white blaze. My skin cracked under the sheer intensity, the pain of my burning flesh mixing with the corruption's invasive chill—but I didn't hesitate.

I slammed my flaming hand onto his face.

Flesh sizzled.

For an instant, I thought it worked. The fire consumed him, searing through skin, the flames flaring brighter as I poured every ounce of qi I had left into the attack. It burned so hot that my skin blackened, my own nerves screamed—but I refused to let go.

Then I saw his eyes.

Not a flicker of pain. No screaming, no frantic attempt to claw my arm away. He just . . . stared. His deadened pupils locked onto mine through the haze of fire, his expression eerily still, as if my attempt to incinerate him was nothing more than an inconvenience.

My stomach twisted.

The fire should have blinded him. The heat alone should have sent him writhing in agony. And yet, despite the flesh peeling from his face, despite the charred, blistering skin, he was still moving.

His free hand rose.

I felt it before I saw it. The oppressive weight of pure killing intent.

I was going to die.

The certainty settled in, cold and absolute. There was no more room to dodge, no more time to counter. His hand, wreathed in the same sickeningly dense demonic qi that had nearly killed my companions, hovered mere inches from my throat. The moment it touched me—

A blur of motion.

Then a deafening *CRACK!*

The next thing I knew, the shadow's body hurtled sideways, crashing into a tree with bone-snapping force. Bark splintered from the impact, debris scattering as the entire trunk shuddered violently, dropping snow from its branches in a resounding crash.

I gasped, stumbling forward, barely able to process what had just happened.

Tianyi hovered above, her wings flaring out as she adjusted her posture midair.

She had drop-kicked him. From the sky.

She landed gracefully a few feet in front of me, her antennae twitching as she studied the fallen figure with sharp, unreadable eyes.

My body was trembling, my burnt hand barely responding, my left arm a mangled mess. The demonic qi in my wound throbbed, the corruption settling deeper, but I forced it aside. I wasn't dead.

My gaze darted to the tree Tianyi had sent him crashing into.

The bald man peeled himself off the bark, his neck cracking as he tilted his head unnaturally to the side. Smoke still curled from the raw, blackened burns across his face, but his expression was eerily calm, as if pain was a foreign concept to him. His empty, sunken eyes flicked between Tianyi and me, taking in the recent development with unnerving patience.

I swallowed hard, forcing myself to steady my breathing. My arm was ruined, and the demonic qi was spreading. If I didn't purge it soon, it would eat away at my body. But there was no time.

"Tianyi—" I coughed, my voice hoarse. "We need to—"

"Heal yourself," she interrupted, never once taking her eyes off the man. "I'll handle him."

Her confidence was absolute, but I knew better than to let that lull me into a false sense of security.

Still, I had no choice. Right now, I was more of a liability than an asset.

I gritted my teeth and pushed off the ground, dragging myself toward my fallen satchel. My breath came in quick gasps, each movement a battle against the spreading corruption. Behind me, I heard the telltale snap of air displacement—a battle beginning.

Tianyi moved first. The bald man barely twisted in time to deflect her blow, his sleeve tearing from the force. But Tianyi didn't relent. She moved like a storm—every motion precise, every strike lethal. Her wings blurred as she attacked from impossible angles, pressing him back with relentless ferocity.

He tried to counter, his fingers laced with that sickening, festering qi, but she was too fast. A swipe of her wing—razor-sharp—tore a deep gash through his arm. For the first time, he faltered.

I didn't waste the opportunity. My fingers closed around my satchel, yanking it open with my good hand. My movements were clumsy, rushed, but I pulled free a vial of Essence Purifying Elixir. With shaking hands, I uncorked it and poured the entire thing over my wound.

Relief was immediate.

The burning, gnawing corruption fizzled as the purifying liquid seeped into my flesh, sending a cleansing heat through my veins. I gasped as the demonic qi was forcibly expelled, leaving behind only the raw, exposed wound and the pulsing ache of overused muscles. The pain was excruciating, but bearable.

I forced myself to focus, assessing the damage. Even with my imperfect execution of Rooted Banyan Stance, the bald man's attack had nearly punctured straight through my shoulder. If I had miscalculated even slightly, I wouldn't be breathing right now.

My hands trembled as I reached for gauze, but my fingers fumbled. The adrenaline, the lingering effects of the corruption—it was all catching up to me. The gauze slipped from my grasp, falling into the snow.

Before I could reach for it, a voice cut through the clearing.

"Kai!"

Jian Feng.

I turned my head just in time to see him emerging from the trees, his sword drawn, his expression a mixture of fury and control. The other Verdant Lotus disciples weren't far behind.

"Cover him!" Jian Feng barked, and one disciple immediately dropped beside me, reaching for my wound with practiced efficiency. I barely had time to process it before movement in my peripheral caught my attention.

Windy.

He struck with terrifying speed, launching himself at the bald man's torso, fangs bared and tail lashing. Tianyi shot forward, her wings leaving a streak of pale blue light as she aimed for the throat.

The bald man moved.

His body twisted unnaturally, dodging Windy's bite, but Tianyi's strike forced him to take a step back. Then another.

The entire scouting team had arrived. He was outnumbered.

For the first time since the fight began, he paused.

Jian Feng took a measured step forward, his sword raised. "Stand down." His voice was cold, authoritative.

Then, slowly, his lips curled.

Not in pain. Not in fear.

In rage.

It twisted his burnt face into something inhuman, veins bulging beneath the raw, peeling flesh. His expression stretched, distorting into a grotesque grimace, as if his very skin struggled to contain the fury beneath. His eyes, sunken yet alight with something primal, burned with an intensity that sent a visceral shudder down my spine. The air thickened, charged with a silent, suffocating malice, as if the mere force of his hatred alone could strangle the life from the clearing.

But he didn't lash out. He didn't scream.

He simply turned.

With a single push off the ground, he vanished.

Snow exploded in his wake, his form disappearing into the depths of the forest in a heartbeat.

Tianyi tensed, wings twitching as she prepared to give chase.

"Stop," Jian Feng commanded sharply.

She turned to him, eyes blazing. "We can't let him go—"

"We need to treat Kai."

I gritted my teeth, forcing myself upright despite the searing pain in my shoulder. "No. We can't let him go."

Jian Feng's eyes snapped to me. "Kai, you're injured. This isn't the time—"

"And when will be?" I shot back, breath ragged but firm. "When he comes back and slaughters the next scouting team? When he finds the village? We lose him now, we may never get another chance."

Tianyi's wings twitched, her gaze flicking between me and the trees where the demonic cultivator had vanished. Windy coiled tightly beside her, his muscles tense, ready to strike again.

The disciples hesitated. They were disciplined, but I could see the flicker of doubt in their eyes. The rational choice was to regroup, to fall back, to ensure I was safe. Every instinct screamed at me to do the same. My body ached, my wounds burned, and my fingers trembled from both the pain and the lingering terror.

But even as fear coiled around my ribs like a vise, suffocating and relentless, another thought eclipsed it.

The thought of Gentle Wind Village encountering that monster.

I clenched my fists to stop the trembling, nails biting into my palms. My breath came sharp, uneven, but I forced my voice to steady. "I'm not saying we chase blindly," I said, swallowing against the dryness in my throat. "But we can't just let him slip away. We need to at least track him."

Jian Feng studied me, his jaw tightening. A long silence stretched between us.

CHAPTER THIRTY-ONE

On Thin Ice Over a Deep Abyss

I hissed as Tianyi's qi surged through me, the warmth sinking deep into my wounds. The puncture in my left shoulder pulsed with pain, but beneath it, I felt something else—reconstruction. The torn flesh was knitting back together, and the bone, which had nearly been fractured from the force of the impact, was being reinforced, stabilizing beneath the careful flow of qi.

Without corruption hampering her powers, it was more potent than most medicine I could make at this moment.

The gnarled burns along my right hand, however, were another issue entirely. Unlike my shoulder, which had suffered direct trauma, the burns were self-inflicted, a byproduct of my desperation. The skin had blackened in some areas, cracked and raw in others. It was only through the quick intervention of the disciples that kept it from fusing together.

Tianyi's antennae twitched as she observed the injuries, and though her face showed little emotion, I could feel just how delicate her touch was as she wrapped gauze around my hand. As though she was afraid of hurting me any further.

"Your shoulder will be okay," she murmured, pressing her palm lightly against my skin. The residual heat of her qi still lingered, but the overwhelming pain had dulled to something more manageable. "You can use your left arm again, but not at full strength."

I flexed my fingers, testing the range of motion. It hurt, but I could move it now. That was enough.

Jian Feng sat across from me, arms crossed, his sword laid neatly across his lap. His gaze, sharp and unreadable, hadn't left me since Tianyi began infusing me with qi.

Windy, meanwhile, was tracking the demonic cultivator with the rest of the disciples. I could feel his presence on the edge of my awareness, following the remnants of the demonic cultivator's trail. His instincts made him uniquely suited for this; if anything, he was better at tracking than all of us combined.

Jian Feng finally spoke, breaking the silence. "We're moving out soon. We've already determined the direction he fled. But you need to return to the village."

I clenched my jaw, already knowing where this was going.

"You're injured," Jian Feng continued. "You've already pushed yourself too far by staying conscious and tracking back here. The Village Head needs to be warned about what happened, and if that cultivator has allies, we can't rule out the possibility of an attack."

I shook my head. "I'm coming with you."

"No. This isn't up for debate."

I exhaled sharply, struggling to rein in my frustration. "I won't slow you down."

"You already have," Jian Feng countered, his voice calm but firm. "You needed healing before we could move forward. That was time lost. We can't afford another delay."

"I'm fine now," I argued, flexing my fingers to prove the point. "And you need me."

Jian Feng arched a brow. "Do we?"

I met his gaze without hesitation. "Yes. I won't be reckless, and I won't put myself at risk. But you will need support. I've done it before—with Feng Wu when we subjugated the Wind Serpents in Qingmu. I kept the front lines stable, poisoned the Wind Serpent, and kept casualties to a minimum. I'm useful outside of a straight fight."

Jian Feng's expression didn't shift, but he was listening.

"I can prepare concoctions for battle," I pressed on. "Tonics for stamina, antidotes in case there's poison, Qi Restoratives—things that could make the difference between surviving and losing. You know I'm right."

The second-class disciple exhaled slowly, rubbing a hand over his chin. "That's not the problem. You could be useful. I'm not ruling that out."

"Then what's the problem?"

"We can't afford to bring dead weight."

I bristled. Wasn't he listening? "I'm not—"

Jian Feng lifted a hand to cut me off. "I know you're not. If you were, we wouldn't be having this conversation. I value your opinion more than before, and I know you're not weak. But that doesn't mean I'm convinced this is the right call. If we engage, you'll undeniably be an asset. But if we need to retreat, can you guarantee your ability to keep pace? I cannot risk your safety, nor can I burden others with the responsibility of protecting you."

The admission should have felt like progress. Instead, it infuriated me to hear his words, as accurate as they were. But this wasn't just a matter of what I was capable of.

"I can't leave Tianyi and Windy alone to face this."

Jian Feng's lips pressed into a thin line.

"I did that once before," I continued, my voice quieter now, but no less firm. "I followed your orders. Stayed behind when I should have been there. And because of that, they almost died."

The words hung in the air, heavier than I had intended. I bowed my head, pressing my forehead to the dirt.

"I know I'm weak," I said, voice steady. "But that doesn't mean I can just stand here and let others die in my place. If something happens, something preventable, and I wasn't there to stop it—I could never forgive myself."

A long silence stretched between us.

I kept my head bowed.

"I'm asking you, Jian Feng," I said, swallowing past the lump in my throat. "Let me go. I'll take full responsibility for myself."

He exhaled through his nose slowly. I heard the faint shift of his sleeve as he crossed his arms tighter, the telltale scrape of his fingers against his sword hilt. We both knew what this was.

It was a bad idea.

A terrible idea.

But some things weren't about what was smart or strategic. Some things weren't about logic at all.

Jian Feng sighed. "You're a pain in the ass, you know that?"

I lifted my head slightly. His expression had shifted. Not softer—he wasn't the type—but something in it had eased. He wasn't looking at me like I was a liability anymore.

"Fine," he muttered. "But don't make me regret this."

I let out a slow breath, nodding. "I won't."

"Then get ready. We'll move once the team sends us a signal."

The moment Jian Feng gave the go-ahead, I didn't waste time. My injuries might not have fully healed, but my hands still worked, and that was all I needed.

I crouched by the supply pile and summoned all the ingredients I had in my storage ring. Although I didn't have my pill furnace, my stock of ingredients was still intact—ginseng, wolfberry, Skyreach Flower, and a handful of other herbs I'd gathered from past expeditions. It wasn't much, but it would do.

Tianyi moved away from me, taking to the skies to monitor the area. I felt secure with her guarding my back.

Jian Feng watched me with thinly veiled curiosity. "What are you doing?"

"Preparing," I said, pulling out a small cauldron from the tent. It was about the size of my fist—meant for simple meals, not alchemical refinement—but it would have to suffice.

Jian Feng frowned. "You're making medicine now? It'll take too long to make anything of use."

I didn't answer immediately. Instead, I took a breath and reached outward with my qi, activating the Alchemical Nexus.

Glowing symbols appeared in the air, surrounding the cauldron in the shape of a cube.

Jian Feng's breath hitched.

I adjusted the formation, guiding the flow of energy. With a subtle shift of my will, I focused on hastening the process. The formations shuddered, then shifted—lines tightening, the glow intensifying. The fire beneath the cauldron responded immediately, flickering brighter, the water inside boiling within seconds.

So this is what it meant by refining without a pill furnace . . .

Even with such a simple setup, I could already tell—it worked.

I reached into my storage ring and pulled out a fresh Skyreach Flower. I'd planned to collect it earlier, but the demonic cultivator's ambush had derailed everything. Now, though, I was glad I had Tianyi pick it for me while we were still in the area.

I extracted its essence, and a fine golden mist rose from the flower. Narrowing my focus, I pushed further, sifting through the gathered essence, isolating only one property—its ability to heighten one's senses.

I moved the remaining, unnecessary parts of the essence into a smaller vial I had on hand.

Then I poured the Skyreach Flower's concentrated essence into the cauldron, adding the rest of the ingredients; ginger and red dates, watching the liquid shift from a pale gold to a rich amber. With my Alchemical Nexus set to hasten the process, the reaction stabilized almost instantly. Within minutes, the potion was complete.

I carefully extracted the liquid and funneled it into a small vial. The result was a Warming Tonic—a potion that staved off cold, improved circulation, and temporarily enhanced strength by invigorating the blood. Simple, but effective.

Jian Feng stared. ". . . That took you less than five minutes."

I grinned, rolling the vial between my fingers. "Convenient, right? A gift from the Interface; I can adjust the formation to either strengthen the effects, quicken the process, or stabilize a volatile process."

His eyes flicked back to the glowing formations still surrounding the cauldron. "I'll admit; our group isn't very capable in this field, and only two of us can use alchemical formations. But even we know there's never been a way to form an array without a physical engraving—at least not at our level."

I shrugged, tucking the vial away. "Then it's a good thing I came with you, huh?"

His expression darkened slightly, but I caught the corner of his mouth twitching just a little.

I took that as a win.

An hour passed in a blur of preparation.

I worked methodically, my hands moving with the practiced precision of someone who had done this a thousand times. The Alchemical Nexus allowed me to refine without a furnace, but it wasn't just the speed that made it invaluable—it was the sheer flexibility. I had set it to hasten the process, but if needed, I could switch to stability or potency at a moment's notice.

In that time, I had produced over a dozen vials. Warming Tonics, Qi Restoratives, and even a few Explosive Elixirs—designed to ignite upon impact, like the ones used in the Grand Alchemy Gauntlet. Admittedly, they were weak in comparison because of the lack of potent ingredients. But the Alchemical Nexus came in handy; raising its potency enough to the point it'd be useful in a fight.

"The disciples are returning."

Just as I funneled the last of the refined liquid into a vial, two of the disciples walked into the camp. Their expressions were tense, breath coming in quick gasps from exertion.

"We found it," one of them said, voice taut with urgency. "The demonic cultivator's base."

Jian Feng immediately rose, his posture straightening. "Where?"

"Northwest, several li away. It's well hidden, tucked between the cliffs, but the sna—er, Windy caught sight of movement. At least three figures. Maybe more inside. The rest of us are monitoring the area and ensuring there are no traps."

That was all we needed to hear.

I tucked the remaining vials into my belt, distributing several to the disciples as we moved. I handed out Qi Restoratives and passed a couple of Explosive Elixirs to Jian Feng, who eyed them with mild surprise before securing them at his waist.

With that, we pressed forward.

We moved quickly, our footsteps muffled by the forest floor. Despite the urgency, there was a heavy tension that settled over the group, an unspoken understanding that this wasn't a simple skirmish.

We passed by the spirit beast bear from earlier. It had finally succumbed to its wounds, its massive form lying still beneath the morning light.

But what caught my attention wasn't just the body—it was what had already found it.

A fox and a badger, their muzzles slick with fresh blood, were already feasting on the carcass.

The bear had been left to die, just like the Iron Boar and Black Tiger. The demonic cultivators hadn't finished it themselves—they had let nature do their work for them.

And as we moved past the corpse, I came to a sinking realization.

They left them to lure others in.

The scent of fresh blood would attract more creatures. Scavengers, predators, even other spirit beasts—none would pass up an easy meal. The demonic cultivators weren't just killing. They were baiting for a larger catch.

A cold shudder ran down my spine.

Just like us.

I clenched my jaw, pushing harder, my feet pounding against the dirt as I picked up my pace.

We thought we were in control, that we were tracking them. But what if we weren't? What if this was exactly what they wanted? What if we were just the next layer of prey, following the scent of blood like every other beast before us?

I swallowed hard, the creeping sense of unease growing heavier with every step.

"Jian Feng," I said, breath coming quicker now, not from exertion, but from the weight of my own thoughts.

He gave a quick grunt of acknowledgment, not breaking stride.

I hesitated, then forced the words out. "What if we're the fox and the badger?"

He shot me a glance, his brows furrowed, but I kept going.

"They didn't finish the bear off. Just like the Iron Boar in Qingmu. Just like the black tiger. They didn't do it because they didn't need to. They let them die on their own, because the scent of blood would do the rest of the work for them."

Jian Feng's expression darkened.

"We're the scavengers," I said, voice lower now. "We think we're tracking them. But what if they're the ones pulling us in? What if we're already in their trap?"

Jian Feng didn't answer right away. His eyes flicked toward the path ahead, toward the cliffs looming in the distance. His jaw tightened.

"I had the same thought," he admitted finally.

That sent a jolt through me. "Then—"

"But it changes nothing. Even if this is a trap, what's the alternative? Turning back? Leaving them to do whatever they're doing out here? Letting them come to us when we're unprepared? We don't have a choice. We have to see this through."

I hated that he was right.

We were caught in a snare of our own making—one we couldn't afford to escape from. Because if we ran now, we wouldn't be the only ones at risk.

I grit my teeth and nodded, shaking off the cold dread curling in my stomach.

"Then we go in knowing what we might walk into," I muttered.

Jian Feng shot me a sidelong glance, something flickering in his gaze—maybe approval, maybe just acknowledgment.

"We go in," he said. "But we don't get careless."

We pressed forward, our pace measured but urgent, our ears straining for any sound beyond our own movements.

Ahead, one of the Verdant Lotus disciples raised a hand, signaling for us to slow down.

"This is where we set our traps. Follow exactly where we step."

Jian Feng gave a firm nod, motioning for me and Tianyi to stay close.

I adjusted my pace, falling in line behind them. The disciples pointed out subtle cues—tiny disturbances in the dirt, thin threads barely visible in the underbrush, small indentations that seemed like nothing until I looked closer.

I exhaled quietly. Even knowing they were there, they were damn near impossible to spot.

As we moved, I distributed the vials I had made, briefly explaining their properties. The disciples accepted them without question, securing them in their robes with practiced ease. Even those unfamiliar with alchemy understood the value of an edge in battle.

The deeper we went, the darker the forest became. The forest itself seemed . . . wrong.

The leaves rustled without wind. The ground underfoot felt softer, almost spongy, like decay had settled far too deep. And the trees—some of them were wrong. Their shapes were subtly distorted, their trunks twisted unnaturally as if something had influenced their growth.

Windy slithered close behind us, alerting us to his presence. Tianyi spoke, listening to the serpent's hisses and relaying his message.

"They are close," she said. "This is as far as we go before they notice."

Jian Feng gestured for everyone to halt. We crouched low, taking cover behind a fallen tree.

From here, the terrain sloped downward, forming a natural basin between the cliffs.

And there—half-shrouded in unnatural darkness—stood the entrance to what could only be the demonic cultivators' hideout.

It wasn't a constructed fortress or anything overtly unnatural. Rather, it was an old cavern, nestled within the jagged rock formations, almost indistinguishable from its surroundings if not for the faint glow emanating from within. A dim, sickly light pulsed faintly at the entrance, flickering like dying embers.

Movement.

I barely caught it—a figure, just at the entrance, shifting in and out of the shadows.

Even from this distance, the air was thick with the same corrupting qi I had felt when the demonic cultivator struck me. It clung to the space around the cavern like an invisible fog.

Something strong.

"What's our plan, Brother Jian Feng?"

Jian Feng exhaled, his expression hardening.

"We're attacking."

He glanced at us all, then explained the plan.

CHAPTER THIRTY-TWO

Courting Death Through Blasphemy

My voice rang out across the clearing, cutting through the thick, stifling air with a confidence I barely felt.

"Oi! Baldy! You still alive in there?" My shout echoed through the trees, bouncing off the jagged rock formations that lined the cavern entrance. I grinned, though sweat slicked the back of my neck.

"That burn must be killing you. What, did you crawl back into your hole to lick your wounds?" I took a step forward, making myself as obvious a target as possible. "Come on, I thought demonic cultivators were supposed to be tough! Or did I misjudge that?"

Jian Feng stood just a step behind me, his sword loose in his grip but his eyes sharp, scanning every shadow in the rock face. He said nothing, his presence a quiet reassurance. He had already explained; we couldn't afford to fight inside that cave. We needed to lure them out.

And unfortunately, I was the best one for the job.

Even so, there was nothing. No movement. No response.

But I could feel them watching.

The hair on my arms stood on end. The sensation wasn't coming from any single direction—it was a weight pressing in from all sides, as if unseen hands were reaching toward me, stopping just short of grasping my neck. My instincts screamed at me, warning me of my impending doom.

I swallowed but kept my stance firm, my fingers curling at my sides. The disciples remained in their positions. Circling the cave so there'd be no way for them to escape. But despite making myself an easy target, nothing ventured out of the cave.

I licked my lips. They were disciplined, even in their madness. But there was something else.

I closed my eyes for half a breath, recalling Tianyi's account of her battle.

Their worship. Their god. The Heavenly Demon.

I inhaled deeply and exhaled just as slowly, shifting my approach.

"Tch. Maybe I was wrong about you all," I said, my tone dropping into something more contemptuous, more biting. The young master persona I'd been cultivating all these years was finally coming in handy. "Maybe I thought too highly of your kind. I thought you all were supposed to be followers of the Heavenly Demon. But what kind of followers are you?"

I let the words hang, let them seep into the silence.

"I expected something grand. Something terrifying. But all I see are rats scurrying in the dark." I spread my arms wide, gesturing toward the cave. "Tell me, is this what your so-called god had in mind for you? Lurking on the outskirts of a province, hiding in caves like cornered prey? Does the great Heavenly Demon reward his faithful with scraps and filth?"

I clicked my tongue, shaking my head. "Pathetic."

I could see Jian Feng looking at me in disbelief from my peripheral vision.

Still no movement. But the weight in the air had changed.

It had sharpened.

The silence wasn't empty anymore—it was seething.

Despite the sheer intent bearing down on me, I kept going. My mind churned with ways to denigrate the Heavenly Demon. *Think*! What would Dian Juan say?

Well, he'd probably piss himself and run away in this situation. But that was beside the point.

"If your god were truly divine, you wouldn't be wasting away in some forgotten cave, skulking in shadows while your betters walk free in the open. No, if your god were real, he would've lifted you up. He would have granted you something more than just . . . this. Tell me, where is your god now? Does he hear your prayers? Does he lift you up? Or has he abandoned you like the wretched pieces of shit you are?"

The change was immediate.

A sharp intake of breath from within the cave. A rustle of movement, the sound of feet shifting.

Then, a single voice, low and rasping, like something dragging itself from the depths of a pit.

"You dare."

A sound like cracking bone echoed from within the cavern, sharp and unnatural. It wasn't just the sound of someone moving—it was something deeper, something wrong. A series of pops and snaps, like flesh contorting, like a body rearranging itself in ways it shouldn't.

Then, a whisper, thin and slicing through the air like a blade to the throat.

"Even a thousand deaths would not suffice for what you have done."

The voice was quiet, almost delicate, but the weight of sheer malice in it made my stomach churn.

. . . Maybe I'd gone too far.

The bald man. His burnt face was still raw and cracked from where I had seared him, the skin blackened and peeling, revealing the flesh beneath. He curled his lips back, revealing teeth stained red. His eyes—deep, sunken pits of ink—locked onto mine with an expression not too dissimilar from an asura.

Demonic qi surged outward as he exploded toward me in a blur of movement, the air distorting around him as if rejecting his presence. He moved too fast—I barely had time to tense, barely had time to react—

Jian Feng stepped in front of me, his sword flashing in an arc—

And then, like a comet plummeting from the sky, Tianyi dropped with crushing force.

The impact sent a shockwave through the clearing, kicking up dust and debris as the bald man was stomped into the ground, his body slamming into the earth with a sickening crunch. Tianyi's foot pinned his chest down, her wings fluttering slightly as she adjusted her stance, antennae twitching in focus.

"Stay," she said simply.

Jian Feng wasted no time. His blade lifted, the arc of his sword gleaming as he prepared to behead him—

But the moment the blade descended, another figure shot from the cavern, blurring into motion.

A second demonic cultivator.

Tianyi twisted, leaping away just in time as the figure's strike cut through empty air. Jian Feng shifted his momentum, twisting mid-swing to block the sudden attack, his blade clashing with the man's claws, sending sparks flying.

Hidden within the snow, his presence suppressed, Windy lunged from below, fangs bared. His body coiled around the second figure in a flash, sinking his teeth into their shoulder before disengaging just as quickly, disappearing back into the cover of the terrain.

The second figure stumbled, their hand flying to the wound.

Three Verdant Lotus disciples surged forward, just as planned. Their movements were coordinated, blades flashing as they pressed the assault on the injured target.

Six versus two. We were just the first line.

Beyond the trees, the rest of the disciples remained hidden, waiting for the signal. Ready to strike when the time was right.

And as the bald man pushed himself up from the dirt, his head snapping toward me, his body trembled with rage. His blank expression was long gone; replaced with bloodlust aimed directly toward me.

The battle had begun.

The second hooded figure stepped forward. His voice began low and measured but rose with growing fury.

"If you had just stayed put, you all could have lived a humble life," he said, his tone laced with venom. "At least until the day our great Heavenly Demon is resurrected."

His hands trembled at his sides, fingers curling into claws as his rage simmered just beneath the surface. Even as the disciples stood poised for battle, ready to strike at a moment's notice, the man showed no fear. There was no tension in his stance, no wariness in his gaze. He did not look at us as an opponent would.

No.

He regarded us in the way one would look at troublesome cattle.

His voice trembled with righteous anger. "But you dared! Dared to speak His name in vain! Dared to mock His divine path!" His breathing hitched, and his head tilted back, his hood falling slightly to reveal a gaunt, sallow face, sunken eyes burning with unholy fervor. "Even our bishop would understand what must be done. To repay your sins, we will exterminate your village. Women. Children. Every last one."

The words sent a ripple through the disciples, but I forced myself to remain still. I couldn't show hesitation. I couldn't let them see the fear creeping at the edges of my mind.

"And we will start," he hissed, his gaze locking onto mine, "with you."

A deep, sickening sound filled the air as he raised his hands, revealing his palms. Etched into the flesh were grotesque sigils, carved so deeply they looked more like brands. A tremor of wrongness rippled through the clearing as he pressed his palms together in a prayer-like gesture.

The air thickened.

The demonic qi in the area surged violently, as if responding to his call.

"Veins of the weeping earth . . . hear me!" he chanted, his voice reverberating unnaturally, layering over itself like a chorus of the damned. "We offer this land! Let it consume those unworthy!"

We moved instinctively, ready to disrupt whatever ritual he was casting—but before I could even take a step, the bald man surged forward, intercepting me with a frenzied charge.

Jian Feng's sword met his attack, sparks flying from the clash of steel and claw, but the hooded man was undeterred. His ritual was complete.

He slammed his palms onto the ground.

A pulse of energy rippled outward, and the snow-covered earth beneath us darkened. A wave of decay spread like ink spilling into water, corrupting everything it touched. The ground beneath my feet softened unnaturally, shifting from solid earth into a tar-like sludge.

The effect was immediate.

Half of our group—including myself—was caught, our legs sinking into the shifting ground. I cursed under my breath, struggling to pull free, but it was spreading too fast. Tianyi, being airborne and swift, avoided it completely, but the disciples nearest to me weren't so lucky.

The bald man's lips curled into a grin as he turned to me, his bloodied face illuminated by the eerie glow of demonic qi. The ground seemed to solidify where he stood; it didn't seem to affect allies.

"You will die first."

He lunged, his claws tearing through the air toward me, a move I had already seen before. The same attack pattern. The same murderous intent.

And thanks to my Refinement Simulation Technique, I knew exactly where it would land.

My mind calculated the trajectory in an instant. Trapped as I was, I couldn't sidestep or retreat. My feet were locked in the sinking ground. But my core was still free.

I bent backward sharply, lowering my upper body into an extreme arch, my back hovering just inches from the corrupted earth. The attack whistled past my face, missing by a hair's breadth. My abdominal muscles screamed from the strain, but I held my position, my breath steady despite the burning tension in my muscles.

Tianyi came forward, grabbing me by the waist and pulling me out. Despite her smaller frame and my immense weight, she wrestled me out with a simple grunt of effort.

"Stay back."

Then she threw me a short distance away, just past immediate danger.

Jian Feng followed up immediately, his sword arcing downward in a lethal stroke, aiming for the bald man's throat.

But before the killing blow could land, the ground warped violently, throwing his attack trajectory off.

The earth trembled beneath them as Jian Feng's strike went astray, narrowly missing the bald man's throat. The demonic cultivator twisted, shifting just out of range before surging forward again.

But Tianyi was faster.

She intercepted him mid-charge, her wings flaring as she kicked off the air itself, twisting and kicking him back, her legs providing a superior reach. The bald man grunted before the impact sent him skidding backward, his feet digging trenches into the corrupted earth.

I landed with a grunt, tumbling across the snow before pushing myself upright. Tianyi had thrown me far enough that I was out of immediate danger, but not so far that I was out of the fight. I sucked in a deep breath, my body aching from the harsh landing.

Good.

I had a job to do.

From my new vantage point, I surveyed the battlefield. The formations had settled naturally—Tianyi and two disciples against the bald man, while Windy, Jian Feng, and another disciple took on the hooded figure.

Windy struck again, launching from the shifting ground like an arrow loosed from a bow. His aim was perfect, his body twisting midair to avoid a counterstrike. The hooded man snarled, swiping at him with his free hand, but Windy blurred—his body slipping through the cultivator's grip as if he were a ghost.

He disengaged, landing fluidly in the snow.

My eyes narrowed.

The earth had stopped churning.

The hooded cultivator had removed his palms from the ground, focusing fully on combat now, and though the battlefield was still difficult to maneuver in, the creeping quicksand effect had stopped spreading. The affected ground remained soft and difficult to maneuver, but it no longer shifted as violently as before.

A slow breath left my lips.

This was still a brutal battle. Despite being outnumbered, the demonic cultivators fought with a single, overwhelming advantage—their complete disregard for their own lives. Every attack was all-or-nothing, with no thought given to preserving their bodies outside of their necks and hearts. They fought to kill, and it seemed if they could take someone with them, that was enough.

The Verdant Lotus disciples weren't accustomed to such savage assaults. The soft earth had thrown them off further, making them hesitant, their movements sluggish compared to their usual precision.

But we were still winning. In fact, none of the cultists had landed a clean hit yet.

Why?

My eyes flicked between the ongoing fights, following every exchange, every clash of steel and claw.

Tianyi.

Windy.

Individually, they were the strongest here—but mostly in raw cultivation level. If it came to the refinement of technique and skill, the disciples were superior.

And yet, their presence had shifted what should have been a hard-fought battle into a slow, but inevitable victory.

Windy struck again, his lithe form weaving through attacks like water through cracks. There was no hesitation in his movements, no fear in his approach. Tianyi's face remained blank as she danced through her fight with superhuman speed; the cultists had to defend against the second-class disciple's attacks, along with her strikes from above.

There was no fear paralyzing their movement.

And that was the difference.

The Verdant Lotus disciples were strong, but they were human. And humans hesitated in the face of something like this. How could they not? A single scratch from these monsters could mean corruption sinking into their bodies. A single mistake could be fatal.

But Tianyi and Windy?

They weren't human.

They had faced death. Survived it.

And more than that—Tianyi had fought these them before. Windy had suffered at their hands. They understood this enemy on a deeper level. And unlike the disciples, they didn't hesitate.

This wasn't a sparring match or a sect competition. This was survival.

The disciples' carefully practiced stances were being eroded by the battlefield itself. But Windy and Tianyi? They fought practically. Cleanly. Without waste.

A battle like this wasn't won with perfect execution. It was won by adapting.

I clenched my fists.

They were keeping us in this fight.

I needed to do my part.

I reached into my pouch, fingers wrapping around the cool glass of a vial. I had spent the last hour preparing for this exact moment.

The disciples weren't at their peak. The winter chill slowed their movements. The terrain was against them. Their fear worsened the quality of their attacks.

But I could change that.

I uncorked the vial with my teeth, tilting it back, then hurled it toward the disciple who was struggling to keep up.

"Sun Yang!" I shouted, catching his attention. His head snapped toward me just in time to see the glass vial sailing through the air. "Drink it!"

He caught it, his movements sluggish from the cold and the corrupting qi lingering in the air. There was hesitation in his eyes, but he trusted me enough to obey without question. He downed the Warming Tonic in one go.

The effect was near-instantaneous.

His posture straightened, the tension bleeding from his limbs. His breathing evened out, and the fog in his gaze cleared. He flexed his fingers, testing the renewed strength in his body.

Then, a shadow loomed.

The bald man's eyes flicked toward me, catching the exchange. His lips peeled back in a snarl as he surged forward, claws bared and wreathed in thick, black qi.

Too fast.

I barely had time to react, let alone move out of the way.

Fine.

I yanked another vial from my pouch.

With a snap of my wrist, I hurled it at his feet.

The Explosive Elixir shattered on impact.

A burst of flame erupted between us, the force sending snow and debris flying. The bald man twisted mid-charge, forced to pivot away to avoid the worst of the explosion.

And that was all the opening Tianyi needed.

She appeared in a blur, wings slicing through the air.

The bald man tried to evade, but the explosion had thrown him off-balance. He avoided a fatal strike, but not completely.

A wet slice filled the air.

His pinkie spun through the snow, severed cleanly at the joint.

The man let out a guttural hiss, cradling his injured hand, but Tianyi had already retreated from his range.

He bared his teeth. "You dare—"

I was already moving, scanning the battlefield, looking for weak points.

Sun Yang, now reinvigorated, had rejoined the battle, his swordplay noticeably sharper. The temporary boost from the tonic had restored his clarity, and he was no longer just reacting—he was attacking.

Good.

I continued my work, weaving through the battlefield as quickly as I could. A support role wasn't passive—it was about control.

I wasn't just throwing out vials blindly—I was watching, predicting, strengthening the key points before they collapsed.

A disciple near the edge of the fight wavered, his stance faltering.

A Qi Restorative landed in his hand.

"Drink."

Another disciple hesitated, his breathing labored from exertion. I gave him a restorative elixir to replenish his stamina.

Meanwhile, Tianyi and Windy ensured that none of my openings were exploited. Every time I moved, they adjusted, intercepting any demonic cultivator that even thought of coming for me.

The two cultists honed their sights on me whenever I neared; whether it was because of my provocations or my support, I didn't know. I used it to my advantage, diving in with resolute trust.

Trust my companions.

Bit by bit, the tide shifted.

The demonic cultivators were forced into tighter positions. They were still ferocious, still lethal, but for the first time since the fight began, they were cornered.

Their backs touched.

Blood dripped from open wounds.

Surrounded.

Victory was within our grasp.

And then—

A voice.

Low, drawling, and cutting through the thick of battle despite being only a whisper.

"Why do the worshippers of the Heavenly Demon struggle against mere insects?"

The air turned to ice.

My breath hitched as a new presence unfurled from the cave.

No.

Not a person.

A monster.

Slowly, it stepped forward, emerging from the cavern's depths.

Despite their injuries, despite their imminent defeat, the two demonic cultists dropped their heads, pressing them to the ground immediately.

Their bloodied forms bowed, their voices trembling—not with fear, but with reverence.

"We apologize, Envoy!"

CHAPTER THIRTY-THREE

The Envoy

The battlefield stilled.

The weight of the Envoy's presence crushed the air itself, heavier than the iron scent of blood or the lingering heat of battle. Even the wind dared not move, as though held in reverence or fear. His hair was long, falling past his shoulders.

He wasn't draped in rippling muscle, nor did he have the hulking presence of a brute who had trained his body to the limits. But somehow, he was more terrifying.

Where the other cultists were frail and gaunt, their skin stretched thin over malnourished frames, he was whole. Not heavy, not bulky, but balanced. Alive in a way the rest of them weren't. He moved with unsettling grace, his body humming with vitality.

However, his face was scarred. Deep, deliberate scars.

Twin lines ran from his brow, down his hollowed cheeks, tracing the path where tears should have fallen. Like his very sorrow had been carved into his flesh, etched in a cruel mimicry of weeping.

Another wound—uneven—cut from his lower lip, across his right cheek, disappearing into the shadow of his hood. It had healed poorly, as if he had never been given the time or the care to let it mend properly.

Yet, despite the disfigurement, there was no pain in his expression. No bitterness or anger.

The cultists stood frozen, not in panic, but in anticipation—their gazes locked onto him, waiting for his decree. They simply . . . waited.

We should've taken advantage; they were utterly vulnerable, injured, and surrounded. But we couldn't move with that *monster* holding our attention. It was like trying to focus on a cornered rabbit as a tiger loomed overhead. My feet dug into the unstable earth, and I gritted my teeth as my body tried to run.

And then—

"You've failed," the Envoy said.

His voice was unhurried. Not a reprimand. Not a rage-filled bellow. A simple, factual statement.

A ripple passed through the demonic cultivators, their hands trembling where they kowtowed.

He took a step forward. Unhurried. Calm. His fingers idly brushed against the cavern wall as he surveyed the battlefield. The bald man, his face half-burnt and his breathing labored, prostrated himself, ignoring his missing finger. The second cultist, despite the number of wounds marring his body, raised his head without hesitation.

"We apologize, Envoy. We have sinned!"

The Envoy tilted his head, eyes flicking over the clearing. He inhaled deeply, as if savoring the chaos, before letting out a sigh.

"It is understandable."

A pause.

"But unacceptable."

The two kneeling cultists flinched. Their bodies shuddered like starving dogs awaiting a beating.

"You were given a simple task," he continued, still unhurried. "To kill the intruders before my prayer is complete. Has the cult truly fallen this far? Unable to deal with rabble?"

A strangled whimper escaped the bald man's lips.

"Use the converts," the Envoy said, with all the interest of a noble selecting which teacup to drink from.

From the cavern, seven figures stumbled forth.

Their bodies were gaunt. Their eyes sunken, skin stretched thin over brittle bones. Their clothes were patchwork—ripped tunics, tattered robes, exposed flesh marred with dark bruises. Some were barefoot, their feet crusted with dirt, yet their lips moved ceaselessly in a droning whisper. Despite the softness at which they spoke, I strained my ears to hear.

"Praise the Heavenly Demon."

They swayed, their hands trembling, their breath ragged. Some were younger than I expected. Some were far too old. Their fingers twitched with the telltale glow of demonic qi, but their gazes . . .

Madness.

Not like the zeal the cultists displayed; it was more scattered than that. They were closer to beasts wearing human skin.

The Envoy lifted a single hand and flicked his wrist. A lazy, dismissive gesture.

"Kill them."

The seven moved. And Jian Feng threw down his vial, creating a plume of smoke.

Movement rustled behind us. The signal for all of them to join the fight.

Twenty versus ten.

The converts were fast, but not like the cultists.

They lurched forward, untrained, their motions jerky and stiff. But their hands glowed with sickly, writhing qi, the same color as the corruption spreading beneath our feet. One of them, a young man—maybe my age—charged at me.

His strike was wild. Untrained. It left his chest open, his weight poorly balanced, but if it hit—

I dodged. His hand barely missed my ribs, passing close enough that my skin tingled from the sheer presence of the demonic qi.

He came again. Fast. Desperate. His feet scrambled for grip in the slush, his breathing sharp and erratic. With my arm injured and my stamina depleting, it was harder than I thought.

I sidestepped his next lunge, my heart hammering against my ribs. He was unskilled. But that didn't mean he wasn't dangerous. The corruption surrounding his hands was enough to rot flesh, enough to cripple anyone who wasn't careful. I dove forward, catching him in the solar plexus with a palm strike. I knew pain wouldn't do a damn thing against them, but as I delivered the follow-up strike—

I saw it.

Patchwork clothes. No shoes. A wooden bracelet was on his wrist. A torn silk ribbon was tied to his arm.

His body was frail. Too thin. Even more so than the cultists.

And his reaction to the blow. Caution, pain, *fear*.

A Verdant Lotus disciple intercepted another convert, his blade flashing—

A clean, practiced slash.

The convert collapsed instantly, a soft gasp leaving his lips.

But before he could die, before his body fully fell into the dirt:

"Thank you."

My stomach dropped.

My pulse thundered in my ears.

"STOP!" My voice tore through the battlefield, louder than the clash of swords, louder than the gasps of combat.

"They're villagers! They're victims! Don't kill them!"

The disciples faltered.

Their movements slowed. Their hands wavered. Their eyes darted toward me in confusion, but I could see it—the doubt. The guilt.

But the cultists—

They did not hesitate.

They pressed forward. Without fear. Without restraint. Without care for their own lives. It was as though their injuries minutes ago had been a lie.

One disciple hesitated—his sword-arm faltering for just a breath—

And a jagged claw raked across his chest, shattering his sword.

He cried out, his body slamming into the ground, blood splattering across the tainted snow.

Another disciple held his blade too loosely—his strike half-formed with hesitation—

And he nearly missed his next target.

The convert, despite his frailty, lunged with everything he had.

The disciple had no choice but to kill him.

His sword sliced through the man's chest, and he staggered backward, eyes wide. His hands shook.

And then—Windy lunged forward, intercepting a second strike from the cultist with engravings on his palms.

The convert's tainted hand grazed Windy's tail.

Windy jerked back, a sharp hiss escaping his throat. I felt the moment the demonic qi latched on through our bond, spreading through his scales like ink bleeding into water.

"Fuck!"

It was my fault. My words caused a change on the battlefield.

We were hesitating. And hesitation in battle was death.

We were being pushed back.

Our footing was unstable.

Tianyi and Windy, under my orders, disabled rather than killed.

Tianyi's strikes were precise—breaking limbs, twisting joints out of place. Windy's venom paralyzed the weaker ones. But even then—

It wasn't enough.

Because while we were fighting with restraint—

The true threats were watching.

The demonic cultivators were waiting. But the biggest threat was *him*.

The Envoy moved.

I barely had time to register the shift before his words slithered through the battlefield, low and unhurried.

"I will deal with the most annoying one."

A chill rippled down my spine.

He reappeared several paces away, just as Tianyi struck a convert. Her strikes were precise; two pinpoint blows to the knees, rendering the man's legs useless. But before he could even collapse, the Envoy's robes flared open, and I screamed.

"TIANYI!"

The moment she disabled the convert, something tore through his chest—and continued its trajectory toward Tianyi's face.

It shot forward, slicing through the corpse like an afterthought, angling straight for her.

With my warning, she twisted midair with transcendent reflexes.

RIP!

The blade clipped her wing.

A deep wound punctured her left wing's membrane, and almost immediately, a pure black qi seeped through the wound, writhing like it was alive.

The Envoy retracted the chain ever so slightly, letting the convert's body hang limply. It was a sickle and chain—carved entirely from jagged, yellowed bones, each link etched with crude engravings.

I was already moving, feet pounding against the slush, but—

Windy was faster.

He lunged for the Envoy, his body a blur of white scales, fangs gleaming with venom.

I fumbled for my satchel, searching for the Essence Purifying Elixir. "Tianyi, take this for your—"

She held up a hand, her gaze sharp with determination.

"Not yet. No time."

With that, she dove back into the fight.

The chain snapped back. The convert's body whipped toward Windy. He dodged effortlessly, slipping past with a flick of his body.

But it was bait. The sickle surged forward, using the corpse as a distraction, inching ever closer to his neck.

Tianyi intercepted it, deflecting the trajectory with a sweeping strike of her arm. A harrowing crack echoed through the battlefield as the sheer force fractured the exoskeleton along her forearm.

The injury wasn't fatal, but the demonic qi spread immediately, dark veins crawling from the wound. With a grunt, her antennae flared with light, slowing the corruption's advance—but not stopping it. A temporary measure.

My breath came fast, ragged. My heart slammed against my ribs, my grip tightening around the vial in my hand.

We were losing control.

For the first time, I felt it deep in my bones—not just exhaustion, not just hesitation—fear.

We weren't just fighting enemies.

We were being made to kill victims.

And the demonic cultivators?

They waited. Using our fear and uncertainty against us. And through that, they overcame the numerical disadvantage.

Like wolves circling a wounded herd.

I clenched my jaw. No. *NO!*

"Disciples!"

Jian Feng's voice rang out, cutting through the chaos like a blade. Despite the dirt and blood marring his face, his eyes never lost their spirit.

"They are forcing you into panic. Victory takes priority! Disable the converts! Kill them if you must!"

I turned, his words hammering into me even as my instincts screamed against them. But I forced myself to focus—because he was right.

"Follow my movements!" he commanded.

His blade flashed. Clean, efficient, merciless.

A convert lunged. Jian Feng parried, his deflection so smooth it barely wasted movement, and his counter sliced through the man's neck in a single breath.

The bald cultist rushed forward, his claws wreathed in dark qi. He used the opening left by the convert's sacrifice.

Jian Feng didn't retreat.

He pressed forward.

A step in, his blade redirecting the momentum. A step out, positioning for the counter.

And that's when I recognized it.

The Bamboo Reprisal Counter.

The rhythm. The flow. Power turned against its wielder.

And in a blur—his blade pierced the cultist's heart.

The first demonic cultivator fell. No matter their inhuman tolerance for pain, nothing overcame a fatal strike to the heart.

But a breath of relief never came.

Because the bald man smiled.

His lips, split too wide, were stained with blood. My instincts screamed.

His hand shot forward, gripping Jian Feng's blade, driving it deeper into his own chest. His whisper coiled around my ear, despite the distance.

"Praise the Heavenly Demon."

His body convulsed. Qi crackled across his skin. Expanding.

I tore the Explosive Elixir from my satchel and hurled it with everything I had—straight between them.

The detonation blasted them apart.

Jian Feng was flung backward, his sword ripped from his grip. His body hit the ground hard, his robes scorched, his skin burned from my intervention.

BOOM!

A second explosion followed—incinerating everything within an arm's length. The cultist was gone, reduced to nothing but ash.

But Jian Feng was alive.

"Jian Feng!" I was already beside him, dragging him upright. His breath came in shallow, ragged gasps. His hands—charred, trembling.

I hurriedly uncorked a vial, pressing it against his lips. A numbing elixir. It wouldn't fully heal him, but it would keep him in the fight.

Before he could speak, I heaved him up, slinging his arm over my shoulder. Pain flared through my injured shoulder, but I gritted my teeth and carried him away from immediate danger.

But the converts didn't allow me to get away so cleanly.

The disciples saw.

And something shifted.

"PROTECT BROTHER JIAN FENG!"

A Verdant Lotus disciple—the same one who had hesitated before—

His blade moved as he put himself between us and the converts.

Another disciple caught the rhythm. Pushed forward.

One by one, their movements steadied. The tide shifted.

Their hesitation fell away like brittle husks, replaced with something sharper. A thousand drills, a thousand mornings of repetition, suddenly clicked into place. Their formation tightened as they drew closer to form a wall between the enemies and Jian Feng.

And they were pushing them back.

The Envoy sighed.

"Futile."

CHAPTER THIRTY-FOUR

Rooted Amid the Storm

We were going to lose.
It didn't matter that we outnumbered them. Didn't matter that we had fought through the converts, taken down one of the demonic cultivators, and pushed this far. None of it mattered when the Envoy hadn't suffered a single wound.

Tianyi and Windy were the only ones keeping him at bay, their movements sharpened to the absolute limit. Their speed, their coordination, their sheer lethality... Despite it all, none of it had landed a clean hit.

Not because the Envoy had an impenetrable defense. In fact, it was the opposite.

He had openings everywhere.

A too-wide step here. A mistimed parry there. The flicker of an exposed throat in the middle of a counter. Gaps that should not have existed in a battle at this level.

But Tianyi knew. Windy knew. And even I knew.

If they took those openings, they would die.

Because that was how they fought.

The demonic cultivators never cared for pain, never flinched from injury. Short of a strike to their neck, they did not defend. They traded. If it took a wound to land a wound, they took that exchange without hesitation.

The way his eyes followed them, measuring, waiting. The subtle twitch of his fingers when they tested his defenses. He was inviting them in.

That was why their battle remained a stalemate. And why, slowly, inevitably, they were being pushed back.

Tianyi's movements remained sharp despite her wounded wing, her footwork compensating as she twisted and wove through the Envoy's strikes. But even glancing blows left their mark—the tendrils of corrupting energy seeping into her limbs, accumulating with every second.

Windy struck with terrifying precision, his serpentine form weaving through attacks, his fangs flashing with venom. But he couldn't commit.

Because if he lunged with everything he had—he would leave Tianyi exposed. So he held back. Just a fraction. Just enough.

And that was all the Envoy needed.

BOOM!

His chain came crashing down from the sky, sending debris and snow flying to obscure their vision.

The battlefield was a ruin of bodies and exhaustion.

The last cultist was barely standing, his body swaying, his breathing ragged, but his eyes gleamed with the same mad devotion, unfettered by the losses on their side.

Five of our own lay on the ground, grievously injured, their moans and sharp gasps cutting through the air. They weren't dead—but they would be soon without treatment.

And yet, even now, Jian Feng pushed himself up.

I had pulled him away, dragging him from the battle, but he shoved me off, eyes dark with unwavering focus. He stumbled slightly before steadying himself.

"I need to fight."

"Jian Feng, you're barely standing—"

His fingers curled around one of the fallen disciples' swords, the metal slick with blood. He didn't hesitate.

"I will fight," he repeated. His tone left no room for argument. "Tend to the others; bring them farther away from the battlefield."

I exhaled sharply, stepping back. "Don't die."

Jian Feng gave the smallest nod before he turned and rejoined the battle.

I had one Qi Restorative Elixir. One Essence Purifying Elixir. And one last Explosive Elixir. As I ran to pull the heavily injured disciples away from battle, I realized that was all I had left.

And it wasn't enough.

The Envoy wasn't just strong; he was fresh. His robe barely had a single tear, his breathing unlabored. Meanwhile, we were injured, exhausted, and barely keeping up. Despite our renewed morale, it was an uphill battle.

"Guh!"

The last of the converts fell, knocked unconscious with the flat of the blade.

All seven converts were disabled or dead, and only two opponents remained.

But as the remaining disciples made a move to intervene and break the stalemate between the Envoy and my companions, the cultist with engraved palms dove forward with unrelenting zeal.

"YOU SHALL NOT PASS!"

He slapped his palms to the earth, the veins on his forearms pulsating and turning purple as the ground shifted under our feet. The disciples faltered, and I hastened my efforts to gather the injured before they sank into the earth and were buried alive.

I grabbed the nearest disciple, slinging his arm over my shoulder and dragging him out of range just as the earth buckled beneath us. The ground groaned, swallowing the corpses whole—pulling bodies, blood, and shattered weapons into its depths.

A choked gasp.

I turned.

One of the fallen converts—one who had his arms and legs broken to stop him from moving—lay at the edge of the sinking ground. His body was limp, barely conscious, but his face twisted in pure, instinctive terror as his head dipped beneath the surface.

"... Damn it."

I pulled the disciple just past the shifting terrain, just far enough to be safe.

Then, with a sharp breath, turned back.

The dirt had already reached the convert's nose. His lips parted in a weak, rasping breath, his fingers twitching uselessly against the slush.

I hesitated. Just for a moment. Then I grabbed him by the collar and hauled him out. He coughed, choking on a mixture of snow and soil, his body trembling violently. But he was alive. The ground stopped shifting as Jian Feng knocked the cultist onto the ground.

I clenched my fists. There had to be something—anything—I could do.

I needed something to turn the tables.

But what?

And then, out of the corner of my eye—

I saw inside the cave.

My stomach twisted.

Bloodsoul Blooms. Dozens of them.

They lined the cavern floor, growing in tangled knots of crimson and black. Their stems twisted unnaturally, their fleshy petals writhing like they were breathing. And at their center—

A decomposing corpse.

Another demonic cultivator, half-absorbed. Their flesh sagged, melting into the roots, their bones barely visible beneath the pulsing plant matter.

My thoughts raced, and I made the split-second call.

"Tianyi, Windy—buy me time!"

I dove into the cave.

The Envoy's composure cracked.

For the first time, he showed genuine emotion. His cold detachment fractured into something resembling anger. His entire body tensed, and his head snapped toward me.

"NO!"

His voice was like a hammer on stone, reverberating through the battlefield. His foot dug into the earth—

And the entire group moved to stop him.

Jian Feng's sword flashed. A Verdant Lotus disciple intercepted with a strike. Windy lunged.

But it was Tianyi who took center stage.

She blurred forward—faster, sharper, more vicious than before. I saw her face for a moment—flushed, almost feverish. And at her feet—

An empty vial of medicinal wine.

Her body contorted as she dodged the jagged bone sickle by a razor-thin margin. And she delivered a clean kick to the Envoy's chin, giving him pause.

I rushed toward the patch of blood-red plants, my palm already reaching outward.

Essence Extraction.

I willed it forward, but just like before, it resisted, blending the line between creature and plant. But compared to the sample I worked with, it was like comparing a cat to a tiger. There was no comparison for its resistance.

My breath came in quick gasps as I pulled. Harder than I ever had before.

"Come on, come on, come on—"

> *Anomaly Detected: Skill Evolution Beyond System Parameters*

> *Essence Extraction—You can extract the spiritual essence of plants, beasts, and metals for the creation of pills and elixirs. You can further extract essences into its different properties and extract from multiple sources at the same time.*

I didn't have time to process it.

I lifted my hand, palm outstretched.

The Bloodsoul Blooms shuddered, then tore free with an audible snap.

Multiple essences at once.

Something I'd never done before.

Their energy coalesced into my palm, spiraling together, dark and writhing. I gritted my teeth, forcing the essence apart and extracting even further for my needs.

I couldn't afford all of it. I only needed two things. Its volatility and unbridled yin qi that gave it power.

I cast everything else aside. The dregs of the extraction fell to the cave floor—rotting the stone where they landed.

I didn't hesitate.

Alchemical Nexus.

The formations formed into place, surrounding my palm. Without a cauldron or a pill furnace, I only had one option and tuned it for stability.

Heavenly Flame Mantra.

I let out a slow breath as the fire flickered across my hand, turning my palm into a heated surface for refinement.

I reached for the Explosive Elixir from my belt and combined it with the Bloodsoul Bloom essence. It was beyond theory. Beyond practice. My Refinement Simulation Technique flared to life, as the reaction that should have torn my arm apart seized as I adjusted the stability at the exact moment of imbalance, using the natural resistance of the demonic plant's essence to bind the energy rather than suppress it.

It was about control. It was about knowing exactly when to let chaos reign and when to impose order.

It was about trusting the process.

> *Your mind has reached Qi Initiation Stage—Rank 4*

The reaction was immediate. My mind worked even faster than before.

A dark, unstable mass took shape—a dormant elixir that held the power of multiple Bloodsoul Blooms.

But it wasn't ready.

It needed a trigger.

My hand trembled. I only had one thing left.

The Essence Purifying Elixir.

The antithesis of demonic qi.

Opposites. Life and death. Creation and destruction. Two forces that could never merge without consequences.

Unless I made them.

I broke the vial, letting the purifying essence mix with the corrupted yin energy.

It fought me. It screamed like the souls of the damned, of the many sacrificed in order to cultivate the Bloodsoul Bloom.

The instability surged, the opposing energies threatening to explode outward—

But I didn't panic.

I let go of control. Of fear.

I let my qi sink into the reaction, not to force it into submission, but to guide it, my body no longer just a cultivator's vessel but a part of the alchemical process itself.

The black and red sphere in my palm writhed, threatening to tear itself apart. The Alchemical Nexus flickered, the symbols inscribed in the air fracturing under the strain.

It wouldn't hold. I had to move.

I was already running before the concoction fully stabilized, my legs burning with exhaustion. The unstable mass pulsed against my skin, scorching my palm. It wouldn't last much longer—it would detonate the moment its balance collapsed.

And I could feel it instinctually. Seconds. That's all I had.

I tore out of the cave, nearly tripping as my vision swam. The battlefield was chaos.

Disciples leaned on each other, barely standing, their robes drenched in sweat and blood.

Jian Feng stood amid them, sword planted in the earth, his breath ragged. Blood seeped through his fingers, pressed against a deep wound in his side. Tianyi still fought, her movements sharp—but her left wing was rotting, corruption eating away at the membrane. Windy coiled low, his tail twitching where demonic qi had spread. And the Envoy continued fighting without pause, his robes torn in several places and blood trailing down his lip.

"EVERYONE, GET BACK!"

Tianyi was already moving. Windy, too. They felt the danger before I even said it.

The disciples hesitated but only for a moment. Jian Feng caught my tone immediately.

"FALL BACK!" His voice cut through the battlefield like steel, and the disciples surged backward, dragging the wounded with them in the split second they had.

The Envoy turned toward me, his sunken eyes locking onto the mass in my palm. Recognition flickered in his eyes.

And for the second time, I saw his composure crack.

I threw it.

Within moments of the sphere leaving my fingers, the fragile equilibrium shattered—

And the world erupted.

BOOOOOOOM!

A deafening explosion tore through the battlefield, shattering the ground, incinerating the last surviving cultist as he leapt forward to protect the Envoy. The wave of heat and pressure blasted outward. The shock wave threw me along with bodies, debris, and corpses alike into the air. The snow melted instantly in the ensuing blast.

I barely braced before I was hurled backward, my body skidding into the cave.

Pain. Everywhere.

My ears rang. I gasped for breath, my body screaming in protest.

But we had won.

The battlefield lay in ruins.

The disciples, though battered, were alive. Some lay unmoving, but their breathing was still there. Blood-splattered, burnt, but alive.

I forced my shaking arms beneath me, my body barely responding as I lifted my head.

The dust was clearing.

And in the center of the devastation . . .

The Envoy was still standing.

". . . No."

I barely resisted the urge to fall to my knees then and there. He stood amid the carnage, his robes in tatters, his body burned beyond recognition. His left arm hung limply, barely attached to his shoulder. His sickle and chain were gone, destroyed in the blast.

His body should've collapsed.

But he was still upright.

His lips twisted into something inhuman.

"Who dares . . ."

His voice rumbled like a death knell.

"Who dares . . . to challenge God's Envoy?"

His eyes burned with something beyond hatred.

I saw it in him.

Desperation.

He wasn't just angry about the fight. He was angry about the cave.

I had destroyed their accumulated Bloodsoul Blooms.

Something they couldn't replace.

His head tilted back. The wounds across his face split further as he let out a guttural, animalistic roar.

"YOUR SIN SHALL NEVER BE CLEANSED, EVEN WITH YOUR DEATH!"

And then he moved. Straight for me.

I couldn't react. My body was beyond its limit. My limbs refused to move, my vision blurred, my breath too shallow to even summon my qi to keep myself upright.

I had nothing left.

I watched as his remaining arm stretched toward me.

His fingers curled, reaching for my throat with a sickly black energy coating his hands.

Move.

My body didn't respond.

Move, damn it!

With the last of my strength, I took a single step.

His fingers brushed past my hair as I stepped forward, just barely avoiding his grasp.

And in that instant—

ROOTED BANYAN STANCE!

I shifted my weight, locked my core, let his momentum carry him into my outstretched fist—

And redirected everything.

> *Rooted Banyan Stance has reached level 7.*

His body lurched past me, his own strength twisting against him.

The technique wasn't perfect. I wasn't strong enough, nor were my reserves enough to complete the technique. My execution was flawed.

But it was enough.

CRACK!

Pain tore through me as my arm snapped under the force. The imperfect stance hadn't negated everything. I felt bone shatter, my body nearly giving out.

But the Envoy wasn't done. Even now. His eyes flashed with the vitality of a man far from death.

"I AM THE EMISSARY OF GOD!"

I watched him surge with qi. I could only raise my head in despair as he moved to grab me.

Tianyi's wings snapped forward, turning into honed blades. With extreme precision, her attack aimed at his neck. The Envoy caught it with his bare hands, cutting deep into his palm, before he crumpled the gossamer wings as though they were paper. Before he could follow up with another attack, Windy struck.

His entire body coiled, his fangs sinking deep into the Envoy's other arm, twisting so violently that bone cracked. The sound was like splintering wood.

And then the disciples moved as one, shadows in my peripheral vision.

They drove their swords into him.

One. Two. Five.

Several blades pierced the Envoy's body.

Even then—he refused to fall.

His head lifted, mouth open, a final curse forming on his tongue.

"PRAISE THE—"

My eyes widened as his qi continued to surge, rising even further to the point I could feel it pressing down on me. His body expanded, the telltale sign of self-destruction.

If the cultists could give their lives to create such powerful explosions, the damage from the Envoy's would undoubtedly . . .

But Jian Feng was already moving. His sword flashed.

A single, clean cut.

The Envoy's head separated from his shoulders, pausing mid-phrase. It rolled carelessly to the ground.

Then his body collapsed, the rising energy dissipating like it was all a lie.

For a moment, no one moved.

The battlefield was silent.

The only sound was the wind howling through the ruined clearing, carrying the scent of burnt flesh and scorched earth. The snow had long since melted from the heat of battle, leaving only blackened, frozen soil beneath us.

Jian Feng remained standing, his sword dripping with the Envoy's blood, his breathing ragged. His grip on the hilt trembled, not from fear, but from sheer exhaustion.

Tianyi wavered, her wings twitching as she tried to fold them back. Her left wing, tattered and rotting at the edges, barely responded to her movements.

Windy was coiled low to the ground, his body rigid, his breathing heavy. His tail, darkened by demonic corruption, twitched weakly.

The Verdant Lotus disciples stood where they were, chests heaving, robes stained red. Then, one of them took a shaky step forward. His sword slipped from his grip, landing in the dirt with a dull thud. His lips parted, his voice raw from battle.

"We're alive," he murmured, almost as if he couldn't believe it himself.

Then, louder.

"We're alive!" His knees buckled, and he caught himself, his breath hitching as he sucked in a deep, trembling inhale. "We won."

The words rippled through the battlefield like a slow wave.

Jian Feng finally let go of his sword. The blade clattered against the ground, his hands falling to his sides. He closed his eyes, tilting his head back as his breath came out in a long exhale.

A sigh of relief. A breath of survival.

I tried to step forward. My legs buckled instantly.

"—!" My vision swam as I stumbled, my body completely giving out. Before I could hit the ground, someone caught me.

Tianyi.

Her hands gripped my shoulders, steadying me. Her fingers trembled.

I barely had the strength to respond. My vision was blurring, my mind barely holding onto consciousness, but I forced myself to look up.

The Envoy's body lay motionless.

His head, severed, lay several feet away, his frozen expression twisted into something between rage and disbelief. Blood pooled beneath him, seeping into the dirt, into the remains of the battlefield.

He was dead.

The last of them were gone.

And yet . . .

I swallowed, my throat dry.

The Envoy was dead. And yet . . . it didn't feel like victory.

Just survival.

Tianyi must have sensed the shift in my thoughts because her fingers tightened slightly on my shoulders.

"Don't think about it now," she murmured. "Later."

I exhaled slowly.

Later.

For now, we were alive.

For now, we had won.

That had to be enough.

CHAPTER THIRTY-FIVE

When Water Overflows

I woke up to the scent of medicinal herbs.

My body ached. A deep, marrow-deep kind of ache, like every muscle, every bone, had been wrung dry and left to mend itself with whatever scraps remained. My right arm was immobilized in a sling, my torso wrapped tightly in layers of bandages. The linen pressed against my ribs with each breath, reminding me I was still in one piece.

Barely.

The ceiling above me was familiar—wooden beams, polished and sturdy, faintly illuminated by the light filtering through the window. The Soaring Swallow. A private room.

I was safe.

For a long moment, I just lay there, eyes unfocused, my mind struggling to make sense of the time between then and now.

My body shifted slightly, and a sharp pull of pain snapped me fully into wakefulness. I hissed through my teeth, turning my head slightly to assess my injuries.

Nobody was in the room with me.

Slowly, the missing pieces began slotting back into place.

Windy had been the one to go back to the village.

I barely remembered giving the order. Everything had been fading into a haze of pain and exhaustion, my body screaming for rest. But Windy had understood. He had slithered away, his slight form cutting through the snow-covered ground, moving faster than anyone else could have.

We needed help.

We needed someone to bring the injured back before the cold finished what the battle had started.

But before Windy had returned, before I had collapsed—

Jian Feng had been the one to reach me first.

I could still feel the way his hand had gripped my jaw, forcing me to stay awake, his voice sharp with something between frustration and urgency.

Don't pass out yet.

He had pressed a vial to my lips, the taste of qi-restoring medicine burning down my throat, forcing clarity into my sluggish mind.

And then Tianyi had been there, too.

She had been pale, her breath unsteady, but she had placed her hands over my worst wounds, her remaining qi seeping into my body. It wasn't much, but it had been enough.

Enough to keep me awake. Enough to keep me moving.

Because the others still needed help.

The injured disciples had been scattered across the battlefield, some shivering from blood loss, others on the edge of unconsciousness. The cold was relentless, leeching the warmth from their bodies, threatening to finish what the battle hadn't.

With Jian Feng, Tianyi, and the few able-bodied disciples to help, I had stumbled from one to another, working as quickly as my broken body allowed. We raided their satchels, their robes, pulling out medicine that they had carried but were too weak to use themselves.

Bandages. Pills. Coagulants.

I had even treated the converts.

Three of them had survived. Their bodies had been broken, battered by the fight, but they were still breathing. I had nearly hesitated before treating them, but the words had already been burned into my mind.

They're victims.

I had forced my shaking hands to move. Applied pressure to wounds. Poured Essence Purifying Elixir onto their injuries, watching the corruption sizzle and fade.

And Tianyi.

I knelt beside her as she slumped to the ground, her left wing trembling, black veins creeping through the delicate membrane.

I had used the last of my Essence Purifying Elixir on her.

The elixir had hissed upon contact, eating away at the corruption like fire to parchment.

I didn't know how much I had saved.

But I had tried.

And then—

Then I had seen them.

A blur of figures cutting through the snow. A familiar voice calling my name.

Elder Ming.

Wang Jun.

Villagers, rushing forward with stretchers and blankets, carrying supplies. Their faces had been twisted with alarm, their breath visible in the cold as they sprinted across the battlefield.

Windy had returned.

Help had come.

And the moment I saw them, the moment I knew everyone would be okay—I collapsed.

I pushed myself upright, gritting my teeth as a dull ache rippled through my body. My right arm, bound tight in the sling, throbbed in protest, but I ignored it. My legs felt stiff, leaden from disuse, but they held my weight as I swung them over the side of the bed.

It was only when I stood that I realized how much my body resisted movement. Every joint felt slow, every breath just a little too sharp, a little too ragged. It wasn't just from the Black Tortoise Tribulation either.

My arms stung, the bruises and bandages pulling at raw skin.

I shuffled toward the door, my fingers brushing against the wooden frame as I steadied myself. The Soaring Swallow's halls were quiet as I stepped out, the inn's usual warmth muted in the early-morning light.

The scent of porridge and boiled herbs wafted from below, mingling with the soft murmur of voices. I followed it, easing down the stairs, my good hand trailing along the railing for support.

As I reached the dining area, the first thing I saw was Lan-Yin.

She sat at a table near the hearth, with a small bowl of sugar water in front of her, a spoon in one hand. Across from her, Tianyi sipped slowly, wings partially unfurled as if to stretch them out. Windy coiled lazily beside her, his long body draped over the back of the chair, chewing on what looked like a piece of roasted meat.

The moment Lan-Yin spotted me, she jolted upright, nearly knocking over the bowl.

"Kai?" Her voice was loud enough that a few heads turned from other tables. "You're awake?!"

I exhaled through my nose, dragging a chair out before easing myself into it. "Seems like it."

Lan-Yin's eyes darted over me, scanning my injuries, as if she half-expected me to collapse again. She didn't say it, but I could hear the unspoken question in her expression: *Are you really all right?*

Instead of answering that, I asked, "What happened to the others?"

She hesitated for only a moment before answering. "They're recovering. The Verdant Lotus disciples had a rough time, but none of them are in critical condition anymore." She paused, then added, "Jian Feng's already started patrolling again."

"And the converts?" I asked.

Lan-Yin's lips pressed together. "They're secured," she said carefully. "Jian Feng had the help of Wang Jun to secure them in their courtyard. Not sure what's happened since."

I glanced at Tianyi. She had been quiet the entire time, sipping her sugar water.

Lan-Yin sighed. "You've been out for two days, Kai. We weren't sure when you'd wake up."

Two days. That explained why my body felt so stiff.

But the real question was—

"No casualties?" I asked.

She shook her head. "None."

The breath I let out felt heavier than I expected. The relief should have hit me harder, should have unraveled something inside me, but it didn't. It sat there, lodged in my chest, like a knot I didn't know how to untangle.

I nodded. "Good."

It was a miracle.

I turned to Tianyi, my gaze flicking to her wing, the one I had poured the last of my elixir onto.

"How's your wing?" I asked.

She shifted slightly at the question. Then, in a slow, deliberate motion, she unfolded it.

The damage was still visible, the edges frayed and uneven, but . . . it was healing. The torn membrane had regrown, translucent, like fresh silk spun in the sunlight.

"It will be slow," Tianyi said, her voice even. "My wings do not heal the same way the rest of my body does."

I exhaled, nodding. It wasn't fully healed, but it wasn't lost, either.

My shoulders sagged in relief, and I bent down to pet Windy.

"I'm going to step outside for a bit," I said. "Get some fresh air."

Lan-Yin frowned. "You *just* woke up. You need more time to rest."

I flashed a lopsided smile—though even to me, it felt hollow at the edges. "I'm more than fine."

She didn't look convinced. Windy's head lifted slightly from where he was coiled, his blue eyes blinking at me lazily, but he said nothing.

I pushed myself to my feet, ignoring the stiffness in my limbs. My body protested, but I forced it to move, heading for the door.

The moment I stepped outside, the chilly air bit into my skin.

The village was already awake. People moved through the streets, going about their day with a quiet sense of normalcy. It was strange how the world could just continue as if nothing had happened.

But the moment I took a step forward, I heard it.

A murmur. A ripple through the crowd.

Heads turned. Eyes widened. And within seconds, the quiet hum of the morning turned into something much louder.

A group of villagers rushed toward me.

"Kai!"

"Are you all right?"

"Should you even be walking right now?"

Their voices overlapped, a blur of noise, but my mind barely processed it. Their faces were familiar, their concern genuine, but I felt . . . detached. Like I was watching this from somewhere far away. I nodded along, answering their questions automatically, my words feeling distant even to myself.

I barely had time to register the voices before another figure shoved his way through the crowd.

Wang Jun.

His sleeves were still rolled up, soot smeared across his arms and face. He must have sprinted straight from the forge the moment he heard the commotion.

The moment his eyes landed on me, his face twisted into something between relief and sheer exasperation.

"You crazy bastard," he muttered, shaking his head. "Of all the things, you really had to dive straight into a death battle with *demonic cultivators*?"

I knew I was supposed to laugh.

The words were lighthearted, meant to be a scolding, but I couldn't bring myself to react the way I normally would.

I exhaled, rubbing the back of my head. "It was a spur-of-the-moment thing."

"One that almost got you killed."

I didn't argue. Mostly because he wasn't wrong.

But before he could keep going, I turned toward the gathered villagers—the people I had grown up with, and the newer faces that had only recently found refuge in our village. Some of them looked at me like I had just climbed back from the underworld. Others, with quiet reverence. It was . . . odd, to say the least.

"I appreciate the concern," I said, forcing a small smile. "But I'd like some time to myself."

They hesitated.

Then, slowly, they nodded.

Respecting my wishes, they dispersed, though not without lingering glances thrown my way.

I turned and continued forward.

My destination was already set, and my steps led me to a familiar set of wooden door.

It creaked slightly as I pushed it open, revealing the familiar warmth of the space inside.

Elder Ming sat at his table, his back straight, a teapot resting beside him. Across from him was Ren Zhi.

They looked up as I entered.

I bowed my head slightly. "Elder Ming. Elder Zhi."

Elder Ming's eyes scanned me, his gaze unreadable.

I forced a weak chuckle. "Sorry for missing morning training. I figured I could take a break for two days."

Before I could straighten, I felt something—a light tap against my head.

Startled, I looked up.

Elder Ming's hand hovered in the air where he had just chopped at me.

"You stupid student," he muttered.

His voice was quiet.

But there was a slight tremble to it.

I stared.

Then, slowly, I noticed it.

The slight redness at the corners of his eyes.

A lump formed in my throat.

Something inside me—something tightly wound, held together by sheer force of will—frayed.

I swallowed, lowering my head.

"I was scared," I admitted, my voice barely above a whisper. "It hurt. I—I didn't know if we were going to make it."

"You should be scared," Elder Ming muttered, voice rougher than usual.

"Because I was. I thought you were going to die."

And just like that, I broke.

The exhaustion, the fear, the overwhelming relief . . . it all finally caught up with me.

My shoulders shook.

Tears welled at the edges of my vision, blurring the familiar warmth of the room.

Elder Ming said nothing.

He just sighed softly. Then, with the same weathered hands that had guided me since I was a child, he reached forward and placed a steady hand on my head.

And for the first time since waking up, I let myself feel it.

CHAPTER THIRTY-SIX

Strong Enough

The clash of battle rang through the morning air.
 Wang Jun's blade arced toward me in a clean, decisive strike—one that would have forced me to retreat just days ago. But I didn't retreat.
 I stepped in.
 His wooden sword came down in a sharp, calculated arc, aiming for my ribs. My instincts flared, old habits whispering at me to evade, to avoid risking an exchange. But something had changed.
 I shifted my weight, my good hand snapping up.
 The moment Wang Jun's blade entered my range, I twisted my wrist and parried it downward with a fist, letting the force dissipate against my forearm. His stance faltered for just a breath, his weight shifting slightly off-balance.
 I bent my wrist downward, like a crane's neck, and pulled my strike just before it could connect with his chin. Parrying and countering with a single move.
 "Again?" He rubbed his chin with a scowl. "I haven't slacked off once, and I'm still getting beaten like a dog."
 I exhaled, shaking out my hand, feeling the faint sting of impact from parrying the sword. A quiet satisfaction settled in my chest.
 Because this wouldn't have happened before.
 Before, I would have dodged. Before, I would have hesitated. Before, I wouldn't have dared step into the space of a blade so confidently.
 But when you've faced the claws of a demonic cultivator, dripping with writhing, corrosive qi—a wooden sword feels almost laughable in comparison.
 I rolled my shoulder, feeling the tension in my bound arm, a reminder of my limits. I wasn't at full strength, not yet. And I knew better than to let pride fool me into thinking I was invincible.

Elder Ming chuckled, his voice carrying the familiar warmth of amusement, but something about the way he looked at me felt different.

"You've made great strides," he said. "More than I expected. But . . ."

He trailed off.

I caught it immediately. "What is it?"

He shook his head. "It's nothing."

I frowned but didn't push. Elder Ming wasn't the type to speak his thoughts unless he was ready.

He exhaled, rubbing his hands together as if brushing something away. "Morning training is finished. You're both free to go."

Wang Jun groaned dramatically, stretching his arms behind his head.

I chuckled, wiping sweat from my brow as I turned toward the Soaring Swallow.

There was another major shift in my routine, something unexpected but welcome—I'd been reading more.

It had started because of necessity. My body still needed more rest than usual, which meant fewer physical activities outside of training. But that time wasn't wasted because Elder Zhi had been providing me with books.

The Soaring Swallow's upper floor was quiet when I arrived, many of the refugees still sleeping in the early morning. I knocked on the door at the end of the hall.

"Come in."

I stepped into the dimly lit room, the faint scent of parchment and ink filling the air. Elder Zhi sat where he always did, his expression serene, his hands resting lightly on the table before him.

"The books are over there."

I nodded, stepping forward to take the small stack of books placed neatly on the table.

Another set.

I ran my fingers along the edges of the bindings, feeling the meticulous precision of each page.

These weren't just any books.

Elder Zhi had explained it to me not long after I woke up—his ability to recreate books from memory, copying down the original contents down to the exact character.

It was something he had done to repay the village, to offer me something in return for the refuge I had helped provide.

But the quality of these books . . .

I had requested martial arts manuals, whatever he had that I could use to train my stagnant Accelerated Reading skill while also furthering my understanding of martial arts.

Instead, I had received something far beyond my expectations.

The texts covered martial philosophy, strategy, formations for group combat, and even deeper insights into the structure of various martial schools—breaking down their core principles in a way that made them digestible yet clearly written by someone with an expert's eye.

I looked up at Elder Zhi. He remained as composed as ever, as if none of this was unexpected.

"You remembered all of this?" I asked, my voice carefully neutral.

He smiled slightly. "Books I read long ago," he said simply. "Ones I remembered well, before I lost my sight."

Before he lost his sight.

I studied him for a long moment. There was more to him; that much was clear.

But I didn't press. However, another question popped up in my head.

"Elder Zhi . . . are you aware of the Heavenly Interface?"

He paused and nodded. "Yes, I have also received its gift."

"How do you perceive it, then? With your blindness?"

"It is difficult to explain to those who have always seen with their eyes, but . . . imagine a world where every word is carved into your thoughts, where every stroke of a character is as vivid as if it were painted across the sky. That is what I perceive."

I frowned, tilting my head slightly. "You mean . . . it gives you an image?"

Elder Zhi nodded. "Not just an image. It is as though the words are sculpted directly into my mind, each one distinct and absolute. No ink, no parchment, but real nonetheless."

I let that settle in, glancing at his face. His scarred eyes remained motionless, unseeing, yet there was an awareness to him that had nothing to do with sight.

"Does it feel strange?" I asked.

"It did at first. But I have lived in darkness for a long time. The Heavenly Interface is simply another way of reading. One that does not rely on what was taken from me."

I studied him for a moment longer. There was something deeply unshaken about Elder Zhi. Someone who had lost so much yet spoke of it as if it were nothing more than the turning of a page.

I shook my head. "Thank you, Elder Zhi. For indulging my curiosity."

He inclined his head with a small smile.

"And for the books," I added, placing a hand on the newly bound texts he had prepared.

"It is no trouble. I will continue to prepare them for as long as you need."

I turned to leave, but just as I reached the door, I hesitated.

The venerable elder had returned to his work, his fingers moving carefully over a new manuscript, his expression serene.

I opened my mouth, wanting to say something. But in the end, I simply nodded to myself and stepped out into the hallway, his words still lingering in my mind. I stared down at the books in my hands, and at the variety of tools he used to assemble and bind these books together.

More knowledge. More refinement. More ways to grow.

The village had settled into a comfortable rhythm, and so had I. My injuries still limited me, but even with one good arm, I refused to be idle.

As I made my way home, I caught sight of Tianyi surrounded by children, her wings shifting slightly as they reached out, hesitant but fascinated. Windy, coiled beside her, looked utterly miserable as a small girl tugged gently at his tail.

I smirked.

Windy's suffering was self-inflicted; he could run away at any time. But despite all his complaints, he tolerated their presence.

Tianyi was far more at ease with them than I expected. She leaned down slightly as one child whispered something to her, then nodded sagely, as if they had just shared the most profound secret in the world.

I shook my head in amusement and walked past, giving them their space.

I had other things to do.

My greenhouse had always been important to me. But now, it had become something more. A place where I had control, despite my injury.

With my abilities improving, I could speed up the growth of herbs at an astonishing rate. The only limit was how much qi I was willing to expend.

I knelt by the raised beds, exhaling slowly before pressing my palm to the soil.

A steady flow of qi seeped from my hand, spreading beneath the surface. I split my reserves carefully, ensuring that no single plant took too much, balancing the infusion between three key herbs.

Ginseng. The backbone of most restorative elixirs. Jadeleaf Lily. A stabilizer in many pill formulas, preventing volatile reactions.

Last but not least, Golden Bamboo. There was no need to speak of its effects.

Its stalks thickened, stretching skyward at an accelerated pace, a deep golden hue shimmering beneath the morning light. It had absorbed my qi more aggressively than expected.

I stood, brushing off my sleeve, and turned toward the clearing where Tianyi still sat with the children.

"Tianyi, mind helping me cut some of this down?"

She turned at my call, blinking before shifting slightly on her feet—then pausing.

Ah.

Her wings.

The damage from the demonic qi was still healing.

I grimaced. I should've remembered.

"No need," I muttered, flexing my fingers. "I'll handle it."

She tilted her head as if debating whether to insist. But in the end, she simply nodded.

And so, I did it the hard way.

An hour later, my arm burned.

Even with only one working arm, I cut down and stripped the bamboo, gathering the usable portions and hauling them back to my workshop.

The freshly harvested bamboo shoots gleamed, still rich with the qi they had absorbed.

With careful precision, I began the extraction, pulling out essences and distributing them in several small vials.

The Alchemical Nexus flared to life.

Formations illuminated the air around my pill furnace, intricate runes shifting as I guided the essence through the refining process.

This time, I wasn't just working with raw bamboo essence. I combined it with a myriad of carefully selected ingredients, adjusting the flow of qi instinctively.

The process felt smoother than ever before; like my body and mind had finally aligned with the act of alchemy itself.

I wasn't just following a formula.

I was shaping it, refining it.

After an indeterminate amount of time passed, three pills settled in my palm, their surface warm to the touch—Golden Drop pills.

Their potency had diminished because of repeated use, but they still carried a powerful effect. Accelerated healing. Deep nourishment for the body and meridians.

I set two aside for Tianyi and Windy.

And swallowed the last one myself.

Night fell.

I stirred from my cultivation, feeling the lingering warmth of the pill settle deep in my bones. My recovery had taken another leap forward. Despite how severe they were, it wouldn't be long before I'd be fully healed.

The disciples recovered faster than I expected as well. Some were already resuming patrolling. And among them, I was well aware of those who lost their fingers, permanently affecting their ability to wield a sword. Or one who even lost an eye, blinding him.

But they were alive and recovering day by day.

Jian Feng had mentioned it in passing, but it was only now, after seeing it firsthand, that I truly understood.

When your body crosses the threshold into the Qi Initiation stage, it doesn't just mean an increase in power or speed. It means you are no longer bound by the same limitations as an ordinary human. The human body breaks. It bleeds. It scars. It weakens with time. That is the nature of mortality. But when you step beyond that, when you begin cultivating qi, your body ceases to be bound by those same rules.

The wounds inflicted by the cultists constantly ate away at our bodies. But with Essence Purifying Elixir, even the most severe injuries would eventually be healed by our internal qi instead of fighting the corrupting effects of demonic energy.

Stretching slightly, I turned toward Tianyi and Windy, who had entered the shop and rested idly by the windowsill.

"Here," I said, setting down the two remaining pills. "These will help."

Tianyi took hers without hesitation. Windy sniffed his suspiciously.

"You saw me make them," I said dryly. "It's not poison."

Windy flicked his tongue, then curled around the pill, swallowing it in one swift motion.

I watched as they both settled into meditation, entering their own form of cultivation.

Spirit beasts and humans cultivated differently—they followed instinct, while we followed technique.

I had asked them before how they circulated qi.

Tianyi had only shrugged. And Windy performed his version of a shrug.

"We just do."

Simple as that.

The words lingered in my mind as I settled onto my cot, staring at the ceiling.

We just do.

Was it really that simple?

I let out a slow breath, my body still thrumming with the lingering warmth of the Golden Drop Pill. My recovery had accelerated, my meridians strengthening with each cycle of qi that pulsed through me.

Even with that knowledge, doubt gnawed at me.

How strong is strong enough?

I had fought and survived a battle that should have killed me. I had pushed beyond my limits, honed my skills, and carved a path forward. But it still felt like I was standing at the base of an endless mountain, the peak obscured in the clouds above.

Essence Awakening? Spirit Ascension? Earthly Transcendence?

What would it take? What threshold would make the difference?

I clenched my fist.

The battle had changed me. That much was clear. But it had also left something behind; a weight that pressed down on me both physically and mentally, even in the quiet of the night.

The demonic cultivators were still out there. There was no telling what they'd do.

The thought sent a chill through me, one that had nothing to do with the cold air seeping through the cracks in the window.

I exhaled sharply, rubbing my temples. No answer would come tonight. Only more questions.

Instead, I focused on what I could do.

CHAPTER THIRTY-SEVEN

Scars

The sack of Golden Drop Pills felt heavier in my grip than it should have. Because of what it represented.

Jian Feng stood before me, his posture straight as ever, despite the signs of exhaustion clinging to his frame. The disciples had been patrolling nonstop, ensuring no remnants of the demonic cult lurked in the region. Despite their injuries, although none of them had fully recovered, they still continued on.

I pulled the drawstring loose and handed him the sack.

"These should help," I said. "They'll speed up your recovery and strengthen your qi circulation. I know it's not much, but I made them smaller to ensure there was enough for all of you."

Jian Feng's gaze flickered toward the sack before accepting it with a nod. "You didn't have to rush."

"I did."

He exhaled softly, shaking his head before offering a small, appreciative smile. "Thank you."

I shook my head. "No," I said. "It's me who should thank you. You and the other disciples went above and beyond to protect my village. If anything, this is just me fulfilling my part of the deal—in exchange for your protection, the Verdant Lotus Sect has exclusive access to my medicine."

Jian Feng studied me for a moment, then nodded. "Even if it won't be enough to mend their worst injuries, it will enhance their cultivation. That alone is invaluable."

I sighed. "I hope so. I'm also working on a potential cure for the converts. Have they shown no signs of getting better?"

He secured the sack to his belt, inclining his head. "No. We've had to alternate shifts constantly. The phrase they keep repeating, it . . . it grates on one's mind."

"I see." My voice was tight as I tried to unravel the mystery of the converts. "I'll work harder for a cure then. I will come and observe them once more after I finish training."

I offered a nod in return before leaving him to his patrols, my steps naturally carrying me toward Elder Ming's courtyard.

The air still carried winter's bite, but it was different now. Milder. Weaker.

Spring was on its way.

As I greeted Wang Jun and Elder Ming, training passed like a blur.

I let out a slow breath, shrugging off my outer robe as I finished the Dance of a Thousand Flames. The bed of heated coals crackled beside me, steam rising where snow had melted around them.

The first thing that caught my eye was my reflection in a shallow pool of melted snow.

Scars.

They stood out against my skin—still pink, still tender. A permanent reminder of the battle.

The ragged scar on my left shoulder, where the demonic cultist had nearly punctured through.

The healed burns along my right hand's palm, where I had pushed the Heavenly Flame Mantra beyond my control.

I flexed my fingers experimentally. The sensation was still there. Faint, lingering, but not gone.

I was lucky.

If this was all I had walked away with, I had no right to complain.

I dropped to the ground, my good hand pressing against the ground.

Then, I shifted my weight, pressing through my palm.

My lower body lifted skyward, legs straightening until I was in a one-handed handstand push-up.

It wasn't just my skills that had changed.

It was my willingness to push myself to the absolute limit.

I thought I had understood what that meant.

I was wrong.

There's a difference between training until you could collapse . . . and training until you *do* collapse.

My breath came slowly and steadily. I pushed. Another rep. Then another.

My muscles burned. My body screamed.

One more.

I pressed up one last time—

A notification appeared in my vision.

> *Your body has reached Qi Initiation Stage—Rank 3.*

My arms gave out.

I collapsed onto my back, staring up at the sky.

For a moment, I just lay there.

Then, I let out a breathless chuckle, my chest rising and falling with exhaustion.

I did it.

I got up slowly, rolling onto my side before pushing myself to my feet. My limbs felt leaden, my breath still uneven from the exertion, but beneath the exhaustion, there was a quiet thrill.

I had broken through. Again.

My body felt different; stronger, denser, like my bones had been reinforced with something more than mere mortal endurance.

"I reached the next level in body," I said, still catching my breath.

Wang Jun scoffed, leaning on his practice sword. "Tch. Guess I'll have to catch up soon." He stretched, the faint flicker of qi shifting around him. "I'm already at the fourth rank of the Mortal Realm, you know."

I huffed a laugh. "Good. You'd better keep up. You had a higher starting point than I ever did!"

Elder Ming, who had been silently observing, tilted his head slightly. His expression was contemplative.

"Tell me, Kai . . . will this be enough?"

I knew what he meant.

The Black Tortoise Tribulation, once an insurmountable weight, was now something I could complete with ease.

Would I remove it?

I clenched my fists. The answer should have been obvious. Any rational cultivator would discard the extra burden now that its benefits had been reaped.

But I hesitated.

"I'd like to hold on to it for just a bit longer," I admitted.

I wasn't sure if I was ready to let go.

Not because I doubted my ability. But because . . . something in me resisted the thought of discarding this growth opportunity so soon. It wasn't as though the weight hadn't affected me anymore. It was still a challenge. And that meant I still had room to improve.

Elder Ming studied me, then gave a slow nod. "I trust your judgment. But remember, Kai—long-term growth is good, but carrying unnecessary weight can be fatal in battle."

I exhaled. "I know. That's why . . . I need to grow faster."

Before the next battle came. Before I was forced to fight again.

Elder Ming sighed but said nothing more.

I wiped sweat from my brow, gathering my things. "I'll be back later."

Wang Jun waved lazily, while Elder Ming watched me leave with the quiet wisdom he always carried. It was time to focus on my task of healing the converts. I'd been pushing it off out of anxiety, but my conscience wouldn't allow it any longer.

As I walked past the partially constructed houses, I noticed how the village was changing.

More homes. More people.

The refugees who had sought shelter here were no longer just guests, they were becoming a part of Gentle Wind Village.

It should have been a comforting thought.

But all I could think about was how much more I had to protect.

I reached the Verdant Lotus disciples' compound and knocked.

A few moments later, the door creaked open.

Miao Hu stood at the entrance.

His gaze flickered to me, and I noticed his left hand missing a finger, the sleeve of his robe folded slightly to hide it.

A twinge of guilt pulled at me, but I pushed past it.

"I want to see the converts," I said.

Miao Hu hesitated. ". . . You sure? Staying around them too long isn't good for the mind."

I nodded. "Just for a moment."

He let out a slow breath, then stepped aside to let me in.

We walked down a secluded path toward the part of the compound that had been set aside.

The air grew heavier the closer we got.

Like an unseen pressure pressing against my thoughts.

"They've been chanting without pause, so we had to put them in the furthest part of the compound, away from where we sleep."

By the time we reached the three restrained figures, I could already feel it, like a persistent scratch in the back of my mind.

Three beds. Three figures.

They were bound; restraints holding them in place. But their bodies trembled, their lips moving constantly in a hushed, feverish chant.

"Praise the Heavenly Demon . . . Praise the Heavenly Demon . . . Praise the Heavenly Demon . . ."

The words crawled against my skin, a foreign, invasive whisper at the edges of my consciousness.

Even bound, even broken, the demonic influence had not left them.

I clenched my jaw.

These are people.

No matter what they had become, no matter how twisted their minds had been, they were still people.

And I was determined to save them.

But how?

The Heavenly Interface materialized before me.

> *Quest: Rescue the Fallen*
> —*Prevent a convert from chanting "Praise the Heavenly Demon" for a full minute without harming them. (0/1)*
> —*Extract and examine a vial of blood from a convert and find its hidden properties. (0/1)*
> —*Use the Essence Purifying Elixir in the cure for the converts. (0/1)*

It reminded me of the first time I had created a healing hydrosol. The system had given me a series of tasks that hadn't made sense at first. But by the end, the pieces had come together, and I had realized the method on my own.

Except this time . . .

I wouldn't simply receive a recipe as a reward.

I would have to create the cure myself.

That meant trial and error, experimenting with the unknown.

And if I failed . . . if I made even the smallest miscalculation, then what would become of them?

I exhaled, suppressing the unease curling at the edges of my mind. One step at a time.

I turned toward Miao Hu. "Has anyone tried to stop them from chanting?"

He blinked, clearly caught off guard. "What?"

"The phrase," I gestured toward the bound converts. "Has anyone tried forcing them to stop saying it?"

Miao Hu hesitated, his brow furrowing. "No . . . I mean, they don't respond to much of anything. We figured that trying to silence them would just be another way of aggravating them. What would that even do?"

"I don't know yet," I admitted. "But I want to try."

Miao Hu gave me a skeptical look, but after a moment, he sighed. "All right. Let me find a cloth."

With his help, we approached the nearest convert—a man whose face was gaunt, eyes sunken, his lips barely moving as he whispered the same phrase over and over.

Praise the Heavenly Demon . . . Praise the Heavenly Demon . . .

I pulled the clean cloth Miao Hu had given me and carefully stuffed it into the convert's mouth, securing it so he couldn't easily spit it out. The second-class disciple moved to restrain his head from moving too violently.

The effect was instantaneous.

The convert's body seized, his entire form trembling as though something had gone horribly wrong. His pupils dilated, his breath coming out in sharp, frantic gasps through his nose. His chest heaved, his hands clenched into fists.

I stepped back immediately, eyes locked onto him. I had expected resistance. A fight, maybe. But fear?

The longer he went without speaking, the worse it became.

His body shuddered violently, his movements growing more erratic, as though his very existence depended on the ability to speak those words.

A minute passed, and his entire body slumped, his head falling forward.

Silence.

Miao Hu tensed. "Is he—"

I quickly checked his pulse. Steady. His breathing had slowed; his body relaxed. His vitals were normal.

He had simply passed out.

I exhaled, stepping back. My mind churned with possibilities.

He didn't die.

That meant that whatever hold the chant had over him wasn't physically necessary for survival. But if its absence caused that level of panic, then it was safe to assume . . .

It wasn't just a phrase. Perhaps it was a compulsion.

I turned to Miao Hu. "This is progress."

"It is?"

"Yes. It means the chant is connected to whatever is keeping them in this state. If we break that connection, we might be able to restore them."

I looked back at the unconscious convert, my mind already racing ahead.

One task down.

Two to go.

And if I wanted to understand what was happening inside them, I'd have to take the next step.

I would need to examine their blood.

CHAPTER THIRTY-EIGHT

Call of the Unknown

The vial of blood sat still on my desk, but I knew better.
It wasn't still at all.
I rotated the glass slowly between my fingers, watching the thick liquid shift within. It was darker than normal blood, darker than it had any right to be. Not just red, but blackened at the edges, thick like ink. I had studied medicine long enough to recognize when something was wrong with a person's blood. Weakness, poisoning, poor circulation—I could usually tell at a glance.
But this . . .
This was something else.
I held it up to the light, tilting it slightly. The way it moved wasn't natural. There was a sluggishness to it, but more than that, a . . . resistance. It didn't just flow like liquid; it pulsed. It shifted. Almost as though it was aware.
A chill crept down my spine.
I exhaled slowly, forcing myself to focus.
This was a mental and physical affliction. That much was clear. But was it the blood itself that caused it, or did it simply reveal what was already happening to them? The human body was a delicate balance, blood vessels intertwined with qi pathways. One could affect the other in ways even the most advanced alchemists struggled to explain.
And as I observed the dark liquid swirling in the vial, I knew.
It behaved too similarly to something I had seen before. The Bloodsoul Bloom.
I turned my gaze toward the shelf where I had stored a vial of extracted Bloodsoul Bloom essence, sitting right beside my usual alchemical ingredients. I remembered how it struggled like a living being when I first extracted the essence.
And now, staring at the blood in my hand, the connection was undeniable.
They had ingested it.

I clenched my jaw, my thoughts racing. If the converts had been force-fed Bloodsoul Bloom, their meridians and blood vessels would have adjusted to its influence, reshaping them into something inhuman. A slow, deliberate process.

It explained why they were already wreathed in demonic qi but clearly didn't possess any sort of martial training.

It explained why they were called converts and used only as a last resort.

And it explained why . . . the cultists we had killed never begged for their lives.

By the time they reached that stage when they became cultists, they were too far gone.

I thought back to the ones we had fought. How they moved with zealous devotion, but their eyes had been mad, empty of anything resembling self-awareness. They hadn't even flinched when we cut them down.

A sick feeling curled in my gut.

Even the ones I was trying to save . . . could I even save them? If the process had already reached too deep, was there even a way back?

I didn't realize how heavy my body felt until a yawn crept up my throat, the exhaustion of the day settling into my bones. I rubbed my temples, looking away from the vial, suddenly weary.

I needed sleep.

I stood, stretching, and glanced outside my window.

Tianyi and Windy were fighting.

Their figures danced against the backdrop of the night, illuminated by the silver glow of the full moon. But this time, they weren't grounded.

They floated.

Windy twisted through the air, his body moving with liquid grace, fangs flashing as he struck, clinging to her like a stubborn scarf. He was just beyond her reach, as she tried to throw him off, darting like a phantom through the night sky.

I watched them for a long moment before shaking my head. That was a problem for another day.

I drifted off the moment my head hit the pillow. But as darkness swallowed me whole, the comforting void twisted.

I was no longer in my bed but submerged.

Not in water. This was thick, viscous, clinging to me like a shroud. The stench hit first—iron and rot—so pungent it burned my nostrils and coated my tongue with a metallic tang. I was waist-deep in blood. An ocean stretching in every direction, a vast crimson expanse under a starless sky.

Then the voice began.

Not an echo, not a sound carried on air. This was something deeper. A vibration that resonated through the blood itself, through my bones, into the very core of my being. It bypassed my ears entirely, slamming directly into my mind.

YOU TRESPASS.

The words weren't spoken in any language I knew, yet their meaning was brutally, instantly clear. A raw, territorial snarl of pure intent.

You stray into depths forbidden. Turn back, mortal, before you are lost.

The crimson tide churned. Not with wind, but as if something vast was stirring beneath the surface. A pressure built, a sense of immense weight descending. From the blood, a shape coalesced, not a silhouette exactly, but a distortion of the very darkness itself. A presence.

It was formless, yet it was there, looming. And it was reaching. Not with hands, but with an unseen force that felt like a crushing weight, a suffocating dread. It was reaching for me.

A heavy weight pressed down on me.

I sucked in a sharp breath, my vision snapping back into focus.

Windy and Tianyi were both on top of me.

Tianyi's antennae twitched, her glowing eyes peering into mine. "You were shaking."

Windy coiled along my side and flicked his tongue in concern.

I swallowed thickly, my pulse too fast. My clothes were damp with sweat. Even awake, I could still feel it. The phantom weight pressing against my bones, the stench of iron clinging to my breath. My muscles were tense, my heartbeat hammering as if I had barely escaped something real.

"It was just a nightmare," I said, my voice hoarse.

I exhaled slowly, rubbing my face. My hands were cold.

Without another word, I reached toward the nightstand and grabbed a sleeping aid, uncorking it and downing the bitter liquid in a single gulp. Although I didn't use it for its intended purpose, it was also good for stabilizing one's mind.

The tension eased slightly.

But the unease remained.

I turned my gaze toward the vial of convert blood on my desk, visible through the crack in my door.

Then to the Bloodsoul Bloom essence sitting beside it.

I shook my head. Whatever this was, it wasn't a good sign.

I exhaled, steadying myself, then turned my gaze toward the window. The night was still deep, the sky an unbroken stretch of darkness, save for the faint glow of the moon. There was no point in trying to sleep again. Even if I did, the dream would still linger in the back of my mind, clawing at my thoughts like an itch I couldn't quite reach.

Fine. If I couldn't rest, then I would focus on something I could control.

I reached for the bundle of dried meat on my nightstand, tearing off a strip and chewing. The taste was all right, but it did little to ground me. I washed it down with a simple herbal tea.

My gaze flicked toward the stack of books Elder Zhi had copied for me. Reading. That would help.

I shuffled through them, debating where to start. I still hadn't fully digested the ones I had already read, but my mind needed something new to latch onto. Eventually, I settled on one near the top, a fresh volume I hadn't yet opened.

I traced a finger over the cover before flipping it open. The script was neat and efficient, the pages filled with precise strokes. The title was simple: *On Footwork and Balance*.

It was a general text, not bound to any one school or style. The author remained unnamed, but from the very first passage, it was clear they had experience beyond simple theory. The words weren't flowery or weighed down by philosophy; they were practical. Meant to be understood and applied.

"The body is only as fast as the feet allow. The hands can only strike where the legs have placed them. To master movement is to master combat itself."

I hummed in quiet approval. Even without specifics, this book held value.

The idea wasn't new to me. I had felt it myself in battle; how a single step could determine the difference between victory and death. How the placement of my weight, the angle of my stance, could either open a strike or expose me to one.

I continued reading, letting my mind settle into the flow of the text. Page after page detailed principles rather than rigid techniques. The importance of shifting one's center of gravity, of understanding momentum—not just one's own, but an opponent's as well.

Then I hit a passage that forced me to stop and reread.

At first, the path is a path. A road walked is a road known. Feet move, and the body follows, simple as breath. The novice steps forward and believes he is moving.

Then, the path is no longer a path. The world moves, yet the feet stumble. The road shifts underfoot, no longer a simple thing. The air resists, the ground deceives. The master takes a step, yet the world sways, and where he treads, the path was never still.

Finally, the path is a path once more. The feet move, but not of their own will. The wind flows, and so too does the step. There is no thought of walking, yet one is already far away. The master does not walk; the world simply carries him.

The words struck something deep within me.

So far, the book had been filled with nothing but practical, straightforward advice. Yet this passage was different. Almost poetic.

I reread it slowly this time. The path is a path. The path is no longer a path. The path is a path once more.

It reminded me of something.

The Dance of a Thousand Flames.

I had learned it from Elder Ming step by step at first, memorizing each motion, each transition, drilling them into my body. But the first time I attempted it on the bed of hot coals, everything I thought I understood had crumbled. My feet had faltered. My balance had wavered. The movement, so fluid in practice, had become foreign, unsteady.

It was only after enduring that pain, after burning myself countless times, that something clicked. I had stopped thinking about the steps and simply moved.

And in that moment, the dance became a dance again.

Mountains are mountains. Mountains are no longer mountains. Mountains are mountains once more.

I inhaled sharply.

It wasn't just talking about footwork. It was talking about learning itself. The cycle of understanding.

A novice followed the form. A master left it behind. But in true mastery, form and freedom became the same.

I felt something shift in my mind.

A notification appeared before my eyes.

Accelerated Reading has reached level 10.
Your skill has reached the qualifications to evolve to the next stage,
Mind's Eye Reading.
Mind's Eye Reading enhances your two abilities and grants you a third one.
Enhanced Comprehension—You can understand and assimilate complex texts and ancient scriptures at an accelerated pace, allowing for deeper insights and quicker learning. You have a minor chance of instantly grasping hidden meanings in texts.
Increased Reading Speed—Your ability to read and process information has significantly improved, enabling you to cover vast amounts of text in a fraction of the usual time without sacrificing retention or understanding. Your reading speed has been further amplified.
Akashic Understanding—Your ability to parse meaning has transcended written language. Concepts and intent are now understood even if the text is written in an unfamiliar language.

I blinked.

For a long moment, I simply stared at the words, absorbing their meaning.

This . . . this was something far beyond what I had expected.

I flipped the page, eyes skimming the text with newfound clarity. *Mind's Eye Reading.* The words didn't just settle in my brain; they wove themselves into meaning, sinking into my understanding before I could even finish the sentence. It was seamless, almost instinctive.

I had grasped and processed the entire passage several times over before I could even blink.

It was like my mind had unlocked another layer of perception, an ability I hadn't even realized I needed until now. With this, I could push through the more complex books Elder Zhi had given me, ones that had previously required careful rereading, detailed revision within my Memory Palace, and even days of contemplation before I could fully digest them.

Now, knowledge settled into place as though it had always belonged.

I leaned back, exhaling slowly, fingers lightly drumming against the cover of the book.

This skill was an incredible boon. But a nagging thought surfaced at the back of my mind.

Akashic Understanding.

It allowed me to comprehend unknown languages. That was undoubtedly useful, but... how often did I come across an unfamiliar language? Most of the texts I had access to were written in common script or variations of ancient cultivator dialects, which I had already been studying. Would this ability truly change anything for me?

A familiar chime rang in my mind.

> *Quest: Return to Origin*
> —*Return to the beginning of the Heavenly Interface. The path will be marked with a series of yellow, glowing orbs only visible to you.*

I stiffened.

The origin of the Heavenly Interface?

Where had it come from? How had it chosen me? These were questions I had stopped asking myself; not because I wasn't curious, but because I had been too focused on surviving, on growing stronger, on seizing every opportunity the system had provided me.

And now...

It was asking me to return.

An icy shiver ran down my spine.

It was a summons.

CHAPTER THIRTY-NINE

Return to the Beginning

Darting between patrols was easy.

The Verdant Lotus disciples had been stationed throughout the village, but they weren't difficult to spot. Their lanterns cut clean paths through the darkness, swaying gently as they moved through their routes. I had already worked out the timing. It was simple enough. Injured and still recovering, their steps were slower, their rotations less disciplined than usual.

That was precisely why I didn't ask any of them to come with me.

I couldn't.

They had fought for my village, endured grievous wounds, and still pushed themselves to patrol, to protect what they could. I had no right to drag them into another reckless endeavor to complete a personal quest.

That's why this would be a solo journey.

I double-checked my satchel, adjusting the straps across my shoulders. I did a mental count of what I had in my storage ring. I had prepared a myriad of elixirs, carefully selected for what lay ahead; ones to restore stamina, to counteract poisons, to restore my qi. But among them, tucked carefully into a reinforced container, was something more volatile.

The Bloodsoul Bloom essence.

I wasn't stupid enough to drink it, but if something in that forest needed another taste of an explosion, I'd be more than willing to oblige.

With everything packed, I exhaled through my nose and turned toward the door.

And immediately stopped.

Two unwavering presences stood like immovable sentries.

I narrowed my eyes. "I don't have time for this."

Tianyi and Windy did not move.

Windy curled slightly, flicking his tongue. Tianyi, arms crossed, stared me down. They both blocked the path to the door.

"You're not going alone," she said simply.

"Yes, I am."

"No, you aren't."

We locked gazes, neither of us willing to back down.

"I'm serious," I said, tightening the strap of my satchel. "It's too dangerous. I don't know what I'm going to find out there, and I can't—"

"Then all the more reason to go with you," Tianyi interrupted. "If it's dangerous, you'll need us."

I sighed. "I can't let you go."

Windy flicked his tail, slithering forward and tilting his head. Although I couldn't understand what he was saying, the intent was clear.

I pinched the bridge of my nose. "Guys, please. I need you to stay behind. If something happens here while I'm gone—"

"I'll tell the disciples."

I froze.

Tianyi's wings fluttered slightly, her tone light, almost casual. "If you don't let us go, I'll go up and tell them exactly what you're doing. Then you'll have an entire squad following you into the forest."

I gaped at her.

She blinked innocently.

. . . They had become very cunning.

Windy, not missing a beat, coiled around my wrist, securing his victory.

I exhaled sharply, rubbing my temples. "You two are insufferable."

Tianyi smiled. "I learned from the best."

I shot her a look, but in the end, I sighed, conceding.

I wouldn't admit it outright, but I felt relief.

Deep down, the idea of going back into the forest alone, where we had fought and nearly died against the Envoy, terrified me. The cold, the trees, the silence that had nearly swallowed me whole . . .

I wasn't sure if I was ready.

But with them by my side, that fear lessened.

"Fine," I muttered. "But you follow my lead."

Tianyi and Windy exchanged a look, satisfied.

With that settled, I turned my attention back to the village. The night was deep, the cold biting against my skin. But the brief switch in patrols gave us just enough time. A few hours before morning practice. That was all I needed.

It was now or never.

The forest loomed ahead, with the trees stretching into the darkness. I pushed forward, weaving through the undergrowth with measured steps, Tianyi gliding silently beside me, Windy coiled around her shoulder.

The yellow glowing orbs marking my quest were unnecessary. I knew the way.

The path was etched in my mind. Not through the system, not through glowing markers, but by memory.

Windy seemed to have questions about where we were going. But in my peripheral, I could see Tianyi having a mental conversation with him. I didn't know how much she knew. But she was there for the ancient ruins, and the subsequent triggering of the Heavenly Interface. It didn't matter.

If they were tagging along, I'd explain it to them once we got there. Once I understood exactly what the Interface is trying to tell me.

Almost a year ago, I had walked this path for the first time. A naive boy, chasing a butterfly, thinking I'd make a fortune by catching and selling her.

Tianyi had led me deeper into the forest than I had ever dared to go.

And now, I was returning.

But it wasn't the same forest.

And I wasn't the same boy.

I moved swiftly, covering several li in silence. The air was cold, but I barely felt it, my focus honed entirely on the path ahead. The trees blurred past, the terrain shifting beneath my feet as the land dipped slightly—

And then I saw it.

The waterfall.

Frozen solid.

A sheer wall of ice, cascading mid-motion, suspended in time. The pool beneath it was buried under frost, the surface unbroken.

I came to a slow stop, exhaling through my nose.

The last time I had come here, I had failed to enter, nearly breaking my skull trying to poke my head through the waterfall and encountering nothing but stone. But now, standing before it once more, I understood one thing clearly.

The Interface hadn't summoned me here for no reason.

How do I open it again?

The first time, it had simply . . . let me through.

I furrowed my brows, lifting a hand, palm facing upward, then pressed it gently against the frozen wall. The ice was solid beneath my touch, cold seeping into my skin.

A quiet glow emanated from my fingers as heat surged outward. My hands trailed a large circle as the ice cracked, melted, and the water evaporated into steam, carving an entrance just large enough for me to pass through.

Behind it—
Nothing.
A solid wall of stone.
I hesitated, then slowly reached out.
Half-expecting solid rock. Half-expecting nothing.
My fingers passed through.
A ripple, like the surface of a still lake disturbed by a single drop.
I inhaled, steadying my breath.
Then stepped forward, Tianyi and Windy flanking me.
And with that, I entered.

> *Quest: Return to Origin has been completed.*

The moment I stepped inside, I was struck by how untouched it was.

It was exactly as I had left it.

Dust hung thick in the air, disturbed only by our entrance. The walls were the same aged stone, the silence oppressive, the faint scent of damp earth lingering like a whisper of time long since passed. My footsteps echoed lightly as I moved forward, eyes tracing over the symbols carved into the walls, the same ones I had seen before but dismissed too quickly.

I wouldn't make the same mistake twice.

Tianyi and Windy moved ahead, curiosity driving them forward.

I followed, stepping closer.

The carvings were old, almost too worn to be legible. Age had left them coated in dust, their edges softened by time. I ran my fingers over one, feeling the uneven grooves, the way the stone had chipped and fractured.

I knelt, brushing off the thick layer of dust before blowing against the surface. A plume of fine particles scattered into the air, revealing the etchings beneath.

Even with the symbols now exposed, parts of them remained unreadable. Sections cracked, missing entirely, or eroded beyond recognition. But as my gaze lingered, I felt something pressing against my thoughts.

Intent.

The words seeped into my mind, not as sound, but as clarity, an understanding that came from somewhere deeper than language.

We did not understand what we had found at first. It was not from our world. It was something greater, older, and powerful beyond reckoning. A fragment of a cosmic script, descending from the Upper Realm.

A cosmic script? The Upper Realm? My mind spun with possibilities. What did they mean by not from our world? Did they mean an artifact? A technique? A piece of divine knowledge?

Or . . . was it the Interface itself?

I exhaled, steadying my thoughts. It made sense. If the Interface was something that transcended mortal understanding, then it had to come from above. But from where? And from whom?

I moved further along the wall, eyes scanning for more. The next section was too damaged to read, the carvings so worn they might as well have been mere scratches in the stone. Frustrated, I kept going.

The next passage was clearer.

"The world was fractured. Knowledge lost. Each era clawing at the scraps of the last. We could not let this continue. If the path to ascension was meant to be walked, it had to be walked together."

I swallowed, the weight of the words settling in. They weren't just recording history. They were justifying something.

So we took the fragment and created a system. Not for one sect, not for one kingdom, but for the world itself. A beacon to illuminate the path, to preserve wisdom, to refine and improve endlessly. To ensure nothing was lost. To bring the world closer to the heavens. And it was beautiful.

My breath caught in my throat.

This . . . this was the origin of the Interface.

A creation.

Not by a single person, but by a group.

A system meant not for the privileged few, not for those hoarding knowledge behind sect walls, but for everyone. A means of preserving, refining, and perfecting understanding so that no generation would be left grasping in the dark.

I pressed a hand against the wall, as if feeling the pride of those who had carved these words.

This wasn't just divine intervention. It was human ingenuity. Or . . . perhaps something in between.

Tianyi had moved ahead, but I barely registered it. My mind raced through the implications. Had they succeeded? Was the Interface the system they had made? If so, what had gone wrong? Why did it only resurface now?

The deeper we went, the more the walls fractured.

The symbols became harder to read.

I stopped in front of another passage, my pulse quickening as I made out the next set of words.

But we were fools. We thought we had found a gift. We thought we had ensured prosperity. They would not accept it.

The missing word. The carved-out space where something—someone—had been deliberately erased.

Who had refused it? Who had seen this grand vision, this attempt to unify knowledge, and rejected it?

I ran my fingers over the gouged-out section, feeling the jagged edges where the stone had been forcefully marred. Someone had not just removed this word. They had erased it. Scrubbed it from history with such force that even the intent pressing into my mind was fragmented, incomplete.

I exhaled sharply, forcing myself to move on.

The next passage made my breath hitch.

It held similarities to another . . . an ancient evil, a name spoken only in hushed tones. Almost a millennium ago, it nearly devoured the world. We had seen records, stories of those who fought against it. A being that thrived on submission, on forced growth through pain and sacrifice.

And then we realized—the script, the source of our Interface . . . it was not the first time it had descended from the Upper Realm. It was not the first time it had been shaped into something greater.

The Heavenly Demon—

The words stopped.

Not because the text ended.

Because something had stopped the writer.

The wall was slashed, the etchings violently defaced, as though someone had carved over it in desperation. I ran my hand over the grooves, feeling the wild, uneven strokes. The intent lingering behind them was urgent, alarmed—and something else.

It took me a moment to place the feeling.

Shock.

And beneath that, a deeper, more painful emotion.

Grief.

I took a slow, shuddering breath, stepping back. The Heavenly Demon. The name alone sent an uneasy ripple through me.

Whispered from the lips of the converts, chanted in their endless fevered prayers.

This was no coincidence.

I swallowed, my throat dry. What exactly had these people discovered? And what had they unleashed?

I turned my head, realizing I had reached the end of the cavern. The tunnel narrowed into the final chamber—the same place where I had first awakened the Interface.

The stone tablet awaited.

Tianyi and Windy were already there.

Tianyi stood still, her gaze fixed on the ancient slab, her wings twitching ever so slightly. Windy coiled beside her, staring as well, his tongue flicking as though tasting something in the air.

I approached cautiously. "Tianyi?"

She didn't look at me right away. When she finally did, her eyes glowed faintly in the dim light. "I can't read it."

I blinked. "Then . . . what is it?"

Her wings flexed slightly before she shook her head. "I don't know. But when I look at it . . . I feel sad."

Sad?

I frowned, stepping closer.

At first, the tablet appeared the same as before—massive, worn from time, yet unbroken. But as I approached, the words carved into its surface resonated.

And I could see them.

They were clearer than the fragmented writings on the walls. The intent behind them was strong, as if whoever had written them had poured the last of their strength into ensuring they remained.

If you are reading this, then we are no longer here.

My fingers curled into a fist.

They came too soon. We did not have time to understand. To prepare. It was just as we made our discovery, the world had only begun to embrace the Interface when the darkness returned. We had thought ourselves safe. We had thought we had ensured progress. But history repeats itself, and we were blind.

Do not forget why the Interface was created. Do not let them twist it. Do not let them turn it into a tool of subjugation. We built this to raise the world, not to shackle it.

Remember us.

The last line was written differently.

The grooves were deeper. The strokes were rougher, uneven, desperate.

As though the writer was running out of time.

Don't let them win.

The words punched through me like a strike to the gut.

This was the work of someone who had dedicated their life to the Interface. Someone who had believed in its purpose, in its ability to uplift, to preserve.

Someone who had watched everything they had worked for fall apart.

And in their last moments, all they cared about was its preservation. Perhaps that's why the quest hadn't given me a reward. Every other quest had a clear aim with a material benefit. Refining a technique, completing an alchemical breakthrough, or testing my limits. This one was different. The Interface sent me here not to reward me, but to show something. Something that couldn't be measured in stats or abilities.

And that truth alone was the reward.

A lump formed in my throat.

Tianyi and Windy observed me. Neither spoke. Neither needed to. But the curiosity was there. A desire to know what made me react like this.

I turned to them, inhaling deeply, steadying myself.

"I'll explain everything," I said.

And with that, I ended the chapter of silence.

And began a story that should never have been forgotten.

CHAPTER FORTY

To Engrave on One's Heart

Silence stretched between us.

Tianyi and Windy sat across from me, unmoving, their eyes reflecting the faint glow of the cavern's entrance behind us. I had just finished explaining everything; the carvings, the warnings, the Interface's creation, and, most importantly, how Tianyi and I had triggered the tablet together, awakening the Heavenly Interface.

I had expected . . . something. A grand reaction, maybe. Shock. Awe. The kind of revelation that shook the very foundation of belief.

Instead, Tianyi's wings twitched slightly, and she tilted her head.

Her first words were not what I had anticipated.

"And when we triggered it, it made you the Interface Manipulator?"

I nodded. "Yeah. That's when I got the title. I don't know exactly what it means yet, or why it chose me, but . . . it's given me access to powerful skills, allowed me to grow faster than anyone else could."

Tianyi's antennae twitched. "That's not right."

"What?"

She frowned, deep in thought. "I was the one who activated it. Back then, I wasn't even bonded to you. I was just a butterfly, and I infused my qi into the tablet. I remember it clearly. I should've received the title too, right?"

Windy hissed beside her, his long body shifting slightly. She glanced at him before translating.

"Windy agrees."

I stared at them, waiting for more.

Nothing.

Just . . . mild offense that I had been the only one given the title.

For a moment, I processed this. Then a quiet chuckle slipped past my lips. Then another. And before I knew it, I was laughing. Genuine, deep laughter that echoed off the cavern walls.

"Why are you laughing?"

I wiped a tear from my eye, shaking my head.

"I just—" A breathless chuckle escaped me again. "I spent all this time thinking about the implications, the weight of it all. And the only thing you care about is why you didn't get the title instead."

"I am being serious. Can I complain to the Interface?"

I laughed even harder. They stared at me, unimpressed.

I exhaled, finally getting control of myself. Maybe I had been expecting too much. After all, my two closest companions weren't human. They had no grand myths or historical reverence for the Heavenly Interface. They didn't see the legacy of what it represented.

To Windy, it was just another weird human thing. Something that had been present since the day he opened his eyes.

To Tianyi, it was a slight against her personal dignity.

That was it.

I smiled, shaking my head. "I don't know why the Interface picked me. Maybe it should've chosen you instead."

Tianyi folded her arms. "Perhaps it did not think I was worthy in that form."

"That's ridiculous. If anything, you were just as deserving."

She simply nodded, as if accepting my words at face value. But deep down, I felt the realization settle again.

Because I was the one who bore this title.

I was tasked with keeping the Interface. With remembering these people who had built it.

How?

How could I live up to something like that?

Now that I knew the truth . . . and its connection to the Heavenly Demon, what was I supposed to do?

I ruminated over the words etched into the cavern's walls. A fragment of a cosmic script, they had called it. The Interface hadn't simply descended from the Upper Realm; it had been created. But by what? By whom?

The Upper Realm itself was something I struggled to fully comprehend. It wasn't just another plane of existence. It was where immortals roamed, where gods, demons, and even Buddha himself were said to exist.

And somehow, a fragment of something from that realm had made its way here, into the hands of mortals, and had been shaped into something greater.

Or something far worse.

If the Interface had been a gift, why had the last words left behind been warnings?

Why had the Heavenly Demon been invoked in the same breath as its origins?

And if the Heavenly Demon Cult had access to the same power—
I shook my head sharply, as if I could physically cast the thought away.
That was a nightmare I didn't want to entertain.
I exhaled slowly, glancing at Tianyi and Windy, who were still watching me expectantly. "It's time to go."
Tianyi nodded, giving the cavern one last glance before turning toward the exit. Windy flicked his tongue but slithered after her without protest.
But I wasn't ready to leave. Not yet.
I took one last look at the chamber. The dust-covered walls. The carvings etched by hands long turned to dust. The words of those who had built something greater than themselves—something meant to uplift, preserve, and never be forgotten.
And now, we were the only ones left who knew.
I stepped back, dragging my gaze over every inch of the walls, every faded inscription, every shattered remnant of their message.
They wanted to be remembered.
So I remembered.
I memorized everything I could, committing the carvings, the patterns, and the layout of the chamber to my Memory Palace, ensuring that no matter what happened, this knowledge would not disappear with time.
And as I turned to leave, I hesitated.
A strange, unspoken pull held me in place.
I swallowed, then bowed my head slightly, whispering, "Thank you."
I wasn't sure to whom I was speaking. The ones who had created the Interface? The unknown writer who had scrawled those last desperate warnings? The Interface itself?
I didn't know why they chose me to continue their memory.
But I would do my best.
I clenched my fists.
"I won't let the demonic cult win."
With that, I turned and stepped through the frozen waterfall, leaving the ruins behind.
The forest swallowed us whole.
The eerie stillness of the cavern was replaced by the crisp sounds of nature. Rustling leaves, the faint hoot of an owl, the gentle whisper of wind through the trees.
The cold was still there, biting at my skin, but it was bearable. The sky had already lightened, hints of dawn creeping over the horizon.
We hurried. The gap in patrols was brief, and we used it to slip back into the village unnoticed.

By the time we reached home, exhaustion was crushing me.

It felt as though I had spent the entire day working, but in reality, the day hadn't even started yet.

I threw my satchel onto my desk, resisting the urge to collapse into bed.

What was I supposed to do with this knowledge? Who could I even tell?

Jian Feng? Elder Ming? Feng Wu? Even if they believed me, what could they do? What could any of us do against something this vast?

The Interface wasn't just some divine gift. It was a tool. A system created to uplift the world—or enslave it.

And if the demonic cultists discovered that I was the Interface Manipulator . . .

A shiver ran through me.

I did not know what sort of magic they could use. If they realized what I was, what if they kidnapped me? What if they had some horrific ritual to extract the Interface from me, to merge it with their own power?

What if they could twist it the same way they twisted the people they turned into converts?

I shuddered at the thought.

No. I couldn't let them find out.

I had no idea why the Interface had chosen me. No idea how or why it worked the way it did.

But one thing was clear.

I wasn't just some cultivator looking to grow stronger anymore.

I was now holding the key to something far bigger than myself.

And if I made a single mistake . . .

The wrong hands would take it.

Time passed.

The crisp morning air carried the sounds of training; the steady rhythm of footsteps on frostbitten ground, the sharp exhales of exertion, heavy rocks pounding onto the earth. I moved through the motions with precision, the Dance of a Thousand Flames flowing seamlessly from one step to the next. My footwork was steady, my strikes clean. My body had long since memorized the drills, reacting out of habit rather than conscious thought.

But my mind was elsewhere.

"You are distracted."

I opened my mouth to argue but stopped. He was right.

I had barely been paying attention. My body had gone through the training by muscle memory alone while my thoughts had remained buried in the ruins, in the words carved into stone, in the weight of a history no one else seemed to remember.

"I . . ." I hesitated. "It's nothing I can talk about right now."

Elder Ming studied me for a long moment before nodding. "Everyone has their right to privacy. If it is something that can be shared, I trust you will do so when the time is right."

"Of course," I said, grateful he didn't press further.

Unfortunately, someone else was far less graceful.

A voice piped up from my right.

"Ohhh, so it's a secret, is it?"

I turned just in time to see Wang Jun waggling his eyebrows, a smug grin stretched across his face. "Come on, Kai. You can't just tease something so ominous and then expect me not to be curious. Why don't you tell me, your best friend?"

I huffed, jutting out my chin so I was looking down on him despite being a head taller than me. "It's not something your feeble blacksmith mind could comprehend."

"Feeble? Feeble?! Need I remind you that I learned how to write before you even knew how to hold a brush?"

"Just because a flower blooms before a tree does, does that make the tree any less significant?"

There was a moment of silence.

Then realization dawned on Wang Jun's face.

"Did you just call me a flower?" His voice turned flat.

I shrugged. "If the analogy fits."

Wang Jun lunged at me.

I yelped as he shoved at my shoulder. Not enough to hurt, but just enough to jostle me off-balance. I barely caught myself, half-laughing, half-protesting as I tried to keep my footing.

"You dare compare me—a master blacksmith—to a flower?!" Wang Jun huffed. "Unacceptable. I demand satisfaction!"

I twisted out of his reach, only for him to grab the collar of my robe and shake me.

"I'm still injured, you brute!"

"I don't see that stopping you from running your mouth!"

Elder Ming watched the great struggle unfold before him with the weariness of a man too old to be dealing with our antics. "Enough. Go wash up. Morning training is done."

I groaned, shaking off Wang Jun's grip as he finally released me, though not without one last playful shove for good measure. He grinned, clearly pleased with himself, while I adjusted my robes with as much dignity as I could muster.

"Unbelievable," I muttered, brushing the dust from my sleeve.

The moment of levity faded as I turned back toward my home, my focus shifting back to the most pressing task.

Curing the converts.

I wasted no time once I returned. I pulled out my notebook, flipping through hastily scrawled theories and notes. This was the last piece of the puzzle; the ending task required completing the cure.

The Essence Purifying Elixir.

I had been so focused on testing the blood samples, on understanding the influence of the Bloodsoul Bloom, that I hadn't considered the elixir's role beyond its name. But now I saw it clearly. The elixir wasn't just a purifying agent; it was a foundation. One upon which derivatives could be formed.

I tapped my fingers against the desk, running through the connections in my Memory Palace.

The convert's blood was infused with demonic qi. But more importantly, it had been changed at a fundamental level. That was what made them more accepting of demonic energy. It wasn't just a corruption; it was a transformation.

That meant I couldn't simply purge the taint. I had to revert the change entirely.

The Essence Purifying Elixir alone wouldn't be enough. It was too simple, too straightforward in its function. But if I combined it into a proper blood detoxification medicine . . .

I inhaled sharply.

"That's it."

I needed to use the elixir as a base, a stabilizing foundation that could be synthesized with other ingredients to act as a full detoxification agent.

The answer was so obvious now that I could see it in its entirety. I needed to cleanse the blood, not just expel the taint. Otherwise, they would never truly be free of the conversion process.

I reached for my satchel, already pulling out dried herbs, ground powders, and a series of vials filled with my prior experiments. I didn't have much room for error—I only had a few ingredients to work with, and I couldn't afford to waste them on failed attempts.

I spent the afternoon running through every permutation in my Memory Palace, mentally crafting and deconstructing the formula. Mixing. Matching. Testing combinations before they ever touched a physical vial.

I was so deep in my work that I barely noticed when Tianyi, perched near the window with a book in hand, suddenly tensed.

She snapped her head toward the door, her antennae twitching.

I followed her gaze instinctively and caught the faint flicker of lantern light outside. Several disciples, converging on a single point far beyond the village's edge.

The darkness around them only made it more ominous.

I rose immediately, shoving my notes aside. I didn't hesitate. If the disciples were gathering like that, something had happened.

CHAPTER FORTY-ONE

Shadows Flicker Restlessly

The wind carried the scent of blood.

It was faint beneath the biting chill of the darkening sky, but I noticed it the moment we neared the gathering of disciples. The distant lanterns cast flickering shadows across the snow-covered ground, illuminating a scene that sent a chill deeper than the cold ever could.

Three bodies, wearing ragged robes with claws outstretched, intending to massacre visible even after death.

Demonic cultists.

Their corpses lay half-buried in the frost, heads severed cleanly from their shoulders.

I stepped forward, my boots crunching against the frozen ground. The disciples who had discovered them stood in tense silence, their weapons unsheathed, eyes darting toward the tree line. I knelt by one body, fingers brushing against the exposed flesh.

The blood pooling beneath them hadn't even fully dried.

"They were killed recently," I murmured. "Within the past day, at most."

Jian Feng, who stood beside me with a grim expression, nodded. "We just found them now, but whoever did this was fast and precise. No signs of a prolonged fight. No struggle."

I scanned the area, taking in every detail. The snow was undisturbed, apart from the drag marks where the bodies had been partially buried. No scorch marks from techniques. No shattered trees or footprints that suggested a chase.

Nothing.

The surrounding terrain was pristine. These cultists had been cut down before they could even react.

I clenched my jaw, the implications sinking in.

Demonic cultists were not easy to kill. Even when they were outmatched, they fought to their last breath, fueled by whatever twisted madness drove them. But this was something else. They hadn't even been able to attack, from the looks of it.

Tianyi landed beside me, her wings folding as her antennae twitched. "I didn't hear anything."

My eyes flicked to her. That meant that even with her enhanced senses, nothing had alerted her. No distant clash. No cries of pain. No surge of hostile qi.

She would have noticed. The disciples patrolling would have noticed.

But they hadn't.

"There's something out there," I said. "Someone who killed three cultists before they even had a chance to fight back."

The thought made my blood run cold.

The demonic cultists were fanatics, but they weren't weak. If something could take them down this easily, without so much as making a sound, then what did it mean for us?

Jian Feng adjusted his grip on his sword. "We should increase patrols. There's no telling if whoever did this is friend or foe."

"Agreed." I met his gaze. "Keep everyone sharp. If this is an ally, I'd like to know who. If it's an enemy . . ."

Jian Feng nodded grimly. "Then we need to be ready."

We stood there for a moment longer. Then, without another word, I turned back toward the village. The patrols would remain on high alert, but I wasn't about to let my guard down either.

Neither were Tianyi and Windy.

As we reached my shop, Tianyi hesitated at the entrance. She didn't go inside. Instead, she perched herself atop the rooftop, wings shifting slightly as she scanned the surroundings. Windy slithered into the garden, curling himself near the entrance, his body coiled in quiet vigilance.

They weren't planning to sleep tonight.

Neither was I.

Hours passed.

The only sounds in my shop were the faint scratch of my pen against parchment and the occasional drip of liquid into a waiting vial.

The recipe for the prototype was ready.

The Essence Purifying Blood Detoxification Elixir. A name so absurdly long I grimaced every time I thought of it. It was taking up valuable space in my head.

I needed something better. Something that was easier to say.

I tapped my pen against my notebook, running through ideas. Blood-Purging Elixir? Too aggressive. Essence Cleansing Tonic? Too mild. Vital Reclamation Elixir? That sounded like something an over-ambitious sect would sell at a marked-up price.

"Hmm..."

I sighed, running a hand through my hair. Maybe something simple would suffice.

Just as I reached for my ingredients to create the prototype, I caught a movement from the corner of my eye.

Tianyi and Windy.

They darted from their posts outside, their figures vanishing into the dark outskirts of the village without hesitation.

My stomach clenched. I opened the window and shouted after them.

"HEY! Where are you guys going?!"

No response. They continued running. I dropped what I was doing and bolted after them.

The night was chilly, the air sharp against my skin as I sprinted after their retreating figures. They were moving fast. Windy glided through the snow, while Tianyi floated with every step.

Something had set them off.

We were nearing the outskirts when I spotted them.

Two hooded figures.

One about the size of an average adult. The other was large, bigger than Wang Jun, broad-shouldered and standing like a monolith against the dark.

They weren't moving toward the village. They were moving carefully, deliberately—until Tianyi struck.

The smaller figure reacted first, brandishing a sword and stepping forward to intercept her. Their blade arced in a clean, practiced motion, aimed to deflect her strike rather than kill.

Tianyi, faster than the wind itself, shifted in midair, avoiding the edge by a hair's breadth before lashing out with a sharp, glowing wing.

The larger figure raised a fist to counter—only to reel back as Windy lunged at them, fangs bared.

I pushed myself harder, forcing my legs to move faster. The moment I arrived, I took in the stalemate.

Tianyi hovered midair, her wings shimmering faintly, poised to strike again.

Windy had coiled himself around the larger figure's wrist, his tail tightening just enough to restrict movement but not break bone. The hooded figure held perfectly still, their stance rigid.

I narrowed my eyes. They weren't struggling.

These weren't demonic cultivators. There was no chance they'd sit idly. They would continue to fight until their last breath.

Even under the hoods, I could see the way they carried themselves. Like martial artists. Their footing was steady, their breathing controlled.

Bandits?

My voice came out sharp as I closed in on them. "If it's grain or food you want, we can give it to you."

The figure carrying a blade stiffened slightly.

I took a slow step forward, my tone turning colder. "But don't lose your life over it."

I wasn't bluffing.

A quiet resolve settled over me. I had spent too long dealing with the aftermath of battle, too long watching others bleed, to hesitate now. If they so much as twitched wrong, I knew Tianyi and Windy would end this before they had the chance to react.

From behind me, I could already hear the distant steps of the second-class disciples.

Reinforcements were coming.

The swordsman hesitated for a fraction of a second—then, to my surprise, he dropped his sword.

His hands rose slowly in surrender.

Windy loosened his grip slightly, still coiled but no longer pressing in. Tianyi remained in place, her antennae twitching as if gauging the situation.

Then, the smaller figure reached for their hood.

Pulled it back.

And spoke my name.

"It has been a long time, Kai Liu."

My breath hitched, a strange pressure settling in my chest. No. It couldn't be. The odds were too absurd. A trick of the dark. My mind grasped for familiarity where there was none.

The hood fell back.

Moonlight sliced through the shadows, casting stark lines over sharp features, ones I almost didn't recognize at first. The angles were familiar, but thinner, harsher. A face hardened by time, exhaustion weighing heavily beneath those dark eyes.

A face I had seen before.

A face I had never expected to see again.

The realization struck like a hammer to the chest.

"Xu Ziqing . . .?"

The scent of roasted tea leaves filled the air.

Lan-Yin set down the ceramic cups with a bit more force than necessary, her expression less than pleased. "Why is it always here?" she muttered, crossing her arms as she stood at the edge of our gathered group. "Of all the places, why does every important conversation happen at the Soaring Swallow?"

I offered her a sheepish smile. "Sorry, Lan-Yin. The drinks here can't be beat."

She rolled her eyes, huffing, before finally relenting and walking away, though I caught the faintest twitch of amusement at the corner of her lips.

I returned my attention to Xu Ziqing and the other man beside him—Ping Hai.

Tense silence lingered between us.

Xu Ziqing was the same as I remembered—his posture disciplined, his movements precise, that same easy confidence in the way he lifted his teacup to his lips. But something in his eyes had changed.

The sharp light they once held had dulled, replaced by something heavier, something I had seen too many times before. The look of a man who had lost more than he cared to admit.

And Ping Hai . . .

The last time I had seen him, he had been a towering figure already, a broad-shouldered third-class disciple built like an iron statue. But now? Now, he looked like he could take down a charging ox with his bare hands.

A deep, jagged scar now marred his face, cutting along his left eye. His arms were thicker than before, corded with muscle, his hands calloused and scarred. His very presence felt weighty, his sheer size making him one of the largest people in the room.

And yet, despite his increased size, despite how he had grown into a figure capable of shattering stone with his fists, he looked tired.

That same exhaustion sat on his features, the same quiet, haunted weight in his posture that I had noticed in Xu Ziqing.

I didn't have to ask why.

The Silent Moon Sect was gone.

I remembered the news I had received weeks before. The one message that left Crescent Bay City. A report of how an entire sect had been erased overnight.

Destroyed by demonic cultivators.

Xu Ziqing set his cup down, his gaze flickering to the gathered figures in the room.

Jian Feng sat to my right, his grip still resting lightly on his sword, his expression unreadable. Elder Ming was watching carefully, quiet as always.

Tianyi perched near the rafters, antennae twitching, eyes fixed on the two men like a hawk. Windy, coiled lazily near my seat, didn't seem aggressive, but I knew better—if either of them made a wrong move, he wouldn't hesitate to act.

The second-class disciples stood further back, their presence a silent warning.

Finally, I broke the silence.

"What are you doing here?"

Xu Ziqing took another sip of tea.

"It's good," he said simply, nodding in appreciation.

I exhaled, waiting.

The second-class disciple's gaze flickered across the table, lingering on me for a moment before shifting to Tianyi. His expression remained unreadable, but there was something behind his eyes.

"I see you've changed," he remarked.

I raised an eyebrow. "What do you mean?"

"The last time we met, you were strong for your level—but now, even without testing you, I can tell. Your foundation has solidified. The way you carry yourself is different. Sharper."

He tapped a finger against his cup, then glanced up at Tianyi, who sat perched in the rafters, watching with silent vigilance.

"But more than you, I find her transformation more interesting. Just a butterfly. And now . . ." His eyes traced over her wings, the slight exoskeletal sheen of her skin, the way she moved with a grace both foreign and familiar. "You've transcended your form."

He turned back to me, that sharp glint returning to his eyes.

"You followed my advice."

I tensed slightly. "What advice?"

He smiled, but it didn't reach his eyes.

"To get stronger. Lest the ones precious to you get taken."

I didn't respond immediately. There was nothing to say.

Because he was right.

I had fought. I had trained. I had pushed myself to the edge and beyond, all so I would never have to see another moment like that again.

Xu Ziqing studied me for a moment longer before exhaling softly, as if the conversation was already done in his mind.

Then, finally, he set his cup down and leaned forward slightly.

"We were on our way to Pingyao. Ping Hai's home village."

I couldn't exactly recall, but I knew the name. Was it close by?

Xu Ziqing continued.

"The Silent Moon Sect has withdrawn its protection from the outlying regions. Every disciple who was outside of the sect was given a single order from Sect Leader Jun."

His gaze met mine, something bitter hidden beneath his calm tone.

"To consolidate. To abandon everything and regroup."

They had abandoned the people under their protection.

"Why? Because you guys were weakened by the invasion? By the demonic cultists?" I asked, voice steady despite the simmering frustration building beneath my skin.

"That," he said, "is what I'm about to explain."

CHAPTER FORTY-TWO

A Myth of a Myth

The words hung in the air like a blade suspended by a thread.

Silence stretched between us, thick and suffocating. My mind struggled to process everything Xu Ziqing had just said. The invasion. The collapse of the Silent Moon Sect. The way the mainland elders had fled, abandoning everything in their wake.

It was one thing to hear it from a messenger.

It was another to hear it from a man who had lived it.

Xu Ziqing was composed, his voice even, his posture as steady as ever. But as I studied him closer, I saw it—the faintest tremor in his fingers as he traced the rim of his teacup. The way his jaw clenched just a little too tightly, as if he had to physically restrain himself from speaking too quickly, from allowing emotion to leak into his words.

Ping Hai, the broad-shouldered warrior trembled, his massive hands gripping his thighs so tightly his knuckles turned bone white. His breath came in slow, deliberate exhales, as if he was forcing himself to stay grounded, to stay in control. But his body betrayed him.

This was not the fear of an inexperienced cultivator.

This was the fear of a man who had seen something so utterly beyond him that no amount of strength could fight it.

I opened my mouth to say something, but Xu Ziqing spoke first.

"The mainland elders ran first," he said flatly. "Whatever knowledge they had of the cult, whatever reason they were being targeted—they weren't willing to stay and fight for it."

"And Sect Leader Jun?" I asked.

"We don't know where he was during the battle." There was something unreadable in Xu Ziqing's tone. "He made the call to abandon the outlying regions afterward. To withdraw all surviving disciples and consolidate."

I clenched my fists beneath the table.

Consolidate. That was a nice way of saying they left people to die.

The table felt unbearably small.

"We had the entire sect at our backs. We had elders. Formation masters. Trained disciples. The Silent Moon Sect was not weak. When the cultists turned their backs on us to give chase to the mainland elders, we had a chance. A chance to strike."

His fingers finally stilled on his cup.

"And yet," he murmured, "we couldn't find it within us to fight back."

A chill crawled up my spine. The great Silent Moon Sect, brought to its knees. Not by overwhelming numbers, not by strength, but by sheer, mind-numbing terror.

Jian Feng's composure finally cracked. He slammed a hand against the table, shaking the cups slightly. "Then why were they being chased?" he demanded. "The cultists. What were they looking for?"

Xu Ziqing didn't immediately answer. His gaze flickered briefly toward Ping Hai before settling back on us.

Then, he said it.

"Phoenix Tears."

A sharp inhale came from the side of the room. One of the second-class disciples stiffened.

Miao Hu.

The man missing a finger slowly sat up straighter, his face pale. "That . . . that's just a myth."

I looked at him sharply. "You know of it?"

Miao Hu hesitated, his throat bobbing slightly. "Everyone does," he said finally. "The Phoenix is one of the Four Celestial Beasts. It represents rebirth, renewal. But one's tears . . ." His voice wavered. "That's a myth of a myth."

The tension in the room deepened.

Jian Feng leaned forward. "Explain."

Miao Hu swallowed. His missing finger twitched slightly as he tapped his good hand against the table, as if trying to recall the exact words. "The legend says Phoenix Tears are the ultimate medicine," he said carefully. "An elixir among elixirs. A single drop is said to heal the most grievous wounds, restore limbs, and cure age-old ailments. Two drops . . ." He hesitated. "Two drops can cure anything short of death itself."

A heavy silence followed.

My thoughts spun rapidly. Phoenix Tears. Something so potent that it defied even the best alchemical creations.

I frowned. "How could the mainland elders possibly have gotten their hands on something like that?"

Jian Feng shook his head. "That's assuming they even had it. The demonic cult clearly believed they did."

That, more than anything, unsettled me.

Because if the cultists had believed the Phoenix Tears existed, then the question became—

"Why would they want it?" Elder Ming murmured, echoing my thoughts aloud.

None of us spoke.

I could feel it, the answer sitting in the back of my mind like a weight I wasn't ready to acknowledge. But the silence stretched longer, thick with unspoken dread, until finally, I forced myself to say it.

". . . To revive their god."

No one spoke.

The meaning was clear. The ruins' warning—*Don't let them win*—it wasn't just about stopping the cult.

It was about preventing the resurrection of the Heavenly Demon.

Because if the cultists were already this dangerous, if even their lowest-ranking members were so terrifyingly resilient, if the Envoy I had fought was a mere glimpse of what they could become . . .

Then what did it mean for the Heavenly Demon himself?

My blood ran cold.

The Envoy had been beyond anything I'd ever faced. His mere presence had warped the battlefield, twisting the air with the weight of his aura. It took the combined effort of Tianyi, Windy, and over a dozen second-class disciples to keep him at bay. The only reason we even won was due to his taking the full brunt of the explosive Bloodsoul Bloom essence I created.

And he was just one man.

A servant.

A fragment of something greater.

I swallowed, my throat dry. My mind flashed back to the ruins, to the desperate warnings left behind by the ones who had come before.

If the path to ascension was meant to be walked, it had to be walked together.
We built this to raise the world, not to shackle it.

They had known what would happen if the cult succeeded. If the Interface was corrupted. If the wrong hands seized it.

And now, centuries later, the cult was on the verge of succeeding.

A low murmur broke the silence. Jian Feng, still stiff with tension, muttered, "This is madness."

Another second-class disciple cursed under his breath.

I clenched my fists under the table. "If the Phoenix Tears really exist," I said slowly, "then it means they've been preparing for this for a long time."

It meant that this wasn't just a recent development. It wasn't just some cultists gathering power over the past few decades.

It was a plan spanning generations.

Xu Ziqing exhaled through his nose. "I'm not finished."

I looked up at him sharply.

He met my gaze, unreadable as always. "After we left the sect, we traveled to Qingmu. That's when I learned you were here."

I stilled. "You came looking for me?"

He tilted his head slightly. "Call it a coincidence. Or call it fate. Pingyao is not far from here."

Something about the way he said that sent a prickle down my spine.

Xu Ziqing set his cup down, fingers pressing against the ceramic rim. "Either way, I've come to collect a debt."

"A debt," I echoed.

"I saved you back at the Grand Alchemy Gauntlet."

My jaw tightened.

That was true.

Back in Crescent Bay City when I had been cornered, when the Narrow Stone Peak disciples had been moments away from attacking me while I was surrounded, it was Xu Ziqing who had stepped in.

I took a slow breath, keeping my voice even. "What do you want?"

He leaned forward slightly. "Elixirs."

I blinked. ". . . Huh?"

He didn't react to my surprise. "I want medicine. Potent ones. We're protecting Pingyao, and we're barely managing as we are. We fought off three cultists before arriving but suffered heavy wounds in the process."

As if to emphasize his point, he pulled back his robe slightly, revealing the deep scars still lining his arms and torso. The faint, lingering traces of demonic qi corruption crawled along his skin, dark and insidious.

I exhaled sharply. "Why didn't you lead with that?"

Xu Ziqing's lips twitched. "Would you have been this agreeable if I had?"

I narrowed my eyes at him but didn't argue. He was probably right.

Ping Hai, silent until now, finally spoke. "We need your help, Kai Liu. Please, it's for my family."

I studied them both.

The Silent Moon Sect had failed them. The mainland elders had failed them. Even their own leader had turned his back on them.

But despite everything, despite the destruction, they were still fighting.

I sighed, running a hand through my hair. "Fine."

Xu Ziqing's expression didn't change, but I could see the tension in his shoulders ease ever so slightly.

"Bring Ping Hai with you," I said. "We'll see what I can do."

He nodded.

The moment we stepped into my shop, I was already moving.

"Take off your robes," I ordered, not waiting for them to comply as I rummaged through my drawers for supplies. "And your hoods. I need to see exactly what I'm dealing with."

Xu Ziqing and Ping Hai hesitated for a fraction of a second before wordlessly complying. The heavy fabric slid from their shoulders, revealing the extent of their injuries.

Even under the dim lighting, it was clear—their bodies were carved with scars. Old wounds healed over time, and new ones poorly treated. Some looked fresh, others barely closed, but all bore the lingering taint of demonic qi. It clung to them like a sickness, slow and festering. It was a wonder how they had made it here without collapsing or even showing any signs. I suppose that was a sign of their resilience.

The bandages and gauze they'd used were amateur work, done with steady hands but lacking proper materials. They had done their best, but it wasn't enough.

"Where did you even get these supplies?" I muttered, peeling away a strip of cloth that had fused to dried blood.

"Qingmu's physician," Ping Hai admitted. "He tried."

I discarded the soiled wrappings and reached for a cloth, dousing it in a bucket of Essence Purifying Elixir diluted in water. The moment the liquid made contact, the demonic qi sizzled, dissipating like mist under sunlight.

Both men tensed.

"Brace yourselves," I warned.

I didn't wait for them to respond before working swiftly, wiping away every last trace of corruption. The elixir burned as it purified, searing the wounds before allowing them to properly close.

Ping Hai flinched.

Xu Ziqing, to his credit, remained composed, but his hands curled into fists.

I nodded toward Tianyi. "You're up."

She stepped forward without a word, placing a palm against Xu Ziqing's back first. A faint glow shimmered at her fingertips as healing qi flooded into him.

His breath hitched.

The qi mended his wounds in an instant, knitting flesh back together, sealing open gashes. When she finished, she moved to Ping Hai, repeating the process.

The moment the corruption was gone, both men exhaled—almost as if they had been holding their breath this entire time.

I dug into my storage ring, retrieving the last of my Golden Drop Pills. I placed two in my palm and extended it.

"Here," I said. "They're body refinement pills. They'll accelerate your healing, but more importantly, they'll help stabilize your foundations after all that damage."

They hesitated.

I understood why. Cultivating was an act of focus, but also vulnerability. Letting your guard down in unfamiliar territory, especially while recovering, was a risk. If anything happened while they were meditating, they'd be defenseless.

Elder Ming's shattered dantian flashed in my mind.

Xu Ziqing was the first to move. He accepted the pill and swallowed it without a word. Ping Hai followed after a beat of hesitation.

I stood, gesturing toward the corner of my shop where I had placed two padded mats.

"Tianyi, Windy, and I will keep watch."

Still, they hesitated.

I let out a breath. "You trusted me to treat you. Trust me to make sure nothing happens while you recover."

That seemed to settle them. Slowly, they sat, closing their eyes, slipping into cultivation.

Hours passed.

I worked in silence.

With every passing moment, I took stock of my ingredients, assessing what I had and what I needed. We had gathered many herbs over the past few weeks, and my garden had flourished under my care, but I'd still have to make choices.

I couldn't afford to waste anything.

By the time Xu Ziqing finally stirred, I had already begun preparing.

He shifted slightly, blinking the haze of cultivation from his eyes before focusing on me.

"You're still working?" he asked.

I glanced at him. "Of course."

He exhaled, stretching his limbs before sitting upright. He inspected his arm, rolling his shoulder experimentally. "I didn't expect this level of treatment. Thank you."

I shrugged, pouring a solution into a small ceramic bowl. "No worries."

There was an awkward silence as I continued to mix and refine. We weren't friends. Far from it. Our relationship had been tenuous from the day I met him in Qingmu, to the day I fought Ping Hai for the beast core, and now. But I couldn't fully bring myself to hate him.

I set down my mortar and pestle. "You already know how this works. The more time I have, the better medicine I can make. If you're in a rush, the quantity will be limited."

The second-class disciple was silent for a moment. Then, he nodded. "Then . . . three days. We'll heal our wounds and strengthen ourselves before we make our way to the village. But the sooner the better."

I nodded back. That was manageable.

I straightened, cracking my neck as I stretched. "Good."

Xu Ziqing followed as I stepped outside, the cold air hitting us the moment we left the shop. We walked in silence toward the greenhouse.

I slid the door open, stepping inside. Warmth enveloped me instantly, and he lingered by the entrance, glancing around.

"This wasn't here before," he remarked.

I knelt by one bed, running my hands over the soil. "Built it after the Gauntlet. Though Narrow Stone Peak almost destroyed it when they came."

He blinked. "What?"

I summarized the situation as best I could. While doing so, I reached toward a cluster of herbs, pressing my palm against the stalks.

Qi pulsed from my fingertips, flowing into the plants.

They responded instantly, leaves trembling as their essence matured in mere moments. Their colors deepened, their scents thickening in the air.

Xu Ziqing observed in silence, watching as I moved from plant to plant, hand-picking the ones I would use.

"I take back what I said back then."

I glanced at him briefly before returning to my work. "Which time?"

"When I called you just some herbalist," he said. "You're not."

I didn't respond immediately. Instead, I focused on the herbs before me, assessing their growth, selecting the ones best suited for the elixirs I needed to make.

Finally, I exhaled. "I am."

I met his gaze, calm but firm. "I am an herbalist. I am also an alchemist. And a cultivator. I take pride in my identity as a whole."

His lips parted slightly as if he wanted to argue, but in the end, he said nothing.

I straightened, dusting off my hands, and then turned fully to face him. "So now that we've cleared that up, tell me—why are you doing this?"

"Ping Hai, I understand. This is his home. His family is there. But you? You were one of Sect Leader Jun's most loyal men. I saw it at the Gauntlet. I saw it in how you carried yourself. I figured if he ordered you to consolidate, you would've done it without question. So why are you here? Why risk yourself?"

For a moment, I thought he wouldn't answer.

Then, Xu Ziqing closed his eyes and let out a slow sigh. "Maybe a year ago, I wouldn't have."

I watched him carefully.

"When I joined the Silent Moon Sect, I believed in its strength. I believed in our principles. In our ethos. That if we followed the structure, we would thrive." His jaw tightened slightly. "But the things I saw . . . the things I heard that night . . ."

He trailed off.

For the first time, I saw it.

Doubt.

Not the wavering uncertainty of a lost man, but the reluctant acceptance of someone who had been forced to confront something ugly—something that had shattered his foundation and left him with no choice but to change.

He met my gaze, his voice quieter this time.

"Maybe I'm being naive. Maybe I'm grasping at something that's already lost. But . . . I'd like to think that doing the right thing still means something."

I stared at him for a long moment.

Then, finally, I nodded.

The conversation ended there, but the message of his words lingered.

CHAPTER FORTY-THREE

Might, Mercy, and the Path Between

"When I went to Qingmu, I learned what you did."

I quirked an eyebrow as I continued to check over the health of my plants. My reserves were already beginning to bottom out from infusing so much of my garden. "Oh?"

"The Iron Claw Sect," he continued. "How you protected them when we couldn't."

I snorted, inspecting the Golden Bamboo with a critiquing eye. "I mostly did it because I didn't want that place turning into a battleground between your sect and theirs."

"Maybe so. But it doesn't change what you did."

He shifted slightly. Then he turned his back on me and looked out into the moonlit sky as he continued his story. "When we got there, it was meant to be a temporary stay. Just a pit stop to recover. We weren't planning to reveal who we were. But that boy from the time with the Wind Serpents; he recognized us immediately."

I huffed a laugh. "Hua Lingsheng?"

His gaze flickered to me, with a faint trace of surprise before he nodded.

I shook my head, grinning. "Figures. He's got a sharp eye; I'll give him that."

Xu Ziqing exhaled, a brief chuckle escaping him, but the moment passed quickly. His expression turned distant, somber. "He recognized us. And despite everything, he welcomed us."

The humor in my chest faded as he continued.

"He gave us a place to stay. Fed us meals. Refused to charge us, even when we insisted. Said we were the ones protecting Qingmu, and that was enough."

I remained silent, listening.

"Even after we abandoned them," Xu Ziqing murmured, "his family treated us with the same grace and respect."

There was something raw in his tone. Not regret. Not guilt. Just . . . something that didn't quite have a name.

"I wished they had said something. Just once. A reprimand. A rebuke. Anything. But they didn't." He exhaled, his hands tightening into fists. "Instead, they just kept giving. Fed us, clothed us, gave us supplies we didn't even ask for. As if our failures didn't matter."

The words weighed heavier than I expected.

I didn't know what to say to that.

Xu Ziqing wasn't looking for a response. He wasn't even looking at me. He was just . . . talking. As if trying to put a story into words rather than expecting a meaningful conversation in return.

The silence stretched, and I let it.

Then, the door creaked open.

Ping Hai stood in the doorway, his hulking frame casting a shadow over the entrance. He looked well-rested, his presence just as large and imposing as ever. "I've finished my cultivation."

Xu Ziqing blinked, as if shaken from his thoughts. He straightened, the faint vulnerability in his expression smoothing over in an instant.

I glanced between the two of them, then sighed, rubbing the back of my head. "It's late. You two can sleep here for the night. We'll talk about getting you a room at the Soaring Swallow tomorrow."

Without another word, the two followed me inside.

The next afternoon, I wasted no time confirming my suspicions.

Xu Ziqing and Ping Hai sat across from me at the Soaring Swallow, finishing what little remained of their meal. Their injuries had healed significantly—at least on the outside—but exhaustion still lingered in their movements, the kind that went deeper than the body.

I folded my arms. "It wasn't you, was it?"

The second-class disciple frowned slightly. "What?"

"The cultists," I clarified. "The ones who were killed outside the village yesterday. You didn't do that?"

"No. We weren't even here yet." He rubbed his temple, expression strained. "And even if we had been, do you think I could've done that? I barely survived Qingmu fending off three disciples with Ping Hai."

I studied him carefully.

For all his skill, for however strong he had gotten, I didn't believe for a second that he had reached the level where he could behead three cultists before they could even react.

Even an elder would struggle to do something like that.

I sighed, running a hand through my hair. "That's what I thought."

Whatever—or whoever—had killed those cultists was still unaccounted for. I pushed the thought away for now. It didn't matter. Not yet.

I stood and gathered my things. "You two do what you want, just don't cause trouble."

Xu Ziqing watched me for a moment, then leaned forward slightly. "Shouldn't we be doing something?"

I paused. "What?"

He gestured vaguely to the village. "I feel out of place here. Sitting around doesn't sit right with me. I want to pay back what was given to us."

I raised an eyebrow. "And why are you asking me? I'm not your leader. And besides, didn't I already tell you? I owe *you* a debt. This is me paying off that debt."

He didn't argue.

"If you really want to make yourselves useful, go to Jian Feng or ask a villager. Don't pay me back—pay it forward to someone else."

Feng Wu's words came to me easily, and I left before either of them could respond.

I had more important things to focus on.

Like the cure.

Miao Hu's words from earlier echoed in my mind. *They've awoken.*

The converts were conscious. Bound. Gagged. Still trying to chant despite their restraints. Some had even attempted to chew through the cloth covering their mouths.

I didn't have time to waste.

I gathered the ingredients—Essence Purifying Elixir, female ginseng, peony root, and a variety of stabilizing herbs.

The process was time-consuming. But it was easy with my current level of alchemical skill. An hour passed before I finally held up three small vials.

A deep purplish-red elixir.

The Blood Purifying Tonic.

Quest: Rescue the Fallen has been completed.
Due to your status as Interface Manipulator, your rewards
will be adjusted accordingly.

A sudden weight pressed against my mind, like a flood of knowledge forcing its way into my thoughts. I staggered slightly, gripping the edge of the table as images, concepts, and techniques poured into my consciousness.

Pressure points. Qi pathways. Meridian regulation. The delicate balance between yin and yang in the body's circulation.

And most importantly, how acupuncture could enhance the effects of the tonic.

My breathing steadied as I focused, parsing through the flood of information.

With the right needle placements, I could guide the tonic's effects, ensuring the corrupted blood was expelled more efficiently. Not only that, but acupuncture could prevent Qi Deviation, something I hadn't even considered when treating the converts.

I cursed under my breath.

Of course. I'd been so focused on cleansing the demonic influence that I hadn't accounted for the shock their bodies would undergo. Their qi pathways, already altered by the conversion process, were vulnerable to instability. If I wasn't careful, the cure itself could cause their meridians to collapse.

That wasn't something I could afford.

I exhaled slowly, rolling my shoulders. But there was a problem.

I wasn't an acupuncturist.

The knowledge was there, sure, but application was different. I had skills in alchemy and medicine, but acupuncture required steady hands, precision, and years of practice. And I only had two of the three.

I glanced toward the vial of Blood Purifying Tonic, my grip tightening around it.

I couldn't afford to make mistakes.

But I didn't have to do this alone.

A realization settled over me, followed by the barest trace of relief.

There was an entire squadron of second-class disciples in the village. Trained martial artists. Many of whom had backgrounds in medicine, healing arts, and battlefield first aid.

Surely, one of them had experience with acupuncture.

Without another moment of hesitation, I set out for their compound. Several were there, going about their training or interacting with the village children who had come over to learn some martial arts.

"Does anyone here know acupuncture?" I asked.

A disciple stepped forward. It was Sun Yang. "I do."

I nodded. "Come with me."

Together, we entered the area where the restrained converts were being held.

One of them lay on a cot, wasting away from hunger, their body trembling as if on the verge of breaking apart. Without the constant empowerment of demonic qi, they were deteriorating.

But I wouldn't let them die.

"Lay him flat," I instructed.

The disciple obeyed, positioning the convert's body properly.

I pointed to several acupoints. "You'll place the needles here. And here. Especially near the heart."

The disciple nodded, carefully inserting the needles with precision.

I took a steady breath and uncorked the vial.

"This tonic will target the corruption through the blood," I explained. "The Essence Purifying Elixir will serve as the base, breaking down the demonic influence. The herbs will encourage expulsion of bad blood while promoting regeneration."

Slowly, carefully, I administered the first dose.

The reaction was immediate.

The convert's body convulsed. Their muscles seized as blackened blood leaked from the acupoints, seeping through the skin. Their mouth opened in a strangled gasp, and they vomited thick, dark fluid.

The disciple flinched at the sight.

But I didn't.

I had expected this.

The corruption had to get worse before it could get better.

Minutes passed. The convert eventually went still, unconscious. His body trembled no more.

But he did not change.

Not yet.

I exhaled, my grip tightening around the empty vial. "We'll have to repeat this for the next few days. We need to keep flushing it out. Let's repeat with the others."

The disciple swallowed. "Understood."

I stepped back, glancing at the other converts.

This was only the beginning.

As I moved on to the next convert, my hands didn't hesitate. The process had already been ingrained in my memory. Positioning, dosage, needle placement. The acupuncturist beside me worked in tandem, inserting each needle with practiced precision as I administered the Blood Purifying Tonic in careful increments.

The same reaction followed. The convert's body convulsed violently, the purging beginning almost instantly. His breath hitched, muscles spasming as dark, putrid blood forced its way out through his acupoints. The stench of decay filled the room, thick and suffocating.

I forced myself to breathe through my mouth.

It was working.

But as I moved from one convert to the next, watching them all writhe under the effects of the tonic, a different thought settled into my mind, one that had nothing to do with the process itself.

What happens after?

These people weren't from Gentle Wind Village. That much was certain.

The village had never reported missing persons, at least not in my lifetime. Which meant these converts were from elsewhere. Other villages. Other homes.

Maybe Pingyao.

I thought of Ping Hai in the Soaring Swallow. I didn't know how far Pingyao was from here, but . . . what if these people were from there?

What if their families were still waiting? Still mourning?

Had they already grieved for them? Moved on? Or were they still hoping, holding onto some desperate shred of belief that their loved ones would return?

My grip on the vial tightened.

How many more had been taken?

Because these three weren't alone. There were dozens, probably hundreds of people out there who had been stolen away, converted, twisted into tools for the demonic cult.

People who never got a chance.

My breath was slow and steady as I moved to the final convert, repeating the process with mechanical precision.

Needles in place. Tonic administered.

The body convulsed.

Dark blood expelled.

Finally, after what felt like an eternity, the last convert stilled. His unconscious body sank onto the cot, breath settling into weak but steady inhales.

It was done. For now.

I wiped my forehead, sweat trickling down my temple. The air was thick with the scent of medicine and expelled corruption.

As I reached for the discarded equipment, the disciple beside me stopped me.

"You've worked hard," he said simply. "Leave the cleanup to me."

I hesitated for only a moment before nodding.

". . . Thanks."

With that, I turned and stepped outside, leaving the compound behind.

The village was quiet as I walked through its streets. The sun had begun its descent, casting long shadows over the frostbitten earth.

I kept moving, my feet following a familiar path, even as my mind wandered elsewhere.

What does it mean to be the Interface Manipulator?

What was my role supposed to be?

Did I have to stand on the very front lines, leading the charge against the cultists? Was that my duty?

The thought sent a cold shudder through me.

"I don't want that . . ."

Did it mean protecting this village instead?

To focus only on what I could control? To safeguard the people around me, rather than concerning myself with the bigger picture?

I frowned. That didn't feel right either.

If I ignored everything outside of Gentle Wind Village, if I ignored what I had learned in the ruins—about the Heavenly Demon, the Interface's origins, and the cult's goal to revive their god—

Wouldn't that just be another form of abandonment?

Like the Silent Moon Sect? Like the mainland elders?

A bitter taste settled on my tongue.

Neither option seemed right.

And yet, I couldn't stay idle.

I clenched my fists and looked down at the floor.

I don't know what my role is supposed to be. I don't know what the Interface expects from me.

A voice called out behind me, breaking me out of my thoughts. "Benefactor."

I turned, catching sight of Ping Hai walking toward me at a brisk pace. The massive man was hard to miss. Towering, broad-shouldered, and moving with a surprising level of grace for someone his size.

I exhaled, letting go of my internal debate for the moment. "You don't have to call me that, you know. We're not that far apart in age."

"I'd disagree. You're nearly five years older than me. You are the same age as the daughter running the teahouse we stay in, yes? I heard she was your childhood friend."

I stopped walking.

Then I turned, giving him a long, long look.

Five years younger.

The hulk of a man in front of me, the one who could likely lift a whole wagon cart if he wanted to, was only a couple of years older than Li Wei?

A slow breath left me. "Five years, huh?"

Ping Hai tilted his head. "You look like you're struggling with that fact."

"I am struggling with it."

He laughed—a deep, booming sound that felt strangely light despite its volume. "Well, regardless of age, I came here to say thank you."

I waved him off. "No need for that."

"I think there is," he said, his voice more serious now. "We have a . . . complicated past. I was on the other side of a wager, and part of the Silent Moon. You had every right to hold it against me. But you saved us. You let us stay. You healed our wounds. That's magnanimous of you."

I huffed, shaking my head. "I don't think I'd call it that. It's simply basic kindness. I owe your senior something anyway."

"I would." His tone was firm. "The Silent Moon Sect isn't like the Verdant Lotus Sect or any of those noble, upright sects. We follow the rule of might makes right. And I once took pride in that. The strong lead, the weak follow—and we never owe debts. We were raised to fight, to claim what we wanted through power. But even we, once, held true to our promises. Even we once understood honor."

He exhaled, his massive shoulders rising and falling, before bowing deeply onto the snowy floor. "And that's why I wanted to say thank you. Not just for the medicine. Not just for the shelter. But because you treated us like people, not just as enemies from another sect."

I didn't say anything at first.

Because, honestly, what was there to say?

This wasn't a conversation about debt. It wasn't a conversation about obligation. It was just two people talking, trying to make sense of the world they had both been thrown into. And yet, somewhere in those words, I felt something click in my mind.

Maybe this is it.

Maybe this is my role.

Not to stand at the front lines, leading the charge.

Not to stay behind, only protecting my own.

But to bridge the gap—to be the one who listens, who learns, and who finds a way forward.

I wasn't a warrior. Or a hero from the tales that Liang Feng weaved.

I was an herbalist. An alchemist. A cultivator who had walked an unusual path.

But paths, no matter how strange, still led somewhere.

I looked at Ping Hai. "Then I'll say this: thank you."

He blinked, surprised. "For what?"

"For reminding me that I still have a lot to learn," I said simply.

A small smile pulled at his lips. "I think we all do."

With that, he gave me a polite nod before turning back toward the Soaring Swallow, his heavy footsteps crunching against the frost-covered path.

I watched him go for a moment before finally heading back to my shop.

The sound of laughter greeted me as I approached.

Tianyi and Windy were playing in the snow—well, if you could call it that. Tianyi was tossing handfuls of it into the air, watching as it fluttered down, her wings, gradually healing, shimmering in the cold light. Windy had coiled himself into the deepest mound of snow possible, his blue-and-white scales barely visible under the frost.

I shook my head, a small smile tugging at my lips.

Even now, even after everything, there was still room for this.

Room for peace.

Room for moments that weren't about survival.

I exhaled, my breath curling into the cold air. I glanced at Ping Hai's back as he walked headed for the Soaring Swallow.

I knew what I had to do.

CHAPTER FORTY-FOUR

The Path Between

The next two days passed quickly.

My hands moved on instinct, measuring doses, adjusting needle placements, refining the Blood Purifying Tonic batch by batch. I didn't hesitate when I pressed the vial against a trembling convert's lips anymore, nor when I wiped away the thick, blackened blood that seeped out from their pores. The scent of medicine and corruption had clung to me so long it felt like it had seeped into my skin.

But it was working.

The converts no longer whispered praises to the Heavenly Demon. Their lips didn't move in fervent prayer. Their eyes no longer held that vacant, mindless devotion. They were still silent, still unresponsive, but they were here.

Then, a sound. Soft, so quiet I almost missed it.

A hoarse whisper.

I glanced over sharply, my gaze locked onto one of the converts. A man, thin and sunken, his skin ashen from prolonged corruption. He stared at nothing, his lips barely moving.

I knelt beside him, heart pounding as I strained to hear.

His voice was weak, dry, cracking with disuse.

"... Sister."

A single word. A single piece of a life stolen from him.

My fingers tightened around the edge of the cot.

It's the first word any of them had spoken.

It took me a second before I murmured back, voice softer than I intended.

"You'll see her again."

I didn't know if he heard me. His eyes slid shut, exhaustion taking him once more.

It would take time for them to find themselves again.

And time was something we didn't have.

Between treatments, I prepared the Silent Moon disciple's supplies.

Rows of elixirs lined my workbench. Strengthening tonics to sustain stamina over long travel. Potent tonics for injuries we couldn't predict. Warming potions to stave off the oppressive winter cold. Not just for them, but for whatever the villagers needed. It wouldn't surprise me if they were suffering from the effects of the long winter. I labeled them all carefully, explaining their effects to Xu Ziqing and Ping Hai.

Ping Hai listened with the focus of a man determined not to fail. Xu Ziqing, ever composed, nodded along, though I could tell he was filing away only the most critical information.

They understood the weight of these supplies. That was enough.

I didn't notice when the others started gathering.

By the time I finished explaining the last elixir, there was a small crowd to bid them farewell.

Wang Jun, arms crossed, watched intently. Lan-Yin frowned slightly as she listened. Elder Ming, his usual quiet presence at the back. Even a handful of Verdant Lotus disciples came, their expressions unreadable. The moment was approaching. And despite having made up my mind, I still felt that familiar spike of anxiety. Of doubt.

I could stay. I could convince myself that the village needs me. That I am more useful here, where I can control the outcome.

But wasn't that what the Silent Moon Sect did?

Withdrawing. Waiting. Consolidating.

And in the end, it changed nothing. It made everything worse.

If I stayed here forever, what would change?

Nothing.

I closed the final box, stacking it with the others. Then, without preamble, I said it.

"But it's okay. Even if you forget, it won't matter because I'm coming with you."

Silence.

Then—

"You *what?!*"

The look on Ping Hai and Xu Ziqing's faces would forever be etched into my memory.

Lan-Yin's eyes widened. "You're joking. You have to be joking."

"I'm not," I said simply.

Jian Feng exhaled, shaking his head. "Kai, think about this. You're still recovering from your injuries. Are you seriously suggesting you leave the village to march straight into another conflict?"

Wang Jun, usually the more reserved of my friends, scowled outright. "That bandage on your arm? *Not* for decoration. The fact that you aren't limping doesn't mean you should be fighting."

"I'm not just going to fight," I said evenly. "I'm going to help. I can stabilize the wounded, supply medicine, reinforce whatever defenses Pingyao has left. If things turn bad, I'll make sure we have the resources to fall back."

"You are the resource," a voice interjected.

I blinked, glancing over—Li Wei.

I hadn't expected him to speak up. The young carpenter stood near the back of the group, his arms crossed tightly, brow furrowed in an expression I hadn't seen on him before.

"The village has no other alchemist of your caliber," he continued. "No other healer, no one else who can do what you do. If you leave and something happens—"

"Then I'll make sure nothing happens before I go," I said, my voice firmer.

Li Wei clenched his fists. "You think you can just 'make sure' of that? You're not a *god*, Kai. What if someone gets sick? What if an attack happens while you're gone? If someone like me gets injured, what then? Who'll build the houses?"

I hesitated. He's not just speaking as a friend; he's speaking as someone who depended on me.

Kai, the alchemist. The healer. The one who had always been here.

My gaze flickered to him, seeing the tension in his frame, the sharp concern in his voice. We hadn't talked much lately. I'd been too busy. Too caught up in my work, my training, the encroaching threat of the demonic cult.

And yet, he had still been here. Building. Helping. Holding the village together in his own way.

I exhaled. "Li Wei, I—"

"Kai, have you made up your mind?"

Elder Ming looked me in my eyes, as if testing my resolve. It was like when I first asked him to train me all over again.

I thought back to my conversation with Ping Hai. To the quiet realization of what my role in all this was meant to be; not a warrior at the front, not a hermit behind safe walls, but something in between. Staying in the village forever, isolated from the larger conflict, would be as much a mistake as running straight into battle.

Something that bridged the gap.

Between sects and villages.

Between cultivators and common people.

Between the present world and the Interface's lost history.

Between destruction and survival.

I couldn't stay here while the rest of the region was under threat. I wouldn't.

I sighed, gesturing toward the two figures at my side. "Yes, Elder Ming. Besides, do you really think Tianyi and Windy would let me go alone? It's not like I'm going there unarmed. I have two powerful and immensely capable spirit beasts by my side."

Tianyi tilted her head, then nodded firmly.

Windy let out an indignant hiss, his tail flicking sharply as if offended by the mere suggestion of leaving me on my own.

There's a brief pause as everyone absorbed that information.

Elder Ming stepped in then, placing a firm hand on the boy's shoulder.

"Kai has decided," the elder said, voice calm but steady. "And I trust him to know his own limits."

Li Wei looked like he was about to argue, his jaw clenching. But then, with a sharp exhale, he took a step back, shoulders tight with frustration.

Wang Jun let out an aggravated huff. "If I didn't know how much stronger you were than me, I'd beat some sense into you."

Lan-Yin muttered something under her breath, crossing her arms but offering no more protest.

Jian Feng, after a long silence, sighed heavily. "Then I'll join as well."

I turned to him, startled.

So did a few of the Verdant Lotus disciples.

They stepped forward without hesitation.

I had expected arguments. Expected protests. But they agreed. Just like that.

I shook my head. "No. This is *my* risk. You don't have to follow. Stay here and protect the village."

Jian Feng met my gaze evenly. "I cannot, in good conscience, let someone I am indebted to go into battle alone." His voice softened. "And I am not doing this as a disciple of the Verdant Lotus Sect. I am doing this as a friend."

"What sort of taoist lets a villager do their job?" Miao Hu protested from further in the back.

My breath caught slightly.

Still, I protested. "The village will be defenseless. I did this on the assumption you would all be here, keeping Gentle Wind Village safe."

Elder Ming looked at me.

"We have more than a dozen disciples staying behind to protect this place. We'll be fine. I trust you, Kai. If you want to go, then go. But don't refuse the help that is given to you."

His eyes held certainty. A quiet, unwavering confidence.

And for some reason, it made me pause.

Why does he sound so sure?

The Verdant Lotus disciples were strong, yes, but they weren't an army. If I—who trained alongside them, who had fought against the same threats—still felt uncertain about leaving, then how could Elder Ming be so at ease?

Did he know something I didn't?

I studied him carefully, searching for the answer. But all I saw was quiet assurance. A belief in something he hadn't said aloud.

Something shifted in my chest.

He trusted that this place would be safe. That much was clear.

And though I didn't understand why, I trusted him.

I let out a breath. "All right."

Then the two Silent Moon disciples stepped forward, their expressions drawn tight.

"You shouldn't," Xu Ziqing said immediately. "This is where your favor to me *ends*. There is no need to put yourself at risk when you have your own village to protect."

I lifted an eyebrow. "Oh? Do you even remember everything I just told you about these elixirs? How to use them? *When* to take them? How to mix them?"

Xu Ziqing's mouth opened. He hesitated. His gaze flickered to the neatly labeled boxes, and I saw the exact moment the realization set in.

He remembered some—but not enough.

"We'll figure it out. We've managed on our own this long." His voice was gruff as he tried to inject some coldness into his words. But now, the longer I interacted with him, the more I could tell it was just a facade.

"Then tell me—what happens when one of you falls in battle? When you don't have time to 'figure it out?' Will you waste precious moments debating which elixir to use while someone bleeds out?"

That was met with silence, and he couldn't seem to find an answer.

"Exactly." I pressed on. "If you plan to protect Pingyao, we will do it together. It'll maximize our chances."

I glanced at the gathered figures, my voice steady. "And in the worst-case scenario, if the village is too dangerous to defend, we bring its people here. It's easier to protect something when we have numbers on our side."

I smiled.

"Well, that's about how it's going to go. Any questions? Concerns?"

Xu Ziqing just stared at me, then at the gathered disciples, then back at me.

"You . . . you're all just deciding this so casually?" His voice was filled with something between disbelief and exhaustion.

Ping Hai, however, reacted differently. His hands trembled at his sides, his lips parting slightly as he took in the sheer number of people standing with them.

His gaze flickered over each face, each person who had, without hesitation, chosen to join this journey.

His throat bobbed as he swallowed hard. He blinked rapidly, as if trying to hold back something he didn't want to show.

"Thank you," he said, voice thick with emotion.

I clapped him on the shoulder, firm but light. "Before we go, I need to make a quick stop."

The banyan tree loomed before me, ancient and unmoving, its roots twisting through the frostbitten ground. My breath curled in the freezing air, dissipating into the sky.

I flexed my right hand, rolling my fingers, feeling the stiffness that still lingered from my injury. It had healed enough. Enough that I could fight, enough that I could move without pain, but not enough that I could afford recklessness.

I exhaled slowly.

Although I wished I could have carried the weight of the Black Tortoise Shell for longer, I knew now that unnecessary burdens only slowed me down. A single moment of hesitation could mean death—not just for me, but for those I needed to protect.

I wouldn't make the same mistake I had against the Envoy.

My fingers curled into a fist.

Then, I *punched*.

The impact shuddered through the tree. Brittle leaves shook loose from the branches, drifting to the ground like silent snowflakes. A clear indentation was left on the bark—not enough to break it, but enough to fulfill the quest's requirement.

A series of notifications swarmed my vision.

> *Sub-quest: The Black Tortoise's Tribulation has been completed.*
> *Quest: Body Refinement (Breakthrough) has been completed.*
> *Due to your status as Interface Manipulator, your rewards will be adjusted accordingly.*
> *The Interface recognizes not only perseverance but the will to surpass limitations. Where others would have ended, you endured.*
> *Where strength was demanded, you forged mastery.*
> *You have gone beyond. Your rewards shall reflect it.*

The weight I'd been carrying. It didn't fade away gently. It was just gone.

For the first time in months, the crushing force that had settled into my bones, wrapped around my limbs, pressing into every motion . . . it ceased to exist.

I inhaled sharply, my balance shifting in an instant.

I felt light. Too light.

The ground beneath me felt distant, unfamiliar, as though my body had forgotten what it was like to exist without restraint. I steadied myself with the banyan, as though I were going to float away without something anchoring me.

A disorienting sensation swept through me. My breath hitched. It was like the dull, unrelenting ache I had carried for so long had become a part of me.

And now, without warning, it had been ripped away.

My feet adjusted instinctively, compensating for a weight that no longer existed.

I clenched and unclenched my fists. Then, experimentally, I threw a punch into the air.

The force of it rippled outward, raw strength bursting forth. I hadn't even infused qi into the strike, and yet wind howled in the wake of my movement.

I blinked.

Then, I laughed.

It was soft at first, just a breath of realization. But then it grew.

Because this was real.

I took one last look at the banyan tree before rolling my shoulders, shaking off the last traces of restraint. It seemed the Interface was taking a while to calculate my reward. I couldn't waste any more time here.

"Let's go."

With a slight bend of my knees, qi surged through my legs with more ease than ever before—

Then I launched forward.

The ground cracked beneath my takeoff, frost shattering as I blurred forward, catching up with the others in an instant.

My heart pounded, my blood thrumming with anticipation.

The journey to Pingyao had begun.

CHAPTER FORTY-FIVE

A Serpentine Dream

Windy drifted into the void of unconsciousness.
At first, he did not realize anything was wrong. He did not know what wrong was. He was simply here; floating, weightless, his long body coiled in on itself without effort or tension. There was no sky, no ground, no up or down. Just the endless, empty white stretching in all directions.

Then—something moved in front of him.

A snake. White, just like him. But it had no features, no distinct markings, nothing that set it apart. A shape, a presence, but utterly devoid of identity.

Windy hissed lowly, his tongue flicking out as instinct demanded.

"Where?" he rasped. "Where is Tianyi?"

He remembered. She had lifted him, her hands careful but firm. There had been pain—sharp, blinding pain—the stench of blood, and warmth. She had told him they were going home. But she wasn't here anymore.

The memory came in flickering fragments, disjointed and strange. The fight. The cultist. Then this. He doesn't know what led him here.

The ground beneath him was solid, but the longer he thought about it, the more unnatural it felt. Cold. Too cold. Ice and snow stretched endlessly in all directions, smooth and reflective, as though he were trapped within an infinite frozen lake. Wind howled through the emptiness, keening and thin, but it touched nothing. No scent. No warmth. No world.

The sky above was a dull, oppressive gray. No sun. No moon.

His unease sharpened.

And then the serpent *lunged*.

It moved impossibly fast, sleek, and fluid, its body blurring into motion before Windy could react. Fangs sank deep into his flesh. Pain. Raw, searing, violent. It spread through his body like fire and ice twined together, flooding every nerve, every muscle. His own blood tasted sharp and metallic in the air.

Then—darkness.

Windy woke up.

The cold. The ice. The endless gray sky. The wind howled through the nothingness. And in front of him . . . the white serpent, waiting.

He stiffened, his coils tensing instinctively.

The serpent lunged.

Windy lashed out, fangs bared, striking blindly. His teeth met nothing. Air, empty and cold. The other snake shifted at the last possible moment, its movements eerily smooth, tilting its head just enough to evade. He barely had time to register it before pain exploded through him again. Fangs tore through his scales, severing muscle, slicing deep into the vital place where his body coiled in on itself.

Darkness.

Windy woke up.

He had felt it. Felt the fangs tear through him. Felt the agony, the fear, the life leaving him.

But he was whole again.

The ice beneath him hadn't changed. The sky, the wind, the empty wasteland—unchanged. And in front of him, the serpent.

Waiting.

Wind struck first this time. He lunged, twisting his body in a coil, using momentum to add weight to his attack. He aimed for the throat—

The white serpent slipped around him like mist. Too fast. Wind barely had time to correct before it coiled tight around him, forcing him into a suffocating grip. He thrashed, instincts screaming, fangs bared and snapping wildly—

Pain.

Darkness.

Again.

He moved without thinking, bolting backward as soon as his vision cleared. The serpent was already moving, its sleek body flowing across the ice, closing the distance effortlessly. Windy coiled back defensively, mimicking Tianyi's light-footed shifts, trying to glide instead of brute-forcing his way through. He twisted, feinted left, then right—

Fangs drove into his throat.

Darkness.

Windy woke up.

Again.

Again.

And again.

He fought. He bit, coiled, lashed out with everything he had. He tried to mimic Tianyi's graceful evasion, tried to remember Kai's technique of redirecting an opponent's attack, the careful timing in his stance. But he was too slow, too predictable, too untrained.

The white serpent was always a step ahead. Always faster.

Again. And again.

Windy tried to flee once.

For a moment, he thought he might succeed. He slithered across the ice, body whipping through the frozen wasteland. The wind howled past him, and he moved, moved, *moved*—

A shadow.

The white serpent appeared ahead of him.

Windy barely had time to register the impossible speed before his world shattered.

The cycle of death blurred into eternity.

Windy didn't know how long he had been here. Days? Weeks? Longer? Time lost meaning when it only stretched from one brutal death to the next.

Each time he fought, he died. Each time he died, he woke up. The pain was real. The wounds were real. But his body remained untouched, whole, as though none of it had ever happened. He did not understand. He could not escape. The only constant was the ice beneath him, the dull sky above, and the waiting serpent that killed him over and over again.

Despair crept in. His fangs dulled with hesitation. His strikes grew sluggish, weighed down by exhaustion that was more in his mind than his body. What was the point? He could not win. He could not flee. He could not even scream into the endless cold.

Then—

Something shifted.

A flicker, a blur, a pattern.

Windy had spent so long reacting, throwing himself into the fight blindly, that he had not watched. The serpent was fast—unbelievably fast—but it was not without rhythm. It moved in patterns. The faintest twitch of its head before a strike. The way its coils tightened just a fraction before lunging.

Windy coiled in on himself, still as the ice beneath him, and focused.

The movement wasn't just speed; it was misdirection. A flicker here, a blur there. A calculated illusion to bait him into striking where nothing existed. His instincts had been lying to him. He had been attacking shadows, not substance.

For the first time, Windy didn't just see the serpent move; he saw where it would move next.

The air shifted before its lunge, the subtle pressure of its body curling in the same way each time, creating an unseen thread connecting past, present, and future motion. It was a sequence; a chain reaction of movements leading to an inevitable result. Not where it was, not even where it would be in a blink, but where the kill could be made.

A direct path. No wasted motion. A perfect strike.

He waited.

The serpent lunged.

Windy struck before it completed the motion.

His fangs met flesh.

The white serpent reared back, hissing, a streak of red painting the ice. But for once, it wasn't his own.

It was shallow. Not enough to kill. But for the first time, it was he who had drawn blood.

The air shifted.

A chime rang through the void, unseen but felt deep in his bones. A sensation he knew well. A welcome reprieve from the unending cycle he'd been met with.

> *You can now use the skill Predator's Insight.*

Windy coiled tighter, his forked tongue flickering out, testing the air. He could feel it now. The subtle, almost imperceptible details of the serpent's motion. The way its body shifted before a feint. The minor tensing of muscle before a strike. It was all clear.

The battle lasted longer.

Windy evaded. Countered. For the first time, he lasted.

The serpent's speed had not changed. But now, he could see.

And the longer he fought, the clearer the patterns became.

This wasn't just instinct. This was learned.

Windy observed. The serpent never wasted movement. Every feint, every flick of its tail, had a purpose. When it struck, it committed fully, a perfect balance of power and efficiency. It knew the most efficient way to kill. It had no hesitation, no wasted energy.

So Windy learned.

He copied the peculiar way it moved. The efficiency of its motions. The precise shifts of weight that allowed it to feint and redirect effortlessly. But he did not just mimic, he refined it. Adapted it for himself.

Windy focused not just on speed, but on reading his opponent's tempo. The way it shifted between offense and defense. The way it controlled the flow of battle with each flick of its body.

His attacks became sharper. More deliberate. He learned to see openings before they existed, understanding the most efficient path to the kill.

For the first time, Windy wasn't just reacting. He was dictating the flow of battle.

The white serpent's movements had always seemed unpredictable, but now he understood; there was an invisible rhythm to it, a song that it had been singing all along. The flick of its tail before retreating, the twitch of its tongue before feinting, the curve of its body just before committing to a strike. Each movement had a response, and each response led to an outcome. Windy followed that rhythm, not just keeping pace but bending it. The moment the white serpent surged forward, he coiled in just the right way, not to evade, but to bait. He let the serpent believe he would be in one place, and then—

He felt his body blur, just for an instant.

For the first time, the serpent struck nothing.

An afterimage stood where he had been a breath before.

The air shuddered. The Interface chime rang again.

> *You can now use the skill Illusory Motion.*

The void shuddered. The frozen wasteland rippled like disturbed water, as though the fabric of this endless liminal space could not contain what had just happened.

Windy stilled, his forked tongue flickering in the frigid air. Something had changed. The cycle had shifted. This was no longer an endless loop of death. He had taken something from this place—something real. A skill. A power. A truth hidden within instinct.

The white serpent, his eternal adversary, had stopped moving. It coiled in on itself, no longer poised to strike. For the first time since this endless battle had begun, it lowered its head and lay still.

Windy did not move. He observed it, expecting another attack, another death, another reset. But nothing came. The tension bled from the serpent's form, and the air around them changed.

Then, he felt it.

The world was fading.

The ice beneath him no longer felt solid. The cold still stung his scales, but it was distant now, muted. The wind's howl grew softer, stretching into silence. The sky, that endless expanse of gray nothingness, dimmed further as if it, too, were unraveling at the edges.

Windy coiled himself tightly, his instincts bristling. He did not understand this place, did not understand what governed it, but he could feel it slipping away. This strange, endless trial was ending.

And then the words came.

They did not come from the serpent. They did not come from the void.

They came from nowhere. From everywhere. They pressed into his mind.

Protect the Interface Manipulator.

The intent behind it felt heavy, but not coercive. As though it were a request.

Windy recoiled, his mind reeling. "Who—?" he hissed, his voice ragged from the countless battles he had endured. "What is—?"

But before he could demand answers, before he could even finish forming the thought—

The world vanished.

Windy gasped.

Scales tingling with sensation. A rush of warmth flooded his senses, jarring and unfamiliar after the bitter cold of the dreamscape. It was overwhelming. The scent of earth. The weight of his own body, real and whole. The sound of breathing—not his own, but another's.

Warmth pressed against him, solid and firm. Not Tianyi.

Kai.

The realization settled slowly, disjointed and dreamlike. He was being held, cradled against Kai's chest, the human's heartbeat a steady, grounding rhythm against his small, coiled form. The warmth seeped into his body, banishing the phantom chill of the void. He was alive. Here. Not trapped in that endless cycle.

"Hold on—Tianyi! Tianyi, he's awake!"

Kai's voice resounded in his skull, giving him a headache.

His mind spun with questions. Who spoke to him? Why had he been given those words? What was that place?

"You're all right, you're all right." The human continued to murmur, pressing him against his chest.

But then—

A terrible, unbearable itch ran down his spine.

Windy's entire body stiffened.

The questions, the mystery, the lingering traces of instinct that had followed him from that realm . . . all of it was obliterated in an instant.

Shedding.

The realization hit like a hammer. His skin felt too tight, his scales tingled with maddening urgency, and his entire body demanded one thing and one thing only.

Rub against something. *Now.*

Windy let out a small, exhausted hiss and weakly pressed his snout against Kai's sleeve, dragging it along the fabric to peel away the suffocating layer of old skin.

Kai made a noise of surprise, shifting slightly. "Windy—ow, stop that, you're—"

Windy ignored him. Bigger problems. Important problems. He needed something rough. Something textured. The edge of a rock, a piece of bark—

His tired body squirmed, rubbing insistently against Kai's arm, then his collar, then—yes. The coarse hem of his robe.

He latched onto it, winding himself tighter and dragging his snout along it with all the force his weary form could muster.

For now, all that mattered was this shedding skin and getting rid of it as soon as possible.

Acknowledgments

Writing a book is and will always be a tribulation. Consisting of sleepless nights and caffeine-addled writing binges. As a habitual procrastinator trying his best to change, writing a book has always been a test of accountability and punctuality (which I still fall short of where I'd like to be).

But I still enjoy it. Every time I think of the next issue, the next character development arc, and the next big villain, I can't help but make sure all my bases are covered so it'll have a satisfying payoff. Whether it's in this book or the ones after it.

Thank you to my girlfriend, Amanda, who's the first to let me know I should be taking a break or resting instead of losing brain cells figuring out the next way I can make Kai miserable.

Thank you to Steven, William, and Susan, for inviting me to their home and letting me experience hot pot for the first time!

Thank you to my friends, who keep me fit as a fiddle and remind me that being glued to a keyboard for two-thirds of my life will eventually make me look like Project Graham.

Thank you to my family, whom I spent a great deal of time with in Thailand after a long overdue reunion, keeping me loaded on Thai iced tea and coffee so I could write every day during vacation.

Thank you to Brent and Randall specifically, who've only solidified my desire to work and write full-time while relaxing on Jomtien Beach.

And finally, thank you to my readers, who are always a source of motivation and thoughtful ideas. Cheers to Volume 4, and prepare yourself for the next one!

About the Author

Carlos Calma is a Canadian author who has been captivated by LitRPG and progression fantasy since he was young. He began reading these genres as a child and started writing his own stories while in high school. This passion has continued into his adult life. Calma resides in Toronto, Ontario.

Podium

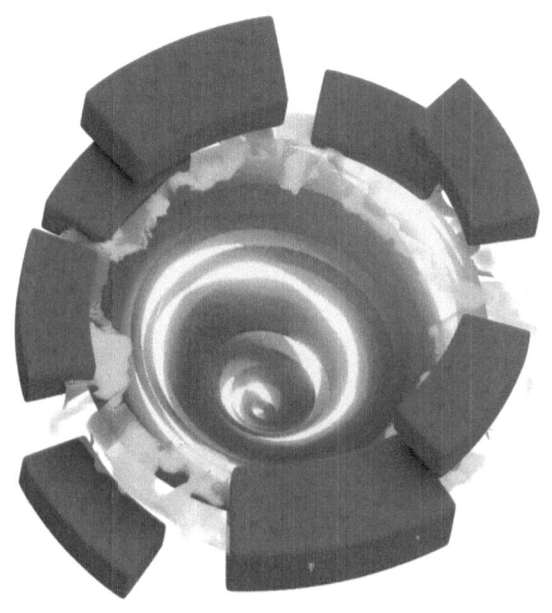

RESPAWN YOUR CURIOSITY
follow us on our socials

 podiumentertainment.com
 @podiumentertainment
 /podiumentertainment
 @podium_ent
 @podiumentertainment

www.ingramcontent.com/pod-product-compliance
Lightning Source LLC
LaVergne TN
LVHW091529060526
838200LV00036B/537